At that, Victoria did yank her arm away, breaking his grip. 'Rockley is no secret, and he is not the weak fool you make him out to be. You needn't stand so close to me.'

'Has he seen your vis bulla?' Sebastian had not moved away, and his hand had shifted between them, below her breasts, to press flat over her shirtwaist against the trembling muscles of her stomach. 'Does he know what it means?'

She shoved against his shoulders and pushed him away. He moved, but barely stumbled backward. He was stronger than she realised.

'Does he know that it means his love walks the streets at night? That she must mingle with those from the dark side to learn their secrets?' Unruffled, nonplussed by her violent reaction, he spoke, his voice low and hypnotic. 'That she kills every time she raises her weapon? That she has a strength he cannot hope to possess?'

'He knows nothing.' Victoria spoke from between clenched teeth. Sebastian had moved in toward her again, crowding her back against the wall, but he did not touch her.

'Has he seen it, Victoria?' The gentle roll of her name's last syllables caused an odd wave in her middle. 'Has he?'

The Rest Falls Away

a&b

The Rest Falls Away

The Gardella Vampire Chronicles

COLLEEN GLEASON

This edition first published in 2008 by
Allison & Busby Limited
13 Charlotte Mews
London, W1T 4EJ
www.allisonandbusby.com

A CIP catalogue record for this book is available from
the British Library.

First published in the USA by Signet Eclipse,
an imprint of New American Library,
a division of Penguin Group (USA) Inc., 2007.

10 9 8 7 6 5 4 3 2 1

ISBN 978-0-7490-7956-7

Typeset in 10.5/14 pt Sabon by
Allison & Busby Ltd

Printed and bound in Great Britain by
Bookmarque Ltd, Croydon, Surrey

COLLEEN GLEASON has been writing for as long as she can remember, throughout school and college, and on and off during her career in health care and small business start-ups. She is married with three children and two dogs The Rest Falls Away is the first book in the historical vampire slayer series, The Gardella Vampire Chronicles.

**Available from
Allison & Busby**

The Gardella Vampire Chronicles
The Rest Falls Away
Rises the Night

Also by Colleen Gleason

The Gardella Vampire Chronicles
The Bleeding Dusk
When Twilight Burns

With love to Steve (here it is!),
Holli and Tammy

Acknowledgements

I cannot thank Marcy Posner enough for taking me under her wing and working with me for the last two years. And a world of thanks to Claire Zion for taking a chance on me and Victoria's story, and for always seeming to verbalise my ideas before I do! Tina Brown has been fantastic with everything from answering simple 'newbie' questions to providing support and keeping everything flowing so smoothly.

My sisters at the Wet Noodle Posse are also top on my list to thank. I've never met a more supportive, loving, talented group of women.

Without Holli and Tammy, I would have been floundering on chapter one for months. Thank you for being there, every single week, and for all of your support and guidance and those darn questions you kept asking! Also many hugs and gratitude to Mom, Jennifer, Linda, Kelly, Diana, Wendy, Jana, and Kate, for being there during this story and countless others. I love you all!

Thank you to my husband and children for putting up with all the times I'm at the computer, or lost in thought trying to work out a plot problem. And thanks to Mary Kay – you know why. And finally, most important, I thank my Creator, without whom none of this would be possible.

Prologue

In Which Our Story Commences

His footsteps were soundless, but Victoria felt him moving.

She grasped the bark of the oak, pressing her body into the tree as if it could suck her into safety. But all she felt was unyielding roughness. She couldn't stay here.

Crouching, curling her fingers around a heavy stick, she eased from the safe shadow of the tree and into the liquid silver of moonlight. The sharp snap of a twig beneath her boot sent her bolting on now-silent feet into another nearby shadow…

She could hear him breathing.

And feel the reverberations of his heartbeat.

It thumped loud, steady, strong, pumping into her ears, pulsing through her body as if it were her own organ.

Victoria moved again, her skirts flapping around her ankles as she dashed away from the sound of her pursuer. She tore through the underbrush, dodging from tree to tree and leaping over fallen logs as though she were a mare given her head.

His solid footfalls came closer and faster as she ran.

A branch tore at her face. Brush snagged her skirts.

She ran and ran and ran in the white moonlight, clutching her stick, and still he came, his heartbeat as steady as his tramping feet.

Before she realised it, Victoria stumbled down a small incline and splashed into a creek. The prop of the stick kept her from falling as she slogged through the thigh-high water, her skirts becoming leaden, weighing her down, slowing her until she could barely take another step.

A cry of rage from behind tore her attention as she staggered up the small incline on the other side of the creek.

As she climbed out, she turned and saw him standing there on the opposite bank. She couldn't see his face…but his eyes gleamed in the dark, and fury and frustration emanated from his body. But he did not follow her.

He did not cross the running water.

* * *

Victoria jolted awake, her heart thrumming madly in her chest.

Sunlight, not moonbeams, blazed through the window.

A dream. It had been a dream.

She smoothed a hand over her face, damp with perspiration, and brushed away the tendrils of hair that had escaped her thick braid.

The fifth dream. It was time.

Her bed was high off the floor, and her feet thumped onto the Aubusson rug as she launched herself from under the coverlet, in desperate need of the chamber pot. Heedless of immodesty, Victoria pulled her sweat-soaked chemise up and over her body and felt the relief of cool air on her clammy skin.

Five dreams in less than a fortnight. That was the sign. She would go to Aunt Eustacia today.

The remnants of the dream dissolved, replaced with a hum of anticipation and a tingle of apprehension. Victoria looked at herself in the tall, cloudy mirror. The warning had come.

Today she would learn just what that warning portended.

Chapter One

Miss Victoria Grantworth's Two Debuts

Vampires.

The Gardellas were vampire hunters.

Victoria was going to hunt vampires.

'Victoria, dear…' Lady Melisande's gentle voice held the barest hint of reproach. 'You may commence with pouring.'

Victoria blinked and realised that her mother had been sitting with her hands folded perfectly in her lap, whilst their two guests waited with empty teacups. 'Of course, Mother. I apologise for my wool-gathering,' she added as she raised the ivory teapot. Her mother's favourite, brought from Italy by *her* mother when she wed with Herbert, Lord of Prewitt Shore, was painted with images of Roman cathedrals.

Fortunately, the two guests at hand were Lady Melly's oldest and dearest friends, and they would not be offended by her daughter's lack of attention.

Three weeks ago, Victoria's biggest concern had been which gown to wear to an evening's event. Or whether – heaven forbid! – her dance card might not fill up.

Or even whether she would land a suitable husband during her debut.

But now…how on earth was she going to hide a wooden stake on her person? One couldn't just slip it into one's glove! Or down one's bodice!

'Not to worry, my dear Melly. I'm sure the chit is just a bit distracted, with her coming-out in less than a fortnight.' Lady Petronilla Fenworth smiled gently at Victoria as she retrieved her steaming cup. Of the three matrons, she bore the sweetest disposition; one that matched her delicate, angelic face and tiny frame. She reminded Victoria of a china doll. 'After waiting in mourning for nearly two years, I am certain she is finally in raptures that she is to debut at last!'

'Indeed she is,' replied Victoria's mother, the celebrated beauty of the trio. 'I have great hopes for her on the mart, for though she is two years older than most of the others, she is certainly beautiful enough to catch the eye of a marquess…or even perhaps a duke!' She looked fondly at her eldest daughter, who had replaced the teapot and now tried to appear interested in the ensuing conversation.

Lady Winifred, who was the other of Melisande's lifelong friends, leant forward to select a biscuit with plump fingers. She looked up, her eyes sparkling with excitement. 'My sister by marriage tells me that Rockley will be seeking a wife this year at last!'

'Rockley!' The other two elder women repeated the name in unison, their tones bordering on a squeal, as if they were the eligible misses instead of Victoria. Since both ladies had been married for nigh on a quarter century (at least until Melisande had been widowed a year earlier), it was quite unnecessary and rather…ear-splitting.

'Victoria, did you hear what Winifred said?' her mother repeated, grasping her hand. 'The Marquess of Rockley is seeking a bride! We must ensure he is invited to your coming-out. Winnie, will your sister by marriage be attending?'

'I shall see to it – and that she insist her husband bring Rockley. Nothing would please me more than to see our dear Victoria steal the heart – and purse – of the elusive Marquess of Rockley.' Winifred, who had been widowed a decade earlier and was childless, had fairly adopted Victoria as her own. Betwixt Petronilla, Winifred, and, of course, Melisande, Victoria had three full-time mothers worrying about her marriage prospects.

She was more worried about whether the small crucifix she sometimes wore about her neck would be enough to deter a salacious vampire.

According to Aunt Eustacia, it would; but as Victoria had yet to come face-to-face with one of the creatures, she wasn't completely convinced. In fact, that had become her biggest source of distraction in the last days – when would she see her first vampire?

Would one simply leap out of the woodwork one evening? Or would she have some kind of warning?

A sharp rapping on the parlour door drew the tittering ladies' attention from discussions of Rockley's physique and his income. 'Yes, Jimmons?' asked Melisande when the butler peered into the room.

'I am in receipt of a summons for Miss Victoria to Lady Eustacia Gardella's home. Her ladyship's carriage awaits the young miss, if she agrees to attend her aunt.'

Victoria set down her teacup with a sharp clatter. More training. And a chance to ask more questions of her aunt.

'Mother,' she said as she rose rather more abruptly than she'd intended. *Fiddlesticks.* The last thing she wished to hear was a lecture regarding the smooth, graceful movements a lady must adopt.

Especially since Aunt Eustacia's assistant, a man named Kritanu, had spent the last two weeks teaching her to move with quick, precise actions. And how to fell a man with the perfect kick. How to take an attacker by surprise by dodging and leaping in a most unladylike manner. Her mother would expire on the spot if she had seen the way Victoria had learnt to strike with her arms, legs, and even her head. 'I would attend Aunt Eustacia, if you will excuse me.'

Melly looked up at her, her round face a version of Victoria's own narrower, more elegant one. 'You have grown quite attached to my aunt in these last weeks, my dear. I am sure it gives the elderly lady great pleasure to have your company. I do hope she does not feel slighted when the Season begins and you are dancing at balls or attending the theatre every night.'

Dancing at balls, attending the theatre, stalking vampires.

Without a doubt, Victoria was going to be an extraordinarily busy debutante.

On the night of her debut – which, due first to the death of her grandfather, and then to the death of her father, had been delayed two years after she had attained the age of seventeen – Victoria sat at her dressing table looking every inch the proper young miss.

Her ink-black hair, a mass of wild curls, had been piled high at the back of her head and pinned to within an inch of its life. It would not dare shift or sag, regardless of the alacrity with which its mistress might dance, curtsy, or otherwise hare about.

Jet beads and the palest of pink pearls had been woven into her curls, and the black beads shone and sparkled when she turned her head, whilst the pearls glowed with the same pale hue of her gown. Matching gems hung from her ears, and a rose-colored necklace of pearls and quartz encircled her neck. Dangling from the front was, instead of a cameo brooch, a small silver crucifix.

Victoria's gown bore the faintest tinge of pink, and fell in diaphanous pleats from under her bosom to the tips of her shoes. The skirt was flowing and very nearly sheer; underneath she wore two more layers of translucent ivory. The dress's low, square décolletage left a rather large expanse of creamy white skin exposed, from choker necklace to the very tops of her breasts. And her gloves, long and virginal white, went past her elbows, nearly touching the tiny puffed sleeves.

Indeed, Victoria appeared every bit the demure, ingenuous debutante that she was…except for the solid wooden stake she held in her hand.

It was the circumference of two of her fingers and nearly the length of her arm from wrist to elbow. One end was sanded smooth, and the other whittled to a needle-sharp point It was too thick to weave into her coiffure, much too long to fit in the small bag that dangled from her wrist.

'Under your skirts, my dear. Slip it into the knee garter under your skirts,' Aunt Eustacia told her calmly. She had a face lined with age, but glowing with beauty and intelligence, as if every bit of happiness from all of her eighty-some years shone at one time. Her hair, still blue-black, she wore scraped back into an intricate mass of coils intertwined with seed pearls, white lace, and jet beads. It was a coiffure more appropriate for a girl Victoria's age than for an ageing woman. Yet Aunt Eustacia carried it well; as well as she wore her high-necked gown of blood-red taffeta.

'Why do you think I gave you the garter? Be quick; your mother is bound to return at any moment!'

'Under my skirts?'

'You must be able to access it quickly and easily, Victoria. It will be well hidden, and with practice you will learn to slip it easily from underneath and have it in your hand when you need it. Now be quick!' Aunt Eustacia did not wait for her to move; she twitched at Victoria's skirts, exposing the ivory lace garter tied just below her knee, and watched as her niece slipped the stick betwixt lace and flesh.

No sooner had they finished than the door opened, and Lady Melisande burst in, followed by her two twittering companions. ''Tis time, Victoria! Come, come!'

'You look lovely! Absolutely breathtaking!' Petronilla gushed, peering at herself in the mirror from behind Victoria and fussing with an immovable curl of her own.

'Rockley is below,' crowed Winifred, bumping into Victoria's elbow as she edged past her to reach for a papery-white clove of garlic that sat amid jewellery, scent bottles, and ornate combs. 'What on earth is this?' she asked, straightening to bring it close to her pince-nez as if to confirm that it was, indeed, garlic.

Glancing at Eustacia in the mirror, Victoria forced

a smile and leant conspiratorially toward Winifred and Petronilla. 'Aunt Eustacia brought it for me,' she said in a low voice. 'She claims it will protect me from vampires.' Deliberately, she drew one eyelid down in a slow wink, and, making a point of glancing over her shoulder as if to be sure her great-aunt wasn't listening, she took the garlic from Winifred. 'I'll just leave it here.'

Petronilla and Winifred nodded, wide-eyed with suppressed humour, and cast amused glances at Aunt Eustacia. Victoria was the only one who saw the elderly lady wink back at her.

'I cannot wait to introduce you to Rockley!' Lady Winnie burbled as they filed out of the room. 'He's danced with Lady Gwendolyn Starcasset more than once in the last week, but he hasn't met *our* beautiful debutante yet! Wouldn't it be a coup if you were to snatch him right from under her nose?'

At the top of the long, curving staircase, Victoria stopped, standing out of sight of the party below. It was the goal of every matron to have such a crush; the ladies Melisande, Petronilla, and Winifred must be in raptures about the number of people crowding the Grantworth home. Despite the fact that Melly was Victoria's mother, the other two had insisted on sponsoring her as well; and as Winifred was the Duchess of Farnham, her reputation sealed the bargain.

Victoria stood alone, waiting to be announced,

nervous and expectant. Tonight was more than her coming-out into Society…it was also her debut as the newest vampire hunter in the ancient Gardella family. Not only must she charm and delight the rich, handsome bachelors and gain the interest of the *ton*, but she must somehow find and stake her first vampire. Here. In the midst of her come-out.

'Announcing…Miss Victoria Anastasia Gardella Bellissima Grantworth.'

Victoria started down the stairs, slowly and regally, her gloved hand sliding along the smooth wooden banister.

She took her time, scanning the crowd of upturned faces, looking for ones she knew…and one that did not belong. Aunt Eustacia assured her that as part of the Legacy, as a Venator, Victoria harboured an innate sense and would recognise the presence of a vampire in normal human form.

As she neared the bottom of the staircase, she felt it: the cool wisp of something over the back of her neck, a breeze, a chill…where there was nothing moving the air. Unable to control her reaction, she turned quickly to look over her left shoulder, behind the staircase…into the shadows where a cluster of guests stood, watching her.

And then she was at the foot of the stairs, her mother slipping her hand into the crook of her arm and turning her to meet a group of distinguished men and women. The formidable Lady Jersey, the Duke and Duchess of Sliverton, the Earl and Countess of Wenthwren, and several others whose names were familiar to her. Victoria did her glowing mother justice: she curtsied and smiled and allowed her hand to be raised and kissed, all the while slipping her attention from the matters at hand and skimming it around the room.

It was a vast area, the foyer of Grantworth House. Four ceiling-high triple-fold doors at the top of a five-step landing had been thrown open to the ballroom. Lamps and candles glinted in every corner, on every surface, from every sconce. The room's pillars were surrounded by potted leafless saplings painted white and hung with glittering garlands. A six-piece orchestra was arranged in one corner of the ballroom, nearly hidden by a cluster of white trees; and a long table decorated with bowls of white roses held punch and other refreshments for the partygoers. Beyond the expanse of the gleaming pine dance floor, three sets of French doors opened onto the terrace. Late May's welcome breeze filtered in, and would have carried the heady scent of lilacs and forsythia if the air hadn't been heavy with French perfumes and floral waters.

'Do you feel it?' Aunt Eustacia had come from behind Victoria, and she hissed in her ear as she drew her from Melly's side.

'Yes. But how can I—'

'You will. You will find a way to corner the creature. You are Chosen, *cara*. You are Chosen because you

have the skills. All you must do is listen to them.'
Eustacia's eyes glittered like the jet beads woven into
Victoria's hair. Her gaze was filled with intensity,
certainty, and Victoria suddenly felt the heaviness of
the weight she bore. Tonight was her first test. If she
passed it, her aunt would reveal all to her.

If she didn't…

That did not bear thinking about. She would
succeed. She had spent the last four weeks learning
how to move and strike at a vampire. She was as
prepared as she could be.

'Good evening, Miss Grantworth,' said a dainty
woman approximately her own age. 'I am Lady
Gwendolyn Starcasset, and I was hoping to make
your acquaintance. I'd like to congratulate you on a
lovely debut. The white-washed trees hung with silver
garlands are a beautiful touch.'

Gwendolyn was daintier and smaller than Victoria,
with honey-blond hair and golden eyes. A smattering
of freckles were sprinkled over her shoulders and
across her back; but the front of her bosom was
lightly powdered so as to hide the ones there. She
had a charming dimple that settled to the right of her
mouth when she smiled, as now.

'Good evening to you, Lady Gwendolyn. Thank
you for your compliment; but I can take little credit
for the decorations. That is my mother's doing. She
is much more comfortable with these sorts of things
than am I.'

Because Victoria had been in mourning for two years, after her grandfather's and then her father's deaths, and the Grantworth family had spent an inordinate amount of time in the country at their Prewitt Shore estate, she knew very few young ladies her age. Of course, that dearth in friendships could have had to do with the fact that Victoria preferred to spend time haring about the countryside – or at Regents Park – on her mare, or reading books instead of making calls and genteelly sipping tea. Regardless, she felt more than a little delighted to have the chance to converse with a girl her own age.

Feeling a renewed shiver over the back of her neck, Victoria took a moment to look out over the crowded room. Where was he?

'So now you can join the rest of us eligible misses and parade around at balls and the like, searching for a husband.'

Victoria stopped scanning the room, surprised at her new acquaintance's bluntness. 'I do rather feel like a prime bit of horseflesh that is being trotted to and fro. I didn't think any of the other debutantes would share such an opinion. Finding a husband is such an important task, or so my mother tells me.'

'As does mine. And not to say that I wouldn't like to marry and bear an heir; it's just the manner in which we're reviewed. Although there are several gentlemen whom I wouldn't mind being reviewed by at all.' Gwendolyn's dimple appeared. 'Rockley, for one. Or Gadlock, or Tutpenney – despite his unfortunate name.'

'Tutpenney?'

'Believe me, he looks much better than his name sounds.' Gwendolyn sighed and added, 'And I was greatly looking forward to dancing with the Viscount Quentworth before the tragedy.'

'Tragedy?'

'Did you not hear?' Gwendolyn grasped her gloved arm, and Victoria looked down at her, surprised to see that the woman's eyes had widened in worry. 'He was found dead on the street near his home. It looked like he'd been attacked by some animal that nearly mauled his head from his neck. But there was a strange marking on his chest that couldn't have been left by an animal.'

Gwendolyn had Victoria's full attention now. 'What kind of markings? And how would you know of this? Surely your mama or father wouldn't have told you this.'

'No, of course you are right. But my brothers aren't terribly prudent about their topics of conversation once they've had a few glasses of brandy, and I'm not so shy about listening in on their talks. That's the only way I get to learn anything interesting.' She looked at Victoria from under her sandy eyelashes as if to read her reaction.

'If I had older brothers – or any brothers – I would likely do the same,' Victoria told her with relish. 'As it is, I must rely on my aunt Eustacia – whom most everyone believes is batty in the head, but who is really quite…enlightening. What kind of markings?'

'Oh, yes…the markings were three Xs on his chest. And I don't believe he was the first victim with this kind of mark—' Gwendolyn likely would have continued, but she was interrupted.

'Victoria,' came a shrill voice laced with barely concealed excitement, 'may I make an introduction?'

'I'll excuse myself for now, Miss Grantworth,' Gwendolyn told her. 'The Duchess of Farnham is heading this way to collect you, and there is Lord Tutpenney, looking ever so lonely. Enjoy the rest of your coming-out.'

Victoria turned to see Lady Winifred beaming an expectant smile in her round, dimpled face. 'May I present my sister by marriage, Lady Mardemere, her husband, Lord Mardemere…and his cousin, Lord Phillip de Lacy, Marquess of Rockley.'

And suddenly, the persistent chill over the back of her neck eased. Victoria felt a sudden burst of warmth spread over her skin, from cheeks to neck to bosom. She held off the urge to look down and see if her skin had coloured darker than her gown.

'My pleasure, Miss Grantworth,' Lady Mardemere was saying. 'What a lovely turnout for your debut! Your mother must be very pleased.'

'She is indeed,' Victoria replied before turning to curtsy for Viscount Mardemere. 'I have hardly had the chance to meet everyone myself.' And then she was looking up into the deep-set, hooded eyes of the Marquess of Rockley.

Lady Gwendolyn had not exaggerated. *Well-turned* did not begin to describe the man who stood before her, raising her gloved hand to his lips. He stood as tall as any man in the room, his rich brown hair gleaming with strands of gold as he tipped his head to press a kiss to the back of her hand. 'If you have not yet greeted everyone, may I dare hope there might be a dance left on your card?' His voice matched his looks – clean, calm, smooth – but his eyes carried a different cadence. Something that made her feel very warm. And…he seemed, familiar to her in some faint way.

'There is indeed, but it is one of the later ones. After supper, if you intend to stay so long.' She looked at him from under her lashes. Victoria did not know where her boldness came from, but it did not appear to dismay the marquess.

'I shall be at a loss to occupy myself until then,' he replied with a meaningful look, 'but wait I shall.'

And then she felt the chill return to the back of her neck, and the weight of someone watching…

Pulling her hand from Rockley's grip, she turned abruptly to look, skimming her gaze over the crowds and pausing at a small cluster of people across the room.

'Victoria?' She dimly heard the surprise in Lady Winifred's voice, echoed by a low rumble from

Rockley: 'Miss Grantworth? Is everything all right?'

There. He was there… A dozen or so of the peerage stood under the downward curve of the staircase Victoria had descended, half-shadowed in the candlelight there, faces bent toward one another, talking, laughing, gesturing.

And then she saw him. He was watching her even as he bent to talk to the slim blond woman next to him. Tall and dark, he exuded power with the mere inclination of his head as he smiled down at his companion. She beamed up at him, openly delighted with his attention, and smoothed her hand along his forearm – helpless and ignorant of the danger she faced.

Just as ignorant as Victoria would have been only weeks ago.

'Yes, yes,' she forced herself to say brightly as she returned her attention to Rockley and then Lady Winifred. 'I thought for a moment that I had seen my mother beckoning to me.' A limp excuse, but since she had offered the apology, it would be accepted. 'Please pardon my distraction, Lord Rockley,' she said, smiling up at him, suddenly realising he was holding her hand again. 'It has been my greatest pleasure to meet you. I will look forward to our dance later this evening.'

He sent her a melting smile and a short bow. 'I will be awaiting the pleasure with great impatience.'

At that moment, Victoria felt rather than saw the

tall, dark-haired man and his companion moving from their position under the staircase. The back of her bare neck was cold, and her fingers began to tingle. They were walking toward the doors that led to the terrace, the slim blond woman looking up at him with a soft, glowing smile. If they went outside…

Victoria started across the room, weaving quickly betwixt and among the crush, slipping past people who wanted to stop and talk. 'Pardon me,' she said when a particularly formidable-looking matron attempted to block her path. 'I must catch my…my aunt before she retires for the evening.'

Because he towered above the rest of the partygoers, Victoria was able to track his movements as the couple wended toward the french doors. They were most certainly planning to step outside to catch a breath of air.

Victoria slipped out onto the terrace, hoping her mother hadn't noticed the beeline she'd made across the ballroom. It would be rather difficult to explain deserting her own debut to wander on the terrace.

And even worse for that tiny blonde if Victoria did not intervene.

Hurrying on silent feet, she clung to the shadows of the noisy, well-lit house as she scurried across the brick terrace. Listening for the murmur of voices, she paused near a statue of Aphrodite, peering around its cold stone base to see if she could spot the man and his intended victim. She had to hurry; he wouldn't waste any time for fear of being discovered.

Then she remembered, and slipped her hand under the silky, flowing skirts to tug free the wooden stake she'd slipped into her garter. Gripping it the way Eustacia had taught her, Victoria left the protective shadow cast by the statue and hurried along the main path, listening intently.

And then she heard a throaty murmur, followed by a husky laugh. Turning to the right, she moved silently toward them and at last came to the end of the path. The couple stood under the canopy of a branch heavy with lilac blooms. The blond woman was looking up at the man, all innocence and delight; and he smiled down at her. Even though it was not directed at her, Victoria felt the power of his beckoning smile. She tightened her fingers on the stake and moved closer.

She was near enough now that she could see the rise and fall of the woman's bosom, and the sharp curve of her target's high cheekbone. He looked like an arrogant aristocrat, standing tall and dark with his handsome face and square-jawed chin.

What would it feel like to slam the stake into his chest? Would she have to shove it through clothing and bone? How hard would she have to push? Or because the heart was his weakness, was it unprotected and easy to penetrate?

She touched her crucifix, praying that she would have the strength. She would have only one good chance.

She couldn't wait any longer. He was smoothing his hands along the woman's bare arms, and she was smiling up at him, curving toward his body. They looked as though they were about to kiss; but Victoria knew better. At any moment his face would change… his eyes would turn a burning red, and his canine fangs would grow, ready to sink into the pure white flesh of the woman.

Now. She must move.

Gripping the stake, Victoria launched herself from the shadows, arm high above her shoulder, her eyes focused on the broad chest of the vampire. And just as she moved, as she was ready to thrust that stake home, the woman's mouth opened with a flash of white.

Stunned, Victoria managed to pivot at the very last moment, whirling toward the tiny blonde, whose eyes glowed red and canines shone lethally. It happened so fast that the vampire did not have the chance to recover from her surprise. Using the force of her sudden change in direction, Victoria slammed the stake into the woman's bosom.

It drove into her skin with sickening ease. Victoria felt a minor resistance, a small pop, and then the weapon slid in. It was like shoving a wooden pike into a bowl of sand.

The vampire froze, her mouth open in shock and pain…eyes wide and glowing red. And then, suddenly, with a small *poof!* the woman disintegrated. She crumpled into dust and was gone.

Just like that.

Victoria stood, panting, staring at the place where the vile creature had been.

She had done it.

She had killed a vampire.

Her knees wobbled. Her breath shook. She looked at her stake to see if there was any blood on it.

It was clean.

'You were going to stake me, weren't you?' came a chill voice.

Victoria looked up and saw that the man was glaring down at her with a decidedly unkind expression. 'I…' What did one say to the victim one had just saved from being bitten by a vampire?

'You thought I was a vampire.'

Victoria forbore to point out that it was an honest mistake; with his gleaming black hair and sharp-planed face, he looked dangerous and untrustworthy. 'One would think you would be a bit more gracious, since I just saved your life,' she replied stiffly.

His laugh was sardonic. 'That would be a fine day…one that I needed a girl to save my life. From a vampire.' He laughed harder.

At that moment, Victoria noticed that he was holding something in his hand. Was that a…stake? 'Who are you?' she asked.

'I am Maximilian Pesaro, master vampire executioner.'

Chapter Two

In Which a Piercing Commitment Is Made

'It was merely a precaution, my dear,' Eustacia said as she lowered her creaking joints and aching muscles into her favourite chair. Favourite, indeed, because of the well-padded seat and generous cushioning on the arms, and because of the small piecrust table next to it where she kept her spectacles, her cross, and a polished white hawthorn stake.

Old habits died hard.

Kritanu was putting Victoria through her paces here in the *kalari*, the well-curtained ballroom of the Gardella home, which had been outfitted as a practice arena. Some of her dark curls had fallen from their moorings, just as Eustacia's had done when she had trained for her hunting activities…oh, decades ago. Victoria wore skirts during these training sessions, since, due to society's dictates, that would most often be her attire. Eustacia knew that trousers made it much easier to spin and kick, but that would come later when she began to learn the Chinese martial-arts technique of *qinggong* in which she would fairly glide through the air, seeming to fly.

Victoria's porcelain skin was flushed dark pink, and her forehead and neck were damp with sweat, but the murderous expression on her face spoke volumes. Eustacia couldn't blame her for being annoyed. Maximilian had chosen the worst possible way to notify her of his presence; but then, that was nothing more than Max's character. Everything was perfectly black or white to Max, whereas most people, including Eustacia, were able to find different shades of grey. It made life more tolerable when one could recognise charcoal or a light mist colour.

Victoria had shown excellent promise with Kritanu in her education and training, or *kalaripayattu*, in the month before her coming-out; but as she'd never faced down a real vampire, Eustacia had felt the need to have plans for contingency purposes at Victoria's debut. It turned out those precautions had been needless; and indeed, perhaps had served to confuse the issue at the ball last night. But Eustacia would have done it again had she the chance.

The pride of a new Venator was a poor price to pay for the safety of her guests.

Kritanu watched with his sharp, dark eyes as Victoria took an offensive stance, then as she flew into action, pivoting, kicking, and whipping her foot into a stack of cushions next to Eustacia's chair. The cushions went flying, and Victoria stopped whirling, hands on hips, right in front of her chair. 'Aunt Eustacia, I nearly staked *him*! Though it would have served him right.'

'Now, Victoria, that's over and done with. You'll need to learn to move on, to put your anger and frustration aside if you are going to be a fierce Venator. Focus and strength, quick thinking and bravery… these are all characteristics you possess, but you must refine them. Learn to use them.'

As a Venator directly descended from the first Gardella, Victoria had been born with the innate fighting skills she would need to be a formidable vampire hunter. Agility, strength, and speed were already inherent in her; the purpose of Kritanu's training her in various martial-arts forms was to refine and hone those skills…draw them forth and teach her how to use them. And the *vis bulla* she would receive would provide her with additional protection and strength.

Victoria ducked and spun about to meet a rear attack from Kritanu, mumbling something like, 'I'd like to refine him,' but of course Eustacia wasn't about to acknowledge that kind of talk.

Instead, she allowed herself the pleasure of watching her lover and companion propel himself into smooth, lethal action as he dodged Victoria's defence and sent her tumbling to the floor. Kritanu, a wiry, muscular Calcuttan nearing seventy-five years old, was a daunting opponent even at his age. He wore an amulet that differed from the *vis bullae* given to Venators, but which gave him additional strength; but even without that, he was still quick and strong.

Nearly sixty years ago, he'd been sent to Eustacia to train her in *kalaripayattu*, the Indian martial-arts form favoured by Venators who fought the inhumanly strong vampires, and the Chinese *qinggong*. He'd remained at her side as her companion ever since. The fact that he also shared her bed was an item that they kept discreet; although Eustacia sensed that Max suspected the depth of their relationship. Kritanu's nephew, Briyani, had been Max's assistant for three years, and the trio of men spent much training time together.

Eustacia looked at Victoria, who was pulling herself to her feet. Her hair straggled over her shoulders, but her face was set with determination. 'Kritanu, I think she's had enough for the day. Thank you.'

He gave a gentle bow, his dark eyes soft and warm. 'I will excuse myself, then.'

Eustacia turned to her niece. 'Set your pride aside for one moment, Victoria, dear. Max was there as a support to you and for safety in the event that something went wrong. You performed well, even after he revealed himself to you. You will make a fine

Venator, *cara*,' she said. 'And together we will put an end to Lilith the Dark.'

The mention of Eustacia's nemesis took the edge from Victoria's eyes, and her annoyance seemed to collapse. 'You promised to tell me more about Lilith the Dark after I executed my first vampire. And about my *vis bulla*.'

'Indeed, and we will begin that as soon as you've had a chance to clean up a bit. Why don't you – ah, he is here already. Now, Victoria,' Eustacia said with a warning look as Maximilian entered the room with a swish and an air of impatience. She hadn't expected him so soon, and certainly wouldn't have had him arrive while Victoria was in dishabille. She was going to have to speak to Charley – the cook and erstwhile butler when Kritanu was otherwise engaged – about that again. She suspected that would be a losing battle, as Charley couldn't comprehend denying Maximilian anything, including the freedom to walk into any area of the house without being announced.

'*Signora*,' he said, squeezing her hand gently while he lifted it to his face and then released her fingers back into her lap. The sweetness of their homeland's language still flavoured his words, and it sounded lovely to Eustacia. She missed Venice. 'I apologise for my cursed punctuality.' He turned to Victoria, and Eustacia watched in fascination as his aristocratic features froze into a mockery of a smile. 'And Miss Grantworth. Our protégé. I bid you good evening.

Apparently I have interrupted some training?'

'Good evening,' Victoria replied stiffly. She didn't bother to hold out her hand, and Max didn't appear to notice or care. 'How does one address…the master of the vampire executioners? My lord? Your grace? Your Stakeness?'

Eustacia intervened before he could reply. 'Max, please take a seat. Victoria was just about to change out of her training gown. Victoria, go ahead. Charley will be along shortly with tea, or brandy if you wish.'

'Brandy? Much as I'd like to indulge, *signora*, you know that I do not partake when I am going on the hunt.'

Eustacia waited until Victoria had gone before she asked, 'Any news?'

He crossed his long legs and leant back into the seat he'd chosen on the settee next to her favourite chair. 'Lilith is here for something called the Book of Anwarth. She has apparently located it somewhere in England. London, to be precise. She's moved her entire entourage here.'

'The Book of Anwarth,' Eustacia repeated. A cold shiver curled at the base of her spine. 'I knew there must be a reason for her to bring her court here. That alone frightens me, Max. For her to uproot herself and leave the safety of her haven in the mountains… I have never heard of such a book, but I will send for Wayren. If Lilith seeks it, it can bode no good for us. She'll send Guardians for it, I'm sure. Imperials, too, perhaps.'

'I'll visit the Chalice. Perhaps I can learn more…'

'Yes, and Wayren will help.' Eustacia gave him a warning look, effectively ending the conversation as Victoria walked in. 'Ah, Victoria. That was quick. We were just about to begin reviewing the history of Lilith the Dark,' Eustacia said briskly, rubbing her knobby hands together. 'Max, I have told Victoria very little about her; I thought it would be best if you were here to assist in filling in the details from your vantage point.'

'Indeed. Please, *signora*, you tell the tale. I will comment as necessary.'

'Very well.'

Victoria leant forward expectantly, and for just a moment Eustacia hesitated. Looking at the beautiful, innocent face of her great-niece, she felt a wondrous sense of pride. She had staked a vampire on her first try. She had taken amazingly well to her training and had accepted all of the darkness and evil that lurked on this earth with a worldly attitude – one that even Eustacia hadn't initially had.

It would be a difficult life. She would give up many of the things other girls her age took for granted. She would be in danger more often than a young woman should be.

Yet, at the same time, Victoria would have a life of unparalleled excitement and adventure. She would face down the most evil creatures ever imagined, and know that she had the strength and cunning to best them. She would lose control of some part of her life, yet gain more freedom than a young woman even in this age could ever fathom.

And it was foretold: only one descended directly from the first Gardella could destroy Lilith.

Max, as formidable and magnificent as he was, was one of the few Venators who did not carry Gardella blood; and that was a fact that made him perhaps even more effective, more determined a Venator.

'Lilith the Dark is the daughter of Judas Iscariot,' Eustacia began. She had told this tale only a dozen times in her lifetime. The first time had been to the pope.

Perhaps this would be the last.

'Judas Iscariot? The betrayer of Jesus Christ?'

Eustacia nodded. 'Indeed, The man who betrayed Jesus for thirty pieces of silver. He is known as the Betrayer; yet the Lord forgave him as he did all mankind. But Judas Iscariot did not accept the forgiveness, and he hanged himself, as you know. He was thus damned to eternal hell. The devil sold him back his corporeal being, and gave him the power to walk the earth in the body of an immortal, a type of demon, in a form we call undead. An undead is damned for eternity once he drinks the blood of a mortal. He cannot be saved.

'In this damned state, caught between life and death, Judas lived in this world for centuries. While he was damned and walking this earth, he turned his daughter into a vampire. That daughter is known as Lilith the Dark. She feeds on human blood and human weakness. Lilith is now the queen of vampires, and she seeks revenge upon us. She lives on the blood of mortals.'

'Because we – the world of Christendom – consider her father a betrayer?' asked Victoria.

'Indeed. There is no name in Christendom spoken with more malice than that of Judas Iscariot. Once a proud name, now it is spit upon, said with hatred and venom. Judas is gone, but Lilith roams the earth, and she builds her army of vampires. She intends to rule the world; her strength is always our weakness. It is our task, our legacy, to keep Lilith and her minions at bay.'

'She and your great-aunt have been enemies for decades. Lilith knows that the only thing stopping her from taking over the world is Eustacia and her powers.' Max's face had deeper lines than usual, Eustacia thought. 'When your aunt first came here from Venice, Lilith couldn't find her. She tore apart Venice, and then Rome and Florence… She sent her people to Paris and Madrid and Cairo, and here to London. It was nearly two decades before she found your aunt. Eustacia's people kept her well hidden, and well protected.'

'You were the best of the lot, Max, young as you were.' Young and determined, he'd been. Angry because he'd lost his beloved father and sister to a vampire; and bloodthirsty in his own way. He chose the path of Venator.

'What is Lilith doing now? Do you know her plan?' Victoria asked. Her hazel eyes were not worried or fearful, as Eustacia had feared. No, they were sharp and calculating. And intense. By God, the Legacy had chosen well.

For the first time in years, Eustacia felt a glimmer of hope. With Victoria as her protégé, and, eventually, successor as the head of the Venators, perhaps Eustacia would soon be able to rest easy.

'In order to succeed, Lilith must destroy your aunt,' Max said. 'At the same time, she has sent hordes of vampires and demons throughout the world to turn as many to their way as possible. In order to feed on their blood, they bite the neck of their victim – not the chest, as is commonly believed—'

'But they leave a marking, don't they?' Victoria interrupted, comprehension dawning in her face. 'Three Xs on the bosom of the victim, as found on the corpse of those men near the wharf. That was a vampire, wasn't it?'

'You are very well-informed for a young girl,' Max commented.

Eustacia hastened to step in. 'Indeed, you are correct, Victoria; although I can't imagine how you would know that. Three Xs representing the thirty pieces of silver Judas was paid for betraying Jesus.'

'Which explains their fear of anything made from

silver. That fool Quentworth was most definitely a victim of one of Lilith's vampires, and we have worked very diligently to keep any hint of vampirism from being attached to his death. It was fortuitous for him that he wasn't turned. As you likely are aware,' Max said, looking down his long, straight nose at Victoria, 'if a vampire feeds on a mortal, it is often deadly... but if he – or she – chooses, he may partake of the human's blood, and offer his own blood back to the human in a kind of mating ritual. If that occurs, the human is sired, or turned into a vampire. So a vampire bite may kill a mortal, or may turn one to an undead. And there are occasions when neither happens, when the bite is not deep enough to kill. Our job—'

Eustacia interrupted. 'Our job is to destroy as many of them as possible while attempting to learn what Lilith is planning to do to seize power. We know that she has moved the bulk of her court to London; where she is hiding I do not know, and Max has not yet been able to ascertain. She is here not only because I am here, but because she seeks something called the Book of Anwarth, which we know nothing about as yet.'

'We Venators have always stopped her in the past. Although in the past, we have not been forced to rely upon young girls newly out of strings,' Max said with uncharacteristic nastiness. 'I do hope you will find time betwixt filling your dance card and selecting your ball gowns to help us.'

Her niece had risen from her seat and placed herself in front of Max, who'd refused to move from his lounging position on the settee. 'Filling my dance cards? Lord Max, or whatever it is that I must call you, I'll have you know that I left my debut – I missed a waltz with the Marquess of Rockley! – in order to protect you from a vampire attack. The status of my dance card remained forgotten as I followed you and your companion out-of-doors—'

'Protect me? Yes, indeed, you were protecting me from my own sharp fangs, weren't you?'

'How was I to know you were a Venator? You did not see fit to divulge that information to me until you could crow with joy at my mistake. But the fact remains that I did what had to be done. And I will do what has to be done in the future.'

'Victoria. Max. Please. We cannot allow ourselves to be divided at this time. Victoria, you must understand. Before you, there have been only three other female Venators in the last century of battle against Lilith. Two of them died hideous deaths shortly after they were inducted into the Legacy and received their *vis bullae*.'

'And the third is sitting here with us as we speak.' Max inclined his head toward Eustacia. 'There are none who could or will hold a candle to you, *signora* – or, if I may say – a stake. You are truly the Chosen one, the Gardella who will unite us and lead us to Lilith's downfall.'

Victoria turned to Eustacia in astonishment. 'You are a vampire hunter? A Venator?'

Max snorted. 'No, of course not. Lilith the Dark fears your aunt because she sits at home and has her hair dressed daily. Of course she is a Venator.'

Eustacia had to give Victoria credit: she did not give a flicker of indication that she had heard Max's derisive comments. 'I didn't realise, Aunt. I believed you were a teacher of sorts, a guide. Like Kritanu. I did not know you hunted vampires.'

'Indeed. And you, my dear, are the next of my direct bloodline, that of the first Gardella Venator, who has been Chosen – and who has accepted the burden.'

'And that,' Max said as he rose to his feet, 'is the precise reason Lilith the Dark has been so determined to find this Book of Anwarth quickly, before you finish your training.' His tone suggested that he didn't understand why Lilith would find Victoria any great threat. 'I must excuse myself now, *signora*. The moonlit streets await.'

'I'll get my stake,' said Victoria.

Max drew himself to his imposing height and looked down his long, narrow nose. He truly was magnificent, Eustacia thought fondly. 'Your offer of assistance is appreciated, Miss Grantworth, but I believe I will be able to handle three vampires without putting you at the risk of tearing your skirt or losing your bonnet. And, alas, it would be no virtue if you mistakenly staked a night watchman or a – what is the name – a Runner.' He drew on his cloak and from its depths pulled out a wicked-looking black stake. 'When you've had a little more practice, and received your *vis* amulet, I am sure you will find yourself on your own patrols.'

With that, he gave a little bow and swept from the room.

Eustacia was almost dreading turning back to her niece – knowing exactly what she would see on her face and in her posture. What had gotten into Max? He wasn't one to mince words, true, and from the expression on his face, he was worried about more than three unexceptional vampires…yet he had been more acerbic than usual with Victoria.

It was almost as if he wanted to discourage her from pursuing the work.

Perhaps that was it. Perhaps he didn't feel she was prepared for her role.

Eustacia reached absently to stroke Victoria's shiny black hair. She felt the same hesitation about exposing her beloved niece to the evil in the world … but at this time, she didn't have any choice.

Victoria had been Chosen, and she'd accepted her fate.

Now they would have to trust that she would succeed.

Two days after Maximilian swept from the room, setting off to fight vampires, Victoria had contrived an excuse to miss an afternoon of making calls in favour of visiting her great-aunt.

Today was a most important day: She had passed her test by staking her first vampire, and she was to receive her *vis bulla*.

Now here she was, about to take the last step toward her destiny. Victoria and her aunt were in a small room on the first floor of the Gardella home. The windows were draped with heavy curtains, and the furnishings were spare and simple, except for a tall cupboard at one end of the room. It was as high as Victoria's forehead, bearing ornate carvings along the edges of the two doors that shuttered its contents.

Candles burnt about the room, and small pots resting above the heat of the flames simmered herbs and water, releasing the scents of verbena and myrrh into the air. A large crucifix hung on one wall, simple yet commanding. It was made of two long pieces of wood fitted together, but with no other ornamentation. A long table held haphazard stacks of old books along with some jars and pots of herbs, oils, and other items Victoria could not identify.

'The *vis bulla* is the most critical tool to a Venator's success,' Aunt Eustacia told her as she sat in her large, cushioned chair. It was the only piece of furniture that looked comfortable. 'Today, as you accept yours, you also accept your destiny of belonging to the Gardella Legacy. You devote your life to the work of eliminating the evil of the undead from this earth, protecting mortals from the persistent creep of Satan and his followers. Upon your acceptance, Victoria, you must understand – there is no turning back.'

'What would happen if I decided not to accept the *vis bulla*?'

Eustacia stilled, looking at her with sudden, sharp eyes. 'Is that what you wish?'

'No, Aunt. I have made my decision. I will accept the Legacy. But I wondered what would happen.'

Her aunt seemed to relax. 'If you chose not to go further, you would undergo a ritual in which your mind would be wiped clean of all knowledge you've received heretofore, and you would lose any and all innate skill or sensitivities you have for being a Venator – skills that you were born with, that merely remained dormant until the dreams came. Those skills and inherent sensations would be given to another.'

'Has anyone ever done such a thing?'

'Indeed, yes. Many times over the years a young man – and in a few cases, a young woman – chose to return to a life of ignorance.'

'And they know nothing about this? Nothing they would see or hear would trigger their mind and make them remember?'

'Nothing. It is to protect them as well as to protect us.'

'Is there… is there anyone I know who was Chosen, but did not accept the *vis bulla*?'

'Yes, Victoria. Your mother was one such person.

And because she chose not to fulfil the Legacy, her powers were passed on to you.'

'My mother?'

Eustacia nodded. '*Si*. She had met your father and had fallen in love with him during her debut season when the dreams began to come. When the time came for her to make her choice, she chose your father.'

'Are there any…repercussions for one who is Chosen and does not accept the Legacy?'

Eustacia took Victoria's hands in her frail, cool ones. 'The only consequence is lost knowledge, and the fact that the powers and instincts will pass on to a descendent. And the powers passed on will be multiplied by the number of generations who have chosen to deny the Legacy. In your case, you are the third in a line of people who have not accepted the Legacy, so it is probable that you have great skill and instinct within you.'

'The third generation? My mother and who else? Who ignored the Legacy and allowed it to be passed to Mother?'

'My brother. Your mother's father, Renald. I was already Chosen when Renald had the dreams. It was very unusual for two people so closely related to be called at the same time. But my brother chose not to accept the task, and then your mother did the same. And so now we are here. You and I, Victoria. The only Gardellas who are directly of the Gardella line. The rest are from far-flung branches of the family. Their powers are more diluted than ours. And there are even some Venators who are not blood-related to us and have chosen at their peril to be Venators.

'Those who are not Chosen by divine order, as we of the Gardella family are, but who choose, must complete great and dangerous tasks… and even then there is no certainty that they will be able to accept a *vis bulla*. But once they acquire their *vis* amulets, they are just as powerful as we are. It doesn't make them any less skilled than we are, but since we are of the original family, we carry the heaviest burden.'

'Are we the only Venators?'

'Throughout the entire world, there are perhaps one hundred Venators, and at this time, you and I are the only living women Venators. And there are thousands upon thousands of undead, and their numbers grow every day, at will. We can never take our ease in this battle, for once we relax our guard, they will surge into strength and power. That is why I called Max here from Venice, for with London being Lilith's stronghold now, I knew we needed more support. The other Venator who had been here in England was killed three months ago.'

'Is Max a Gardella? Is he a real Venator?'

Eustacia speared her with her eyes so sharp that Victoria nearly stepped backward. She had never seen such a fierce expression on her aunt's face. 'Max is more of a Venator than you are, Victoria. He chose this path at great peril, and he is at this time the most powerful of the Venators…after myself. Yes, I am called *Illa Gardella*, and you will be too someday when I am gone. But I…my arthritis and age keep me slow. It is only his lack of Gardella blood that keeps him from being the Chosen one, the head of the Venators – the most powerful one of us all. Someday it will fall to you, Victoria.'

Her face gentled. 'Now, my dear, if you have had enough of your curiosity assuaged, perhaps you would bring me the book from the cabinet.' Her perpetually curling finger, the one part of her body that visibly betrayed its age, jabbed toward the mahogany cabinet standing against one wall in her private salon.

Victoria went to the slick breakfront and carefully fit in the tiny key that her aunt usually wore on a strong gold chain about her neck. *Click click, clunk…* the key turned and the lock tumbled open.

She had never gone to the cabinet on her own before, and had certainly never been given the key to unlock it. She realised she was holding her breath when she pulled both doors open as if she were the butler, sweeping a clique of guests through a set of French doors into the dining room for dinner.

Inside the cabinet, on its gently inclining display, rested an old book. The Holy Bible.

It was heavy, with gilt-edged pages that shone stubbornly despite its age. The leather corners were creased and bumped, but the spine was true, and three faded silk bookmarks fell lifelessly from their places.

Victoria brought it to Aunt Eustacia and placed it on her lap so that the older woman could read it.

'If you fulfil your destiny, Victoria, you will be victorious for us all.' She laughed softly. 'You are aptly named, my dear. Perhaps that is yet another sign.'

She opened the front cover and pointed to the words written in ink of varying shades of black, brown, and sepia. 'These are the names of the Gardellas who have accepted the Legacy,' she said, tracing across the lines with her curling fingers. 'The original pages of this Bible were given to the family during the Middle Ages. Six hundred years ago.' She looked up, her dark eyes sharp. 'You understand, there have been Venators in the Gardella family since Judas Iscariot hanged himself and was brought back to earth by Satan. But we had no place to record our history until a Gardella monk scribed this book in the twelfth century. The pages have been bound and rebound, and we have added more pages as the decades have gone by.'

As her aunt carefully turned the crisp brown sheets, they crackled like a gentle fire. Victoria saw images on some of them; and on others fading script, line after line. Ornate lettering, patterns, and illustrations in faded colours decorated the first letters of each book of the Bible. She saw the way hers and Aunt Eustacia's lines in the family tree fell directly beneath that of the first Gardella, and how other Venators appeared randomly throughout other branches.

'This book holds not only the word of God, but

also the secrets of the Gardella family, including the prayers and incantations that will empower your *vis bulla*. So now, my dear, are you ready to begin?'

Victoria's heart pounded, but she nodded without hesitation.

'Good,' Eustacia said. 'I will call the others.' At Victoria's look of surprise, she continued, 'The power behind your *vis* is not one that can be conducted only through me. Others who know of this matter and who, though not Venators, are nevertheless skilled and knowledgeable, await in the parlour. Victoria, you must lie on that lounge there. You are already garbed appropriately. Come, lie down. I will call the others.'

Victoria did as she was told, and settled herself on the long half chair that propped her back at a low angle and allowed her to extend her legs. She looked down at the training gown she wore. It was loose-fitting and buttoned from neckline to ankle.

After that, things happened both quickly and infinitesimally slowly. Aunt Eustacia moved about the room, which had suddenly, become much dimmer; lit only by candlelight. The other participants stayed in the shadows, but Victoria recognised Kritanu and Maximilian, as well as Briyani, Kritanu's nephew, who also remained near the perimeter. Something sweet burnt in the air, and Victoria felt relaxed and expectant.

'Now we will begin by calling to mind the purpose

for which we gather.' Eustacia began to speak in some language that it took Victoria a moment to identify. Latin. The others joined in and it continued. The smells in the room became stronger, and then Eustacia moved to stand next to Victoria.

Her stomach shrank back toward her spine when she felt Eustacia's warm, curling hands touch it. Then there was coolness as one, then another button was undone. The cloth of her gown was pulled apart just over her belly, and from her angle Victoria could see the oblong patch of skin that included part of her abdomen and exposed her navel.

'Forged from silver in the land of the most holy of places,' said Eustacia, 'this *vis bulla* will provide you uncommon strength and healing, Victoria Gardella. It will give you clarity and power when you need them the most, as you fight against the forces of evil that threaten our world.'

Victoria watched as Kritanu pushed a small table next to her aunt, and she took a small jar filled with a clear liquid. Something glinted in the bottom of the jar. 'This holy article, stored in holy water from the Vatican, taken from the Holy Land, will be your strength.' Dipping her fingers in, she pulled out the small silver item: the *vis bulla*.

Though the light was low, Victoria could easily see the small silver cross that dangled from a thin silver hoop. The hoop was narrower than the size of a ring she might wear on her smallest finger.

As Victoria watched, Kritanu picked up a thin silver wand, perhaps the length of one's palm and as slender as a needle. It curved gently, making a semicircle. Kritanu's hands were warm on her abdomen, and Victoria felt her breath become more ragged. He was gentle and quick, and with one swift, neat movement, he dipped the needle into and through the top lip of skin at her navel. Eustacia handed him the *vis bulla* and, with a quick pinch, he slipped it into place.

The silver cross felt cold resting in her navel, but the pain from the piercing was already waning. Aunt Eustacia made the sign of the cross over Victoria's belly, and then she buttoned up her gown. The other participants said one more prayer, and then they filed out of the room, silent, leaving Eustacia and Victoria alone.

'There,' her aunt said. 'This gift is given you in recompense for your life of dedication and the sacrifices you will make. As long as this amulet of strength touches your skin, you will be physically strong and quick to heal; Your movements will be swift and powerful; your mind will be sharp and clear. It does not make you invincible, nor does it make you immortal.'

She helped Victoria to sit up and drew her into her arms, embracing her with surprising strength. 'Wear it well, Victoria, and go with God as you do this work.'

Chapter Three

Miss Grantworth Miscalculates

'Our lovely debutante has scored the attention of the most elusive bachelor in London!' squealed the Duchess of Farnham in a decidedly unduchesslike tone as she poked over the tray of tea treats. 'Rockley could not take his eyes off her all night at the Roweford dinner party!'

'He was on her card a second time, but Victoria disappeared for some ridiculous reason and he could not claim the dance,' Melisande complained. She lifted her favourite, a blackberry scone, and scooped clotted cream over it. 'He appeared quite disappointed. I could not find her anywhere, and when she came back, she told me some foolish story about helping one of the other girls look for her cloak.' Tsking, she took a genteel bite of the scone, dabbing at the cream that stuck to the corner of her mouth. 'I reminded her that her only concern ought to be landing a good husband…and these other girls are nothing but competition!'

'Was that not the night that Mr Beresford-Gellingham disappeared?' asked Petronilla, eyeing the plate of tea cakes and biscuits mistrustfully, as if one were about to leap into her hands and force its way down her slender throat. 'That is the third incident in less than a month!'

Winifred, the duchess, had forgone Melly's technique of nibbling in favour of the one-step process; thus her mouth was full of lemon-basil biscuit, and she resorted to nodding vehemently. When she swallowed and washed the last dry crumb down her throat with tea, she said, 'He disappeared and has not been heard of since! No one seems to have a clue as to where he has gone off to.'

'And those horribly disfigured people with the Xs on their chests!' Melly gasped. 'Left to die near the wharves! I cannot imagine what might be causing such devastation.'

Petronilla leant forward, her blue eyes sparkling and her voice low. 'There is only one thing that can cause that kind of destruction. Vampires!'

Winnie jerked back in her seat and inhaled a mouthful of biscuit crumbs that set her to coughing. Her chins and jowls wobbled and trembled as she stared bug-eyed over the rim of her teacup.

'Don't be ridiculous, Nilly,' Melly told her. 'Despite

my mad aunt's propensity for carrying holy water and pressing garlic on anyone who will take it, there are no such things as vampires. You have been reading too many gothic novels.'

'Surely the Runners would stop them if there were vampires,' Winnie managed to choke out. 'Perhaps I ought to consider wearing my cross again.'

'The Runners couldn't stop them,' Petronilla told her calmly. 'Vampires have superhuman powers. They are stronger than the strongest man, and they have an allure that cannot be resisted.' She smiled complacently and copped a dreamy look. 'According to Polidori's book – and everyone knows he is the expert on vampires – a vampire can seduce a woman with a mere look. From across the room.'

'Nilly, have you been into the sherry this afternoon? There are no such things as vampires!' Melly exclaimed. 'You are frightening Winnie, and the servants will think you daft if they hear you fantasising about evil creatures that don't even exist. We have much more important things to worry about – such as how to push Rockley's interest in Victoria. I don't expect that he will darken the door of Almack's, but perhaps we will see him at another event this week.'

Winifred eagerly seized upon the change of subject. 'He will be attending the Dunsteads' ball tomorrow night. If you haven't been invited, I can arrange for that.'

'We have been invited and plan to attend. And this time I will not let Victoria out of my sight until she has danced two dances with the marquess!' Melly said with determination.

'We will help you,' Winnie said, sipping her unsweetened tea. Sugar tended to add unwanted pounds to one's hips if one didn't take care. 'If there are vampires lurking in the darkness, the last thing we want is Victoria coming face-to-face with one!'

'Miss Grantworth…at last the opportunity to collect my lost dance.'

Victoria turned at the sound of the warm, mellow voice and found herself face-to-face with the Marquess of Rockley. He wore a gently flirtatious smile, and his blue, heavy-lidded eyes glinted with satisfaction.

'My lord,' she replied, returning his smile, 'how kind of you to remind me of my abominable manners from the other night.'

He must have appreciated her sense of humour, for he offered his arm and responded, 'How else would I goad you into seeking my forgiveness? After all, begging off merely because your elderly aunt was feeling unwell…well, one might believe it was only a handy reason for abdicating your dance.'

'Hmmm,' said Victoria, slipping her fingers around his arm, 'I didn't realise my excuses were so transparent. Perhaps next time I'll be forced to invent a fatal disease or something of that nature!'

'It is my hope, Miss Grantworth, that you won't be inventing any further excuses for missing a dance with me, as I assure you that I am not about to tread on your toes, despite the fact that my feet are thrice the size of your own.'

'Ah, you have found me out... 'Twas for that very reason I made certain I was not available when your dance came up. The rumours of black-and-blue marks on the feet of the other debutantes...well, they are quite frightening. Alas, I shall have to chance the tenderness of my toes, as you have caught me dead to rights.' Laughing, she tightened her fingers around his arm, surprised at how solid and warm it felt, even through her gloves and his fine woven jacket. Looking up at him, she again felt a hint of familiarity, as if she had known him another time.

'It appears to be a waltz, Miss Grantworth...Lady Melisande, do you permit your daughter to waltz?' He was looking over her shoulder.

Victoria turned back to her mother and Duchess Winnie, who'd both been watching her banter with Rockley whilst wearing complacent smiles.

'Of course, Lord Rockley, of course,' trilled Lady Melly. 'My lord, I hope you will enjoy your dance!' Her eyes gleamed.

'She certainly does,' muttered Victoria as Rockley swept her away.

She bumped gently against his tall form as they turned, and he looked down at her with a knowing smile. 'She certainly does what, Miss Grantworth?'

'Hopes that you will enjoy your dance with me; but I am certain that you are no more hard of hearing than I am. It must be difficult for you, now that you, the elusive Marquess of Rockley, have announced you are seeking a bride. All of the matchmaking mamas have lined up, conniving and scheming to bring you into their fold.'

They stepped onto the dance floor in the ballroom of the Duke and Duchess of Dunstead's home. With a fluid, practiced motion, Rockley slipped the arm she clung to around and behind her, pivoting her to face him. 'You cannot imagine being in such a predicament?' He grasped her fingers, and they stepped into the time of the music.

'No, I truly cannot.' She looked up and found his eyes fastened quite quizzically on her.

'But are you not in the very same position? Being put on display for all of the young…and not so young bucks,' he added with a rueful smile, 'looking to wed and father an heir? Surely you must feel the same pressures our society imposes on all of us who are gentrified and also unwed.'

The dull ache of the ring through her navel was a reminder of the biggest pressure of all. She'd executed two vampires since receiving her *vis bulla*: one at the Roweford ball (causing her to miss Rockley's second dance, to her dismay) and one during an intermission at the Drury Lane Theatre. Both stakings had been frightening and exhilarating at the same time. The most difficult aspect, however, had been creating a reason to slip away and do her duty. Fortunately, Aunt Eustacia had been in attendance at both events and had been able to help her make her escape.

Victoria returned the marquess's smile. 'I may feel the pressure, but I have no intention of succumbing to it.'

He looked startled. 'You do not wish to wed? Does your mother know this?'

'It isn't that I do not want to marry; that I definitely intend to do,' she explained truthfully as he twirled her around the floor. 'It's that I have no intention of being *rushed* into making a decision that will affect me for the rest of my life.' Especially since she'd just made such a decision in accepting the Gardella Legacy.

But that was different.

It wasn't as if any other woman – or man – crowding the ball tonight would have such a choice to make.

The surprise in his face evaporated. 'I can certainly understand that sentiment, Miss Grantworth. I'm not certain that your mother, who is, at this moment, watching us with a definitely plotting expression on her face, would agree with you, but I can fully relate.'

Victoria smiled up at him, a burst of pleasure trilling through her at the joy of being spun gently across the floor by the Marquess of Rockley, no less. Surely Rockley was the handsomest, most charming, and wealthiest unattached man at the ball. And he was looking down at her with quite obvious interest.

'Miss Grantworth, I have a confession to make.'

'Oh?' she asked, raising her eyebrows delicately.

Every time she looked at him, she felt a gentle churning in her stomach – an expectant, pleasant churning.

'We once met long ago…and I have not been able to forget you.'

'It does feel as though we've met,' she replied. 'I have been wondering on that myself…but I must confess that I do not recall when or where it was.'

'Your forthrightness pains me, Miss Grantworth, but I must tell you the story. Perhaps it will stir your memory. Some of my father's holdings abutted Prewitt Shore, your family estate, I believe. And one summer many years ago – I was perhaps sixteen – I was riding one of the stallions from the stable. One that I was not, of course, supposed to ride,' he added with the hint of a proud smile, 'but, of course, I was a daredevil and I did. I came barrelling across a meadow, not realising I had strayed onto the lands of our neighbour, and – ah, but you do remember now, don't you?'

Victoria's face had lightened with a smile. 'Phillip! I knew you only as Phillip; you did not tell me you were the marquess's son!' The image was with her; it had been buried in the recesses of her mind, that summer when she was but twelve, but now it came back as though it were yesterday: a sturdy, dark-haired young man flying across the fields on a hot summer day. 'You jumped over the fence and your mount landed, and so did you – on the ground in a tumble!'

He laughed ruefully, his square jaw softened by the movement. 'Indeed, and I suffered for my boldness. But I met you, the pretty, dark-haired girl who rushed to my aid and made certain I was cared for. And you even chased down Ranger, the stallion, so that he would not return to the stables without me and tell the tale of my deceit. If I recall…once you were sure that I wasn't gravely injured, you spent the next ten minutes chastising me for my foolishness. The image of you standing above me, calmly holding the reins of that large chestnut gelding, and flaying me with your tongue, has stayed with me always.'

Victoria looked away demurely. 'I must have been quite bold to speak so to a man I did not know.'

'Indeed, and it was your boldness and your fearlessness that intrigued me. I have not forgotten you, Miss Grantworth, for you made quite a lasting impression on that young man. And,' he added as the dance music came to a close, 'it has become clear that you have lost none of your boldness, nor your opinions, nor your originality…for I am quite certain that there is not another debutante in this room, or in the *ton*, that is as unconcerned about finding a husband as you are.'

'And I have never truly forgotten the young man who rode with such carefree abandon in a manner that I only dreamt of doing. I envied you that. And I can hardly comprehend that you are the same boy that I knew for a few weeks! The marquess's son – I would never have known it.'

He smiled down at her, and warmth returned to her face. 'Someday, perhaps we will ride together, Miss Grantworth. And you can try your hand at leaping over fences and bounding across fields. I promise, I will tell no one.'

'And that is a promise on which I will hold you to your gentlemanly word.'

When they finished dancing, Lord Rockley returned her to her mother and Lady Winnie. 'I am rather thirsty; perhaps you are as well. May I provide you with some lemonade, Miss Grantworth? And, of course, Lady Melisande and Your Grace?'

'Oh, do not trouble yourself, Lord Rockley,' Victoria's mother warbled. 'But I am sure Victoria would love something to drink.'

Victoria gave Lord Rockley a surreptitious wink, but slipped her hand from his grasp. 'I'm sorry, my lord, but I see my next dancing partner approaching. Perhaps you will be thirsty later?'

'Of course, my lady. I'm certain I'll have a thirst for the remainder of the evening.' His eyelids swept to half-mast and he gave her a meaningful smile as he captured her gloved hand and lifted it to his lips.

Lord Stackley was Victoria's partner for the quadrille, and he led her through the paces with alacrity, if not with skill. Despite the fact that he stepped squarely on her feet twice during the first set with all of his solid weight, Victoria barely noticed. The *vis bulla* was not only good for fighting vampires…it was protection against clumsy gentlemen!

After Lord Stackley, she danced with Baron Ledbetter. Another quadrille. And then with Lady Gwendolyn's eldest brother, Lord Starcasset, Viscount Claythorne.

But it was during another waltz, with the tall and gangly Baron Truscott, that Victoria felt a familiar chill lift the hair at the back of her neck. Until that moment she had almost forgotten the fact that there were things to worry about other than whether her toes would be mangled before the night was over.

As Truscott spun her around, not nearly as elegantly as had Rockley, but with some efficiency, Victoria scanned the dancers and the others in the room. She would not make the same mistake as before, assuming the predator was the one who looked most like she'd expected a vampire to look: tall, dark, and arrogant.

After a moment she was fairly certain that a man with brown hair and a rather hooked nose, who stood with a young woman she didn't recognise, was the vampire whose presence she'd felt. She kept one eye focused on the couple as Truscott managed their way betwixt and between the other dancers. As long as they remained in the room, the young woman was safe. It would give Victoria time to extricate herself from Truscott and figure out a way to get the vampire alone.

She couldn't exactly stake him in the middle of the ball.

It was a curious thing: vampires were not allowed to enter the home of someone who hadn't invited them, or someone acting for the owner of the home. Gatherings such as this ball at the Dunstead home were by invitation, and only to the members of the *ton*, of course. So how did a vampire manage to get himself or herself into the ball?

She supposed it was due to the comings and goings of servants and staff, and the masses of people invited to events such as this. There were many ways to be 'invited' into a home…for something as simple as delivering a bouquet of flowers or the side of beef to be served for dinner. And once the invitation was extended, it was permanent as long as the homeowner did not change.

Victoria was thankful when the dance ended, but dismayed when Truscott manipulated their exit from the dance floor to be near the tables filled with drinks and cakes…completely across the room from where the vampire stood, watching.

Watching *her*.

Victoria realised with a start that his cold eyes had focused on her. Unblinking. Tugging at her from across the room.

He curled one side of his mouth in a half smile, still staring at her. A little nod. And then he slipped his arm around the woman next to him and began to lead her away.

A challenge.

If the chill on the back of her neck had merely raised her nape hair, it was now standing straight up. And ice was forming.

'Lord Truscott, I must excuse myself,' Victoria said quickly, pulling her arm from his grasp and ignoring the glass of lemonade he was offering her. 'I…I believe my gown has a loose ribbon, and I must…see to it.'

'But Miss Grantworth—'

'Please excuse me.' She slipped away, hurrying as quickly as she could without drawing attention to herself as she pushed through people edging the dance floor. It would be faster to move through the dancing couples, but that would only cause a stir. Pray God her mother or her two cronies didn't see her!

She kept her eye on the vampire's dark head, which was more difficult than when she'd been stalking Maximilian, for this man was only average height, and got lost among some of the other partygoers. The couple walked through an alcove, strolling at a comfortable pace, and turned down what appeared to be a hallway.

Victoria's skirts wrapped around her ankles, and would have been flapping if they'd been made of something heavier than light chiffon. Bending quickly, she slipped her hand under the hem of her skirt and pulled the narrow wooden pike from its garter on her calf.

The stake felt solid and comfortable in her hand. This one was more slender than the one she'd used to stake the vampire at her own coming-out party, but according to Aunt Eustacia, was just as potent as the thicker one. The trick was, she had told her, to find a stake that was light enough to carry and hide easily, but strong enough that it wouldn't break when being stabbed into the vampire's breastbone.

Victoria hurried along the hallway, listening with her ears and her instincts. She wasn't sure which room they had disappeared into...but when the ice at the back of her neck became almost painful in its intensity, she paused outside an ajar door.

He would be expecting her; but stealth wasn't as imperative as skill and cunning. Could he sense her in the same way she could sense him? He must, or how else would he have known her?

She toed the door open and waited. From her vantage point in the hallway, near the wall, she could see into the chamber. It appeared to be a den. A fire burnt across the way, and several large sofas flanked a red-and-orange Persian rug. A glimmer of movement caught her eye, and she watched as the faint shadow shifted.

Was the shadow the vampire...or his victim, acting as a lure?

The vampire could be hiding behind the door, waiting for Victoria.

She knew how to solve that. She kicked the door hard, and it swung open, slamming into the wall behind it and leaving the entire expanse of the room to her view.

'Ah. I see you have found us.'

The woman sat on one of the settees, and the vampire stood menacingly behind her. Victoria's heart thumped. Here she was, face-to-face with an undead. No advantage of surprise – and the additional problem of a victim.

Then she heard footsteps hurrying down the long hallway. And her name, called low, with urgency. 'Miss Grantworth?'

Good gad. Rockley!

She leapt into the room and slammed the door shut, keeping her attention on the vampire, and her fingers wrapped around her stake. Drawing in a deep, cleansing breath as Kritanu had taught her, she froze in an offensive stance and looked at the vampire.

'Release her,' she said, gesturing with her head toward the woman, who'd not moved one whit. Scared stiff, she was.

'I think not,' the man purred. He stepped from around the settee and Victoria suddenly, fully understood what Aunt Eustacia meant when she spoke of the allure of the vampire. It crackled in the room, this awareness she felt, an inexorable drawing toward him. As if he held her strings in his hands and was tugging ever so gently.

Without conscious thought, she dropped her hand to her belly and touched the *vis bulla* through the froth of her skirts. The headiness lessened. Her fingers gripped the stake. He stepped closer.

His eyes, still normal, but gleaming with a fierceness she'd seen only once – in the gaze of a mad dog that had had to be shot – never left hers. A smile curled his mouth.

'So you are the one. A woman Venator.'

'You seem to have the advantage of me,' she replied coolly. 'But that's no matter, as you won't be around long enough to enjoy it.'

A low laugh issued from his mouth, and she saw the gleam of fangs. His eyes narrowed, the pupils pinpointing and the irises burning pale pink, then delicate ruby red.

'I've never had the taste of a Venator before. I'm sure it will be most fulfilling. Quite delectable.'

Without warning he launched himself toward her, moving with such lightning speed that it seemed as if he'd flown on a breath. His hands closed over her shoulders, taking her by surprise. She dropped the stake, and he laughed when it fell onto his boots. His grip was painful, his sharp nails digging into the soft parts of her shoulders as she struggled against the agony and the fear.

Before you, there have been only three other female Venators in the last century of battle against Lilith. Two of them died hideous deaths shortly after they were inducted into the Legacy and received their vis bullae.

She was damned if she was going to give Max the satisfaction of her being the third.

Victoria tipped her head back, then slammed her forehead into the face of the vampire, thanking Kritanu for making her practise this move so many times. She felt the squash of his hooked nose giving way beneath the onslaught, and his reaction to the pain allowed her to jerk from his grip. She lunged to the ground and closed her fingers around the smooth ash stick, but before she could rise, he recovered and sent her sprawling.

Frothy pink skirts wrapped around her legs as she rolled onto her back; then they slid back like skates on ice as she drew her knees to her chest and kicked out with both feet. She caught him in the chest as he rounded on her, and propelled him away into a small table. The table fell over, scattering its contents over the rug. The vampire landed on the floor and she followed him, rolling after him on the rough Persian rug, stake at the ready.

She was just about to plunge it into his chest when something wrapped around her neck from behind: a strong, slender arm, ending in a white glove. Skirts of blue – a colour that did not match Victoria's dress – tangled around her feet.

As the arm pulled on her, Victoria slammed her head back, cracking into the woman's face. But the male vampire was reaching for her shoulders again, yanking her down toward his bared teeth.

She kicked out with her feet, blindly, not in the measured way Kritanu had taught her, and felt panic begin to clamp her chest. Two of them! She'd been fooled again!

She felt his hot breath on her neck, felt the tug of his calling, the promise that if she would just relax… just let go…there would be no pain, only pleasure. Ecstasy. Release.

His breath hypnotised her; his burning eyes scored into her, promising.

She vaguely felt a movement behind her, and then the jolt as he pushed someone away, growling in anger. The woman, she thought in the back of her mind. *He wants me for himself.*

The smooth wood slipped from her fingers. He breathed again, drawing in her strength. Her head swam.

She closed her eyes.

Chapter Four

The Marquess's Thirst Remains Unquenched

Maximilian brushed past the butler, who would have announced him if given the chance, and hurried down the wide, sweeping staircase at the Dunstead home.

Two Guardian vampires on the loose and here he was, chasing down a novice Venator who was more concerned with filling her dance card and juggling beaux than wielding a stake. Only the slight chance that the vampires might find her first had convinced him that he must notify Miss Grantworth by tracking her down at a bloody dance.

A quick scan around the crushed ballroom told him she was not attempting that ridiculous waltz. The back of his neck remained neutral: no vampires in the vicinity. Frowning, Max pushed around a cluster of tittering debutantes who gawked at him from behind fans in every shade of pink. He flung them a glower meant to send them cowering, but more than one of them looked at him with promise in her eyes and a pout on her lips.

Blasted English twits. Nary a thought in their minds but what was in a man's purse or his pants. Or both. No wonder so many of them were targets of vampires. Easy marks.

Max pushed through the room. He had the urge to leave, to get back on the street and track down the Guardians, but he also had to report to Eustacia that he'd first done his best to locate Victoria. He'd make his way through the entire perimeter of the room, perhaps stick his head out onto the terrace, as it wasn't out of the realm of possibility that the virginal Miss Grantworth had found an excuse to walk in the moonlight…and then he'd leave.

He'd made his circuit and seen nothing of his quarry, and was just about to slip out onto the terrace when he felt the barest coolness on the back of his neck. Max stopped. The chill was faint, just barely there; but since there was no draft and his nape was thoroughly covered with a healthy mass of hair, there was no mistaking it. He looked around, scanning the room again, and then down the hallway that stretched away up five steps. There.

He bounded up the steps and started down the hall that made an L turn after only three doors. The hair on the back of his neck was standing now, and at least he knew he was on the trail. The fact that

Victoria was missing from the ballroom intensified his urgency; she was either with the vampire – or vampires – or outside kissing one of her beaux. Either way, Max would have to handle the problem.

A novice Venator was no match for a Guardian vampire; God help her if she was battling both of them.

As he hurried down the hall, he saw one of the English fops Victoria had been swooning over at her ball.

'Miss Grantworth?' the man called, tentatively opening one of the doors.

Either he had an assignation with the girl or he was chasing her on *her* assignation. Regardless, Max had to get rid of him, for it was now obvious that Victoria was in this proximity.

'Are you perchance looking for Miss Victoria Grantworth?' asked Max pleasantly, belying his urgency. His nape was positively icy.

The man – the Marquess of Rockford or something of that nature – straightened as if caught with his hand down a lady's bodice. 'Indeed I am.' He looked at Max with a hint of challenge in his deep-set eyes.

'I believe I just saw her walking that way… She appeared to be returning to the dance,' Max told him. The last thing they needed was an interfering hero type, which was exactly what the Marquess of Wherever appeared to be. 'She looked to be making much haste.'

The marquess measured him, then gave a brief nod. 'My thanks to you, sir.'

Max barely waited until the man had passed him before hurrying off down the hall. His instincts pushed him on and he knew when he found the right door.

Flinging it open, he rushed in, pulling a stake from his pocket.

He was just in time to see a vampire poof into dust across the room; but he had no chance to take in the details, for a second Guardian had turned as he burst in and flew toward him with instantaneous speed. He stopped her in mid-leap with a stake to the chest, and she was gone.

Shutting the door behind him, for it had all happened so quickly he'd left it wide-open, he stepped in and surveyed the scene.

Victoria was in a tumble of skirts on the floor; but she was pulling herself to her feet by the time he took two steps. Her curling black hair was still anchored high at the back of her head, intertwined with some fripperies that appeared to glint when she moved. One thick corkscrew had escaped and fell over a white shoulder. The delicate fabric of her skirts was crinkled beyond repair, and her fair English skin cast a paler glow than usual.

'Maximilian,' she said, standing straight, holding on to the back of a settee. He noticed that her hand trembled ever so slightly as she pushed away a loose black wave that dipped over her eye. 'How fortuitous that you should arrive just in time to see my great escape. Or' – she lowered her chin and looked at him from under her lashes – 'was it that you came to rescue me? Sir Stakes-a-Lot saving the helpless damsel?'

She was white. And the faint quaver in her voice gave away her strain. And… 'Bloody *hell*!' Max was at her side, roughly pushing away the errant black curl that hid… 'You've been bitten!'

'Ouch!' She jerked away, still clutching the settee. 'I'm well aware of that…and it hurts, so don't touch it!'

Maximilian ignored her and pulled her toward one of the gas lamps so he could get a better look. 'He didn't feed much.' He smoothed his fingers gently over her warm skin, feeling the steady pumping of her vein under his rough fingerpads. When he brought his hand away, a smudge of crimson coloured his fingers. 'Damnation!'

He jammed his hand in his pocket and scrabbled his fingers around until they pulled out the vial. 'Do be still, Victoria,' he snapped, twisting the cork from the small bottle. He pushed her head none too gently aside so he could see the wound. Before she could react, he had sprinkled the four small red circles of the bite with the water.

Victoria shrieked in pain and jumped away, clapping her hand over the wound. 'What are you doing?'

'Washing the bite with holy water and salt, of course. And yes, it does sting, but it's the only recourse at this time. You'll be all right, but we've got to get you to Eustacia immediately. She has a salve—'

'Of course. I know that.' The look she gave him was dark. She let go of the settee and shook out her skirts. 'My gown is ruined! I cannot walk out of here and through the party in this condition! Everyone will think…Well, they'll think the worst!'

Max closed his mouth. When he spoke, his jaw was tight. 'I will fetch your cloak—'

'No, you'll never be able to find it. I'll go with you and we can cover up my gown. But my mother—'

'Eustacia will send her a note explaining,' Max replied, ushering her toward the door. 'Come, we have time, but not that much time. The holy salt water will only slow the Guardian's poison for a short time.' He fairly pushed her out the door and followed her directions down the hall, back toward the party.

When she'd found her cloak and arranged it to cover her gown, he took a moment to adjust the fallen piece of hair, tucking it firmly into the collar of her cloak so that it would hide the bite.

Moments later he was propelling her across the ballroom, dodging anyone who appeared eager to stop and talk, when the Marquess of Rock-something materialised. Victoria froze; Max could feel it all the way along the arm he'd been using to steer her through the crowd.

'Miss Grantworth. And…er…ahem.' He looked pointedly at Max. 'I was looking for you.'

'Lord Rockley,' Victoria said, with a gentle note in her voice that Max had yet to notice in any of his conversations with her, 'I apologise for disappearing, and I regret even more that I am being called away to my great-aunt's bedside. She is ill again.'

Rockley – so that was his name – looked at Max again, then back at Victoria. 'I see. Well, my lady, I regret that I was not able to quench your thirst this evening. Good night.'

'My lord, wait.' Victoria pulled away from Max and reached for the marquess's arm. He stopped and looked down at her, and even from Max's view, he appeared cool and untouched, although surely one of the most beautiful women in the room was pulling him back. 'May I present to you my aunt's personal guard, and my *cousin*' – Max heard her stress that last word – 'Maximilian Pesaro. He came to fetch me to her side. Urgently.'

Rockley gave Max another of his measuring looks, then the barest trace of a bow. 'Phillip de Lacy, Marquess of Rockley, at your service, er, sir.'

Max's patience was gone. The niceties of society and the flirtation between a debutante and a titled fop meant nothing in the grand scheme of things – namely that the beloved niece of Eustacia Gardella was currently carrying a vampire bite on her neck. 'My pleasure, I'm sure. Victoria, I must insist we be on our way. Your aunt is in desperate straits.'

To his surprise, Victoria allowed him to practically tow her off in his wake; she had to take quick steps in order to keep up with him, but she did so with a minimum of fuss.

'You appear to have no concept of how little time we have to address the situation in which you've so foolishly placed yourself,' he snapped, shoving her into the coach that had been waiting for his return.

Victoria stumbled in and crawled over to a far corner, dragging her skirts and cloak. Despite her bravado in facing him, she looked more than a little terrified about the result of her weakness. However, she recovered much too quickly.

'I suppose you will have some sort of nasty remarks to make regarding my weakness,' she said as the coach lurched into movement. 'Regarding my failure as a Venator. Bitten by a vampire. A great laugh for you.'

Max stared at her from his seat across the coach. A small lantern hung in the corner, casting a soft glow over the interior, enough that she could see his mouth set into a thin line.

He hesitated for only a moment; then he reached toward his throat and whipped the cravat from its perfect anchor, stripping it away and tossing it aside. Victoria watched, dumbfounded, as he snapped open the buttons on his collar and yanked it wide, exposing his neck. He turned to one side, displaying the four small marks of a vampire bite: two from the top fangs, two from the bottom.

With a steady look, he turned in the other direction and showed her the other side of his neck, right at the juncture of his shoulder. The one that had not quite healed.

'The reason I carry a vial of salted holy water.'

He settled back in his seat and turned to stare out the window.

Victoria closed her mouth and said not another word.

Victoria could not forget how easily she'd succumbed to the vampire's allure. When his lips had touched her neck, she'd softened, swayed, under his influence. His teeth, needle sharp, had played there…scraping gently over her skin, taunting, stroking, glancing over her pulse point as she lay in his arms, malleable and soft as a puddle of wax.

And then, just as he sank his fangs into her skin… as the painful pleasure flooded over her, into her… she gathered every last bit of reality that swam in her mind, and closed her fingers over the stake. He moaned in ecstasy, and she struck.

Poof.

He was gone, and suddenly Maximilian was there. And now he'd brought her to Aunt Eustacia's house.

'The Guardians had found her by the time I arrived,' Max explained as he hustled Victoria into the salon. Her neck was still throbbing, thanks to another generous application of Max's salted holy water during the ride in his carriage, driven by Briyani.

'Guardians?' Victoria asked as he directed her toward a chair. She sank into it and sat placidly while Eustacia and Kritanu bustled about the room. They were preparing something that smelt nasty and she expected would soon be plastered over her bite. Or, worse, that she would have to drink.

'Guardian vampires,' Kritanu told her in his gentle accent. 'Fierce and loyal to Lilith, they are her elite guard. She turned each of them herself; they are her personal servants. Many of them have been undead for centuries or more. A common, less powerful vampire has eyes the colour of blood. You can tell a Guardian by the colour of his eyes – they are not so red as that, but lighter, ruby pink.'

Victoria nodded. 'Is that the only thing that makes them different from other vampires?'

'Guardians carry a poison in their fangs, unlike other vampires and Imperials. If it is not stopped, it will cause death – even in a Venator. That is why Max was so determined to bring you back without delay.'

'Imperials? What are they?' asked Victoria. 'You did not tell me there were different types of vampires.'

'Guardians and Imperials are not common, and since there is so much you must learn, I felt it necessary to focus your time on learning to fight them, and teach you other aspects of the undead as time goes on,' Aunt

Eustacia confessed. 'I see that I have done a disservice in trying not to overwhelm you, Victoria. You might have been better prepared to recognise them tonight.'

'Imperials are the oldest vampires,' Kritanu explained kindly. 'Many of them are centuries, even millennia old. They carry swords, and they can fly or move about with such speed that they appear to fly. Their eyes are dark red-purple, and although they do not have the poison that the Guardians do, they are the most fearsome of the vampires. And the rarest.'

'And that is why I did not feel you needed to know that so soon.' Eustacia looked over at Max. 'I did not expect them to be so bold. Usually the Guardians stay close by Lilith; and Max has not fought an Imperial for two years.'

'It was obvious they were looking for Victoria; they sought her out at the ball.'

'Did you execute them?' Eustacia asked as she bent toward Victoria's neck, bringing a lamp so close it heated her skin. 'You did well, Max,' she added, brushing her fingers over the sore area. 'Your quick thinking will make this much less painful.'

'Victoria staked the one who was biting her. I happened to stop the other.' Max appeared to be perusing the page of an open book quite studiously. The page whisked as he turned it.

Eustacia looked at Max, then at Victoria. 'You staked the Guardian who bit you? *Sorprendente!* Kritanu, the ointment.'

'Yes…they were both attacking me, but he pushed the woman away. Then when he…' She glanced at Max, who looked as disinterested as if she were describing a new gown. Nevertheless, she dropped her voice. She didn't want the depths of her weakness to be so…evident. 'When he bent to bite me…I let him. He…hypnotised me, I think. I felt him pulling me – Yeow!' she squealed. And she didn't even think about how mortifying the sound was. It *hurt*.

The ointment wasn't merely cold and putrid-smelling…it stung as if it were drilling into her skin. It burnt ten times worse than Max's salt water, and Victoria couldn't hold back the tears of pain.

'I know it's uncomfortable, my dear, but this will keep the scarring to a minimum and destroy most, if not all, of the Guardian poison. With any luck, it will look like no more than some faint blemishes. And along with the fact that you executed the vampire who did it…well, there should be no harmful effects.'

Victoria resisted the urge to look at Max, who had turned three more pages. He'd rebuttoned his collar and retied his cravat. But she remembered the scars on his neck. They were much more noticeable than a faint blemish. The man was fortunate that high starched collars were in style.

Eustacia turned away to clean her hands and Kritanu gently wrapped a cloth around Victoria's neck, covering the paste that still felt as if it were ravaging her skin. 'Breathe deeply and slowly, in and out,' he told her quietly. 'In and out. It will help to ease the discomfort.'

Victoria did as he suggested, and it did, indeed, lessen the pain.

'You'll want to sleep here tonight,' Eustacia told her. 'I've sent word to the Dunsteads for your mother, so she won't be alarmed. I'll tell her I sent a coach for you myself, for if I know Melly, if she ever found out you'd ridden alone with Max, she would be quite beside herself.'

She took Victoria's hands. 'You staked a Guardian vampire while he was biting you. If I had any reservation at all about your calling as a Venator, Victoria Gardella Grantworth, it would be gone now. As it is, I suspected from the beginning that you were special. Now I know you are. If anyone can stop Lilith, it will be you.'

Chapter Five

In Which Miss Grantworth Finds an Unexpected Ally

'My lady! You've been bit by a vampire!' Verbena's eyes goggled in the mirror over Victoria's shoulder. With her round face and abominably frizzy red-blond hair, the maid looked like a babe just awakened from her sleep.

Before Victoria could think how to respond, let alone grasp that her maid had recognised the bite, Verbena bent to look closer. 'It looks like it'll heal just fine,' she said, nodding sagely. 'Put salted holy water on it, did ye?'

'Verbena…how…' Victoria collected herself. 'You aren't shocked at all.'

'No, my lady, and why would I be? With all the fuss about crosses, and stakes lying around, and that cross ye've got in your belly, what kind of maid would I be if I missed them clues? I've been waitin' for ye to ask me to find a way to hide garlic in your gloves!'

'That wouldn't smell very pleasant at all,' Victoria replied slowly. She wanted to shake her head to clear it. But she didn't think that would help.

'And why you're not carrying your own salted holy water, I've been wondering meself. And how did ye manage to get bit anyway? I thought Ven'tors didn't get bit?'

'How did you know I was a Venator?' Tired of looking at her maid through the mirror, Victoria turned on her stool and faced her.

Verbena stabbed a finger toward her abdomen. 'You carry the sign, of course, my lady.'

'How do you know about all of this? Vampires and Venators?'

Verbena shrugged. 'Who doesn't know about 'em? Vampires, I mean. Most peoples do, just they choose not to believe they exist. Unless they get bit; then they believe – but by then it's too late, in most cases. Everyone knows you got to stab them in the heart with a wooden stake, and everyone knows about the cross and holy water. I know most peoples think vampires are ugly, fright'nin' people who claw up your chest, but that ain't so. I've seen a bit before in me lifetime, I have. Me cousin twice removed, Barth, he knows lots about vampires, and he's been telling me stories since I was a little one. And he sees 'em a lot, too, over to the places in St Giles. He carries a big crucifix, he does. Holds it out in front of him when he walks on the street. Looks pretty funny to me eyes, but it's better walkin' safe than lookin' smart.'

It seemed once Verbena was given leave to talk, she took it. Greedily.

'Well, Verbena, I must say it is quite fortunate that you are so…er…well accustomed to the idea, as it will make things much easier for me. Because, of course, Lady Melly mustn't know anything about this at all.'

The maid bobbed. 'Yes, my lady. Your mother would up and faint dead away, then ship you off to the country for good. And then where would we be? There ain't no vampires in the country that I know. An' I've already been thinking about other ways to dress your hair so we can put a stake in there, if need be, so's you can pull it out real easy if you need it.

'An' there's prob'ly a way to put in two, 'cause I'm sure it could happen when ye might lose the one, and then what would ye do? Fortunate ye are to have such thick, heavy hair, so we have lots to work with. And until that bite is healed…well, my lady, that's going to be a challenge with these low styles that show off your neck and bosom, but I have some ideas, and we'll manage it. You just let me worry about that.'

'Indeed.' Victoria turned back to her mirror. For, after all, what else was there to say?

'I can appreciate her devotion to her aunt, but if Victoria continues to disappear at inopportune moments, she will lose all chance of landing the marquess – or any other prudent marriage contract!' Lady Melisande was pacing the parlour of Grantworth House.

'Now, now, Melly, don't fuss,' Petronilla urged. 'Surely the fact that your foyer and sitting rooms are filled with flowers indicate that Victoria has intrigued more than one potential beau!'

'Indeed, but none of them are from the Marquess of Rockley! He did not call today, and I am fearful that Victoria's leaving the ball early last night has cooled his interest.'

Winifred reached for a ginger cookie, a large crucifix thunking against her chest as she sat back. 'You said your aunt is ill?'

'I do not know – but she sent her friend Maximilian Pesaro to fetch Victoria to her side last night, claiming that she was. I do not wish to interfere, for my aunt has a vast fortune she will leave to us…and…well, she can be a bit frightening…but it could not have been a more inopportune moment for her to call Victoria away!'

'Maximilian Pesaro? I do not believe I know him,' Winnie commented, looking with interest at the lemon icing on a plate of chocolate biscuits. She had yet to make her selection, for fear of choosing one with a lesser amount of icing. 'Who is he?'

'He was the frightfully tall man who came striding through the room just after dinner like he was on a mission somewhere important. Dark hair, swarthy skin, and an expression that was like to send my heart pounding from my chest!' Petronilla replied, hand clasped to said chest as though to keep the organ in place. 'He looks terrifyingly dangerous. Like a pirate!'

'At least you did not say he looked like a vampire.' Melly took a seat on her favourite chaise. 'He is a particular friend of my aunt, and has recently arrived from Italy, perhaps six months ago.'

'He could be a vampire,' considered Petronilla, her eyes gleaming. 'I wonder if he is! Your aunt seems to know an awful lot about them.'

'I have taken to carrying garlic in my indispensable, on the recommendation of my butler's sister's mother-in-law,' the duchess confessed. 'I do not wish to be a victim of those creatures!'

'A duchess carrying garlic. How ridiculous!' Melly laughed. 'Winnie, there are no such things as vampires. In fact, the latest I have heard from my cousin Lord Jellington is that the Runners believe those people left for dead by the wharves were attacked by some kind of mad dog, and that the claws made the marks that people think look like Xs. They shot and killed one just two days ago, and there have been no more attacks since.'

'And what about the people who have disappeared? Beresford-Gellingham and Teldford?'

Melly put her teacup down rather a bit too abruptly. 'And what do you believe happened to them, Winnie? They turned into vampires themselves? That's ludicrous. Beresford-Gellingham likely took himself off to the Continent to get away from his creditors, and Teldford is foolish enough to have tripped and fallen in the Thames, never to be seen again. Just because two or three people have not given their whereabouts does not mean there are vampires about!'

'My maid told me she heard of a woman who was visited by a vampire in her bedchamber,' Petronilla breathed. Her hand fluttered at her throat. 'She said that it wasn't frightening at all…that he was very gentle and…passionate.'

'Gentle until he sucked all of her blood out with his fangs!' exclaimed Winnie in shock. 'Nilly, I assure you, it would be no sweet picnic to have a creature suck the blood from your chest!'

'I would agree if I believed they even existed. Now, enough of that ridiculous topic. Tell me what I shall do to ensure that Rockley regains his interest in Victoria,' Melly said, forgetting her habit of nibbling. She stuffed a whole ginger cookie in her mouth.

'Rockley was so attentive last evening, and the way he spoke about fetching your lemonade and having a thirst all night…well, I was certain he intended to ask you for a second dance, Victoria. I can't imagine what could have happened,' Lady Melly said as they settled in the carriage that evening.

'I can't either, Mama,' Victoria lied.

'Unless that girl Gwendolyn Starcasset has caught his eye again. He did dance with her twice at Lady Fiorina's ball three weeks ago.' Lady Melly's eyes narrowed and her lips pursed. 'You must invest greater effort into catching his attention, Victoria. Unless something has put him off, which I can't imagine what, you should have no problem regaining his attention. He finds you very attractive; he had his eyes on you whilst you were dancing with that dreadful Lord Truscott I warned you about.'

'Lord Truscott wasn't so dreadful.'

'Hmph. He hasn't the money nor the looks of Rockley. I do hope you will pay some attention to the marquess the next time we see him at an event. Perhaps you should not have left the ball early last night.'

Victoria nodded and agreed. Once her mother was put to something, she was put to it. And apparently Lady Melly was determined to make a match betwixt her daughter and the marquess.

In all honesty, Victoria had to admit that it was a pleasant thought. She'd danced with Rockley several times, and spoken with him at other social engagements, and she found nothing about him lacking. He was agreeable enough. Handsome enough. Witty and kind and charming, just as he had been that summer long ago when she knew him only as a young man – certainly not a marquess! – who seemed carefree and bold. They'd met every day for a fortnight, and he'd never let on that he was more than a boy from the village. He thought she was interesting and original and he had sought her out, based on his memory of her. That meant something, did it not?

Or perhaps his memory of her had been so perfect – although how a young woman harping on him could be considered perfect, she wasn't sure – that the reality of who she was today, grown into a young lady, did not meld with what he remembered. Perhaps she was a disappointment.

At least he hadn't tried to entice her into a secluded alcove and thrust his tongue down her throat and his hand into her bodice, as Viscount Walligrove had done at the Terner-Fordhams' dinner party two nights earlier. Victoria had dealt with the lecherous man and his bloated lips quite neatly. He hadn't known what came at him when she used some of the *kalaripayattu* moves Kritanu had taught her. Combined with the added strength from her *vis bulla*, Victoria's defence techniques had left the viscount in a heap on the floor, with a black eye, a broken nose, and a sprained ankle.

Perhaps he'd think twice about groping an innocent girl in the future.

'We are going to have to see about procuring a different maid for you, Victoria,' continued Lady Melly in a completely different vein. 'That girl –

Verbena – is much too careless in her work. Look at you – your hair is already falling down, and we haven't even arrived at the Straithwaites' yet!' She leant toward Victoria, her hand reaching toward the thick curl that rested over Victoria's shoulder.

'Mother, please.' Victoria moved quickly out of reach; though that meant huddling further into the corner of the seat she shared with Lady Melly and crinkling her silk skirts even more. 'I have no need to replace Verbena. She arranged my hair this way purposely; I wanted to try a different style. Perhaps we'll start a new fashion.' She smiled, even as she toyed with the offending lock of hair to make sure it still covered the four red marks on her neck.

'Hmph.' Lady Melly settled back in her seat. 'I can't say as I like the style for myself, but there is something to be said for being an Original. If you need to be an Original in order to catch Rockley's eye, then so be it. And I suppose the Straithwaites' musicale is one of the better places to debut a new style, if there is one.'

Victoria couldn't argue. Lord Renald and Lady Gloria Straithwaite were distant cousins of Lady Melly, and every year they displayed the substantial musical talents of their four daughters at a performance carefully choreographed to show them at their finest. The eldest had made a successful match last Season, and the Straithwaites clearly intended to continue the trend.

Because the Straithwaite daughters were triply endowed — with talent, funds, and curves — the musicale was fairly well attended by the marriage-seeking bachelors of the *ton*.

Shortly after arriving at Stimmons Hall, Victoria found herself seated in the ballroom. Tonight, however, though there would be music, there would be no dancing. The rows of chairs and the few settees along the side walls made it clear that all attention was to be focused on the four Straithwaite sisters.

She couldn't help but crane her neck to see if perhaps Rockley had elected to attend, but she did not see his dark head anywhere. Victoria settled in her seat to peruse the elegantly lettered program that had been rolled up and tied with pale pink ribbon. When she unscrolled it, she understood why. By the time one sat down and opened the program, it was too late to make an excuse to leave.

Ten pieces were listed.

Ten.

Victoria stifled a groan. She appreciated Mozart and Bach as much as anyone, but to sit through ten different pieces — each with three movements — was just too much for her. She cast a covert glance at the other attendees to see if there were any other shocked faces, but there weren't.

She was just going to have to suffer through it.

At first Victoria listened. She truly tried to listen. She sat primly next to her mother, taking as much time as possible to arrange her delicate skirts in gentle folds over her knees and the chair. Then she clasped her hands neatly in her lap, with her reticule tucked under her fingers. She could feel the outline of a small glass vial in the little pouch, which reminded her of the screeching pain in her neck when Max had poured his salted holy water on the bite. Verbena had somehow acquired a small bottle and filled it for Victoria so she would have her own.

Seething over Max's supercilious comments, and the pain he'd inflicted on her without warning, occupied Victoria's mind for approximately three movements of one of Mozart's quartets. It was only when she realised she'd gone beyond crumpling her reticule with annoyance and on to mangling her silk skirt that she knew she would have to think about something not quite as inflammatory as Max.

Maybe there would be a vampire here tonight and she would have an excuse to slip out of the room. Victoria held her breath and concentrated on the sensations at the back of her neck.

It didn't feel the slightest bit cool.

Or…maybe another lecherous gentleman would try to take advantage of one of the young ladies, and Victoria would be able to teach him a lesson.

She tried again to listen. And she succeeded in paying attention to each of the four Straithwaite daughters and the array of instruments they played throughout a Bach piano concerto. For the whole three movements, she managed to follow the melody and its ebbs and flows…and Victoria felt that was quite an accomplishment.

But then she looked down at the program and realised that the musicale was not even half over.

And her neck was still warm.

Submerging a sigh, she commenced to thinking about Rockley.

It was a delicious pleasure to recall the way they'd glided smoothly over the dance floor, his strong arms holding her just close enough to be proper, close enough that she could feel his warmth and smell the slightly smoky tang of his jacket. The way he looked at her from those heavy eyes made her want to close her own and slip into the memory.

She definitely wanted to kiss him. She knew that a kiss shared with the marquess would be nothing like the one Viscount Walligrove had imposed upon her. Fantasies about kissing might not be appropriate thoughts for a young lady, but then again, most young ladies didn't wear ash stakes in their hair and seek out vampires.

Nor did they have the strength and ability to instantly cut a grown man to his knees.

It was a heady power.

The only thought that marred her enjoyment of the memory of her dance with Rockley was the way he'd looked at Max.

And that thought brought her back to brooding

about the master vampire slayer. His arrogance and sharp tongue grated on her nerves. And the way he looked at her when she even breathed the mention of a ball or dinner party, as if being a Venator and having a social life were mutually exclusive options… Her fingers crinkled her skirts again.

She felt a sharp elbow in her side, and turned to look at her mother, who was frowning and glaring down at Victoria's hands. She smiled at Lady Melly and made her fingers release the poor cloth and tried once again to focus on the music.

The seventh piece out of ten. More than half done. But…she looked closer at the list. There were four movements to each of the last three selections, instead of three.

Victoria closed her eyes and then reopened them. She looked down at the list and counted again, and saw that indeed she'd been correct.

Vampires seemed to be making their way through Society events; why couldn't one be attending the Straithwaite musicale?

There was no question that the music was beautiful; it was, and it was elegantly presented. The musicians were lovely to look at, each dressed in a different shade of blue: ice, robin's egg, cornflower, and sapphire. But one could listen to a trilling piano and a singing violin, viola, and cello for only so long without wanting to get up and walk around. Or stake a vampire.

Disappointment had her looking back down at the program again, willing the musical sisters to begin playing Mozart's Piano Concerto in D Minor, the last piece on the list.

At that moment, Victoria felt a shift of air over the back of her neck. It was cool. She straightened in her seat, no longer drowsy and bored. At last. Something to occupy her mind!

She tried to look around without appearing to do so. Then she realised the coolness was gone. And she saw that the shift in the air had merely been the faint lifting of breeze through an open window, which someone had blessedly had the sense to open.

Victoria stilled, waiting, breathing with long, slow breaths so she could focus all of her attention on the barometer at the back of her neck. Surely she'd felt something cool. It wasn't just the breeze.

But nothing changed.

When the Straithwaite sisters at last began the final selection in the program, Victoria felt a change behind her – as if someone were looking at her. The hair at the back of her neck tickled, sending shivers down one arm.

It wasn't a vampire, no. She didn't sense that. It wasn't an uncomfortable feeling. It was…

Victoria dropped her program and, ignoring her mother's frown, bent to pick it up, turning to look behind her as she did.

It was Rockley, standing at the back of the room,

obviously a late – very late – arrival to the musicale. Victoria didn't know whether to be annoyed that he hadn't had to sit through the whole program, or delighted that he was there. Of course, there was no reason to believe he was there because she was.

Victoria looked at the three unmarried Straithwaite sisters with new eyes. Was he here to court one of them? They were all beautiful, even though the youngest was rather young, at just sixteen, to be debuted. And they were wealthy – much more so than Victoria was.

Now she was not only bored, but annoyed as well.

Then the last movement of the concerto ended. The string musicians pulled their bows away from their instruments for the last time. The pianist pushed back the bench and stood to join them in perfectly choreographed curtsies.

Everyone was applauding and standing up, at last. Victoria assumed it was from relief that the show had ended. But when she would have stood, Lady Melly snatched at her arm and pulled her back down into her seat.

'Rockley is here,' she hissed into her ear.

'I know that, Mother.'

'He's coming this way, Victoria. Remain seated. I am sure he will make his way to us.'

But what if he didn't?

Then… 'Lady Grantworth,' came the smooth voice from behind her. It sent lovely prickles down her spine and sounded warm and familiar. 'How lovely you look this evening. I trust you enjoyed the musicale?'

Then suddenly he was there, in front of her, standing in the small space between the rows of seats. Victoria didn't hear her mother's response to his question; she presumed it was one designed to take his attention off herself and direct it onto her daughter. 'Miss Grantworth,' he said with a bow and a delicious smile. 'I find that I still have quite the thirst from last evening. Would you care to accompany me for some lemonade?'

Looking up at him from her spot on the red velvet chair, Victoria felt a smile of relief and pleasure relax her face. He was looking at her as if they were old friends…perhaps more than old friends. When he offered his hand, she stood, and he pulled her up. The cloth of their gloves slid against each other with a dull friction, but she was certain that wasn't the only reason her hand felt suddenly warm. 'I am terribly thirsty,' she replied, slipping her hand around his arm. It felt comfortable, as if it belonged there. 'Lemonade sounds lovely, Lord Rockley.'

Asking for permission to be excused was a moot point, for Lady Melly nearly pushed them away and turned to speak with an acquaintance.

Victoria, feeling her face warm from embarrassment, looked up at the marquess and said quietly, 'It is no secret how my mother feels about your thirst. Indeed, I fear that she might be willing to send you to the desert in order to ensure that you are not quenched.'

'Indeed. I feared she might drag me from my seat to yours if I did not find my own way quickly enough.'

Victoria bumped into his arm as he tugged her gently around a corner, following the others out of the ballroom, and looked up at him, mortification heating her face. 'Oh, dear…I spoke only in fun, my lord! My mother is indeed like a sharp-toothed bulldog. I shall call her off immediately—'

'Miss Grantworth, *I* was only jesting. It gives me great pleasure that not only did I have the serendipity to see you two nights in a row, but more so that I was able to make it through the crowd to your side and sweep you away before any of your other beaux might do so.'

His words were light, but as they strolled through an entryway into the dining room, she read a different expression in his eyes. Under those heavy lids that on another man might have made him look lazy or insouciant, Rockley looked at her with a heavy concentration that made her feel almost faint…nearly as light-headed as the vampire had, just before he bit her last night.

At that thought, Victoria reached up quickly, grabbing at the curl that hung just so over her shoulder, to make sure it was still in place, covering the four red marks. She pulled it straight with nervous fingertips, then let it spring gently back into a concealing corkscrew.

And she realised he'd asked her a question. And was awaiting an answer.

'Too many to count, then, Miss Grantworth?' His voice levelled, and even over the rising noise from the other musicale attendees, she could hear its different inflection. 'Apparently I should have resisted the urge to visit Tattersall's today, and instead made my presence known at Grantworth House.'

'My mother and I would have welcomed you most graciously had you chosen to attend us today.'

'I am well aware that your mother would have done so…but I fear the question is more complicated than that, Miss Grantworth. You told me quite directly that you are in no haste to marry, and while I find that refreshing and a bit off-putting…I should rather know for certain how difficult it would be should a gentleman wish to urge you along that path.' They'd stopped walking now, and were standing near a cluster of people crowding the tables of food and drink. Three dozen people milled about, but for all of that, when Victoria looked up at Lord Rockley, she felt as if they were alone.

His arm had clamped her wrist close to his body as they walked, but now he allowed it to slide free as he turned toward her, standing with his back to the room as if protecting her, shielding her from the crowd.

Victoria felt a large, beaming smile work itself out from inside. 'Lord Rockley, I would have been *particularly* delighted had you called on Grantworth House today.'

The austerity in his face lessened. 'I am pleased to hear that, Miss Grantworth.' He reached for her hand and slipped it around his arm. 'Shall we find that lemonade I've been promising you?'

As they stood in line to wait for lemonade, Rockley nudged her gently with his elbow as if to gain her attention. She looked up at him, suddenly overwhelmed by a feeling of comfort. Here was a kind, handsome man who appeared to be interested in her as a potential wife...and whom she felt the urge to come to know better. To kiss, even. A man her mother would approve – no, thrust upon her. A man who had remembered her for more than seven years.

'You appeared to have been entranced by the music,' he said with a fond smile. 'I must admit, I would have been hard-pressed to sit for such a long period of time, only listening to Mozart and Bach.'

'Ah.' Victoria smiled back at him. 'That is the explanation, then, my lord.'

He handed her a white teacup filled with lemonade. 'Explanation of what?' Cupping her elbow, he gently steered her away from the tables and toward a pair of chairs at the other end of the room.

'Your tardiness in arriving at the famous Straithwaite Musicale. I'm sure the three eligible sisters were devastated that you missed most of their performance.'

'They might have been, but that is not my concern, Miss Grantworth. You see, I have a reasonable excuse for arriving here so late.'

Victoria took a sip of the lemonade, pleasantly surprised that it was perfectly tart and chilled enough to be refreshing. She looked at him from over the top of her cup, and when their eyes met she felt her knees weaken. 'Truth to tell, my lord, I am more than a bit envious that you had such an excuse; for if I had one, I would have arrived just as you did.'

'As always, Miss Grantworth, I find your honesty refreshing and amusing…but don't you wish to know the reason for my tardiness?'

Victoria considered him for a moment. He had a very pleasing smile, especially when his lips turned up just like that at the corners, ever so slightly. Now that she'd been reminded of the memories they'd come flooding back, and she recalled him smiling at her that way the day after they'd first met, when he brought her forget-me-nots in thanks for her help in chasing down his mount. The first time she'd received flowers from a man.

Victoria thought she might still have the pink satin ribbon he'd tied them with. She smiled up at him, as much at the memory as from the question he'd just posed. 'Of course I am interested in the reason for your tardiness, my lord, if you should like to tell me.'

'The reason that I arrived nearly two hours after

the musicale began was that it took me that long to discover where a certain young lady was going to be tonight.'

Victoria felt the rush of heat sweep over her, surely colouring her fair skin. 'Indeed?'

'Indeed. Miss Grantworth, may I call on you Thursday?'

'I wish that you would.'

Apparently, the young man from years ago was not the least bit disappointed in the woman she'd become.

Chapter Six

In Which Miss Grantworth Stands Her Ground

'Did you dance with your marquess last night, Victoria?'

She looked up from the stake she was whittling into a lethal point. Max sat in a large chair, drinking something the colour of topaz, and studying what appeared to be an ancient map of tunnels on a table next to him. He didn't even look up as he spoke. Aunt Eustacia and Kritanu had left the parlour moments earlier to retrieve a book and tea, respectively.

'If you are speaking of Lord Rockley, I'm sure it will delight you to learn that I did not.'

'Pity.'

Victoria considered the stake for a brief, delicious moment, then regretfully rested it on the table. She had four new polished ash stakes, each to be painted a different colour so that they could complement her various gowns. Verbena had suggested ivory, pink, pale green, and blue, and was advocating further decoration using flowers, feathers, and beads.

'I didn't dance with him because we attended a musicale, and there was no dancing. But he has asked to call on me.' She didn't care if she sounded like a petulant child.

For the first time Max looked up at her. His expression was forbidding. 'You are playing dangerously, Victoria.'

'Hunting vampires is playing dangerously. Being courted by a rich, handsome man is not. And in either case, I am well able to take care of myself.'

Max's gaze dropped pointedly to the side of her neck, where the four red weals had begun to heal. 'Your ability to take care of yourself has yet to be conclusively proven; however, that is not what I meant. You are playing dangerously with the marquess and his attentions.'

'Why do you begrudge me the pleasure of the company of a perfect gentleman?' Victoria asked. They had begun using each other's familiar names almost immediately after the incident with the Guardian vampires. It felt ridiculous to be formal with someone who hunted the undead in tandem with her. 'Is it because you never move in the circles of Society, so you look down upon anyone who does?'

He settled back in his chair and looked at her. The golden liquid in his glass streamed in the light, shifting as he gently moved his wrist in small, circular motions, as if he were thinking how to respond. 'Victoria, you completely misunderstand my motivations. I begrudge you nothing. If I had my way, you would have nothing to worry about but the next ball and whether to allow your marquess two dances in one night. But surely you realise that you cannot go on the way you have been.'

'I do not understand what you mean.' There was a shift in the air now, and the discomfort that always seemed to snap between them had ebbed into something lethally serious.

'I see that you do not.' He appeared genuinely surprised. 'Victoria, you cannot think to marry the marquess, so why do you continue to play with his affections? It is clear that he is smitten with you. Perhaps not in love, but at least smitten.'

'I cannot… Not marry him? I fear it is much too early to be discussing such a possibility, but should it come to pass, there is no reason I could not accept his proposal. I realise that, coming from Italy, you may not understand the machinations of Society here in England, but—'

'It has nothing to do with your position in Society.' The level tone was gone from his voice; now he merely sounded angry. 'Do not be obtuse, Victoria. You are a Venator. You cannot marry. You cannot even take a lover!'

Though she later berated herself for it, Victoria

could not stop her gasp at his words. Warmth billowed up her neck and into her cheeks as she responded, 'You needn't be crude!'

'Crude? As if being bitten by a vampire isn't the greatest form of crudeness. Victoria, you are a hunter of violent creatures. You cannot allow yourself to be divided or distracted by something so mundane as a husband or family.'

Victoria could hear the return of footfalls. She spoke quickly and quietly. 'If I choose to love or marry a man, I will do just that. And I'll continue to kill vampires while I do it.'

The door opened and Kritanu strode in, carrying a very large tray. He glanced curiously at Victoria, and then Max, likely noticing the tension in their faces, but he said nothing. Placing the tray on the sideboard near Max, he gestured to the teapot and cups. 'Please, Miss Victoria, you may pour your tea and perhaps help yourself to a biscuit.'

At Aunt Eustacia's home, it was an informal affair, as they were all treated as equals in the fight against Lilith.

'Eustacia will return momentarily. Our guest has arrived.'

'Guest?' Victoria asked, assessing Max. Yes, he'd known – just as he knew the purpose for this meeting, and she did not. Why did everyone appear to know everything except for her?

As she poured her tea, adding a dollop of cream,

Victoria stewed. Certainly she was the newest Venator, but Aunt Eustacia had made it clear that she was an instrumental part of the group. Why, then, did the rest of them talk about things that she knew nothing about? Keep information from her?

It was Max. He'd said it earlier – if he had his way, she wouldn't be a Venator; she would have turned away the opportunity to wear the *vis bulla* and help rid the world of vampires. Why was he so set against her? Merely because she was a woman? And young?

Were they testing her? Keeping things from her until she proved herself?

All of the Venators were equally skilled, and all had the innate skills and sensitivities to fulfil the Legacy once they received their *vis bullae*. Did Max truly believe she thought of nothing but balls and gowns and beaux? When she knew that there were hideously evil creatures wanting to take over the world?

True, many young women her age did think of little but finding a husband; after all, that was what had been drummed into their heads since the moment they were out of leading strings. But surely he'd seen by now that she was more than just another debutante. After all, she'd staked a Guardian vampire as he was biting her!

The door to the room opened and in walked Eustacia, followed by a tall, sapling-slender woman. She appeared to be several decades younger than Eustacia, but older than Max by a decade or more, and she brought with her an unusual, earthy scent. Her pale blond hair, as fine as the most delicate of silk threads, was gathered away from her face in a decidedly unstylish tail that hung down the centre of her back. She wore a flaxen gown that looked more like a night rail; it was floor-length and fell straight from her shoulders to her feet, yet still managed to portray the shape of her body. Her grey-blue eyes glinted intelligently in a pale, serious face, and her lips were a surprisingly vibrant colour of pink. She looked ethereal and clear-sighted, as if she could see things that others could not.

'You are Victoria?'

'I am, but I am afraid you have the advantage of me.' Victoria didn't know whether to stand and curtsy, or remain seated with her cup of tea as the woman moved to stand in front of her. The earthy scent, which was not un-pleasing, followed her.

'Victoria, this is Wayren. She is not a Venator, but she is a valuable help to our cause,' Eustacia explained. 'She has deep knowledge of ancient cultures, legends, and mysticism through her extensive library. She acts as a resource to us when we need her assistance.'

'I'm very pleased to meet you,' said Victoria, meaning it.

'Hello, Max,' Wayren said, turning. Max stood, and although she was a tall woman, he loomed fully a head taller than she.

He took her hand and raised it to his face, gently

brushing it with his cheek instead of his lips, then releasing it. 'Wayren, how wonderful to see you again. You look well.'

'And so do you, Max,' she replied with a smile that transformed her face into one of delight and humour. 'It has been well over three years since the last time we worked together. Apparently you are no worse for wear.'

Max laughed gently and Victoria stared. It was the first time she had ever heard him laugh with real delight. 'Indeed not. Now, you are here to tell us about the Book of Anwarth.'

Aunt Eustacia gestured to a chair, and when Wayren took her seat, Victoria noticed that she carried a large satchel that appeared to be quite heavy. It thumped awkwardly when she let it slump to the floor.

'Yes, and also to determine what Lilith wants from it. Eustacia contacted me as soon as she learnt that she was trying to obtain the book. It took me some days of travel to arrive.' Wayren looked at Victoria. 'I come from a long distance.'

'Did you find anything in your library that might help?' asked Eustacia, taking a seat herself in the chair that was always reserved for her, next to the piecrust table.

Wayren leant down toward her satchel and, flipping it open, pulled out a sheaf of paper and a battered book. 'My library is organised in such a way that it is simple to locate nearly anything by following a number system by topic. I found several mentions of something called the Book of Antwartha; Max, is it possible that you misunderstood the word and that it is Antwartha instead of Anwarth?'

He nodded. 'I would say. I was in a situation that did not provide a perfect environment for listening.'

'I am not surprised to hear that.' Wayren smiled. 'That makes things easier, as I wasn't able to find anything referencing "Anwarth". Apparently…' She paused, and dug back into her satchel. When she straightened, she was wearing a pair of square-shaped spectacles that gave her face a completely different look. More austere than fey, Victoria thought. 'The story behind this book has its origins in the Indus Valley, in the country of your ancestors.' At this she nodded at Kritanu, who had taken a chair next to Eustacia. 'You were correct that there is a connection with the goddess Kali.'

'Kali…yes, she is known in India as the Queen of the Dead. She rules over death, but she is not an evil goddess, as death is a state that we all must encounter. Legend has it that she bore a child who was half demon and half god. This child was known as Antwartha.' Kritanu's shiny hair, pulled into a short club at the back of his neck, gleamed blue-black as he nodded at Wayren, as if passing the tale back to her to continue.

'It is this demonic child of Kali who legend says gave his early followers the so-called wisdom in the

Book of Antwartha. The book contains rituals and rites for utilising the blood of the living as sustenance for the immortal followers of Antwartha – known as *hantus*, or, in your language, vampires.'

'Lilith believes this ancient book is in London; that is why she's here, isn't it?' Victoria said. 'How did an ancient manuscript get here? From India?'

'Likely in some manner of trade between England and her colony of India,' replied Max. 'Ships back and forth between London and Calcutta could easily have carried it here.'

'Yes, I can see that. But why now? How did it happen that Lilith just now found it?'

Wayren shook her head. 'I do not know; Max, do you?'

He frowned. 'My…source wasn't as willing to give information as I was to receive it, unfortunately, and at some point I had to put her out of her misery. All she told me was the name of the object Lilith is seeking, and even then I did not hear her properly. It is fortunate that Wayren was able to translate my miscommunication.'

'If the book is indeed in London, our first course of business, whilst Wayren continues to study her resources, is to locate the book before Lilith or her Guardians do,' Eustacia spoke. Victoria noticed that Kritanu had closed his fingers over her hand as if to provide support.

'That is imperative.' Wayren pulled her spectacles

away and looked at each of them in turn, including Victoria. 'According to my information, the Book of Antwartha contains powerful spells and incantations utilising malevolent power. If Lilith obtains this book, she will have the ability to raise demons at will by the legion. There will be no way to keep her at bay, even if we call all Venators here. She will overcome the world of mortals and we will all become her slaves... or worse.'

Chapter Seven

The Marquess of Rockley Presses His Suit

'Now, then, don't you look pretty as a picture!' Verbena gushed, leaning in toward Victoria and adjusting a curl that had fallen from her hairstyle. 'The feathers are just the touch!'

Victoria had to agree. Her maid was truly a genius! She'd slipped the pale blue stake straight into the thickest part of her hair, after affixing three soft feathers to the dull end. Thus, from the front, it gave the appearance of gentle white decoration shifting and flowing at the back of her crown. The beauty of the arrangement was that she could remove the stake from her coiffure easily and quickly, without disrupting the style.

'Wonderful, Verbena! It looks lovely.' Rockley was to pick her up for a drive in the park, and she was pleased that her hairstyle looked demure yet flirtatious.

'And now that your bite is near healed, well, tucking this light scarf around your neck will do just fine. Though I know you won't need the stake during daylight hours, 'cause them creatures don't come out then.'

Victoria turned. 'Oh, no, Verbena, that is not exactly true. Some of them do come out in daylight hours.'

Verbena's eyes turned into large circles and she sat on the bed suddenly, as if her knees had given out. 'No, my lady! You're funning me!'

Rather pleased to know something about vampires that her maid didn't, Victoria hurried to assure her that she was indeed correct. 'It's true. There are some rare powerful vampires, very few of them, who have lived for centuries and who have become somewhat accustomed to the daylight. They can actually move about in the sun, as long as they are covered or shaded, although they cannot remain in the light for very long, or allow the sunlight to touch them directly. If it does, they begin to burn.'

'My gracious word!' Verbena's round cheeks had turned furious red, and her flyaway peach-coloured hair seemed to vibrate with her anxiety. 'Me cousin Barth is goin' to have to start carryin' his crucifix during the day too? I don't know how he's goin' to get his work done, havin' to hold that thing up in front of himself all the time, and drivin' the hackney as he does! My lady, are you quite certain about this?'

'Aunt Eustacia told me so, and I believe she would be one person who would know!' Then a thought struck her. 'Verbena, did you say that Barth lives in St Giles? And he sees vampires there?'

'Yes, my lady, he sees more'n he wants to, that's for sure. But they leave him alone, because of his crucifix and the garlic he hangs from his neck.'

'Can you take me there?'

'Take you there?' If Verbena was horrified at the thought of vampires in the daylight, she was utterly traumatised at this request. 'St Giles is *no* place for a lady, my lady!'

Victoria stood, and felt the feathers waft in the air. 'Verbena, I am no lady. At least, I am not so much of a lady as I am a Venator. We have to find the Book of Antwartha before Lilith does, and if there are vampires in St Giles, it is possible that I might learn something from them. I wear a *vis bulla*, don't you forget. Max is not the only Venator who can hunt down vampires and make them tell him their secrets.'

Verbena opened her mouth to say something, and Victoria braced for another round of defence; but it was unnecessary. 'If yer going to St Giles, I'm going with you. And you're not wearing a gown, my lady. You'll dress as a man.'

'Of course. Thank you, and no need to worry. You will be safe with me. There is no time to waste, so we'll go tonight.'

'Tonight?' Verbena's eyes goggled. 'At night? Oh, my lady—'

'Tonight, Verbena. And you say your cousin drives a hackney? That is perfect. Can you arrange for him to pick us up at midnight?'

'Midnight?'

Victoria could actually see the rampant pulse racing in her maid's throat. 'Midnight tonight, Verbena, when the vampires are on the prowl.'

Phillip de Lacy, Marquess of Rockley, settled into the seat next to his companion. 'Miss Grantworth, you look utterly charming,' he told her as they set out for the park. His tiger and her maid were seated on the small raised seat in the back of the cabriolet, leaving Phillip and Victoria in the front.

'I might say the same about you, Lord Rockley.'

'You say? It must be due to the company I am keeping.' He glanced over again, just for the pleasure of looking at her. Her fair skin had the faintest pink tinge that he hoped was due to the delight of his company. And how did her slender neck hold the weight of all that dark hair? He imagined what it would look like if it weren't piled at the top of her head. How long was it? He remembered from that day in the meadow, when she had lectured him, how it billowed and blew in a mass of dark curls around her shoulders and arms, in ringlets from one end to the other.

'It is a beautiful day.' She sounded a little breathless, uncertain. Perhaps this was the first time she'd ever been alone – or nearly alone – with a man.

He smiled at the thought, pleased about it, then looked up at the sky and laughed. 'A beautiful day is it, Miss Grantworth? With those puffed grey clouds, laden with rain? Despite the sun peeking through occasionally, I had the concern that you might decline to ride out with me today for fear the rains would come and ruin your gown.'

He watched as she looked up to see what he'd seen: pillowlike grey-and-white clouds filling the sky, making it colourless rather than blue.

'I rather like the rain,' she replied stoutly, but with a hint of smile. 'It makes me appreciate the sunny days more.'

Phillip continued to grin. 'Nice save, my lady, and honest as always. And here I thought for a moment there that you were going to slip into the convention of talking about the weather instead of other, more interesting things. Can you smell the moisture in the air?'

'I never noticed it before, Lord Rockley, but the breeze does carry a scent that portends the rain shower.'

'Never believe that I have forgotten my promise to take you riding across the fields and meadows…but I feared for the weather to drown out our ride, and knew that the carriage would protect you better.'

'Lord Rockley, it is my turn to make a bit of a confession.'

He turned to her with interest, noticing that she was alternating between looking at her fingers, then ahead of them, and then at him. Where was his bold lady now? 'I am most intrigued. Please, confess what you will.'

And then the thought struck him that perhaps he would not appreciate her confession. What if she felt the need to divulge the name of another beau?

'I'm certain you recall the day after you fell from your horse, meeting up with me in the same meadow. I had gone there hoping to see you again, but not at all certain you would be there, of course.'

He smiled, relief lightening his grip on the reins. 'You would likely have found some other way to track me down and apologise for your harsh words, right, Miss Grantworth?'

She laughed, and he was pleased that she'd read the humour in his speech and remembered that she had not even thought to apologise for flaying a layer from his back. Good. That was part of what made her so interesting to him. She was not a shrinking violet, this Miss Grantworth whom he remembered...or whom she had become. He was more than pleased.

'As it was, I did not need to hunt you down, nor to apologise, as I recall, Lord Rockley, for you met me in that field, and you were the apologetic one.' She looked him fully in the eyes. 'That was the first time

I'd ever been given flowers by a man…and I still have the pink ribbon you tied them with.' As if to prove her point, she lifted her hand and tugged away the cuff of her glove, displaying a bit of her wrist and a pale pink swatch of satin tied around it.

'Your confession, such as it is, delights me, Victoria.' Propriety be damned; he'd called her by her Christian name for those weeks that summer. It felt foolish to be formal when they were reliving those moments.

He'd navigated them from the main drag of Regents Park and turned off into a more private area. Stopping the cabriolet next to a small thicket of lilac and forsythia, he gently wrapped the reins around the small post there for just that purpose.

Reaching for her gloved hand, he said, 'Miss Grantworth, I would be most appreciative if you would call me Phillip, as you did before.' He was aware of his voice deepening, as it did when he became serious, and he forced himself to look at her with a nonchalant expression. Perhaps it was too familiar too soon, but, devil take it, he must have fallen in love with her years ago, for he'd never forgotten her. Couldn't get her out of his mind. Had practically made a fool of himself tracking her down at the Straithwaite musicale the other night. Thank God he'd arrived late enough to miss the damned thing.

And it appeared, once her faulty memory was jogged, that she had not forgotten him.

'Phillip is such a strong name,' Victoria replied, looking not at him, but at the way his fingers traced each of her own gloved ones one by one. 'It suits you. And you may continue to call me Victoria, as you did when we were younger.'

And then, as if her words were some offstage signal, the clouds opened and the rain blasted down in sudden, loud torrents. The startled squeak from Victoria's maid at the back of the cabriolet drew her attention, but Phillip stopped Victoria from turning back to see to her with a gentle hand at her cheek. Any excuse to touch that flawless white skin.

'My tiger will take care of her,' he said. 'And their moment of distraction will allow me to do this.'

He leant into her sphere and touched his mouth to hers. She smelt like flowers and some kind of spice, and though he barely got a taste, her lips were warm and moist with surprise.

She did not start or move back, but instead pressed closer, angling her head to one side so their mouths fit better. Much better.

The rain streamed down around them, spraying fine mist onto the edges of the seat and onto their shoes. The tip of her nose, cool from the damp air, brushed against his warm cheek as their lips moved together. He released her hand and closed his fingers gently around her upper arms, bringing her closer to him so that her lovely breasts brushed against his jacket. Not close enough, but he was patient.

Or perhaps he wasn't.

She tasted as delicious as he'd imagined, and he wanted to sample more. He deepened the kiss deliberately, testing her...and she did not fail. She opened her mouth to him, and he felt the rush of want as their lips and tongues tangled. The brocade of her cloak crumpled under his fingers, and he closed his eyes when she reached up to touch his jaw.

When he released her and moved back, he looked down into green-and-brown-flecked eyes, hazy and heavy-lidded, and he felt a rush of satisfaction. She bore the stamp of his possession there in her face and wet on her swollen lips, not to mention in the faded ribbon around her wrist.

He was going to marry this woman, by God.

The freedom of wearing trousers!

Victoria had attained the age of twenty never experiencing the full range of movement, the loss of the fear of tripping over one's skirt, and the pure naughtiness of having one's nether limbs encased and defined in such an improper way.

She felt incredibly scandalous and powerful as she climbed into Barth's hackney without any assistance other than what appeared to be a heavy walking stick that had been sharpened to a point at the end. Verbena followed after her, looking like a moonfaced, wide-eyed boy, clutching a thick stake in one hand and a large silver cross in the other. With her hands otherwise engaged, it made her activity a flurry of useless motions until Barth lost patience and shoved her inside.

Scrambling into a seat across from Victoria, Verbena tried to adjust her cap while still holding the stake and cross. One peach braid stuck out, doing little to support her disguise.

'What makes 'em afraid of silver?' she asked as the hackney jolted into motion.

'Because Judas Iscariot betrayed Jesus for thirty pieces of silver,' Victoria replied. She was not nervous, but her senses were on edge. She hadn't told Aunt Eustacia of her plan to visit St Giles tonight, afraid that she would either forbid her to go or, worse, send Max along too.

'And garlic?'

'I do not know that, but I suspect it is because of the odour. A vampire's smell is much keener than a mortal human's. Perhaps it is acutely displeasing to them in their undead state.'

'Can you recognise one? When we're there…will you know if there's one before they try 'n' bite us?'

'I can always sense if there is one nearby,' Victoria told her maid, realising that the girl was plying her with questions to steady her nerves. 'Most of the time I can tell who the vampire is, and I am getting better at doing so. Don't worry, Verbena: I do not think they will attack without provocation, especially if we are seeking them in a public place.'

After a brief, difficult discussion with Barth, Victoria had convinced him to take them not only to St Giles, the vilest and most dangerous neighbourhood in London, but specifically to a place where he'd encountered vampires in a social rather than a predatory setting. Since Barth had seen and in fact transported vampires many times without being attacked, Victoria realised that he must know where they gathered.

It was only because she was a Venator that Barth agreed to take them to the Silver Chalice.

'If'n anyone can pr'tect himself, it's gonna be a Ven'tor,' he said by way of acquiescence.

When the hackney jerked to a halt (if Barth hadn't been Verbena's cousin, and guaranteed trustworthy for that reason, Victoria would have hired a driver with more finesse), she opened the door.

It was after midnight, but the street was as busy as Drury Lane would be after the theatre let out. The smells were much worse, however, and Victoria wondered how the vampires could stand it. The back of her neck had been cooling, but once she opened the door it became so cold she felt as though icy picks were thrumming on her nape. Turning up the collar of her man's jacket, as if that would help, she adjusted her hat to make sure none of her telltale curls were escaping.

Although it was a cloudy night, the street wasn't dark, due to random gas lamps swaying outside some of the establishments. Victoria used her lethal walking stick as leverage as she stepped down from the hackney, then moved to talk with Barth and instructed him, 'Stay, regardless of what happens.

'Where is the Silver Chalice?' she asked, noting that it seemed an odd name for a place that attracted vampires.

'Down there.' Barth pointed a shaking finger, whilst the other hand clutched his cross.

Victoria turned to look as Verbena stumbled out of the hackney, jostling her as she landed on the ground. 'I see nothing but a burnt-out building.'

'Down *there*, behind it.'

Victoria stepped closer and saw what he meant: an opening two doors wide, barely noticeable near the foundation of the burnt-out building. As she moved toward it, something bumped into her from behind, nearly sending her sprawling. Her walking stick raised, she pivoted to see Verbena shrinking away from three menacing creatures. Her maid's mouth was open wide in a silent scream, and Victoria had to swallow her own automatic reaction and remind herself that she was not helpless. She was a Venator.

'Wot brings two such dand'fied young men to this part of town, do ye think?' asked one of the three men. Something gold flashed in his mouth along with a grin that looked decidedly lascivious. Then something else gleamed silver in his hand.

The three men had circled around them and stood

close enough that Victoria could smell the fumes of alcohol and other unpleasant odours. All three were dressed in dark clothing that appeared to be, whilst not so very clean, at least in fairly good condition. They weren't vampires; vampires didn't need knives. A stake might not stop them, but Victoria knew she was stronger than three mortal men. Still…her gloves dampened under her palms. She hadn't thought to bring a non-vampire type of weapon.

'I b'lieve I heard the young men say they be looking fer the Silver Chalice,' replied his companion, as if Victoria and Verbena were no more than a disinterested audience to their conversation.

'We've found it,' she said, deepening her voice. 'We'll be on our way now.' Verbena bumped into her again, and Victoria resisted the urge to bump her back. She didn't need a clinging maid knocking her off balance if she had to shift into a fighting stance.

'Ye cannot enter without a token,' said the third of the men. He'd needed a shave at least three weeks ago, and his forehead and cheeks shone grimy and sweaty in the low light. 'If ye two lovely men wish to come with us, we'd be pleased to 'elp ye pr'cure one.'

'For a fee, I presume,' Victoria replied. Verbena bumped her again, and she nearly turned to shout at her…then she realised why the girl was standing so close when she felt something cold and heavy next to her hand. She wrapped her fingers around it. A pistol.

Victoria shifted and suddenly had the weapon pointing at the closest of the three men. She was calm, her breathing steady, but her fingers trembled. 'I don't believe we'll be paying you gentlemen any fees this evening. Now, disperse yourselves, sirs, before my finger becomes impatient.'

Although Aunt Eustacia had never taught her to use a pistol in her training, Victoria knew how to handle one. She'd seen it done. Pull the trigger and the thing would spit out a bullet whilst kicking back in her hand. Whether she would actually hit anyone was another matter; but the three men were so close, she was not concerned.

Of course, that was assuming Verbena had loaded it.

The men apparently believed her threat, and although they didn't disappear, they did melt into the darkest shadows of the stubby building next to the burnt-out ruins above the Silver Chalice.

Victoria slipped the pistol into the deep pocket of her cloak and, gripping the walking stick, started toward the double doors that led, she hoped, to the Silver Chalice.

The doors were closed, but when she and Verbena each pulled on one, they opened easily to reveal a steep staircase leading down into the earth. At the bottom was, fortunately, a dim glow of light, but certainly not enough to easily light their way.

But vampires had excellent night vision, so it likely

wasn't a hardship for them to make their way down a stairway so dark and straight one couldn't see two steps below. Victoria's neck was painfully cold, and the chill was beginning to creep up into the back of her skull. She reached back automatically to touch it, rubbing her fingers over her nape in hopes of easing the frigidness, but it made no difference. With a last look at Verbena, she started down the steps, thankful again that she wasn't wearing dragging skirts.

As she descended the twenty stairs, sounds from below became louder and more distinct. People talking, laughing, shouting…the clinks of metal tankards clattering together…the thuds and thumps of hands slamming onto tables or walls…and a wistful sort of music coming from a perfectly tuned piano.

When she reached the bottom, she had to turn a corner, and then she found herself in the Silver Chalice.

Although Victoria's experience with inns and pubs wasn't extensive, she had dined in two during her travels, and this one didn't look all that different from what she'd experienced in the mortal world.

Tables crowded the stone-walled room, which had a lingering dampness from being below the ground. Lanterns hung from ropes and chains from the planked ceiling, and the floor beneath was hard-packed dirt. Along one side, to the left and around the corner from the entrance, was another doorway that likely led into another room; although it was possibly another exit.

Next to that door was a long bar, behind which two women hurried back and forth, filling tankards and slamming them onto the counter.

No, if it weren't for the frozen feeling on her neck, Victoria would think she'd merely stepped into a travellers' inn that was just a bit darker and danker than she was used to.

No one seemed to have noticed her and Verbena, and for that she was thankful. Wanting to get a feel for the establishment and its clients, she hoped to remain incognito for a bit longer. She scanned the room, identifying which people were vampires and which were not. To her surprise, a good portion of the clientele weren't undead blood drinkers, perhaps as many as half was her guess. That portended well, for Victoria had been wondering what they might serve to drink at this establishment. Though she'd had more than one sip of brandy – the most notable time was after her father's funeral – she wasn't the least bit interested in partaking of anything vampires might drink.

At last she saw a small table stuffed in the corner a short distance from the piano. Grabbing Verbena's cold fingers, she tugged her to follow, and began weaving her way to it. As they passed the piano she noticed the musician, who hadn't stopped playing since she and Verbena had walked in: a female vampire with a long fall of silvery hair and an unhappy face, alternately bending over the keys, then turning her face up to the ceiling as if completely enraptured in the music. The song was sad and longing and beautiful in a haunting way.

When they sat, Victoria chose a chair so that she could see the rest of the room. It was rather a letdown that they had walked into this pub and found a seat with nary a glance or flare of interest from anyone in the room.

That, then, answered a question Victoria had been meaning to ask Aunt Eustacia: could vampires sense the presence of a Venator? The answer, apparently, was no.

Now that they were in the Silver Chalice, surrounded by vampires who might possibly know about the Book of Antwartha, Victoria realised she had planned no further than this. Perhaps she'd never quite believed she would actually get to this position. But she was…and she needed to act before Verbena fainted with fright.

Apparently they hadn't arrived completely unnoticed, for they'd barely settled in their chairs – it was much easier to flip up the tails of her coat while sitting, rather than gently lay out the skirts of a gown – when a serving wench elbowed her way to their side.

'Wot'll it be.' It was decidedly not a question – a bored, impatient statement, more like. Victoria looked at Verbena, at a loss for how to respond. Since she'd left her reticule at home, she had no coin with her.

'Two house ales,' Verbena responded smartly. She

slapped two coins onto the sticky table, a proud grin ticking the corner of her mouth.

Victoria looked at her. That was twice tonight Verbena had come to the rescue of the Venator. Perhaps Victoria had been a little hasty in deciding to come on her own.

But now...now that the niceties had been handled, Victoria could decide the next step. She was going to prove herself to Aunt Eustacia and the sullen Max and the waiflike Wayren, who looked at Max with such big blue eyes it made Victoria's mouth curl. It was abominable that he should lecture Victoria about being distracted from her mission.

As it turned out, Victoria didn't need to decide any next steps, for just as she finished patrolling the room with her eyes, a movement came into her peripheral vision, and a man sat down at the table with her and Verbena.

At first she'd thought it was Max.

But no. Not Max. No, this gentleman was most definitely not Max.

'Good evening, gentlemen.'

The dulcet voice, flavoured with a Parisian accent, belonged to a handsome man who immediately struck her as being an intriguing mixture of gold and bronze – from his tanned skin and amber eyes to his blond-tipped auburn hair and the chocolate-coloured waistcoat and fawn breeches that were clearly stitched by a tailor of immense talent.

He sat next to Victoria, very close; she wondered if men normally sat this close to each other at their private clubs. His leg touched hers under the table and it felt uncomfortable. Yet she didn't move hers away.

She made certain her voice matched his tenor when she replied, 'Good evening, sir.' When men were alone, did they require to be introduced before they conversed? Or did they simply have the freedom to talk without such formalities?

'You appear to be newcomers to the Silver Chalice. Since it is so difficult to find, we don't often have the pleasure of new faces. Have you come for any… particular reason?'

Was he warning them off or merely attempting to be friendly? Victoria did not know the appropriate way to respond, so she decided to be direct. The sooner she learnt whether the inn would be helpful to her, the sooner she could get Verbena back to Grantworth House. 'We are looking for information.'

At that moment the server reappeared and slammed two metal tankards down in front of them. The ale sloshed out onto the table, slapping onto the man's wrist and the edge of his sleeve. 'Damn, Berthy, can you not have a little care? This is alençon lace!'

'Ye shouldn't wear such fine things in a place like this,' Berthy snapped, swishing away with a twitch and a twaddle.

The man whipped out a handkerchief and dabbed

at the lace edging of his cuff. 'If she weren't so damn good at her job, I'd toss her into the streets.'

Good at her job?

Toss her into the streets?

Victoria wasn't sure which statement surprised her more, but she chose to focus on the latter. 'Do you own this place?'

'Indeed I do, though I'm not always proud to admit it. Among other establishments, might I add. Sebastian Vioget…sir. At your service.' He extended a hand, his attention focused on her so heavily Victoria nearly forgot to offer her own.

'Victor Grant…son. Victor Grantson,' she repeated more smoothly. His fingers closed around hers, swallowing them tightly for longer than she thought necessary. Or perhaps it was just the discomfort of knowing that her slender hand, even cased in black gloves, must feel much more fragile than most hands he'd shaken.

'And what kind of information might you be looking for…here?' His attention did not lessen in intensity; Victoria felt as though he were looking deep into her mind. The only thing that kept her from being apprehensive was the knowledge that he wasn't a vampire.

He most definitely wasn't a vampire…yet that did not explain the odd pull he had for her. It was not unlike the sensation she'd felt just before the Guardian vampire sank his fangs into her neck.

Victoria resisted the urge to shake her head; but she did shift slightly away from Sebastian Vioget under the guise of reaching for her mug of ale. Should she come right out and tell him what she was looking for?

Why not? Boldness in words and actions were the hallmarks of a successful Venator; although there were times when one must sit back and plan, she assumed. 'I am looking for the Book of Antwartha.'

Apparently her boldness was the right tack. 'And why would you think to find information about such a thing here? An old book would be found at Hatchards or Mason's. You have come to the wrong place.' He leant toward her, so close she could see the dark flecks in his golden eyes, and so near she could feel some kind of energy heavy in the air between them.

'I did not say it was an old book,' Victoria replied, 'though it is apparent that, despite your admonishments, I have indeed come to the right place.'

He laughed then, a low, rumbling, self-deprecatory chuckle. 'Indeed. In fact, I may be able to help you in your quest…but first, may I make a suggestion?'

She nodded, wary now that the glint of humour in his eyes seemed to have become focused on her.

'Wearing ill-fitting trousers and a hat does nothing to obscure your gender, and in fact calls attention to it. You have fooled no one.'

Chapter Eight

In Which an Unexpected Visitor Throws a Wrench in Miss Grantworth's Plans

'Perhaps it wasn't my intent to fool anyone,' Victoria replied. 'Perhaps I've come to the conclusion that trousers are much more comfortable than skirts.'

He laughed again, and under the table his leg shifted against hers. It was warm and heavy, and Victoria moved away. He looked at her and smiled knowingly, but fortunately did not comment.

'Since we've covered the niceties regarding my choice of clothing,' she said, feeling more confident now that she didn't have to maintain the unfamiliar guise of a gentleman, 'will you tell me who can help me find the Book of Antwartha?'

'If you would be so kind as to keep your voice more…temperate…I may be able to be of assistance. No, as I can see that won't be possible, we must go somewhere we can speak more comfortably.'

The thought of going anywhere with this man made Victoria uncomfortable…in a warm, improper sort of way. Perhaps it was just because Phillip had kissed her today that she kept noticing how Sebastian Vioget's mouth moved, and its shape. And noticing how close it was to her.

Just then someone turned the corner from the bottom of the same staircase she and Verbena had descended, and paused, standing a short distance from their table. Even though he was not facing them, she recognised his tall, dark figure, perhaps because she'd half expected to see it anyway.

Max.

Victoria swiftly turned away to hide her face. 'Do you have a place in mind?'

'Excuse me for a moment,' he said, standing abruptly. 'If you would be so kind as to walk through that door, I will join you shortly.' He drew her attention to a narrow door that Victoria had not noticed earlier; it was quite obscured to the casual observer, as it was nudged into the corner of an alcove. 'It is unlocked.'

Victoria watched as Sebastian moved easily, quickly, but without appearing to hurry, directly toward Max. An uneasy feeling churned in her stomach, but she stood as directed, hoping to slip out before Max saw her. If Sebastian was right, and her disguise was so patently false anyone would see through it, it would ruin all of her plans if Max merely looked in her direction.

Something tugged at her sleeve as she stood, and Victoria pivoted. She had completely forgotten about Verbena! How could the girl have so easily slipped her mind, sitting there next to her?

The answer was clear when she turned and saw that during her conversation with Sebastian, her maid had adjusted her chair closer to another nearby table and appeared to be quite companionably sitting with three other people, including the vampiric piano player.

'Is that not your cousin Max, speaking with Mr Vioget?' asked Verbena. Her breath smelt like the ale she'd ordered, and the sparkle in her eyes told Victoria she'd been having a grand time.

'Yes, it is, though he is not really my cousin. I must leave before he recognises me. Tell your friends farewell and come with me.' Victoria stood, gripping her cane-stake, and moved quickly through the door Sebastian had pointed out. Verbena followed.

Even as she curved her fingers around its rough edge to pull it closed behind them, Victoria paused to look back. Sebastian and Max stood talking in the same place Max had been standing since he came into the room.

Their conversation consisted of short bursts of speech shifting from one to the other, with little animation or expression on the part of either man,

Max being the taller of the two. Neither appeared to be on the offensive, yet neither appeared to be particularly agreeable toward the other.

As the two men moved apart with curt nods and without handshakes, she slipped back behind the door. Closing it after her, she turned to look, for the first time, to where Sebastian had directed them.

Verbena stood, leaning against one grey brick wall, still holding her tankard of ale. Or was it Victoria's mug? It was full enough that it appeared not to have been touched.

They were in a hallway with a curved brick ceiling and sconces studded every fifteen paces or so. Before Victoria had the chance to explore further, the door opened again and in came Sebastian.

'Your friend can wait without,' he said, glancing at Verbena. 'She will be quite safe with Amelie and Claude.'

Victoria would have declined, but Verbena was already starting toward the door. 'I would prefer it, my la – lord,' she said quickly. 'Amelie is the piano player and she has already fed tonight, so I am not afeared of her.'

'No harm will come to her if she is with Amelie,' Sebastian repeated. 'And what I am about to tell you is meant only for the ears of a Venator.'

Victoria started, then quickly recovered. Had Max seen her after all, and told him who she was?

'I will be safe as a bug,' Verbena told her with a

bright smile, and against her better judgment Victoria nodded her assent.

Verbena nearly slammed the door after her in her enthusiasm to return to her newfound friends, and Victoria was suddenly quite alone with Sebastian Vioget.

He reached toward her, and it was all she could do to keep from flinching; then she felt the top of her head cool and lighten as he swept her hat away.

'I have been wanting to do that since I first saw you,' he told her, dropping it carelessly. 'Now, if only…' He reached behind her, and this time she moved, just as his fingers touched one of the pins at the back of her head. She wasn't quick enough, for as she shifted the pin stayed in his grasp and pulled from her hair.

Sebastian tsked. 'I am one of those who thinks it a shame that women must hide the beauty of their hair.'

Victoria felt the pistol in her pocket and pulled it out. She didn't aim it at him, just pulled it out so that he could see it. 'That may be well and good, but I am no longer interested in your commendations regarding my clothing and coiffure. If you cannot help me with my quest, I will excuse myself from your presence and find someone who can.'

Sebastian laughed and dropped the hairpin. Victoria felt the heavy mass of hair slip at the back of her head, and she had to resist the need to touch it, to push it back into place. 'You are worthy of your legacy, my dear. Now, before we continue, I should like to know your real name.'

She saw no harm in telling him. 'Victoria. And I should like to know what makes you think I am a Venator.'

'I know quite a lot about everything. Including the fact that you… Ah, yes, indeed, it is true.' He was reaching toward her again, and before she could stop him he'd pulled back the high, starched collar of her man's shirt. His hand was not gloved, and it brushed warm against her bare neck.

Victoria took a measured step back. She was not going to react the way her body wanted to: quickly, jerkily, in panic. She would not let him know how he affected her with his insouciant way of touching her.

She was a Venator, and she was stronger than he. Whoever he was.

'Are you going to help me, or shall I just leave?'

'And risk your cohort out there recognising you? Without your hat, you look like a delicate young woman wearing her brother's clothing. Ridiculous, and an affront to your beauty. At least its brim hid some of that flawless skin and the line of your jaw.' He offered her his arm, turning toward the hall that stretched before them. 'I'm sure you aren't willing to take that chance. Why, I wonder, did you not want him to see you?'

Victoria did not take his arm, but she turned to walk along with him. The passage was wide enough that they could stroll shoulder-to-shoulder without brushing against each other, and for that she was grateful. As she walked, the unstable mass of her hair bobbed with the rhythm of each step. 'Do you know him?' She purposely did not say his name.

'Maximilian? Of course I do. He comes in here occasionally, and I have told him he may patronise the place as long as he does not cause a disturbance or hunt my clientele. Just as I have warned my other clients not to hunt their prey in my establishment. See? We all get along famously.'

They walked along the hallway, Victoria holding her cane-stake in one hand and the pistol in the other. She felt confident that she was prepared for whatever threat might come her way.

'In here, my dear,' he said, stopping in front of a door near the end of the hall. There was another option across from this entrance. Both doors appeared to be identical.

Victoria tightened her fingers on the stake as she stepped over the threshold into a well-furnished room that appeared to be an office. Bookshelves lined one wall; on another was a desk. To one side was a settee and two chairs clustered around a low table, near a fireplace. The wooden floor was covered with a rug. The only disconcerting thing about the chamber was the fact that there were no windows – and only one exit.

'I see that my study meets with your approval,'

Sebastian said. 'Please, have a seat.'

'You brought me here for what purpose? Surely the Book of Antwartha isn't sitting on the shelf there.'

'No, of course not. But it truly was important that we are not overheard in our conversation. Because' – he held up his hand to stop her furious response – 'I can tell you exactly where the Book of Antwartha is. And how to get it.'

Victoria closed her mouth and sat down. She rested her cane next to her and slid the pistol beside her on the cushion.

'Very good.' He smiled and chose a seat next to her on the settee. 'Now, then, if I give you this information, what will you give to me in return?'

Prickles erupted over her skin. 'What would be of value to you?'

'Two things. Two very simple things, Victoria Gardella. Ah, yes, I know exactly who you are.' Sebastian smiled and he looked at her with the gold-orange eyes of a tiger. 'The first requirement is…you cannot tell anyone where and how you obtained the information. You cannot tell your cohort Maximilian; you cannot tell your aunt. If you do, *I will know*. And it will go very badly for you. You see, no one else at the inn knows who you are. No one would know we have met. No one would know how you came upon this information unless you divulged it.'

Victoria nodded. 'I promise.'

'And I should trust you?'

'The same way I trusted you when you told me my maid would be safe. And the same way I've trusted you, bringing me back here.'

He chuckled again, that knowing laugh. 'Ah, yes, as a Venator you are in such jeopardy from me.' His words were mocking, yet there was an edge to them that told Victoria they weren't as careless as they sounded. 'But you were right to trust me regarding the safety of your maid. She is truly in no danger. As I told you, I do not allow preying on the unwilling in my establishment.'

'What is the other requirement?' The prickles on her arms rose in anticipation of his response.

'I wish to see your *vis bulla*.'

Victoria's throat went dry. Not what she had expected. But much, much worse.

'Would not a kiss suffice?' she asked boldly, a red haze clouding the edges of her vision. After all, she'd already kissed one man today. She could not imagine…opening her man's shirt and showing this stranger her middle.

'Are you offering me an additional favour? If so, I will gladly take it. In addition to my original request, of course.'

'Not in addition, but instead.'

'It is a tempting thought, as I have never kissed a Venator…but no. I wish to see your *vis bulla*.' The expression on his face told her he hadn't even considered making the change. 'And then I will tell you all you need to know.'

'How do I know what you tell me will be the truth?'

'You will have to trust me.'

It was Victoria's turn to laugh. 'And why should I trust you for something of that nature? And why should you help me?'

'As for helping you…I of course have my reasons, but sharing them with you is not part of the bargain. It is of no matter to you why I should help a Venator. And…if the information is wrong – which it is not, I assure you – what will you have lost by merely showing me your *vis bulla*?' His voice dropped to a disturbing low at the end, a deep almost-whisper.

'Or…' His voice was stronger now, steadier. 'I can simply give Maximilian the information. I am sure he would be appreciative.'

'He wouldn't show you his *vis bulla*' Victoria responded, suddenly realising that Max had one just like hers, dangling from his navel.

'I don't wish to see his.'

Victoria felt the harsh thumping in her chest. It was just modesty that prevented her from showing him. Just modesty. And if she did, she could return to Aunt Eustacia and Max with valuable information… or even the book itself.

Sebastian was watching her from a relaxed position in the corner of the settee, but she felt the tension as he waited for her response. And suddenly, as if giving up under his intense contemplation, gravity won out over Verbena's work, and her hair slid down from the back of her head into a loose mass around her shoulders. He smiled in satisfaction. 'Just as I had envisioned it.'

'Tell me something and I will decide if the information is worth a kiss…or the sight of my *vis bulla*.' Her own voice sounded rusty.

'Lilith knows where the book is. She will be sending her Guardians for it tomorrow night when the moon is high. Either you will stop them, or Lilith will succeed and have it in her possession. Now, will you play this game or will you not?'

Victoria angled back slightly against the arm of the settee, her torso turned toward Sebastian while her feet remained planted on the floor. The pistol was an uncomfortable lump under her hip, but she didn't care – she rather preferred knowing exactly where it was. She took off her gloves. Spreading the edges of her jacket, she pulled it away from the crisp white shirt that hung from the collar nearly to her knees.

Her fingers rested on the cloth at the centre of her belly, and she paused to look up at Sebastian. He hadn't moved, but rested quietly, watching her. His chest rose and fell under his own coffee-coloured jacket and pale shirt.

Victoria's fingers moved deftly as she pulled the shirt loose from her trousers. She could not look at him as she drew the edges of her shirt up, felt the cool shift of air over her suddenly bare skin.

The holy silver gleamed against the white of her flesh, nestled in the shadowed hollow of her navel. She heard Sebastian draw in his breath slowly, and then free it slowly.

He moved just as carefully, and although Victoria wanted to, she couldn't release the cloth she held open, couldn't pull it down. He reached toward her for the third time that night, and though her stomach shrank and dipped away, his fingers found the silver cross and caressed it…then slid to touch the gentle rounding of her belly, circling in an echo around her navel.

Warm, heavy, intense…his palm covered her skin.

The red haze at the edge of her vision turned dark and she could barely breathe.

Chapter Nine

Miss Grantworth Becomes Frightfully Chilled at a Most Inconvenient Moment

When Victoria opened her eyes, Sebastian was still looking down at his hand on her stomach. Blinking, trying to clear her head, she realised he hadn't even noticed she'd…what? Fainted?

Only a moment had passed – she was sure of it – since everything went dark. A brief second. An anomaly.

But whatever had caused it – whether it was her own sensitivities or some other weakness – she didn't want to chance that it would be repeated. She grasped Sebastian's hand by the wrist and removed it from her lifted shirt. He looked at her then, his eyes the rich colour of strong-brewed tea, all remnants of the golden colour gone.

'You wanted to look. You said nothing about

touching.' If she weren't so wary, she would have been jubilant that her voice came out strong and sure, with a hint of the mockery Max often carried in his tones.

He bowed his head in gentle acknowledgment and drew away.

'I will be grateful to you if, now that I have upheld more than my share of our bargain, you will tell me what I need to know.'

'Indeed I will, Victoria.' He clasped his hands over his chest, relaxing back into his position at the opposite end of the settee, and seemed to gather his thoughts.

That was fine with Victoria, for she wasn't sure she would be able to hear or remember anything he might say over the rush of wind in her ears and the pounding of her heart.

At last he spoke, and when he did it was brief and to the point, as if he, too, felt uncomfortable continuing to be in her presence. 'The book is currently in the possession of a man recently returned from travels in India. While there he purchased an old castle, and the book was included in the estate's library. A protection was placed on it centuries ago, and the book cannot be opened until the protection is broken. It also cannot be removed from the possession of its owner by a mortal human.'

'But an undead could steal it?'

'Yes, that is the case. You must thus wait for Lilith to send her accomplices to take the book, and that is when you must apprehend them, after they have already stolen it. Else, if you attempt to take the book on your own, you will die as soon as you touch it.'

Victoria looked at him, considering. 'But I am to believe that once a vampire removes the book from the owner, it is safe for a mortal to touch.'

'Indeed.'

'And…how is a vampire to steal it from this man if it cannot cross the threshold of a home uninvited?' Scepticism laced her voice.

Sebastian gave a bare nod, as if acknowledging her cynicism. 'That is why it will happen two nights from now. The owner of the house will leave on his travels, and the person staying there in his absence will invite the undead into the home.'

'This person who will invite the vampires in…is he aware that they are vampires? And the purpose of their visit? Will this person be harmed?'

Sebastian's shoulders moved in a careless shrug. 'That is all the information you will need, Victoria. You may act on it or choose not to.'

'And if you are lying to me, or mistaken in your information, I will suffer the consequences.'

Sebastian stirred, sitting up and leaning toward her, his eyes dark slits. 'Victoria, I intend this to be only the first of many times for us to meet. Thus, I assure you, I am not lying. And when it comes to matters such as these, I am never mistaken.'

* * *

Victoria and Verbena did not arrive home until the sun was peeking over the eastern edge of London's profile. Weary, exhilarated, and unbalanced by the events of the night, Victoria did not speak during the ride home, and instead contemplated her next course of action.

Sebastian had given her the direction of the man who had the Book of Antwartha. He also reiterated that the vampires were to steal it in two nights, which was now the very next night, because the owner would be away. If his information was accurate, Victoria had visited the Silver Chalice none too soon. Perhaps that was why Max had been there last night.

Should she tell Aunt Eustacia and, by telling her, inform Max, so that they could work together to obtain the book? Or should she lie in wait for Lilith's men herself, in the event that the information Sebastian gave her was false?

At Grantworth House the hackney pulled up at the curb by a yawning Barth, and Victoria and Verbena slipped down and onto the walk. Hustling toward the servants' entrance, Victoria followed Verbena through the back way, which had been left open by pre-arrangement, and managed to slink into her room without being noticed by any of the servants. Lady Melly would sleep until after noon, and to her knowledge, Victoria had come home from a dinner party with the headache.

Verbena helped her undress, and Victoria fell

gratefully onto her feather bed. Just as she was drifting off to sleep she remembered: tonight she was to see Phillip at the Madagascars' ball. Perhaps there would be an opportunity for him to kiss her again.

She smiled into her pillow.

'Why is it,' Phillip murmured as he drew Victoria close to his side, 'that I must always beat a path through a throng of bucks if I wish to dance with you?'

Her wrist tucked betwixt his arm and his side, she allowed her hip to sway against his as they strolled away. 'They were not there to speak only to me,' she replied, turning up her face to smile at him. 'Gwendolyn Starcasset has quite a following as well.'

'That may be so, but most of them were panting over your hand, not hers.'

'You are too kind, sir,' she replied with a coy smile.

His arm tightened hers against his side. 'I am not kind whatsoever,' Phillip replied. 'In fact, I have not one whit of kindness toward those fops.'

'And what of the mamas and belles who moon over your handsome face and bulging purse?'

'I am soon to put them out of their misery. Would you care for something to drink, Victoria?'

She could only nod and try not to stare up at him. *Soon to put them out of their misery?* Could he mean what she thought he meant? Her skin flushed warm and she was grateful for the cup of punch in which she could bury her face.

It was only yesterday that he'd kissed her in the park, and despite her unsettling experience at the Silver Chalice, Victoria had awakened late in the day today remembering the taste of his lips. Wondering if tonight he would take the opportunity again.

A proper lady wasn't supposed to think about kissing a man to whom she was not married, or at least betrothed. But since she'd received her *vis bulla*, Victoria had moved far beyond being a proper lady. Killing vampires. Wearing trousers. Walking the streets at night.

Showing her navel to strange men.

What would Phillip think if he saw her *vis bulla*!

Her face grew hotter than ever, and Phillip must have noticed, for he said, 'Are you feeling quite all right, Victoria? Shall we step outside for some air?'

'Yes, I would like that.'

Just outside the ballroom's grand french doors, Victoria and Phillip paused on the terrace. Two other couples stood at the waist-high railing, looking down over the weaving pathways and clusters of hedge that made up the Madagascars' walking garden. A gentle sweep of steps led from the centre of the stone terrace down into the vegetation below.

Phillip released Victoria's arm and slid his around the back of her waist, guiding her along the railing. A gardenia tree, laden with creamy white blossoms, grew up from below and was near enough that he could choose a flower and offer it to her.

'For my lady,' he said, holding it out to her. 'I wanted to bring forget-me-nots, but they are out of season.'

Victoria smiled as she accepted the gardenia, amazed as always by the intense fragrance that came from a single flower. She noticed that Phillip had moved them along the terrace to a more private corner, still within the bounds of propriety as they stood out in the open in a well-lit area, but away from the wide-flung doors and chatter of the ballroom. The other couples lingering in the night air appeared not to notice their presence. She recognised one of them as Lord Truscott of the inept feet and Miss Emily Colton.

Phillip turned to face her, crowding her gently toward the railing, and she tipped her face up. His dark hair rose well above his forehead, not one lock daring to fall from its high-brushed moorings even when he looked down at her. The look in his half-mast eyes made her hands damp, and she smiled nervously.

'Victoria,' he said in a rumbling voice that carried to only her ears. 'You must know that I have never forgotten you, and my regard for you has grown since we have renewed our acquaintance.'

At that moment Victoria felt a prickle of cold air over the back of her neck. She started, so sudden was the sensation, and so unexpected. Why *now*?

Phillip was looking at her in concern, 'Victoria?'

'Go on, please. You…were saying?' She smiled. Perhaps it was only a chill spring breeze.

He took both of her hands then, and drew each of them, one at a time, to his lips, pressing a brief kiss onto the back and then the palms of each one. 'When I made the decision to look for a bride, I anticipated that it would take me nearly as long to settle on one as it had taken me to decide to look.'

It was not a breeze. The chill had become harsher, more intense. Victoria, who stood with the railing behind her and the light of the ballroom spilling out in front of her, tried to keep her attention on Phillip. She smiled up at her suitor, even as it became clear that the vampire was not in the ballroom.

He or she was here, outside. Likely with a chosen victim.

She had to do something. Her fingers tightened in Phillip's grasp, and she looked back up at him. 'Phillip…I feel a bit of a chill.'

He stopped, as her words had interrupted his, and looked down at her. 'Could we…I should like to speak with you on something before we go back inside. I have something I wish to ask you.' He released her hands and boldly placed his fingers around her bare arms, gently moving his hands up and down as if to warm her.

Victoria swallowed. She wanted to hear what he

was going to say…but how could she listen now?

'Victoria,' Phillip had continued to speak, 'as I said, I expected it to take me a long time to find the right woman to marry…so imagine my surprise and delight when I realised I'd found her…only weeks after beginning my search. Because, in truth, I had found you long ago.'

The cold at the back of her neck was unbearable; it was all she could do to keep from pulling her arms from Phillip's grip and rubbing her nape while dashing off into the gardens below.

For that was where the vampire was.

And how was she going to get away to get there?

'Victoria, will you be my marchioness?'

'Yes, Phillip! Yes, I will…but would you please get my wrap? I am frightfully chilled!' She couldn't help that her voice came out with a panicked note; she had to stop the vampire.

He looked down at her, surprise stamped on his face, as if he didn't quite know how to react.

Victoria had to think: she *had* accepted his proposal, hadn't she?

'Yes, of course, my lady,' he replied slowly, formally. Victoria felt a pit in the bottom of her stomach.

He started to turn away, but she grabbed his arm and pulled him back. She flung her arms around his neck and pulled his face down for a kiss, murmuring, 'Yes, I will marry you, Phillip. I want to marry you.' A great burst of joy flooded her. She was in love, and she was going to marry Phillip!

He kissed her in return, and then she pulled away, the frigidity at the nape of her neck calling her back to duty. 'My wrap, please, Phillip, so that we can stay out here for a bit?' She smiled, biting the inside of her lip, silently entreating him to *go now* so she could slip down into the gardens.

He was smiling too, now, not so formal, and she knew she'd saved that moment…now if only she could save the victim. Go now!

He did, striding quickly from the terrace back into the ballroom, and Victoria barely waited until he was inside before hurrying down the steps into the dark gardens below.

Chapter Ten

Wherein Miss Grantworth Takes Herself Out of Training

When Phillip returned to the terrace carrying Victoria's filmy wrap, she was gone.

He stood in the pie-shaped wedge of light that spilt over the stones and looked around to be certain she hadn't moved into a more shadowy corner...but she was nowhere to be seen. The other couples had disappeared. The patio was empty.

Just then he heard a faint scream from down below, in the gardens.

He ran down the steps, her shawl fluttering in his hand, his feet crunching on the pebble-stoned path, spewing up a scattering of stones with each step.

'Victoria!' he called, dashing to the left, where he was sure he'd heard the scream – a sound so faint that if he'd been inside the building for one more moment, he would not have heard it.

Why had she left the terrace? What had happened?

Had someone taken her?

As he rounded a bend in the path, he nearly collided with a figure in skirts. She was staggering, half bent, sobbing, clutching at her gown. Without thinking about impropriety, he grabbed the woman's shoulders. 'Victoria?' he said, giving her a soft shake.

She looked up. It was not Victoria but Miss Emily Colton, who had been standing with Frederick Truscott on the terrace only moments before. Her face was a terrified mask, and something dark, like a scratch, marked her neck. She was babbling something incoherent, clutching at him as if she were drowning and he was pulling her from the water.

Phillip was torn. Victoria was still out there, but Miss Colton needed him too. And what had happened to Truscott?

'Come,' he said, pulling her after him, back toward the house, calling for help along the way. Over her muffled sobs, he listened fearfully for another cry from the dark.

'Did you see anyone else?' he demanded urgently. 'Another woman? Miss Grantworth?'

She seemed to nod, to give an affirmation, but he wasn't certain what she was saying between her sobs and trembling. When they came in sight of the terrace, he gave the woman a gentle push and called for help, then turned and dashed back into the darkness.

'Victoria!' he called. 'Victoria!'

He rounded another corner, and nearly ran into her.

'Victoria!' he exclaimed, grasping her shoulders and pulling her to his chest, crushing her there in gratitude that she wasn't the one sobbing, frightened. 'What happened? Are you all right?'

She seemed to be breathing hard, but she did not appear to be in any distress, and she disengaged herself from his death grip more easily than she should have been able to. She was looking at him, surprise and something else...intense...in her beautiful face. For a moment he forgot his worry and just enjoyed the perfection of her countenance – and wondered why her eyes carried such a predatory glint.

'Phillip? I am fine. I am not hurt at all. What is wrong?'

'I heard someone scream, and I thought it was you! You weren't on the terrace when I came back.' He realised he'd dropped her wrap somewhere along the way, and he slipped his arm around her waist. After all, she had accepted his proposal. Although it wasn't official, they were engaged. It was proper enough.

'I dropped my indispensable from the terrace, and when I went down to get it, I heard a woman...talking, arguing – she sounded as if she were in danger.'

'So you went after her to help?' Phillip wanted to shake her, his fragile love. 'You could have been hurt!'

'But I was not...it was Emily Colton. She ran past me. Did you see her?'

'Yes; she is frightened, but appeared to be unharmed. Foolish girl,' he said, squeezing her close to him with his arm around her waist. He should have expected nothing less of one who would dress down a young man half again as tall as she was when she was only twelve – her beauty and her boldness, her charm and her tendency to think for herself and not as Society would dictate. No wonder he loved her. 'You were brave to go to her aid, but you could have been hurt yourself! You should have called for assistance.'

Victoria nodded against him. They were walking up the steps of the terrace, and Phillip was pleased to see that the terrace was still empty. Miss Colton would be taken care of after her fright, whatever it had been – perhaps something as simple as a branch catching at her or an argument with Truscott, wherever he had gone off to – and he and Victoria could stand on the patio alone.

And start again where they had left off.

He looked down, ready to gather her back into his arms. 'Victoria, what is that in your hand?'

He saw even in the half-light that her cheeks flushed light pink. She looked down at the slender piece of wood she held as if wondering how it got there. 'I...it was falling from my hair as I hurried to help Miss Colton. I'll just put it in my indispensable, for only my maid knows how to repair my hair.'

Phillip thought that the stick looked rather large and unwieldy to be part of such an intricate coiffure, but what did he know about how women dressed their hair? He appreciated the results, but had little interest in the mechanics.

He was just pulling her close to him, tipping her chin up with a gentle nudge of his thumb, when he realised she was looking over his shoulder into the ballroom. 'Phillip…I really must go check on Miss Colton and make certain she is unhurt.'

Disappointment rolled over him. 'I am certain she is being cared for. Although I do not know what became of Lord Truscott.'

She pulled easily from what he thought was a firm grip. 'Phillip, I promise…I will return in just a moment. I feel responsible for her. Won't you come inside with me?' She smiled so prettily, and hugged his arm so close to the length of her body, brushing against the side of her bosom, that he couldn't refuse.

Back inside the Madagascar home, Victoria quickly excused herself from Phillip. Frantic with the delay he'd caused by catching her in the gardens, she hurried through the throngs of people, knowing that she would have to offer more explanation to him later.

She was relieved that there didn't seem to be a massive sense of panic or outrage from the party goers; more clusters of people were talking than dancing, but they did not seem to be upset. It appeared that possibly Miss Colton had made her way to the ladies' changing room without causing too much of a commotion about the vampire attack that had happened only yards away from the merrymaking.

Victoria prayed that was the case, and hoped that Miss Colton was in no frame of mind to speak of what had happened…or ask about the whereabouts of Lord Truscott. She wasn't sure how she was going to explain that he'd poofed into a cloud of ashes.

It was perhaps too much to hope that Emily Colton hadn't realised what was happening before Victoria arrived upon the scene; but she did indeed hope. It had happened quickly; Lord Truscott was just bending his face to her neck when Victoria burst upon them.

Emily escaped, disappearing into the brush with a shriek, before Victoria had come face-to-face with Truscott and plunged the stake into his chest.

Now she hurried down the hall and reached the ladies' retiring room. Pausing to collect her breath and pat down her hair, Victoria eased the door open and found a small cluster of women around a white-faced Emily Colton.

'Emily,' Victoria said, slipping inside and closing the door behind her. 'How are you?'

'Oh!' shrieked Emily, leaping to her feet and throwing herself at Victoria. 'You are unhurt! I was so frightened for you!'

Victoria gently extricated her from the other woman's arms. 'I am not hurt at all. And how do you feel?'

Emily ignored the question and began babbling to the others, pointing at Victoria with a shaking finger. 'She came right in at the moment he attacked me! I ran away; I shouldn't have left her, but I was too frightened to think!'

The five other ladies looked from Victoria to Emily and back again, as if measuring the difference in their demeanours. Victoria was careful to keep her expression gentle even though she needed to know what Emily had seen, and whether she'd realised what happened.

Emily was still speaking rapidly, as though she had to let the words loose or she would lose them. 'What happened? Did Lord Truscott—?'

'I do not know what happened to him,' Victoria replied, clasping her fingers around Emily's hand. 'As soon as you ran, he turned and disappeared in another direction. He did not hurt me.' That, at least, was true.

It appeared that Emily accepted this explanation; and the others had no reason to question it. The word vampire had not been uttered; she need give no explanation for Truscott's disappearance. Now Victoria could excuse herself and find Phillip.

It would be easy to return to her betrothed; but it would not be so easy to accept that she had killed

Lord Truscott of the soft brown eyes and clumsy feet.

'It has happened!' Lady Melisande burst into Winnie's drawing room without waiting for the butler. 'Oh, glory be, it has happened! Victoria is to be a marchioness!'

'Rockley has come up to snuff?' Winnie leapt to her feet with surprising agility for one so well cushioned. 'Oh, Melly, I am enraptured for you! And for Victoria, too, of course!'

'Victoria is to marry Rockley?' Petronilla exclaimed at the precise moment the duchess squealed. 'Get out of my way, Winnie, so I can hug her too!'

The ladies danced around the room, the china and knickknacks clinking in their wake.

'He came just shortly ago to get my blessing – as if he needed to ask!' Melly, out of breath, huffed as she sank into a chair.

Winnie, who had snatched up two blueberry scones, did not pause in her enthusiastic prancing until she'd poured tea for the newest arrival. Then she plunked down next to her.

'We shall have to begin planning the wedding immediately. It will be the event of the Season!' Petronilla said. 'But do tell, did Victoria have any details about the incident at the Madagascar ball last night? It is the talk of the town!'

Winnie slammed a hand to her chest, closing her

fingers around the crucifix that rested on the shelf of her bosom. If possible, it was an even bigger cross than the one she'd been wearing last week. 'Nilly was just telling me about it. I'm certain it was a vampire attack!'

Melly looked at them. 'Whatever are you talking about?'

'Miss Emily Colton was attacked last night, in the gardens at the Madagascars' house. She was not hurt, but frightened, and her escort, Lord Truscott, has disappeared,' Winnie explained.

'Why do you think it was a vampire attack?' Melly said, rolling her eyes. 'Lord Truscott likely got too familiar with Miss Colton and she sent him on his way…and did not want to confess that she'd been walking in the garden alone with him. Miss Colton has been known to be a bit loose, you know.'

'But no one knows where he is,' said Winnie. 'And it was in the dark. And her neck was scratched.'

'Perhaps Lord Truscott is a vampire,' said Petronilla. Her eyes gleamed like sapphires. 'Perhaps he was overcome by lust and could not resist any longer, and tried to seduce Miss Colton in the gardens…'

'What nonsense! Nilly, Winnie, I declare, if you would rather go on about vampires instead of helping me to plan Victoria's wedding, then I will leave you two to it!'

'No, Melly, we'll stop. I don't want to talk about them anyway,' Winnie said, shooting a look at

Petronilla. 'There's nothing about them that fascinates me on any level. They are evil bloodsucking creatures, dirty and smelly with claws and long hair—'

'They are not! Mrs Lawson's daughter's neighbour's sister was the one who had one in her bedchamber, and she said he smelt like liquorice and that he was clean-shaven and—'

'I thought you did not want to talk about them!' Melly interrupted, standing. 'I am going to leave if either one of you mentions the word *vampire* again.'

Winnie clamped her mouth shut. Petronilla raised her teacup to her lips and sipped, gazing innocently out the window.

'Now,' Melisande said, settling back into her chair, 'which modiste should we have make the dress?'

'Victoria always looks well with Madame LeClaire's designs,' replied Petronilla.

'I was not talking about Victoria's gown! I meant my dress!' said Melly indignantly.

'Well, in that case, I suggest we take ourselves out of here and down to Bond Street for a shopping excursion!' said Winnie.

And they very happily did just that, with Winnie clutching her crucifix the whole way.

The sun was lowering when Victoria climbed out of Barth's hackney only a short distance from the home of Rudolph Caulfield, the man who owned the Book of Antwartha. Sebastian had clearly indicated that the vampires acting on Lilith's behalf were to arrive at night, but Victoria was taking no chances that they might come and go before she got there.

Verbena had helped her to dress, not as a man this night, nor as a debutante, but as a Venator, in a costume the maid had specially prepared. It consisted of a split skirt that appeared no different from any other day dress, but which would allow her more freedom of movement. The sleeves were firmly anchored to the shoulders of the dress's bodice, unlike the filmy, frothy ones that were often barely basted onto normal evening apparel. The cloth was dark blue, with very little ornamentation, and of a soft cotton, so there would be no rustling noises of taffeta or charmeuse. Its length was a bit shorter than what Victoria was used to wearing, several inches from the ground.

The most unique aspects of the costume were two small slipknots into which Victoria could slide stakes to hang at her waist, and two deep pockets hidden in the folds of the skirt, where she might put salted holy water, a crucifix, and other accoutrements.

When Victoria slipped out of the hackney, she left her cloak behind; it was a balmy summer evening, and the excitement of the adventure would keep her warm. Barth was given his instructions, and she turned from the coach.

Earlier in the day she and Verbena had travelled to Caulfield's home, known as Redfield Manor, in order to ascertain its location, its geography, and an appropriate place where Victoria might wait and watch without being noticed.

Verbena, quite into the spirit of things after her evening drinking ale with vampires at the Silver Chalice, approached the servants' door in an attempt to learn what she could about the household schedule and layout. Victoria wasn't sure how she managed to extract the information, but she learnt that the servants were leaving with Rudolph Caulfield that afternoon, and that the gentleman coming to stay at the home would be bringing his own retinue.

And, as Victoria slipped behind a tall iron gate, she was grateful that Verbena had also learnt that the garden was very rarely used…and thus would be the perfect place to wait.

Finding a stone bench thrust under a small tree that had refused to sprout buds that spring, Victoria sat and slid to the edge so she could watch the house. From this vantage point she could see anyone approaching the front door. She assumed that Mr Caulfield and his servants had left and been replaced by his houseguest during the afternoon.

As she sat, trying to ignore a persistent bee that was determined to find nectar in the vicinity of the dead tree, Victoria felt a stab of guilt. She had argued long and hard with herself and with Verbena about whether to tell Aunt Eustacia and Max about her plans for the evening…but in the end she had decided not to. She could take care of herself – Kritanu had trained her well. She knew what she was doing.

So she'd decided to do this alone, for several perfectly logical reasons.

First, if Sebastian's information was wrong, she would feel foolish having dragged Max to the site of Redfield Manor; for it was certain he would have been the one to accompany her, not Aunt Eustacia.

Not to mention the fact that she would have to be in his company the entire evening.

Second, Victoria was certain she would be able to handle two or three vampires alone – particularly since the element of surprise would be in her favour. She could determine when and how to strike.

Third, she had braved the dangers of the Silver Chalice on her own to get the information, and Sebastian had warned her not to tell anyone. If she had told Aunt Eustacia and Max, they would have demanded that she divulge her source. Once she had the Book of Antwartha in her possession, no one would care how she got the information.

And fourth…Max and Aunt Eustacia all seemed to be willing to keep their own secrets from her. So why should she not act on her own if they were not going to include her in all of their plans? After all, she was a *vis bulla*ed Venator, and she *had* staked a Guardian vampire whilst he was biting her.

Never mind Verbena's clicking tongue or wagging chin. Victoria was comfortable with her decision.

So she waited and turned her thoughts toward

more pleasant items, such as the passionate kisses she and Phillip had exchanged on the terrace, and in the carriage, and on the front doorstep of Grantworth House. She was to be married! She could scarcely believe it had happened so quickly, so easily and wonderfully. She'd always thought fondly of the young man she'd met that summer; perhaps even then she'd given him her heart. Whatever had happened then, whether she had felt love for him or not, did not matter, for she loved him now.

The sun seemed to move infinitesimally slowly toward the ring of trees that edged the street. Victoria watched, noticing each person as he or she walked by, knowing that she would recognise the vampires when they approached.

Suddenly her attention was caught by a movement at the corner of her eye…from the back of the garden. Victoria held her breath and shrank more closely into the shrubbery surrounding her bench, slipping quickly to a crouch on the ground.

The backyard was shaded in this late afternoon, and would soon be dark, so the shadow that eased from a crack in the stone wall was at first indiscernible. It moved with speed and grace, and as it drew closer to the back of the house and became recognizable, Victoria's mouth dropped open from behind a boxwood.

Max.

There was no mistaking his height and spare,

measured movements as he made his way toward a set of wooden cellar doors.

A bolt of fury shafted through her, and Victoria slammed her teeth together so hard a crack of pain shot through her jaw. She was surprised he didn't hear the loud snap; and she was glad he didn't.

What was he doing here?

Not looking for her; he would easily have found her if he'd cared to look.

Somehow he must have learnt about the book, that it was here and that the owner was gone.

In the moment that the blankness of shock and the red haze of anger burst over her, Victoria had missed his next move. When she refocused her attention toward the house, toward where Max had been approaching the wooden doors, he was gone.

Had he gone in?

Or had he found another hiding place, as she had, and would also lie in wait for the vampires?

He was a blasted fool if he thought she was going to wait here by herself.

Victoria eased from her hiding place, gratified that, although the sun hadn't set completely, the shadows were long enough in this garden that they afforded her a protective cover as she hurried along in Max's path.

As she approached the building, one of her questions, at least, was answered when she saw a tall, unmistakable figure pass in front of a window at the back of the house. Max was inside, in the servants' quarters, if one were to judge by the size and placement of the window.

Did he think to snatch the book from under the vampires' noses? Before they had the opportunity –

Oh, God. Max was going to take the book himself! If he touched it before it was out of the house, he would die!

Victoria launched herself from her shield of bushes before she realised that she couldn't go haring into the house willy-nilly.

And she realised quite suddenly that she had made a mistake. She should have told Aunt Eustacia and Max.

For if she did not stop him in time, he would die… and she would be to blame.

Chapter Eleven

In Which Maximilian Encounters Dust Bunnies

Max paused, listening intently. He'd made it inside Redfield Manor with no problem at all. Not any surprise. This wasn't the first time he'd slipped into a building undetected, and it certainly wouldn't be the last.

From his resources at the Silver Chalice, he knew that the Book of Antwartha was to be stolen tonight from this very location, and that Rudolph Caulfield had left the city, taking his servants with him, leaving an unsuspecting houseguest to watch over his belongings.

This was their only chance to get the book before Lilith did; once she had it in her possession, hidden away wherever she was holding court, it would be impossible to retrieve it.

He could not fail tonight.

Satisfied that his presence hadn't been detected, and that there was no one about to come strolling around a bend in the servants' hallway, Max hurried along the passage. Although he wasn't familiar with the layout of the house, logic suggested that something of a valuable nature would be kept in a study, where it might be locked away, or in a private parlour in the personal quarters of the owner of the house.

Max was hoping it would be the latter, as the private quarters would be on an upper level and less likely to be inhabited by the houseguest or investigated by his staff.

The servants' staircase was accessible and would lead to the upper floors. The pale blue door that ended the passageway was made of warped and buckled wood, and it creaked faintly when Max opened it. He slipped through and dashed with light feet up the narrow steps, pausing at the top to listen.

When silence continued to reign, he cracked the door and put his ear to the edge. A dull thump from near the front of the house, below, told him that at least someone was not in the vicinity. But then he heard the doorknob on the warped door below as it turned with a dull clink, and he couldn't wait any longer – he pressed through the narrow aperture and found himself in a blessedly carpeted hall on the second floor.

On cat feet he hurried down the hall, pausing at each entrance to listen, gently open its door, and peer in. The rooms were dark and uninhabited, the furnishings covered with sheets or other protection, as if they hadn't been used for years. Mr Caulfield had recently returned from India – which was how the Book of Antwartha had made its way from the colony to the mother country – and it was obvious his home had been closed up for that purpose. This would make Max's task easier, for the items brought from India, including the book, would stand out as new additions to the room, and would likely be in a chamber that was obviously in use.

Max had three more rooms to search when he heard the door at the top of the servant staircase open at the far end of the hall. He pivoted through the door at which he stood and closed it swiftly and silently after him. Turning, he faced the room, hoping to heaven it was empty, for he hadn't time to check… and found himself in a bedchamber that had been used recently.

Fortunately for him, it was empty, but Max couldn't be certain it would remain so. He heard footsteps moving down the hallway; they were barely discernible, but his hearing was nearly as acute as a vampire's.

Max dove under the high bed, sliding the chamber pot, which fortunately was empty, out of the way and closing his eyes against the puffs of dust he'd stirred up. It tickled his nose and made his eyes water as he fought to keep from sneezing; any little bit of disturbance of the air seemed to go right into his nostrils. He pinched the bridge of his nose, right under the innermost edges of his brows, and felt the urge to sneeze dissipate.

The door to the room opened, and someone came in. The back of Max's neck remained unchanged, so he kept his hand on the pocket where his pistol was. He couldn't see the person, couldn't look at his shoes to tell if it was a servant or the houseguest; but when he or she strode across the room and then back out, Max exhaled slowly. Likely the valet bringing some laundered clothing to the room, or even the houseguest coming up to retrieve something he'd forgotten.

Good. He hadn't relished the thought of an altercation with a mortal. Vampires he could stake without a second thought; but fighting with or injuring a mortal was something he tried to avoid. He'd seen too much violence, and preferred staking vampires to fisticuffs because it was much neater. No blood, no cracking of bones, no mess. Just a small pile of ashes.

Yet…to get the Book of Antwartha, Max would do whatever was necessary, because if he did not, an infinite number of mortals would be in danger.

He waited until the quiet footsteps disappeared before he slid from under the bed and pulled himself to his feet. Brushing the dust from his dark pants, Max hurried toward the door. He had two more rooms to search on this level, and then he could move on to the third floor. It was a less likely location for something like the Book of Antwartha, but at least he could eliminate it before having to slink around on the main area, where he was more likely to be found out.

He poked his head out of the room and looked up and down the hall. Once again satisfied that he was alone, he stepped out and turned the knob of the room across the hall – and found himself in a library.

Ah. He smiled in satisfaction. Crates and boxes stood against the wall, and next to a great armchair was a haphazard stack of books that certainly hadn't been sitting there for the years Caulfield had been in India.

On one of the tables, he saw a box the size of a large book, open, like a treasure chest. Red silk wrappings spilt from its interior, and with a complacency borne of certainty, he started toward the table.

The Book of Antwartha. It had to be.

He approached the table eagerly, even as he kept one ear turned toward the hall, listening for unwelcome footsteps. Fingering a pistol in one pocket and a stake in the other, he bent toward the box to look in. Empty.

He turned and then he saw it. By a tall window grey with twilight, in front of the wingback chair, it had been hidden from his view when he walked in. But this was certainly it: a large, dusty brown book with an embossed A on the cover, sitting on the table by the chair as if the person reading it had set it down in front of him. He moved closer, his ear still cocked toward the door, eyes on the book.

He was just reaching for it when something flew from behind the long draperies and knocked him aside. He tumbled into the wingback chair, and the force followed in a tangle of skirts.

'Don't touch it!' hissed a female voice that he suddenly, shockingly recognised.

'Victoria? What in the bloody hell are you doing here?' He forgot to keep his voice down, and she slapped a hand over his mouth, jamming an elbow into his chest as she struggled to pull herself upright. Damn. She might not weigh much, but her elbows and hips were sharp as her tongue.

'Be quiet!' she hissed, her mouth much too close to his ear. 'I just saved your worthless life, you blasted fool. We don't need to be heard.'

Max disentangled himself from Victoria, slipping out from under her and letting her sag into the chair by herself. He stood, glaring down at her, and adjusted his jacket. 'I repeat,' he said from between clenched teeth, albeit at a lower tone than previously, 'what in the blazes are you doing here?'

'I repeat,' she whispered, standing upright and shaking out dull, dark skirts, 'I was saving your life. You cannot touch the Book of Antwartha,' she cried as he reached for it. Her fingers closed over his wrist, barely wrapping around its circumference, and she gave him pause with her surprising strength.

Ah, but yes…she wore a *vis bulla*. How could he forget?

Max curled his lips into a smile that he knew wasn't pleasant in the least. 'We have the chance to get it out of here now. Or is it that you want to be the one to bring it back? If that's your game, then I won't stand in the way – grab it and let's go!'

'If I wanted to do that,' Victoria replied pertly, 'I would have let you touch it, then stepped over your dead body to take it to my aunt.'

He would have replied, but they both heard it at the same time: low voices and dull footsteps making their way down the corridor. Before he could react, Victoria snatched at his sleeve and pulled him with her toward the long draperies from which she'd come bursting forth.

She shoved him toward one, and she ducked behind the other, and they stood like sentinels on either side of the window. If he turned his head he could see her profile, as she was backed against the wall. He wanted to shake his head to clear it.

Max peered down and over his shoulder, trying to look through the window, and realised that it was cracked open. He could feel the faint brush of air on the fingertips he curled up behind him, on the sill. Slipping his fingers under the bottom rung of the sash, he pressed up gently, and felt the window move.

If he could get it open…perhaps they could snatch the book and make their escape.

He felt the window give more easily, and turned to see Victoria looking at him. She was pushing up with her fingertips as well, and with their combined strength they were able to lift the window…silently, slowly, surely.

The back of his neck had chilled. The voices were closer now; they would be coming through the door at any moment if this chamber was their destination.

He looked at the large bound manuscript, then back at Victoria, measuring his chance…but her hand whipped from behind the drapes and slammed into his chest. 'No!' she hissed, drapes roiling about her. 'I'll not say it again, you arrogant fool!' Then, just as the door opened, she snatched her arm back behind her covering curtain, pulling it straight and still.

Max inched the drapes away from the shadowed side of the window where the sliver of his face peeking out would be less likely to be noticed. They filed in one after another. There were three of them; two Guardian vampires and one mortal.

Sebastian Vioget.

He should have known.

The man always seemed to be where he should not be.

Max realised his fingers had closed around the drapes in a fierce movement, and he released the heavy brocade slowly so as not to draw attention. So far, he had escaped detection; this was not the first time he was grateful that vampires could not sense the presence of a Venator.

But then... Vioget looked directly toward him. Max did not move, merely watching as Vioget transferred his attention to the other side of the window, where Victoria stood, then continued his conversation with the vampires.

'I believe this is the item which you seek,' Vioget was saying, and he gestured to the table only inches away from Victoria.

One of the vampires grunted and stepped forward to touch the aged tome, and Max felt Vioget look toward him again. He groped in his pocket for the pistol; he'd use it if he had to. He could not let those vampires take the book.

While the three were bent over the table, one of the vampires thumbed carelessly through the ancient pages as though confirming it was the real thing, Max chanced a glance over at Victoria. She was not looking from behind the curtain, but stood rigidly against the wall, as far away from the draperies as possible.

Was she frightened? She damn well ought to be! If she hadn't stopped him, they would have had the book and been out the window by now.

Max considered his options. He could burst from behind the curtains and attempt to take them by surprise. Vioget's hands were both in view; he at least did not have a weapon at hand, although he might have one on his person. That would be like him.

The vampires were bound to be two of Lilith's strongest and smartest Guardians; she would not send any but the best for this task. He'd get one for certain, the second one easily if Vioget did not interfere.

Or Victoria. Why could he not touch the book? Blasted woman.

And then suddenly Max's options evaporated with a swish of the curtains as Vioget flung them aside, exposing him.

'Maximilian. I did not expect to see you here this evening,' he said with a condescending smile.

But Max had his pistol out and was pointing it at the blondish French fop before he could finish his thought. 'I highly doubt that,' he responded, stepping fully from behind the curtain, pistol in one hand and stake in the other. He did not look back, but his peripheral vision told him that Victoria had not moved. Perhaps she would be smart enough to come to his aid. Not that he needed her assistance, but it was better to be safe than to lose the book.

'Now,' Max said pleasantly, 'if you will step aside I promise not to hurt you, Vioget, as I know that the continued safety of your person is your greatest concern. But these other two…gentlemen…well, they may not be so lucky.'

He barely had the words from his mouth when the two vampires, ruby-eyed and with fangs gleaming, were on him. The pistol was of no use; he allowed it to drop to the floor as the force of the launching vampires knocked him to the rug.

One of them pinned the wrist holding the stake to the floor above his head, using two hands, whilst the other straddled him at the waist, fighting to capture his other hand. Max grunted, drawing his knees and feet toward his body, and with one quick, strong movement, hooked his feet around the front of the vampire's neck and whipped him into a backward somersault. The vampire crashed into a table behind him.

Max rolled to the side, slipped a second stake from the sleeve of his shirt, and slammed it into the chest of the vampire still holding his wrist down before the Guardian knew what had happened.

Before the ashes hit the floor Max was on his feet, facing the other vampire, who was coming at him with a gleaming sword and a feral smile that sported two fangs digging into his bottom lip. With a quick glance at the rest of the room – Vioget was watching in amusement, his arms folded over his middle, and Victoria was nowhere to be seen – Max returned his attention to the vampire as the blade sliced in the air in front of him.

He leapt aside, vaulting over the wingback chair, then, standing behind it, hefted it by the arms and shoved it at his adversary. Max followed the momentum of the chair and came after the vampire, slamming him into the floor only inches from

Victoria's draperies. He didn't need her assistance. She was probably cowering behind, too frightened to move.

She should have stayed home with her marquess.

Anger surged through him, and he used it to drive the stake into the second vampire's heart.

'*Et voila!*' Vioget murmured as Max rose to his feet, breathing deeply, but by no means winded.

Keeping a steady eye on the other man, Max started toward the table where the book had been jolted to the edge during the fracas. He wished briefly for his pistol, but as Vioget stood with no indication that he would attempt to stop him, Max thrust the concern from his mind.

He reached the table and stretched out his hands to lift the heavy book...and stopped.

Two things occurred to him at that moment. First, Victoria's warning had been vehement. Second, Vioget had not touched the book himself, even when the vampires were looking through it. But the vampires had touched it.

Then a third realisation: Victoria had been in the room before he had...she could easily have taken it if it had been her intent to one-up him. She, at least, believed there was a reason he should not touch the book.

He made a show of adjusting his sleeves, taking the opportunity to shift slightly to one side so he could better see Vioget from the corner of his eye, and reached for the book again…and again paused. Yes, it was there: the almost imperceptible change in Vioget's stance. Oh, he hid it well, but not well enough.

Yes, there was something about the book. Victoria, it appeared, had been right. And, Max realised with a suddenly bitter taste, quite possibly had saved his… what had she called it? His worthless life.

'You did come for the Book of Antwartha, did you not?' asked Vioget in that falsely pleasant tone.

Max stepped away from the table. What was Victoria waiting for? 'You seem particularly interested in its fate,' he replied. Perhaps giving it to Vioget would draw her out. 'Did you not come for it as well?'

'What would I do with such a book? I won't stop you from taking it, Maximilian,' Vioget told him. 'I don't wish Lilith to have it any more than you do.'

Before Max could reply, or make sense of that comment, he heard something that drew his attention from the matter at hand. From outside of the open window…a shout, a low scream.

Victoria?

He dashed to the window, yanking back the curtains. She was gone.

He looked down and in the darkness, broken only by a partial moon, he heard rather than saw an altercation below.

She'd gone out the window and gotten herself into a fight. She'd probably been gone the whole time he was fighting the Guardians.

Max cast a quick glance at Vioget, who'd turned, but made no move toward the window. 'Go. The book will be safe here.'

Max trusted Sebastian Vioget like he trusted a beggar in a room with a case of gems, but he had no choice. If he couldn't touch it, neither could Vioget.

Max looked out the window. If Victoria could go out this way, so could he.

Chapter Twelve

Our Heroes Commence with Much Poofing and Slicing

There were ten of them.

And that was after Victoria had staked two; so an even dozen to begin with, plus the two that were in the house. With Sebastian.

Blast! Sebastian was here!

She tripped the vampire with bared teeth who came at her with his eyes glowing, and he went sprawling over the garden bench she'd been sitting on only a short time before. Whirling to face the one coming up behind her, she stabbed at him, missed, and kept her momentum going until she got the one behind him in the chest. *Poof!*

Nine to go.

The only good thing about there being so many was that they couldn't all jump on her at once; there wasn't enough room…so if she could just hold one or two off at a time, and send them to their destiny with her ash stick, maybe she could hang on until –

Victoria stifled an un-Venator-like shriek as something landed on top of her from the tree above. *Make that ten left*, she thought as her face slammed into the ground. Her breath knocked out of her for a moment, she couldn't move. But when she felt him, or her, pulling her lopsided twist of hair away from her neck, she found new strength.

Kicking back with the heel of her foot, she caught the vampire at the base of the neck, hard, and then a second time in rapid succession, but she was unable to dislodge him. Victoria felt a clawing of panic when another vampire swooped down and, crouching next to her, grasped one wrist in each hand, immobilising her. Her nerveless fingers released the stakes she held.

Her cold neck suddenly felt bare and vulnerable, and she twisted and fought with less skill and more blind panic – opposite the way Kritanu had trained her. One hand grasped a hank of her hair, pulling back, baring her throat as a knee in the base of her back kept her hips grinding into the ground with her struggles.

She swallowed a thick, choking sob, difficult to do when one's neck was craned backward, looking up into the fiery eyes of a blood-craving undead, and gave one last thrust of effort. *Wham!* She brought both heels up as hard and fast as she could, her hips coming off the ground, and knocked the vampire forward so that he lost his balance and jostled into the one who held her wrists.

Victoria, huddled under two vampires struggling to gain their balance, twisted frantically and tried to slip from underneath, but strong hands grabbed her ankles, and all she could do was buck at the hips.

Then she felt a stirring in the air, a new presence, and in an instant her ankles were released. The unmistakable *swish*, the faintest crunch, and another *poof*. The one who'd been on her back was gone.

Her wrists were free, and she rolled half to one side to grab one of her stakes just as another vampire lunged toward her. She lifted the stake and he impaled himself. She leapt to her feet, pushing the hair from her eyes just in time to see Max stake two more undead in one smooth, brutal motion.

And then there was silence.

It was just the two of them, facing each other, breathing heavily, grasping lengths of pointed wood in the garden of Redfield Manor.

'You didn't touch the book.'

'What in the blazes were you doing?'

They both spoke at the same time.

Then silence again. His face, harsh and handsome in the shadowy light, glistened with a stripe of perspiration. He wiped it away from where it clung to the edge of his jaw.

Victoria slipped her stake back into its loop at her waist and, using both hands, pulled all of her heavy hair back from where it drooped over her face and shoulders. Verbena was going to have to find a better way to contain it, or she was going to cut it all off. Long hair flying in her face was a liability, and she couldn't chance its obstructing her view as it had tonight.

Max stepped toward her, looming tall, blocking what little of the moon showed as he bent closer. One hand came up and grasped her jaw before she realised what he was doing, turning her head to one side, his long fingers sliding along her chin and brushing down the side of her throat. 'You're not hurt,' he said, then released her and stepped back. Several steps back.

'You didn't touch the book,' she said again, resisting the urge to rub the skin he'd just touched.

'No. You told me not to. It's still inside, I believe. How many did you get?' His breathing had slowed, but the harsh, measuring look was still on his face. A dip of too-long hair brushed one cheekbone near a narrowed eye.

'Five, perhaps six. I lost count. There were twelve out here, and another two inside.'

'I got the two inside. And four out here. There are still at least two.' He turned to look up at the window from which Victoria had escaped the room. 'But they've gone off. You climbed down that tree?'

Victoria nodded, then bent to pick up her other stake. Her breathing had gone back to normal, and it was just sinking in that not only had she been overwhelmed by the number of vampires and nearly lost the battle, but that Sebastian was the houseguest who let them in.

What was he doing here?

She dared not ask Max; to do so would be to admit that she knew Sebastian, and she was fairly certain that would be in violation of their agreement.

'Tell me what you know about the book.'

'It's going to be stolen tonight by two – or more – undead. Once they remove it from the house of its owner, it is safe for us to take. But if a mortal takes it, touches it to steal it, he or she will die.'

Max stared at her for a moment. 'Where did you learn this interesting bit of information?'

'We should not be standing here,' Victoria replied, starting to walk toward the front of the house. 'If there are at least two vampires left, they are still after the book. We will have to take it from them once they leave the house.'

'Victoria.' His voice was pitched threateningly, meant to stop her.

But she paid him no heed and continued toward the front side of the house. If she stood in a certain place, she could see the front doorway and remain hidden…whilst also having a view of the garden.

Max stalked after her; she couldn't see him, but could feel the annoyance in the way he moved, silently, but purposefully in her tracks. She picked a place in the shadows of a spreading oak, standing behind its trunk. Max stood just behind her, looking over her head. A piece of bark drifted onto her shoulder from where his fingers touched the tree.

'Victoria, where did you learn this information?'

'It doesn't matter. And besides, I have not asked you how you learnt what you know,' she replied, still looking straight ahead at the house, trying not to shift. He was right behind her. 'Do you think they will remove the book tonight?'

'I don't have the same information you apparently have received, but it would be my expectation that they will not return to Lilith without the book.'

'Undead have to remove it from the house. If there are only two or three of them, we should have no trouble relieving them of their burden.'

'Theoretically, yes.'

They fell silent, waiting, watching, breathing steadily and smoothly at last.

And then…Victoria started when Max's hand appeared in her periphery, a finger, pointing silently.

Three of them, walking toward the house, in the centre of the street as if they owned it. Broad, tall, long hair gusting with each stride. Even from where she was, Victoria saw the whiteness of their skin, the deep, violet-red glow of narrowed eyes. And the long glint of metal swords drooping from their hands.

Her neck felt as if a wedge of ice were pressed against it.

Her stomach tightened and she surreptitiously

rubbed her damp palm against the rough bark of the tree.

'Imperial vampires.' Max's voice was in her ear, barely audible.

But she hadn't needed to be told; Victoria already knew. The vampires closest to Lilith, closer than her elite retinue of Guardians, and so powerful they could pull the life energy from their victims without using their fangs – just their eyes.

Lilith was indeed taking no chances.

They didn't move as the Imperials approached Redfield Manor. It was fortunate they were downwind from the vampires, and that there was a gentle breeze. It might keep the three from scenting her and Max. Victoria watched them, her neck burning with chill. They were still a distance away, but even now she could feel the power, the hate…the evil. She stifled a shiver.

For the first time she was truly glad Max was there.

The Book of Antwartha was still inside the house, and would need to be removed by one of the undead, for Sebastian would not have been able to take it.

But why was he here?

Lilith knew that she and Max would do anything to stop her from getting the book. Perhaps there were even more surprises awaiting them tonight. Victoria had an uneasy feeling that although they were prepared, the queen of the vampires was one step ahead of them.

If she had gone to Aunt Eustacia or Max to share what she knew, they might have been better able to plan their strategy. After all, Max had some experience with Imperials. But Victoria had gone solo, and so had Max, and now they were at the mercy of Lilith's determination.

How did one fight an Imperial? Her heart seemed to pound through her whole body. Surely the vampires must sense it!

As if reading her thoughts, one of the Imperials paused at the stoop of Redfield Manor, turning toward them and sniffing the air. Victoria held her breath and felt Max tense against her.

Then the vampire turned back to his companions, and they separated. Two went up the steps, and the one who'd faced them remained at the bottom, standing near the street. The length of his sword was a third leg, stretching from hip to ground.

The door of Redfield Manor opened and the two Imperials went in. The third was alone.

She nearly jumped when Max's fingers closed around her arm and he breathed into the vicinity of her ear, 'Me first. Wait; then you follow.' Without waiting for her response, he stepped from the shadow of the tree and began to walk boldly toward the Imperial.

He had no sword, no weapon but the ash stakes and a long, slender branch that had a jagged end.

Victoria watched as the Imperial turned to face

Max striding across the grass that had somehow become damp. His burning eyes no more than slits, the vampire stood ready. Even from her distance, in the glance of light from the moon, Victoria could see the smirk of readiness, the indolent stance that said he was ready for a fight.

When Max came within two arms' breadth, the Imperial lifted his sword. Yes, he had brutal strength that matched Max's, but to fight a Venator, who carried a pike of wood that held death, Lilith took no chances. She armed her vampires with metal pikes, swords. Thus they were evenly matched. Wood to metal. Holy strength to inhuman might.

Victoria understood Max's plan, and though her heart picked up speed as she saw the two tall, broad figures face each other, she waited. The Imperial would have scented their presence; by Max announcing himself and approaching the vampire, it was obvious he hoped Victoria would remain unnoticed.

Metal glinted in the light, and Victoria saw that they were engaged, fighting for life. Or undeath.

She'd been wrong. They were not evenly matched.

Max had the disadvantage. The skin of her palms dampened. While his weapon would kill only if he got a clear slice through the chest, the sword wielded by the Imperial was lethal in any manner.

And if he drew blood, its smell would attract the other Imperials and Guardians from inside Redfield Manor…and any that lurked on the streets.

They moved as if choreographed, seeming to leap and almost glide through the air at times, blocking and thrusting, each with their staff of death, spinning, leaping, banking off a nearby tree one time; gliding up the side of the house and down another time. Almost as if they were puppets on strings, lifting into the air and careening back toward each other in lethal ballet movements.

She watched, amazed, as Max seemed to skim and glide on the air in the graceful movements of an art form she had not yet learnt. She kept her eyes trained on them, praying she would know when to step from the shadows and come to his aid. Praying she would be quick enough.

And then the constant ice at the back of her neck changed, pulling her attention from the battle. She felt something behind her and turned just in time, her stake at waist height. With a quick thrust she jabbed it up and into the chest of the very ordinary vampire who'd had the foolishness to come up behind a tense Venator, a woman who he'd thought would be easy pickings.

That would be his last street hunt.

Victoria turned back around, realising that her movement would have alerted the Imperial to her presence, just in time to see his long metal blade arc through the air and tumble to the ground. In a move that took her breath away, Max vaulted from the vampire and snatched up the blade. Straightening, he turned and, with one clean swipe, cleaved the Imperial's head from his neck.

The vampire poofed.

All was still.

Except for Victoria's ramming heart and dragging breaths.

Max turned as she came across the grass toward him.

'One down. Two to go,' he said, meeting her halfway. To her great annoyance, he was barely out of breath. 'We're better matched now. You take that side. I'll take this one.' He gestured to the boxwoods that flanked the stoop of the house.

'You were flying.'

He looked at her, eyebrows raised. 'In a manner of speaking, yes. As much as you might think you know, you still have much to learn, Victoria. Now take your place.'

'Wait.' She grabbed his arm, her breathing steadier now. Something shiny dampened his sleeve, and she saw that it had been sliced open and blood spilt. 'He got you.'

'Of course he did,' Max snapped, pulling his arm back to his side and stepping into the protective shadow of another tree. 'How else was I to distract him to twist the sword from his grip? One quick flip of my stake at that angle and he had to drop it.' Under his annoyance there was an air of satisfaction and smugness.

'Congratulations,' Victoria replied just as briskly. 'But if we don't bind it up and stanch the bleeding, it'll attract every other undead in the vicinity…not to mention the ones inside with Sebastian.'

She could have bitten her tongue, but that would have meant more blood scent on the air. And Max wasn't about to allow it to slip by.

'How do you know his name?' He rounded on her.

Victoria refused to be cowed. 'Later, Max. First, let's take care of—'

But she never finished her sentence. The door beyond them opened and two Imperial vampires stood at the top of the stoop.

The vampires had to step out of the house, carrying the book, before it would be safe for Victoria and Max to take it from them.

They exchanged looks under shadow of the boxwoods, satisfying themselves that the other understood this.

Although the first Imperial paused at the door's threshold, he did not wait long; the one behind him appeared just at his shoulder and they both stepped out. Their hands were empty but for the swords they still carried.

They looked around as if searching for their missing colleague; since he'd popped into ash, they would see no sign of him. But perhaps they would smell the lingering dust in the air.

The Imperials strode down the steps, only feet away from Max and Victoria – they must smell them, Max's blood, too, for certain – looking around, the nostrils of one flaring as if testing the air for scent.

Just as one turned toward the bushy, shoulder-high boxwood that sheltered them, Max leapt from behind it, brandishing the sword, and beheaded the vampire in another clean stroke.

As the third and last Imperial whirled about, holding his own silver blade, another face peered around the doorway. Victoria saw him and crashed from behind the shrub, dashing up the steps before he could close the door.

He came out onto the stoop to meet her, and she saw that he was not carrying the book himself; but that did not matter, as now she had to fight him to his death. Or hers.

Dimly, through her own battle with the Guardian vampire, she was aware of the fierce clashing of swords below as Max and the Imperial faced off. A shout, and the one moment of distraction caused her to glance away. The next thing she knew, her opponent had her by the waist. He lifted and threw her so she half stumbled and half flew down the steps, landing in a breathless heap on the ground near Max and the other vampire.

She scrambled to her feet just as Max shouted her name; this time it was clear, and she looked over in time to see him point behind her; then he was back into the throes of defending himself.

Victoria turned and saw the figure of a man dropping from an open window of the house, carrying something large and bulky under his arm. She turned, and before she could lift her foot to take a step, she was knocked to the ground, facedown on the grass.

Groping hands, colder than the chill at the back of her neck, curled around her hair and pulled it from her nape. She whipped her hand around behind her and stabbed at the vampire.

Instead of plunging into his heart, the point of her stake popped into his eye like a stick into a plump grape. He cried out and she slipped from under him, staggering to her feet.

With only the briefest of glances at the embattled Max, she took off running.

Victoria ran faster than she had ever imagined a human could run; the *vis bulla* had to be helping her. Or perhaps it was Divine Providence.

Whatever it was, she managed to keep the running vampire in her sight. He wasn't too far ahead of her; when they reached the corner of a mews he took a sharp turn, and she followed, plunging into a dark, narrow alley lined with thick bushes and shrubs that blocked what little illumination the partial moon offered.

Her night vision wasn't as powerful as that of a vampire, nor did she have the sense of smell…but she pushed her way blindly down the passageway. She couldn't stop – if she lost him, the book was lost. It was Lilith's.

She could not let that happen.

When she got to the end of the mews, Victoria had to pause. Which way had he gone? Nowhere to be seen…then the ever-present chill at the back of her fleck heightened, and she felt him behind her. He'd ducked into the brush to wait for her to pass.

His mistake.

She turned and started back slowly. He wouldn't be able to squeeze all the way through the bushes; they were too dense, and on one side was the wall of a garden. She was thankful he was only a Guardian, and not an Imperial, some of whom could shape-shift. Guardians were fierce fighters and had strong pulls of energy, but they were more easily bested than an Imperial.

There he was.

She turned, thrust into the brush, and felt something solid. Not his chest – he leapt out and they were suddenly grappling on the ground, rolling across the pebbled pathway and into the brush. He had his hands around her neck; he wasn't wasting his time going for a bite, she thought as they tightened.

Her breathing became more difficult, and the edges of her already dark vision clouded more. She grasped the stake. One shot… Her fingers felt soft and wobbly. She clasped them, ordering them to tighten even as her mind fizzled.

Wham!

She struck as she had earlier, and got him in the eye. Two blinded vampires to her credit tonight; but that wasn't enough. Victoria rolled to her feet as he pulled himself up, one hand over the injured eye, struck…and then he was gone. *Poof.*

Panting, Victoria stood for a moment to catch her breath. Drawing the oxygen back into her lungs, she thought nothing had ever felt so good. And she listened.

Nothing.

Silence.

Only the faint rumble of a horse clopping on a distant street.

The book.

He had to have dropped it. Victoria grappled through the brush until she found it. She reached, hesitated, then, holding her breath, picked it up. Nothing happened.

With a sigh of relief, she hitched up the bulky bag and tucked it under her arm.

Now what?

Should she go back and see if Max needed help?

What if he didn't? What if he'd been…

No, she'd best get the book safely home, and then she would find out what happened to Max. If he was all right.

God, she hoped he was all right.

If he wasn't, it had been a noble sacrifice.

If he wasn't, she was on her own.

Victoria stepped from the mews and into the open night.

Chapter Thirteen

The Marquess Makes an Unwelcome Announcement

A hired hackney – not Barth's – took her home. Victoria kept the Book of Antwartha on the seat next to her in the carriage and tried not to think about Max. As he'd taken great pains to impress upon her, he was more than capable of taking care of himself.

And she knew he would rather she take care of the book, now that it was in their possession, than take a chance on losing it while coming to his aid.

When the hackney reached Grantworth House, Victoria alighted quickly, carrying the heavy bag under one arm and slamming the door of the carriage behind her. The windows of the house were dark except for the one lamp burning in the front parlour window. It was nearly four o'clock; her mother should have arrived home from the ball she'd attended by now and likely was snoring in her bed. Victoria slapped a coin in the hand of the driver and turned to start up the steps to her house.

And felt a blast of chill over the back of her neck.

Bloody hell

Again?

She groped for the stake she hadn't thought she'd need again this night and turned to look up the street. Now her entire body went cold.

Her mother was home, indeed. But she wasn't in her bed sleeping.

No. The Grantworth carriage sat gleaming green and gold under the street lamp, where it should not be. And the man sitting in the driver's seat, holding the reins of the abnormally still horses, was not the Grantworth groom.

Victoria glanced reflexively down at the bundle she held, then immediately back at the carriage. How many were there? How could she fight them with one hand holding the book? She couldn't put it down.

'Venator!' shouted a voice.

Victoria turned and saw four vampires – Guardians, she judged, based on the fact that their eyes were more ruby than garnet – stepping from behind the carriage. One of them, a tall, crimson-haired woman, had spoken.

'I hope I haven't kept you from your nightly excursions,' Victoria replied with a calmness she did not feel. 'It took a bit longer than I planned to finish this evening's task.' As she spoke, she was looking around, her mind calculating even as she struggled to comprehend that her mother was in the custody of five vampires.

How many of the damned creatures were there in London?

The absurd thought was a testament to her weariness and frustration; but Victoria could not indulge it now. Mother was in the carriage and Victoria had to save her.

The crimson-haired vampire now stood close enough that Victoria could smell her dusky, dusty, dry scent. Taking care not to look her directly in the burning eyes, Victoria readied herself for any sudden moves. The other vampires flanked behind her in a V arrangement.

'We provided your mother with an escort home this evening,' the leader said in an unhurried tone that matched Victoria's. 'She is well; we've resisted the urge to feed on her until now, Venator, because we knew that if you succeeded in your task and obtained the Book of Antwartha, you'd need a compelling reason to turn it over to us.'

With a flick of her chin she gestured, and the carriage door opened. Lady Melly stumbled out, tangled skirts and all, tripping as she tried to descend the steps. But she was well, unharmed except for the bruises she would likely have on her knees and elbows from the fall.

'I can't give you the book,' she said simply. 'But I

can give you your life…such as it is. If you prefer to keep it, and not to go the way of…oh, a dozen of your colleagues, you'll just toddle off into the night and find another tired Venator to harass.' If there were any other Venators in London…tired or not.

In the back of her mind, she heard Big Ben strike four. In sixty minutes or a bit more, the sun would begin to rise…

Could Victoria stall them long enough?

And then a hackney cab turned the corner, bumbling along at an unusually fast clip. Victoria recognised its driver. What was Barth doing here?

But before she could form the question, the cab dashed by without pause, and a splash of water burst from its open window, catching four of the vampires.

Suddenly they were screaming and clawing at themselves wherever the water had touched them. Almost before she grasped the fact that someone – Verbena, perhaps – had dashed a bucket of holy water on them, she flew into motion with her stake.

By the time she'd stabbed two of the undead, the hackney had turned around and come back. Another splash of water drenched the vampire sitting in the driver's seat, and a smaller wave fell onto the last two companions standing in the street.

They were in such agony, it was easy – too easy – to take care of them; but Victoria didn't have the energy even to feel grateful for the simple, satisfying ending to a busy night.

Barth's hackney finally stopped next to her on the street, as Victoria wrapped one arm around her blank-faced, uncharacteristically silent mother and the other around the precious bundle of an ancient tome and worked her way up the steps to Grantworth House.

A frightened Lady Melly was just one of several things Victoria would have to deal with in the morning, not to mention what to do now that she had the Book of Antwartha – and the fact that her engagement was to be announced at a ball that evening.

But for now…she wanted the comfort of her feather bed, and a safe place to hide the book.

And the assurance that Max had survived the night.

As it turned out, handling Lady Melly was much easier than Victoria had anticipated. Verbena, who had indeed flung the holy water on the vampires, prepared and administered a sleeping draft for her that dropped her like a stone.

By the time Victoria woke in the morning, Aunt Eustacia had arrived at Grantworth House. She'd been summoned by Max, who had indeed survived his third Imperial in one night and who had arrived at Grantworth House only moments after Victoria hustled her mother off to bed. He'd come for his own assurances, of course; and once notified by the suddenly important Verbena that her mistress was home, unhurt, and in possession of the object of Lilith's desire, Max slipped off into the night, presumably to seek his own feather bed.

Aunt Eustacia had her own ways of dealing with the shock of vampire victims. Holding a small gold disk etched with a spiral design in front of her niece's face, she spun and swung it until Melly's face grew blank and her eyes unfocused.

'Why,' asked Victoria when her great-aunt was finished erasing the memory of red-eyed, long-fanged undead from her mother, 'must we do that? Would it not be better for those who aren't Venators to know what the risks are? To know that vampires do exist?'

They were sitting in the parlour of Grantworth House; it was nearing noon, and it was the first moment the two women had had alone.

'To have the panic spread, as it surely would? To give Lilith that added benefit of frightened humans, weakened by their fears? Or to give untrained, unprepared would-be heroes the false belief that they could kill and hunt vampires as easily as a Venator? To have unworthy ones call for their own *vis bullae*? No, Victoria, it is much better to keep the knowledge from those who are helpless to work against it. With the exception of a very few,' she added as Verbena bustled into the room.

Then her sharp black eyes focused unwaveringly on Victoria. 'But it is no use changing the subject, my dear. I understand you have achieved the goal which we had all been working toward. May I offer you my deepest congratulations, my heartfelt thanks, and—'

'—And my gravest anger.'

Max, of course, standing tall and forbidding in the open door of the parlour. Verbena stood goggle-eyed and spasmic-haired behind him, and behind her was Jimmons, the red-faced butler, who should not have allowed the visitor entrance without warning. Although, knowing Max, Victoria acknowledged that she wasn't terribly surprised that it had happened.

He stepped fully into the room, dressed all in black, including his shirtwaist – Victoria didn't even realise they *made* black shirtwaists – and shut the door smartly behind him, nearly pinching Verbena's inquisitive nose.

'Just what did you think you were doing, Victoria?' he snapped, stalking toward her.

'Max—' Aunt Eustacia began, but Victoria overruled her.

'Saving your life…or have you so easily forgotten?' She stood too, upturned face to his furious one.

'Saving my… Victoria, if you had shared your information with me *prior* to the moment when it nearly cost me my life, the saving of it would not have been a factor! In fact, we would have determined the best way—'

'—for *you* to obtain the book, while I sat home and tended to my fripperies and furbelows, no doubt!'

'Of course not! It would have been a team effort, with a plan—'

'Easy words from the man who did not share *his* information with me either! What kind of team effort did you have in mind, Max?'

He opened his mouth to respond, but Eustacia had had enough. She shot out of her chair at Victoria's last words and placed herself quite straitly betwixt the two of them, a hand out in either direction. 'Sit down, both of you,' she ordered in a thunderous voice that Victoria had never heard before.

She sat. And so did Max. But, she noticed, he didn't look the least bit cowed.

'Let me make this clear,' she said, spearing each of them with her eyes in turn. 'The two of you are our only real hope here in England, and you must learn to work together, or we will find ourselves splintered by dissension. Now, I am not going to discuss further what happened last night…except to congratulate you both. And to breathe a great sigh of relief. We have the Book of Antwartha, and Lilith does not. You executed three Imperial vampires, Max, and that, I believe, is a one-night record. The most I ever did was two in one night,' she added with a twitch of a rueful smile. 'And numerous other Guardians, I am aware. Thanks in part to your resourceful maid.'

Victoria nodded in agreement; she had expressed the very same gratitude to Verbena, which, must have, in part, caused the maid's newfound officiousness.

'What is to be done with the book now that we have it?' asked Max easily, as if the outburst and scolding had never happened.

Before Aunt Eustacia could respond, a proper knock came at the parlour door and Jimmons opened it to peek in. Victoria nodded, and he widened the opening and said, 'It is too early for calls, but the gentleman would not be dissuaded from being announced, Miss Victoria. The Marquess of Rockley.'

Warmth suffused her face before she could catch it, and without looking at Max or Aunt Eustacia, Victoria replied, 'Please show the marquess in, Jimmons. I expect this shall not be the first time he calls outside of normal polite hours.'

From the look on his face, Max dearly wanted to say something…but before he could, the door opened again and Rockley came in.

Victoria rose eagerly, but managed to catch herself before rushing to Phillip's side. Their engagement was not yet announced; it would be unseemly for her to act so until after this evening's ball. But a great part of her yearned to put her arms around him, to bury her face in his chest and lose herself in his normalcy…in the non-vampiric, stake-less, well-lit comfort of *normalcy*.

He, too, seemed to need to restrain himself from touching her; but when he saw the other occupants of the room, Phillip stiffened into a more formal persona and took an offered seat not so far from the one in which Max sat.

'I am sorry to call so early,' he said after the appropriate introductions – or, in Max's case, reintroductions, 'but I heard what happened last night and I came to be certain all was well.'

Victoria stared at him. How could he know about what had transpired...how?

But Phillip was still talking, his bluish-grey eyes serious and concerned. 'Is your mother here? Is she safe?'

And then she began to understand. 'My mother is fine. She is sleeping well upstairs, and I do believe she has put the whole event from her mind.' Literally. 'What and how did you hear of this?'

'The word was that her carriage had been stolen, with her in it. That was the only news, and it was not until early this morning that I heard. I am glad she is here, and well. And you...Miss Grantworth, you must have had an awful night of it.' Because they had not yet announced their betrothal, he used her formal title, but there was no mistaking the personal, intimate way he spoke it.

Max shifted in his chair. 'If you heard of the carriage being stolen only this morning, I wonder why the news that Lady Melly was arrived home safely did not also reach your ears.' He smiled pleasantly.

Phillip returned the smile. Pleasantly. 'You've found me out, Lor—er, Mr Pesaro. It was merely an excuse to assure myself that Miss Grantworth was suffering no ill effects from what must have been a terribly trying night.'

Victoria covered Max's short bark of laughter with her response. 'How kind of you, my lord.' She sent him a smile that matched the intimate timbre of his voice. 'I can assure you, although my evening was difficult in more ways than one can imagine, I am feeling quite the thing now that it is morning and the sun is high in the sky.'

Phillip looked at her, then at Aunt Eustacia, and glanced over at Max before returning his attention to Victoria. 'I am certain that after last night's frightening experience, you will need to rest and take your time preparing for the ball tonight. I am hopeful that this evening will be just as exhausting, but in a more pleasant way. We will have much help in celebrating our news.'

'News?' Max asked delicately, springing to the bait. 'Another ball? Celebrating what?'

'Why, our engagement, of course,' Phillip replied blandly. 'Victoria and I are to be married in one month's time.'

Chapter Fourteen

Whereupon an Alliance Is Suggested

Victoria wore a gown of the palest of icy purple, with dark violet rosebuds and lace trimmings along the flounces of her skirt. Verbena dressed her hair in all manner of intricate coils and braids, made all the more labyrinthine by its corkscrew nature, and anchored it at the very top of her head. Two strands hung free, one on either side of her face, curling from her temples to rest over her collarbones.

Sparkling behind them were clusters of amethyst and diamonds hanging from her ears. A large, square amethyst rested in the hollow at the base of her throat, tied there by a white velvet ribbon.

She carried a small indispensable of pearlescent silk, into which was tucked a faded pink satin ribbon, and draped a thin alencon lace shawl around her elbows.

She did not carry a stake. Or holy water. Or even wear a cross, except one tucked deeply into her bodice...and dangling from her navel.

Tonight she was not a Venator.

Tonight Victoria was the betrothed of the Marquess of Rockley.

Perhaps it was an impetuous decision, but Victoria wanted one night to enjoy being a woman in love with a handsome, charming, wealthy man. She wanted one night when she did not have to consider how a vampire might enter the ballroom, or how she might make a quick exit...or even whether the breeze at the back of her neck was a gust of summer wind or the sign of an undead.

She wanted to be normal.

Nevertheless, she had brought a stake and had hidden it with her cloak in the family parlour. Just in case.

Phillip had never looked more handsome as he led her to the dance floor after their betrothal was announced by his closest relative – his deceased mother's brother – halfway through the ball. He swept Victoria gracefully into his arms and they began the first waltz of the second set, surrounded by a combination of beaming and surprised faces.

At first they were the only couple on the dance floor. Through five measures, Victoria felt the weight of half the *ton*'s gaze on her, assessing the wife-to-be of the Marquess of Rockley, one of the most sought-after bachelors of Society. He looked down at her as if she were the only woman he'd ever seen – or would see – as they turned around the oblong dance floor in an elongated triangular path.

By the time they'd come near the edge of spectators three times, other couples had begun to ease their way out to take their own turns to the waltz, and Victoria did not feel so much like a trophy on display.

Phillip lifted his gaze periodically to meet the eyes of friends, family, and acquaintances as he guided her through their paces, but his attention always returned to her. It made Victoria feel warm and tingly, the way he looked at her with promise and steadiness. She smiled, turning her face up and looking only at him, trusting that he would direct her through the steps without her having to notice where they were going or near whom they were stepping.

A wonderful feeling…allowing herself to let go. To not have to be aware of her surroundings. To not have to listen to her instincts and wonder when that chill would creep across her neck, and to not have to calculate how she would slip from the room to do her duty.

'Your aunt and your cousin did not appear to be pleased with our news,' Phillip said after they had been dancing for a moment and there were others on the floor.

'I believe you simply took them by surprise with your announcement. They expressed their overwhelming emotion after you took your leave.'

'I thought perhaps they would have wanted to attend tonight to celebrate with us. I am disappointed that they did not accept the invitation to join us here at St Heath's Row.'

'Aunt Eustacia does not move about Society all that much anymore,' Victoria replied. 'She has come here from Italy in only the last four years, and she does not know very many people. And Max…he chooses not to attend functions such as these. Just as you did… until recently.'

'I cannot fault your cousin for that; although had I known I would have found you, I am certain I would have made an effort to fend off the matchmakers much sooner '

'A lovely thought, Phillip, but I cannot agree. You know that I have moved very little in Society for the last two years, since I have been in mourning for my grandfather and father. If you had indeed bestirred yourself to move about thus, I fear I would have lost you before I found you.'

'Never. Victoria, there would have been no one but you for me.' He sighed, smiled, and continued, 'I fear it is time that I make another confession.'

As she had the first time, she raised an eyebrow. 'Another one?'

'Another one. My last, Victoria, so enjoy it.' He tipped his head and looked down at her. 'The reason I chose to put myself at the mercy of Society this year is because I knew you had finally ended your mourning and were to come out. I wanted to meet the young girl I'd known long ago and see if she had grown into the woman she promised to be. She had; and I fell in love with her.'

When he looked at her like that, with his shining blue eyes so steady and sure, she felt as though nothing would ever be so certain as Phillip and his presence. As if the reality of vampires and Lilith and the Book of Antwartha didn't have to exist in a world that Phillip and she lived in.

But of course, it could not be. She already knew those evils existed. She had already fought them – and fought them successfully.

While she couldn't leave them behind, couldn't be hypnotised out of them as her mother had been, Victoria knew she could survive the split world as long as she had Phillip waiting for her on the other side.

'Max, I don't recall the last time I saw you so disturbed.'

'Disturbed? That's much too polite a word to describe the way I'm feeling,' he snapped at Eustacia. He'd been stewing about it since yesterday, when Rockley had blithely announced the news at Grantworth House.

'Victoria cannot marry – and a marquess, no less! What has addled her brain?'

'I don't disagree with your sentiment, Max, but

the fact remains that there is no law against a Venator marrying anyone, marquess or no.'

'No law but common sense. Of which she apparently possesses none.'

Eustacia had not moved from her chair; but despite her calm, measured words, he saw the concern in her ageless face. She might not rail and stalk as he did, but as she said, she was no more pleased than he was.

'We have the Book of Antwartha,' he continued. 'And I will admit that she played a much larger role in its recovery than I had expected…but she likely believes that all threat is now abolished, since we have the book, and she does not have to play at being Venator any longer.' He flicked his finger over the sleek black stake he'd just slipped from his favourite hidden pocket.

'It is no more than I suspected when she was first called – she would find it exciting and exhilarating for a time, and then become bored with it,' he continued. 'And then she would want to return to her simple world of poetry-spouting beaux and pink furbelows and dance cards. This is precisely why women should not be Venators. Present company excepted, of course, Eustacia, as you always are the exception that proves the rule.' He gave a short bow, for he recognised the beginnings of fire in her onyx eyes.

'Victoria has given no indication that she believes

the threat is over, Max; you must admit you are being unfair. She did save your life during the process of getting the Book of Antwartha; and although it would have been preferable for the two of you to stop trying to cut the other out and work in tandem, you did indeed work together and succeeded. Brilliantly.'

'That is my point exactly, Eustacia. Just as she is beginning to show the skill of a truly gifted Venator – and yes, I'll freely admit that she has the potential to be as good as you or I – she is going to be entering into a marriage! Where she will need to account for her every moment to the marquess, and where she will have greater strictures and parameters placed on her life. Not to mention the distraction of being In Love. Have you seen how love-sopped people look at each other? And at no one else, and nothing around them? We cannot afford another near miss like we had two nights ago.'

'You said as much to Victoria yesterday when she – or rather, the marquess – told us they were getting married,' Eustacia reminded him with a calmness he did not understand. 'But, Max' – she spoke louder, raising her voice for the first time and stepping over his arguments – 'I cannot and will not order her not to marry. It is her decision and I have to let her make it. Although I do share the same concerns as you, I know that I must step aside and let her do as she will. We all have that freedom, as Venators, and she is not the first to love and want to marry. Some of us love, but do not marry,' she added, giving a bare glance toward the door through which Kritanu was due to come at any moment.

'And the truth is, Max, perhaps she will succeed where we do not expect her to. Perhaps Victoria needs that balance of the light with the dark; the ordinary with the horrific unordinary. Perhaps that will make her stronger, more adept…just as your own grief and anger feed your strength.'

'I can't agree with you, Eustacia. The life of a Venator is like that of a priest – we are called and we are solitary. And we must remain so in order to fulfil our destiny.'

'And what of me, then, Max? Have I not fulfilled my destiny because I am not alone?' Eustacia asked gently, as if she suddenly understood what was at the core of his disheartenment.

Max recognised an unanswerable question when he heard one, and swiftly changed the subject. 'Victoria recognised Sebastian Vioget. How does she know who he is?'

Eustacia lifted an eyebrow. 'That is interesting. My assumption would be that wherever and however she learnt about the book and its protection was where and how she learnt who Sebastian Vioget is. And it concerns me that he was there at Redfield Manor.'

'It concerns me that he would have allowed me to pick up the book,' Max replied with sarcasm. 'He was nearly salivating at the thought.'

'It's too bad you cannot see to form an alliance with him. It might be to our benefit. Perhaps that is something Victoria should consider.' Before Max could speak, Eustacia brought up another unpleasant topic. 'How is your neck?'

He caught himself reaching to touch the old bite. It had indeed been paining him in the last day, throbbing with a constant dull tic. 'I felt no need to mention it has been hurting; it would be no surprise to you, considering the events of the last few days.'

'No, but I could give you more salve,' Eustacia replied gently, as though speaking to a young child. 'There is no need for you to endure the pain.'

'It is nothing.' Perhaps he would have said more, but at that moment Kritanu opened the door from the hall and Wayren glided in.

'Felicitations, Eustacia and Maximilian,' the blond librarian beamed. Her long medieval sleeves would drag the floor when her arms hung at her sides; but now, as she had them raised in delight, the flowing cuffs served only to wrap themselves around Eustacia and then Max, in turn, as Wayren embraced each of them. 'You have succeeded in retrieving the book! And so quickly!'

'Yes, it was quite fortuitous,' replied Max as she stepped back.

'And your bite?' asked Wayren, giving him the same assessing look Eustacia had.

'It is tender,' he admitted.

The door opened again, and Kritanu ushered in the second guest – Victoria, of course. Max looked over and said, 'Ah, there she is. And…alone? You did not bring your better half, Victoria?'

'Oh, no, Phillip sends his regrets. He is much too busy trying to decide which way to tie his neckcloth for the wedding,' she replied sweetly.

Max had to bite his lip to keep back his surprised delight at her smart rejoinder. She was quick. He couldn't fault her there.

As he sat down in his favourite chair next to the highboy where Kritanu kept the brandy, he looked blandly at Eustacia, who had given him a less than pleased look at his sarcastic comment.

'Your better half?' asked Wayren, settling next to Max but speaking to Victoria.

'Max is speaking of my betrothed husband, the Marquess of Rockley. He – Max – appears to be under the impression that when I take my vows I will forget those I have already made to the Gardella Legacy.'

Victoria, whose hair was dressed in a way that Max had never seen, pressed a kiss to her aunt's cheek, and then one to Kritanu's, before selecting a chair directly opposite Max. Instead of being piled high on her head, with every black curl stuck in place and intertwined with gems and ribbons, her hair fell in a simple, long plait down the back of her dress. She had to move the braid out of the way or she would have sat on it.

Max noticed that she was carrying a leather bag,

and as she settled in her chair, she drew it onto her lap.

'That is the book?' he asked, desirous of getting their discussion onto more important things than the impending wedding.

'It is.' Victoria drew it out and held it for a moment before offering it to Eustacia. 'What shall we do with it now that we have it? Is there anything in it that could help us?'

Wayren watched the battered leather tome with the same avidity Max's old dog watched the table for a bone or other scrap to fall – or be pushed – to the floor. She sounded almost breathless when she spoke. 'I will have to study it to know for certain... but I would venture to say that there is little in there that would promote living in the light. It is the book of Kali's evil child, and as such has only recipes for promoting evil. Still, knowing what value it has for Lilith may help us to understand her next move.'

'Indeed,' Eustacia agreed. 'Merely having it in our possession is the greatest of advantages. And in fact, I have been thinking long and hard about where we should hide the book until we have decided what to do with it.'

'Won't you keep it here, Aunt Eustacia?' asked Victoria, surprise lighting her face.

Max did little to disguise his snort of disgust. 'Eustacia's home, or mine, would be the first place Lilith would look for it; Or yours.' He was not disappointed; a jolt of enlightenment changed her face. Ah, perhaps she did understand the severity of the situation. That the game was not quite over yet…and, in fact, would not be over until Lilith was annihilated. 'She knows who foiled her plan, and I can only imagine her fury with us.' Actually, he could imagine it quite well. Better, in fact, than he wished.

'Wherever it is kept, you must place it out of direct sunlight, especially while transporting it,' Wayren said, 'or it will crumble into dust. It is an evil book, and therefore it thrives in the dark…and disintegrates in the light. And before you take it, I would like to reverse the protection on it as well, in order to give us additional security.'

'Reverse the protection?' asked Victoria. 'You can do that?'

'That is part of Wayren's charm,' Max interjected. 'No pun intended.'

Wayren tinkled a laugh at his jest, and he was partially mollified when Victoria narrowed her eyes as if not sure what to believe. He felt a perverse pleasure in keeping himself one step ahead of her.

'I would like to destroy the book,' Wayren added, 'and then we need not fear Lilith finding it and retrieving it, but before we do that I want to do a bit more investigation in order to make sure there will be no adverse effects if we do. Or whether there is anything in the book that we might find advantageous. So if there is a place that it can be kept safely for a bit longer...'

'I have come to the conclusion,' Eustacia interrupted pointedly, 'that the best place is to hide it away in a church or holy place of some sort. She can't go there if it is protected enough, and she cannot send her minions.'

'If you do not have a place in mind, I have a suggestion,' Victoria spoke. 'There is a small chapel on the grounds at St Heath's Row – Rockley's estate,' she added, looking pointedly at Max. 'I could hide the book there, and make certain that there are enough holy relics and images to keep them away, even if they were to determine it was there. I will be becoming quite familiar with the entire chapel, including its decor, as that is where we are to be married.'

The way her lips curved in a mocking smile made Max's blood pressure rise. He gave no indication, however; just picked up his black stake and slapped it against his palm. It was time to leave.

He stood. 'Well, then, since we have settled that, I must be on my way. Lilith will have sent her people out to gather victims for her feeding, and I've a mind to put her on a restricted diet.'

He expected Victoria to leap up and insist upon going with him, and he had a rigidly polite response ready to sally off to her...but she didn't. She just looked up at him with those clear hazel eyes in a delicate, creamy face that should not belong to a woman who'd killed eight vampires two nights earlier.

'Take care, Max,' she said, surprising him again this evening.

'I will.' And he left, glad to be out in the night doing what he was born to do. At least he would have no distractions.

Victoria wanted to make another visit to the Silver Chalice, but that was easier conceived than actually realised.

Her retrieval of the Book of Antwartha had happened six days ago, and since then she had been balancing the requirements of being the future Marchioness of Rockley, duties to her mother, who was milking her new status for all she could, and meetings with Aunt Eustacia, Kritanu, the waiflike Wayren, and, of course, Max.

As promised, she had taken the book and hidden it under the altar at the chapel at St Heath's Row, which was the extensive Rockley estate that sat on the very edge of town. Wayren had been given leave to visit the chapel at any time so that she could study it in safety; Phillip had been told that she was a distant relative of Victoria's who was offering a novena in her name for the success of their marriage, and wished to spend time in the chapel.

Max was not so easily managed. He had tried several times to bring up the fact that she'd mentioned

Sebastian's name during the events at Redfield Manor, but Victoria had been stubbornly closemouthed. She was furious with herself for such a blunder, but as long as she continued to sidestep Max's inquisition, she could keep the damage to a minimum. In fact, she found it a pleasure to see the annoyance on his face when she sweetly dodged his queries.

It was when Aunt Eustacia began to ask questions that Victoria had more difficulty.

'Max tells me you have met Sebastian Vioget,' her aunt commented one afternoon when Victoria had managed to slip away from Grantworth House before Melly dragged her off to another tea. It wasn't that she didn't like sharing biscuits and gossip with her peers; it was that she'd done so much of it in the last week that Victoria felt ill at the thought of more lemon curd and clotted cream slathered on various baked goods. Not to mention the fact that her stays were feeling uncomfortably tight.

And how was she going to fit into a wedding gown if she kept eating five or six rounds of tea during daily visits?

'What makes Max think I've met him?' countered Victoria innocently.

Aunt Eustacia gave her an indulgent look that told her she would allow her to play the game of splitting hairs. 'You recognised him at Rudolph Caulfield's home, so Max assumed you knew him.'

'I did recognise him, but that doesn't mean that

I have met him. What do you think he was doing there?'

Her aunt clasped lace-edged hands in her lap and looked directly at Victoria. 'I thought perhaps you would have the answer to that.' The indulgent look had vanished.

'I truly don't know why he was there. I was as surprised as Max must have been. Unless Max had expected him…?'

Her aunt watched her for a moment as if to gauge the veracity of her statement, then seemed to make a decision – obviously in Victoria's favour, for she said, 'Sebastian Vioget is very powerful and he could be a valuable ally to our cause. If we could trust him.' Aunt Eustacia was looking at her with such scrutiny that Victoria felt her face grow warm. She felt as though her aunt was waiting for her to say something, but Victoria did not know what…and she knew that anything she said at that point would be inadvisable.

But Victoria, at least, had no reason not to trust Sebastian. The information he had given her had been correct – as far as she could ascertain.

It wasn't that she *did* trust him. It was that she didn't not trust him. That splitting-hairs problem.

'Why don't you trust him? He's not a vampire.'

Eustacia swept at her a look that reminded her of the sharp swipe that Max had used to behead the Imperials. 'No, he is not a vampire. But the mere fact that he was at Rudolph Caulfield's home, in the midst of this transferral of the Book of Antwartha, has given both Max and myself reason to wonder at his involvement. Victoria, what do you know about Sebastian Vioget? Have you had any interaction with him?'

Victoria opened her mouth to speak, then closed it, Sebastian had warned her about divulging where she'd gotten her information…but how could she keep such information from Aunt Eustacia? Especially when asked so directly?

She struggled, knowing that her aunt was watching her, and knowing that the fact that she'd delayed answering her question had already given her aunt the information she sought. So she made the decision.

'I visited the Silver Chalice to try to find information about the Book of Antwartha, and I met him at that time. He made it clear to me that I was not to tell anyone we'd spoken, so I did not.'

Aunt Eustacia nodded once. To Victoria's relief, she asked for no further details. Instead she commented, 'If you should have occasion to meet him again, it would not be remiss if you were to attempt to establish some level of cooperation. It could be to our benefit.'

With that, Victoria knew she needn't put off visiting the Silver Chalice any longer.

She would go tonight.

Chapter Fifteen

Miss Grantworth Acquires the Headache

It wasn't quite as easy getting to the Silver Chalice as Victoria had envisioned it.

She'd forgotten that her fiancé was taking her to the theatre that evening. And she'd rather been looking forward to seeing the latest rendition of Master Shakespeare's *The Taming of the Shrew*.

She told herself that the odd squirming feeling in her middle had nothing to do with the fact that she would see Sebastian again…it was because she hoped Phillip wouldn't question her when she claimed the headache immediately at the end of the play.

That way she could see the program, but then be required to return home immediately instead of arriving late at a post-theatre ball or taking a stroll through Covent Gardens. The curtain rose at seven thirty and the theatre normally let out by eleven.

If Barth were there with his hackney by midnight, that would give Victoria plenty of opportunity to pay a visit to the Silver Chalice and return home in time to get several hours of sleep before her wedding gown fitting.

Perfect.

And it actually worked according to plan. There weren't even any vampires at the Drury Lane Theatre, nor did even the slightest chill skitter across Victoria's neck during the trip there and back. In fact, there had been a dearth of vampires since the fights at Redfield Manor, and Victoria began to wonder if she and Max had fairly cleared out a good portion of Lilith's army. Perhaps the vampire queen had gone into hiding and was licking her wounds, or, better yet, perhaps she'd left the country.

'Are you certain there is nothing I can do for you?' asked Phillip as he led her up the walk to Grantworth House. He was clearly disappointed at having their evening cut short, but he'd handled it with grace and concern, as she'd known he would.

'Thank you, darling, but a bit of rest and Verbena's peppermint tea is all I need. I am sure to be fresh as a daisy tomorrow,' she told him. 'And I had best be so, for Madame LeClaire is attending me for a gown fitting.'

Jimmons had opened the door for them, and Phillip followed Victoria over the threshold. 'Now that, my lovely, is something I would pay dearly to see.' His smile, warm and crooked, told her that he knew it was only a matter of time before he would have his desire fulfilled.

Glancing about as if to assure himself that Jimmons had retreated, Phillip took her shoulders, and under the gentle pressure of his fingers she stepped toward him. Her breasts brushed the buttons of his coat, the folds of her skirt jutted around and between his trousers, and one foot slid between his.

Another guiding movement from his fingers, and she came closer and had to draw in her breath because they were close, touching at hip, thigh, and foot. And then mouth. Warm, slick, tender, he kissed her.

If she'd truly been suffering from a headache, Victoria was sure it would have flown as easily from her head as all other thought actually did.

'I know you aren't feeling quite the thing,' he murmured near her lips when they paused, foreheads heavy against each other, 'but I can't resist.' His nose slid against hers as he dipped to kiss her again.

When he finally set her away from him, just as carefully as he'd drawn her near, Victoria opened her eyes. She had to blink in order to focus, and was deliciously pleased to see that his normally half-lidded eyes were even droopier. He looked as though he wanted to slip back into her arms with the same ease and comfort of sliding into a feather bed. But warmer. More inviting.

'Good night, Phillip,' she heard herself say as he stepped away, still holding her hand. Her palm, then fingers, then the very tips of them, slid through his grip as he released her. The door was behind him. Still looking at her with those half-closed eyes, meaningful and determined, he reached for the knob, turned it, and slipped out into the night.

'Well, if that wasn't a kiss of true love, I don't know what is.'

Victoria spun to see Verbena standing at the bottom of the staircase – lud, she hadn't even heard her approach! – with a decidedly wistful expression on her face. 'Love's not necessary to a well-matched marriage,' Victoria said firmly, 'but it certainly doesn't hurt. Now, is Barth here?'

'He's been waiting just around the corner for the marquess to leave,' Verbena replied. 'Are you certain I cannot go with you tonight?'

'No, I thank you, Verbena, but I will go alone. Barth will deliver me safely and I'll be home before dawn. You'll need to be here in case my mother asks for me. She was concerned when I left the theatre, as I told her I wasn't feeling well. Now, I had best be on my way if I hope to get any sleep tonight.'

'Barth will wait while you change your gown.'

'No, but I will take my dark red cloak. Its hood will help to hide my face.' In the event that Max was also at the Silver Chalice.

* * *

When she alighted from Barth's hackney forty minutes later, Big Ben had just struck half past midnight. Under the heavy cloak, Victoria held the pistol she'd remembered to bring this time – there would be no Verbena to come to the rescue tonight. She also had three stakes in various locations on her person; her indispensable, which held a vial of salted holy water; and a large crucifix tucked into her relatively high bodice. That last had been at Verbena's insistence, for if she was not allowed to go, she would ensure that her mistress was well protected.

Well protected she would be from vampires. And armed with the pistol, she would be safe from other predators.

But for some reason, when she thought about Sebastian Vioget, she was not altogether certain how secure she would be.

The Silver Chalice had more empty tables than it had the last time Victoria had been there; but since there'd been only one at that time, and there were three this time, she did not think it was any indication of a dearth of business.

Under the cloak's hood and the low coil of her hair, Victoria's neck bristled with chill as though an arctic wind blasted it. At the bottom of the steep stairs she paused to glance around, looking for anyone she knew.

Amelie, the platinum-haired pianist who'd sat with Verbena the last time, was at her place to the left. She bore the same melancholy look Victoria remembered from before, and played the same sad, drawn-out music. Max was not here, and neither, as far as she could see, was Sebastian.

Drawing back the hood of her cloak, Victoria stepped from the shadows near the stairs and started toward a table. Berthy, the rude serving woman, remembered her, even though Victoria had been dressed in man's clothing the last time. Apparently Sebastian had been right about its not hiding her gender. Berthy sloshed by with two hands full of tankards and gave Victoria a nudge that resulted in a splash on her cloak. 'He said to come to the back rooms.'

Victoria didn't waste the energy wondering how Sebastian knew she'd arrived; perhaps he'd told Berthy to give her those instructions regardless of when she came. She started toward the brick wall where the door was, then changed her mind and selected a seat at an empty table with three chairs.

On her way back to the bar, Berthy paused by Victoria's table just long enough to ask, 'Wot's it to be?'

'Cider,' replied Victoria to the back of her head; but Berthy nodded, and she knew she'd heard her.

Letting her attention wander the room, Victoria amused herself by identifying which patrons were undead and which were mortal. To her surprise it was fairly evenly split, and there were even tables at which the two kinds mixed. Why a mortal would willingly interact with an undead was something she couldn't comprehend. It was rather like the fly sitting down for tea with the spider: likely to be dangerous and messy.

When Berthy swooped back by, her hands full again, Victoria watched as she slammed down two tankards at a table with vampires. Something too opaque to be red wine slopped over the sides and ran down onto the table. Victoria felt the hair on the back of her arms rise, and she looked away as one of the undead drank eagerly.

Placing the cider in front of Victoria, Berthy gave her what appeared to be a smile and leant close enough to say, 'Makin' him come to ye, eh? 'At's the way to teach 'em.' And then she was gone.

Hiding her smile in the wide metal mug, Victoria took a sip of the fermented drink. Not bad. She'd remembered her coins this time, and pulled out a farthing to leave on the table for Berthy.

Just then Max – dressed in black, of course – appeared from around the corner of the descending stairs. As Victoria had done, he looked around the room, and, recognising the inevitable, she raised her hand to draw his attention.

He didn't appear surprised to see her; in fact, the speed with which he made his way to her small round table betrayed the fact that he'd been searching for her. Eustacia must have told him.

'Good evening, Max,' Victoria said as he slid into

the chair next to her. 'Shall I ask Berthy to bring you an ale? Or would you prefer what they're drinking?' She gestured to the vampires next to them. 'It looks a bit thick to be a chianti.'

He leant toward her, his elbows on the table next to hers, his eyes scanning the room even as he spoke. 'I cannot believe you came here alone, Victoria.'

'I'm a Venator, Max, same as you.'

'I don't know what Eustacia has put into your head, but Sebastian Vioget—'

'—is delighted to welcome you to his establishment.'

Max's intensity evaporated. Victoria literally felt it ooze out of him; he was sitting close enough that she felt the ease in his taut muscles, the gentle, deep breath he took. 'Vioget. What impeccable timing, as always.'

Victoria glanced at Max. His body relaxed, lean and long, in the chair next to hers; he looked as though his best friend had just wandered up and mentioned that the sun was beaming. His smile showed even white teeth and a gentle dent in the skin next to the corner of his mouth...but she recognised the edge to that innocuous smile.

'And who is your lovely companion?' Sebastian slid into the third seat at the table, to the left of Victoria. The three of them sat in a wide V, with Victoria at the apex, facing the open room.

Before Max could reply, she had to save the

moment. 'I must have the advantage, then, Mr Vioget. I am Victoria Grantworth, and I must confess I am aware that you are the owner of this establishment. I saw you the last time I was here.' None of which, strictly speaking, was a lie.

Approval glinting in his eyes, Sebastian reached over and took her gloved hand. 'I am very pleased to make your acquaintance, Miss Grantworth.' He raised her hand to his lips and pressed a kiss to it, watching her with his golden eyes. It brought to mind the last time she'd visited the Silver Chalice – when she'd been dressed as a man, and they'd shaken hands, her slender one in his wide-palmed one.

And then she had a flash of memory of that same bronze hand, fingers splayed, brushing over the warm skin of her ivory belly. Her stomach tightened involuntarily, as if he were reaching to touch it again, and their eyes met as he released her fingers. His expression had changed to amber, and she knew he remembered too.

'How about some of that whiskey you keep in the back,' Max said, his voice still low and smooth. But Victoria could feel him scanning her as if trying to read between and under and around the polite words they'd spoken. His unruffled manner merely underscored the power she knew was hidden. The question was whether Sebastian was aware of it.

Sebastian caught Berthy's attention, and somehow she knew what he wanted, for moments later she slammed down the whiskey bottle and two small glasses. This time she did not slosh on his lace cuffs.

'So you have retrieved the Book of Antwartha,' said Sebastian after he tipped his glass back. Light from the wall sconce behind him glowed at the edges of his curling hair, giving him an oddly angelic appearance. 'I must offer you my congratulations. It was a bit of a moment, there, Pesaro, when you might not have succeeded.'

Max's arm brushed hers as he tossed back a healthy swallow of the golden liquid. Placing the glass with deliberate care, he watched Sebastian closely, yet his words sounded nonchalant. 'Did you know of the protection on the book? That a mortal must not steal it from its rightful owner?'

Sebastian's response was equally as cool. 'I had heard something of that nature.' Their gazes met steadily, neither willing to give way.

'Kind of you to have mentioned it.'

Suddenly Victoria's attention was drawn to a cluster of movement near the bottom of the staircase entrance. She glanced over and her heart stuttered to a halt.

No.

No! Impossible! Still staring at the entrance, she could barely get the words out. 'It's Phillip! Rockley! He's *here!*' Victoria grabbed blindly at Max's wrist. 'My God, he's here!'

Max had been focused on Vioget; now he turned

to look at her, then toward the entrance, where she was still watching in shock. She felt her nails bite into his warm skin.

The marquess was standing just at the bottom of the staircase. He appeared to be holding a pistol at his side. And he had drawn the attention of more than one of the Silver Chalice's occupants.

How could this be? She had to get him out of here… but she couldn't let him see her! Victoria dragged the hood of her cloak up over her hair and shifted back into the shadows, realising that she was going to have to ask Max for help. Her fingers were icy. She felt ill. How had he come here? How could it be?

'Someone you know?' asked Sebastian lightly in his French accent. He was watching them closely, as if feeling his disconnection from the two of them. 'I do hope he is not planning to cause trouble.'

'Miss Grantworth's fiancé,' Victoria dimly heard Max explain as her brain fumbled for a solution. 'She must leave before he sees her.'

Thank goodness he understood. And he was right – she had to leave before he saw her! The shock began to wane, replaced by focus and determination.

Sebastian looked at Victoria in surprise. 'Sneaking around on your betrothed? Tsk, tsk, my dear Miss Grantworth.' Lifting his eyes, he caught Max's. 'I will show her another way out, so she'll not be seen.' Apparently Sebastian understood too.

Max appeared ready to argue, but Victoria took

his arm again, looking at him from under the hood of her cloak. 'Max, you must see to him. Please. Make certain he gets out of here, and home safely. He doesn't belong here.'

Sebastian stood, pulling Victoria to her feet without waiting for Max's agreement. 'Come with me, Miss Grantworth,' he murmured, closing his fingers firmly around her arm.

Victoria sent Max one last pleading look – much as she hated the fact that she had to ask for his help – and allowed Sebastian to lead her two paces from their table and through the door to the hidden hallway.

Max would make sure Phillip was safe.

Max watched Vioget whisk Victoria from the main room. *Damnation.* What the hell did Rockley think he was doing?

It didn't matter how or why…now the only concern was getting the fop out of here before the vampires decided to take offence at the pistol he was holding.

During their murmured conversation, Rockley had only scanned the room and taken three uncertain steps farther into the pub. If he'd seen Victoria, it had been only as a shadowed figure.

'Rockley,' Max said as he approached the man, who still stood at the entrance, looking around and gathering the attention of every undead in the room. Fresh blood was always better than the kegged stuff

Vioget kept in the back. 'May I offer some advice? Put the weapon away. You won't need it here.'

The fop looked at him, and Max was gratified to see that there was no fear in his eyes, nor was there the jumpiness that often accompanied men who waved pistols around in the form of courage. His look was not only steady, but unsurprised at seeing a face that he recognised.

'It was necessary to get from my coach to the door to this place,' Rockley replied, tucking the pistol into his pocket. 'And I'll use it if I need to in order to find Victoria and get her to safety.'

Here was where Max had to show his skill as an actor – better, he thought snidely, than Victoria and Vioget had done earlier with their demonstration of a first meeting. 'Victoria? What in the bloody hell are you talking about, Rockley?'

'She's here somewhere. I followed her, and I cannot imagine what she is doing here! In a place like this.' Even as he spoke, his sharp eyes darted around the room again, as if to assure himself she hadn't reappeared. 'What are you doing here?'

'I haven't seen Victoria,' Max said unequivocally. 'I've been in this seat for well over an hour, and if she were anywhere around, I would have seen her. I won't even ask the question why you think she would come to a place like this, in the middle of the night. You must have some reason for thinking so, ridiculous as it is.'

'I followed her from her house. I saw her get out of a hired hackney, for God's sake. A hackney! Your cousin got out of the hackney and came down here.'

That was right; he couldn't forget that Victoria had told him they were cousins. 'How long ago was this?' asked Max, knowing that there had been a lapse of time between his arrival and Rockley's; and Victoria had already been here when he came back into the Chalice after a quick patrol through the neighbourhood. Max had been waiting for her since eleven o'clock.

'Some little bit of time,' he replied. 'I fell into an altercation when I first came out of my carriage, and had to persuade a few gentlemen that I was coming down here, either with their permission or without.'

That explained the pistol.

'As I have said, Rockley, she is not here. Indeed, if I had seen my cousin come into an establishment such as this, I would have escorted her home immediately. This is no place for a woman, nor for most men either.'

'I followed her from her house,' Rockley said stubbornly. 'She said she was feeling ill, so I brought her home after the theatre. But she left her wrap in my carriage, and I came back to return it and saw her come out the front entrance and climb into a hackney.'

'You must be mistaken. It must have been her maid you saw, or someone else leaving her house. It's ludicrous, Rockley, simply ludicrous to think

Victoria came to a place such as this.'

Max noticed that one of the larger vampires had been eyeing Rockley with more than curiosity. He needed to get the man out of here before he found himself in the middle of a brawl. The truce the undead and mortals shared here at the Silver Chalice was tenuous; once strained or stretched, it quickly disintegrated into a melee. He'd seen it happen.

In spite of the fact that it would be more than an inconvenience to Sebastian Vioget, Max couldn't let that occur. He looked at Rockley, who, for all his every-hair-in-place appearance and perfectly folded cravat, appeared ready and able to protect himself.

Acting the hero was all well and good, and it certainly must be attractive to the ladies...but the Marquess of Rockley was not the least bit equipped to deal with the particular dangers here. Max had plenty of experience and little patience with such naive do-gooders.

The only thing to do in a situation like this was buy some time, get the man a drink, and put *salvi* in his whiskey. That would make him much easier to manage.

'You did not tell me you were engaged,' murmured Sebastian in the flickering light.

Victoria felt the cold stone wall of the passageway behind her, and the warmth of his words on her face. He'd closed the door behind them, and they were alone in the curved-ceilinged hall. His fingers still held her gloved arm betwixt her wrist and elbow; she could easily snap his grip with one tug.

'And you did not tell Max about the protection on the Book of Antwartha,' she replied. 'We all have our secrets.'

He smiled. 'Is it a secret that you are engaged to a rich dandy? One who must be rescued from the darkness like a debutante fending off an overzealous suitor?'

At that, Victoria did yank her arm away, breaking his grip. 'Rockley is no secret, and he is not the weak fool you make him out to be. You needn't stand so close to me.'

'Has he seen your *vis bulla*?' He had not moved away, and his hand had shifted between them, below her breasts, to press flat over her shirtwaist against the trembling muscles of her stomach. 'Does he know what it means?'

She shoved against his shoulders and pushed him away. He moved, but barely stumbled backward. He was stronger than she realised.

'Does he know that it means his love walks the streets at night? That she must mingle with those from the dark side to learn their secrets?' Unruffled, nonplussed by her violent reaction, he spoke, his voice low and hypnotic. 'That she kills every time she raises her weapon? That she has a strength he cannot hope to possess?'

'He knows nothing.' Victoria spoke from between clenched teeth. Sebastian had moved in toward her again, crowding her back against the wall, but he did not touch her.

'Has he seen it, Victoria?' The gentle roll of her name's last syllables caused an odd wave in her middle. 'Has he?'

She could not look away from his tigerish eyes, could barely move her lungs to breathe. The damp, rough wall jutted into her cloak and through the cloth of her flimsy gown, just as the pressure of his hand had come through the front of her skirt. She felt a trickle of sweat from the stones seeping into the back of her head. It was cold and musty.

'No,' she whispered.

Satisfaction glowed in his expression. 'I see.'

He stepped away suddenly, as if he'd been yanked back. As if her proximity had suddenly become too much. Victoria was able to breathe and to move, and she leveraged herself from the wall, shifting away from him.

'Come. Let us go before your Venator comes back to check on us.'

He turned and strode down the passageway, leaving Victoria to follow; so different from the first time, when he'd led her by the arm. She hesitated, as she had then. The choice between Scylla and Charybdis: solid Phillip and the maelstrom of Sebastian. Which was the lesser of the two challenges?

In the end, she followed Sebastian. Phillip was a bigger part of her life, one she would not risk jeopardising. Sebastian was merely a man.

Chapter Sixteen

The Marquess Wins the Shell Game and Makes a Grave Error

Phillip de Lacy was no fool. Not a bit.

He knew something was amiss; what he did not know was whether Victoria's brooding cousin Maximilian Pesaro was the cause or the cure.

The man seemed capable and intelligent; he did not appear sly or devious. By firmly suggesting that Phillip put away his pistol, he had likely saved him from causing an altercation here in this filthy place – something that Phillip had missed in his concern for Victoria. He had to give him credit for that, if nothing else.

The way some of the patrons here were looking at him, as if he were a young hare ready for the spit, made Phillip more than a bit uneasy. He was no light-footed jackrabbit, skittering off at the slightest hint of danger. But there was something wrong about this place. Something that made his blood run cold.

He'd seen Victoria leave her house; despite Pesaro's arguments, he was certain it was she. The way she walked, her height, even her movement as she closed the door behind her…he would recognise Victoria anywhere, in any disguise. And that garnet-coloured cloak was fine wool; surely she would not loan it to her maid.

Thus he'd followed the hackney, at first with a jealous twisting in his heart – was she going to meet someone? A lover? This was not the first time she'd left an evening early or cut short her visit. Uncertainty borne of his need for her, and worry for her safety, drove him to follow her. He did love her; he could not bear it if there were someone else who possessed her heart.

When the hackney took a turn to the worst part of London and finally rolled to a stop in this dark, dingy place, Phillip no longer worried that she was meeting a lover. Instead he realised that whatever called her to this part of town went much deeper than lust or passion.

Whatever she was involved in she could not, should not handle alone. She must be frightened out of her mind to travel to such a place; and it could be only the worst of circumstances for her to be unwilling to confide in him. But he would take her home and convince her to tell him…for they were to be married, and he to be her husband. He would take care of her. He would fix whatever needed to be fixed.

That, at least, had been his plan until he walked down the stairs into this hellhole of a pub that smelt like rusting iron and must. The cousin had drawn him to a table in the most shadowy corner and ordered him a drink. It wasn't until he saw, from the corner of his eye, Pesaro's hand shift over Phillip's own drink, ever so quickly, so slightly – but enough that he recognised the movement – that Phillip realised Pesaro had his own agenda. And when Phillip took a sip of the whiskey and felt Pesaro watching him, he knew it for certain.

So when the other man turned to speak to the massively well-endowed serving woman, Phillip exchanged their glasses.

And when Pesaro turned back, Phillip offered a toast, watching as the other man drank of the same drug he'd attempted to foist upon him, all the while wondering why Pesaro would do such a thing. Was he trying to kill him, or merely drug him?

He supposed if Victoria's cousin wanted him dead, he wouldn't have advised him to put his pistol away, or drawn him away from the centre of attention in the room.

No matter. He would either ask him or, if he died, it would be a moot issue.

Unsurprisingly, Pesaro appeared eager for Phillip to drink his whiskey; so he obliged, but only if the cousin drank with him. It was when their glasses were nearly empty that he began to see signs of the other man's edges wearing down. His eyes drooped; his words came slower. Whether he was being poisoned or merely drugged, Phillip did not know… but whatever it was, the other man had attempted to foist it upon Phillip, so he felt very little remorse.

'You switched glasses,' Pesaro said, his voice slurred and his eyes glistening with anger. 'Damn fool.'

'It is only what you deserve. Why have you tried to poison me?'

'You do…not know…danger… Keep you… safe… Fool.'

He waited until Max gave up, his head slumping to the table. 'Now I will find Victoria.' Phillip dropped a few coins on the sticky wooden planks and they clattered to a stop next to the man's half-curled fingers. Then he stood and walked away without looking back.

It was clear that his fiancée was not here, if she ever had been. He crossed the room, hurrying toward the stairs, fingering the pistol under his cloak.

Phillip couldn't wait to get out of this cloying, depressing place; he rushed up the steps, needing to breathe the clean night air. He had to clear his mind, which now had many more questions than when he'd arrived – including the reason Victoria's cousin would try to drug him.

When he reached the top of the stairs, Phillip heard

heavy steps behind him. He turned and saw one of the patrons, large and pale-faced, stalking up the stairs.

Slipping through the door, Phillip was back in the night. He closed the door and turned to hurry away; but the man came through more quickly than he could have imagined. Suddenly he was right behind him, and Phillip felt hot breath on his neck…even though it was covered by his cloak, and the man was not touching him.

He turned, pulling the pistol from his pocket and pointing it at his stalker. They were standing in the middle of a narrow alley, and there was nowhere for him to run but back down the stairs to the Silver Chalice…or past the man who blocked the street entrance of the alley.

'Stay back, or I will shoot,' Phillip warned, his finger tightening on the trigger. His aim was steady, his senses alive and singing even as a confident calmness flowed through him. He did not wish to hurt the man, but he would do what he must to protect himself… and find Victoria.

The man took another step forward and Phillip pulled the trigger, aiming for his shoulder. His aim must have been off; the man kept coming. His vision swam, and he felt an odd tightening in his chest, as if his lungs were not his own…as if someone else inflated and deflated them.

He could not look away, could not move away from the man coming toward him.

Something glinted red, but Phillip could not see it…it curled at the edges of his blackening vision. Phillip could not focus; he aimed blindly ahead, hoping for the man's chest, and pulled the trigger.

His attacker's eyes were burning an odd colour… like glowing wine. He reached for Phillip, who tried to pull away, but the man had inhuman strength; Phillip could not shake him, could not dislodge his grip even slightly. And then something white gleamed in the dim light as one hand closed over Phillip's head, pulling it to one side.

Sharp white teeth, descending toward his neck.

'Why did you not tell Max about the protection on the Book of Antwartha?' asked Victoria. She stood fully across the room from Sebastian, in the same den-like chamber they had been in before – the one with a single entrance.

He looked up from where he was pouring two small glasses of something pale pink. The settee on which she'd sat before, and where he'd touched her *vis bulla*, bisected the space between them like the low stone fence that kept the sheep in their fields at Prewitt Shore. Victoria wasn't certain who was the fenced-in lamb and who was not.

'I wanted to see if you had kept our bargain,' replied Sebastian, stepping toward her. Victoria moved so that the sofa remained between them, and reached across to take the glass he offered. She was careful not to allow their fingers to touch. 'If he knew about it, it was because you had told him.'

'I kept our bargain, but he could have died without the knowledge.'

'But he did not, for he did not touch it. He knew.'

'I told him only to save his life. He didn't believe me.'

'His life is of such value to you?'

'Any life is of value to me. What is this?' She looked at the glass. The liquid pooled into a ruby colour at the bottom of the tiny tulip-shaped vessel, but as the glass widened up, it became the palest of pink.

'Only a bit of sherry. Try it; I believe you will find it to your taste.' He raised his glass in a mock toast and tipped its entire contents down his throat. When he looked back at her, he nodded to the settee. 'Have a seat, Victoria.'

'No, thank you.' She set the glass down and stepped farther away; now she was standing behind the settee and he in front.

'Are you frightened of me, Victoria?'

'What have I to be frightened of? I am a Venator.'

'Indeed. I wondered the same thing myself. In fact, perhaps it is I who should be wary of you.' He looked at her and held her gaze for a long moment. 'Perhaps I should.' He broke away and swivelled to the table to pour another glass of sherry.

When he came back around, his face was shuttered,

closed. He offered another sardonic toast, but instead of downing the whole glass, he merely took a sip and sat on the settee. Half turned, he arranged himself in its corner so that he could see Victoria, standing behind the protective fencing of the sofa's back, her hand resting on its chintz covering.

'Why did you come here tonight?' he asked.

'You were expecting me. I was a bit surprised.'

'I told you the last time you were here that I would see you again. I knew you would come back. But I am curious as to why.'

'Perhaps to thank you for the information that helped us to get the Book of Antwartha. If I had not had your information, Max and I might have died in the effort.'

'So you come bearing tokens of gratitude?' He shifted himself onto one knee on the sofa cushion and covered her hand with his fingers, holding it gently in place on the top of the back. 'I am pleased to hear that. And particularly thankful that Eustacia sent you rather than Maximilian for that task.'

Victoria wanted to pull her hand away, but she controlled the urge. 'I get the impression that you and Max aren't the best of friends.'

'I wonder why that is,' Sebastian murmured, but he sounded as if he couldn't care less. 'I'm more interested in finding out how you planned to express your gratitude for my assistance than what thorn sticks in Maximilian's craw.' With his free hand, he reached up and began to tug her long glove down past her elbow. 'Did I mention how much better you look when dressed as a woman than a man?'

He released the wrist he'd held on the top of the settee, but not her glove, and when she pulled away the glove came off, turning inside out from her fingers. Her hand and arm were bare.

She stepped back, out of his reach. Sebastian was not the type of man to climb over the settee after her.

But he wasn't looking at her; he was holding her forlorn white glove between his hands, stroking his fingers down over its length as if smoothing his touch over her arm. Then he wrapped it gently around one of his hands and looked up at her.

'Where is your ring?'

At first she thought he was speaking of her *vis bulla*, the ring in her navel…but then she realised he was looking at her bare hand. Her left hand.

'I don't have one…yet. Did you know I was there in the room at Redfield Manor?'

'Of course. I also knew the moment you went out the window; Maximilian was too busy staking vampires to notice. But I saw the twitch of the drapes and knew you were gone. I understand you killed seven vampires that night.'

'It was eight. And Max defeated three Imperials on his own.'

'Bravo, Max.' Sebastian rose and she stepped farther away. 'Victoria, you are annoying me. I am not going to leap across the room and ravage you.' He did indeed look angry, an unusual expression in a face that was normally bent on wooing or charming.

He tucked her glove into his pocket and walked with rather harsh footsteps back over to the table where he'd poured their drinks. Turning to face her, he leant back against it, crossing his legs at the ankles and his arms over his middle. He looked all bronze and golden and utterly dangerous. His hair gleamed dark near the crown, but tawny and blond and even silvery at the curling tips, and his mouth was set in a harsh line, the upper lip shadowing his lower one to a dark toffee colour.

There was silence for a long moment. Victoria had expected him to demand some sort of additional recompense for the information that led to their obtaining the Book of Antwartha, but he did not. His enticing, engaging manner had evaporated and now he merely looked displeased.

'I am sure it is safe for me to leave,' Victoria said at last. 'I'm certain Max has managed to get Phillip away by now.' She looked at him, expecting an argument.

But instead he reached into his pocket and pulled out her glove, offering it to her.

It lay draped over his open palm, but when she reached for it his fingers closed over her bare hand. And tugged.

Perhaps it was surprise at his sudden movement; perhaps it was curiosity. Perhaps she was just tired of fighting it. But Victoria allowed herself to continue forward until she was standing as close to Sebastian as she had been in the hallway.

Transferring her hand to his other, as if unwilling to chance her escaping, he tucked the glove back in his pocket and looked down at her. Humour glinted in his golden eyes. 'That was easier than I expected.'

'Sebastian—'

He turned her bare hand palm up, lifted it, lowered his face…and touched his lips to the inside of her wrist. They were soft but firm, gently damp, and feather-light. They almost tickled. Then they moved, opening, tracing the texture of the veins and tendons in this demure region. He nibbled on the narrow edge of her wrist, gently bit the full pad of her palm at the base of her thumb.

Victoria couldn't pull her arm away. No, that wasn't true – she could; she knew she could break his grip easily – but she could not force her muscles to move. Her eyes closed; her other hand reached out blindly, to catch herself, and flattened against a solid, warm, breathing chest.

'I have always wanted to taste a Venator,' murmured Sebastian, moving up to look at her. His lips were no longer thin and harsh; they would never look thin and harsh to her again after this. After feeling them.

He still held her fingers, which curled helplessly around his, and he traced his thumb over the top of her hand, looking at her.

And then they both heard it, and just as the noise registered in her mind, the door slammed open.

In the doorway stood Max, leaning heavily against its side. 'Rockley's been attacked,' he said, then slid to the floor.

Chapter Seventeen

In Which Miss Grantworth's Bedchamber Sees Much Activity

The next thirty minutes were a blur of activity. Max, although confused and weak, was still coherent enough to explain that he'd managed to stop a vampire in the midst of an attack on Phillip.

'Was he bitten?' asked Victoria, wrapping one of his heavy arms around her shoulders so that he leant against her and one hand dangled free just below her left breast. She was helping him out to his unmarked carriage – not as difficult a task as it would have been if she didn't wear a *vis bulla*.

'No…got there in time. Staked the bastard.'

Victoria assumed he meant the vampire, not Phillip. Although she wasn't completely positive.

Max had saved Phillip, hustled him into Barth's hackney, and given the driver explicit instructions on how to get him home and what to do once there. Phillip was unhurt, but confused and nearly unconscious from the ensuing scuffle.

'What will he remember?' asked Victoria as she helped Max climb into his carriage.

'Nothing. Used the...pendant.'

She pushed him into his seat, then climbed back out of the carriage to say good-bye to Sebastian, who, although he hadn't been much help getting Max outside, had not hindered her effort either. He'd come along, showed her another way out from the back area, and helped to call Max's carriage around.

'Thank you,' she told him, although she wasn't sure what she was thanking him for.

'Until we meet again,' he said simply. He made no move to offer her glove, and she didn't ask. Victoria turned and climbed into the vehicle. Sebastian closed the door behind her.

The carriage lurched as they started off, and she tipped onto the seat across from Max.

He was slumped in the corner, a rumpled lump of black and grey. As the street lamps flashed into the interior, she saw that his eyes were closed.

Had he been bitten? She hadn't even thought to ask...she'd been so worried about Phillip since Max's dire announcement.

Victoria stood carefully, coming over to his side of the carriage, and nearly fell in his lap when they went around an unexpected corner.

She was just reaching for his collar when he opened his eyes. 'What are you doing?' he asked, pushing himself upright.

'I thought you might have been bitten.'

'Sit down.' He glowered at her. 'I haven't been bitten in…years.'

'Then why do you carry salted holy water? And why does that bite look like it's new?'

'So that if I am with anyone who's bitten, I can pour it on their bite.' He seemed to be suddenly more alert.

'What happened to you, then, if you weren't bitten?'

He drew in a deep breath, folding his arms over his middle. 'I was drugged. By your marquess.'

Victoria's eyebrows rose. 'Really. So a mere slip of a marquess got the best of you, when a nasty vampire couldn't? And you freely admit this?'

Max opened his mouth as if to speak, but appeared to change his mind. He turned to look out the window, his profile flashing every time a street lamp illuminated the carriage interior. She looked at the haughty slope of his nose, the set ridges of his mouth, the unruly mess of dark hair. He looked beat.

'What happened, Max?'

'I did what you asked, Victoria. We needn't discuss it further.' He did not look away from the window. 'Your marquess is safe and will suffer no ill effects – and very little memory of what happened, because I took care of that too. He was trying to shoot a vampire with a pistol.' Scorn laced his voice. Then, 'Where is your glove?'

Victoria looked down; both of her arms were hidden under her cloak, the bare one and the gloved one. 'I...Sebastian took it.'

Max turned to look at her. 'And what else did he take?'

Victoria's heart thumped faster. She shook her head.

'He expected payment for his information; what else did he take?'

Liberties. Liberties her fiancé hadn't taken. And in a way, he'd taken yet another piece of her naiveté. Shown her exactly why women wore gloves. All the time.

'Victoria.'

'Nothing. He has my glove, and has taken nothing else. I am a Venator, Max. He is no match for me.'

It might have been a laugh that issued from his lips; Victoria wasn't sure. But he said nothing, just turned and looked back out the window.

They rode in silence for a time; then she spoke. 'Thank you. For what you did tonight.'

That drew his attention from the passing scenery. He looked at her, dark and angry, from his corner across the narrow space. 'Rockley had no idea what he'd walked into tonight. This is exactly the reason you cannot marry, Victoria. Your two worlds simply cannot intersect as they did tonight. Continuing on this path will only cause more destruction.'

And with that, he turned back to the window and said nothing more.

Victoria did not sleep well that night. Her dreams were filled with a storm of images melding together: Phillip and Sebastian, Aunt Eustacia and Max, and words and voices running together: *I've always wanted to taste a Venator... You cannot marry... That is something I would pay dearly to see... Does he know you walk the streets at night?... What else did he take?*

She woke to find sun streaming through the window, nothing at all like the dark dinginess of her clash of memories. It was nearly eleven o'clock. Madame LeClaire would be arriving in two hours for her gown fitting.

Her wedding gown fitting.

Victoria passed a hand over her eyes. Was Max right? If she married Phillip, was she attracting more destruction?

Emptiness clawed her belly, and it was not because she'd had nothing to eat. How could she not marry Phillip? Charming, funny, handsome Phillip? The man who made her laugh, who jested with her, who helped her to see the humour in the society she was forced to live in. Who'd brought her flowers after she lectured him. The man who did the right thing, what was expected. A man she could understand.

He had followed her last night. Followed her into a den of vampires with little thought for his safety and no understanding of the world he was entering. If she married him, would she be able to keep her secret? Would she have to? If he knew she was a Venator, and safer than anyone on earth, would he understand?

He had made his confessions…harmless they were. Did she owe him the same?

Sebastian's words haunted her. *Does he know that it means his love walks the streets at night? That she must mingle with those from the dark side to learn their secrets? That she kills every time she raises her weapon? That she has a strength he cannot hope to possess?*

How could he understand? It had taken her weeks to understand, and she was called to this duty.

He was so good, so proper. How could he be married to a woman who stalked evil? Who was violent…who killed? He could never accept that in a wife – he should not have to.

He couldn't understand her world. Aunt Eustacia, and Max, and Kritanu…even Verbena and Barth… they understood. They were all a part of that world, that life.

Phillip was not, and could never be.

She drew a deep breath, knowing what she would do.

A heavy knot settled in her middle as she began to consider life without Phillip. A life that consisted of lurking in dark streets, in subterranean pubs, the need to always hunt and kill. The end of dancing and laughing and no hope of having someone to love, someone to care for her.

Perhaps that explained Max: his demeanour, the undercurrents of anger, and his ripping sarcasm. He was so alone. Victoria had believed it was by choice. Perhaps she was wrong.

Perhaps she had no choice either.

A loud slam from below, and the sound of pounding footsteps rushing up the stairs, caused her to turn toward the door to her bedroom.

Shouts; they sounded like Jimmons, and even Verbena, and suddenly her door flew open, slamming into the wall.

Phillip.

'Victoria!' He stood there, tall and wild, his cloak whirling about him and his hair falling over his brow. 'You are here, and safe!'

She was so aghast she did not move even to close her jaw; Verbena and Jimmons and Maisie the housekeeper were standing in the doorway, all speaking at once, explaining how it had happened that Phillip had made his way up here.

'Send them away,' he said to her, striding toward her where she remained in bed, her blankets pulled over her nightgown. 'I am your betrothed; we are to be married in three weeks…send them away!'

She had never seen him like this, the unruffled and proper Phillip in such a stir. 'Go ahead; you may go.'

She waved at Jimmons and Verbena. Then, amazingly, considering the situation, she had a logical thought. 'Is Mother up and about?'

'She will be now,' replied Verbena.

'Keep her from me, then. Tell her whatever you wish, but keep her from here until the marquess leaves.'

'But it is not proper—' began Maisie.

'Go. Please. It will be fine if no one speaks of this.'

Only after they left did Victoria allow herself to look at Phillip. The knot in her stomach had twisted tighter. She had thought to have more time to decide what to do…how to respond to Phillip. How to tell him she could not marry him.

But her decision was made. It was the right one.

'Victoria, Victoria.' He stood next to her bed, hands behind him, as if trying to keep himself from reaching for her. 'I am so sorry, but I could not wait. I needed to make sure you were here, were safe.'

'Phillip…' She shook her head, closing her eyes for a moment. What could she say? 'Phillip, I am fine. You see me; I am safe. I only had the headache.'

Where had that come from? She hadn't planned to continue her charade.

He looked at her from above, standing over her, his blue eyes sharp but still wild. 'Victoria.'

'Phillip, sit down. Here.' She smoothed her hand over the French-knotted coverlet, making a space for him next to her hip.

'I don't know if I…should.' He looked at her, and she saw something in his gaze she'd never seen before. 'If it's proper.'

Victoria laughed; she couldn't help it. 'Phillip, don't be absurd…you are already here, in my bedchamber. In three weeks I will be in yours.' Their eyes met and her mouth dried. Had she really said that? That lie?

He sat, his solid weight heavy on the edge of the bed, tilting her toward him. Through the layers of blankets his leg touched hers.

'In three weeks. I don't know that I can wait so long.' He reached over, touched her unbound hair, and let his hand trace her cheekbone before curling it back next to him. 'But I must know, where did you go last night, Victoria? Are you in some kind of trouble?'

'I wasn't feeling well,' she told him. Why was she still lying? She had to let him go.

'Victoria, I love you and you will be my wife, but one thing I cannot tolerate is dishonesty.' He was angry, an emotion she'd never seen in him before. True anger, layered with a sort of desperate concern. But not frightening. No, this was an anger she could live with. 'What were you doing in St Giles last night? Tell me the truth.'

Then her tears burst forth. Everything she had held back in the last weeks, since she had had those dreams. Since she had learnt of her calling.

Racking sobs, shaking, and trembling – the results

of fear she'd submerged so deeply when fighting for her life – everything poured out of her into Phillip's shoulder, for he'd gathered her close, the bedsheets falling away as he wrapped his arms around her.

'Victoria, Victoria,' he crooned, smoothing his hand over her head, down over the tangled curls of her hair, bumping along her spine. 'My God, Victoria, what is it? I will fix it; just tell me. I will make it right. I am not without resources; I will use them all if I must.'

When she pulled away from his drenched coat, he had a handkerchief ready to mop her face and wipe her nose, as if she were a child. She felt like a child being cared for. For the first time in almost two months she felt like she didn't need to be in charge. In control.

The strong one.

She had never loved Phillip more than she did in that moment.

'Thank you,' she said with the soft hiccup of her last sob.

He dropped the handkerchief and grabbed her shoulders. 'What is it? Tell me. I cannot bear to see you like this.'

'I cannot.' She drew in a long, hitching breath. 'I cannot tell you, Phillip, but I swear it is nothing you can change. Even if you had all the money in the world, and you reigned over this land, you could not change this.'

He stared at her for a long moment, his eyes darting

from side to side as if to get a better view inside her own gaze. The whites of his eyes were pink, cracked with red.

'You must tell me.'

'I cannot.'

'Last night I came after you. I know it was you, despite the arguments your cousin made. At first I was afraid you were meeting a lover, and I followed you…because I had to know. I had to know if your heart was given to another. I thought even then that if it were, if I just knew it for certain, I would still want to marry you. I would find a way to drive him from your mind.

'But when your hackney – my God, Victoria, don't you know how dangerous it is to use a hackney? – stopped in St Giles, I didn't know what to think. You wouldn't meet a lover there, no matter who he was. I saw you get out of the hackney and go through a door into one of the most dangerous-looking places I've ever seen. I would not have gone there if I hadn't known I must protect you. I had to use my pistol to convince some of the street men to let me by.

'Your cousin saved my life. I am not sure what happened; it is all quite a muddle in my mind. I just know I left to look for you, and then I woke up at home. How I got there is very unclear. I dreamt about red eyes…

'You see, my darling, I don't understand what happened last night, but I did not come here with accusations or preconceived notions. There is nothing you can tell me that would change the way I feel about you. Please.'

She could give him something; maybe it would help him to understand. 'Do you believe in destiny?'

He nodded, a bare hint of relief tangible in his face. 'Of course. It was destiny that first brought us together years ago.'

'Destiny is unchangeable. It's indelible, written in stone. Power and money and resources cannot change it, Phillip. You cannot alter it. And that is why I cannot tell you, no matter how much you beg, what I was doing in St Giles last night. Because that is my destiny.' A destiny he could not accept – a wife who killed, a world of evil and darkness. Phillip was too much in the light…she couldn't destroy his world.

'Victoria!'

She was shaking her head. 'I love you, Phillip. But I cannot.'

He looked stricken. 'Victoria, with all that I am, I ask you to please tell me. I will not be angry, no matter what it is. But I cannot have this between us if we are to marry.'

Now. Her hands frozen under the warmth of the blankets, she drew in her breath and closed her eyes. She would not look at him whilst she said it. 'Then perhaps we should not marry.'

He was still, so still. Even his breath stopped; she could hear nothing in the darkness of her closed eyes but the faint voices from below-stairs. And the rapid, painful thudding of her heart.

'Victoria.' The anguish in his voice opened her eyes. Phillip was not looking at her; he looked out the window at the sunshine pouring on the rooftop of a nearby garret. A blue jay, with its unpleasant squawking song, fluttered to a stop on a nearby tree limb.

'I'm sorry, Phillip.'

He stood abruptly, spinning away from the bed, stalking to the door. She watched him through pooling eyes, and he paused at the threshold. 'If you change your mind…' He spoke to the door.

'I can't.' She forced the words from her throat. She wanted to call him back.

Phillip didn't look at her; he went through the door, closing it with a soft finality behind him.

Victoria didn't understand. She would have slammed it.

Chapter Eighteen

Interlude in a Carriage

Victoria sent a note to Madame LeClaire, cancelling her fitting due to illness. The word would be out soon enough, she knew, that the engagement of the Marquess of Rockley had been broken. It would be in the paper within days – either the Society tattletale section, or the announcements; it depended who got the news first.

She didn't have the heart to tell her mother. Not yet. Perhaps in a day or so, when the pain wasn't so raw. Lady Melly was so happy to be bringing a marquess into the family, Victoria didn't have the heart to tell her she'd called it off.

Verbena tsked over her red eyes, but said nothing save, 'I'm so sorry, miss. It's not the same, but I felt pretty bad when I lost my Jassie to another woman. Leastwise you know it ain't that.'

If that item was supposed to make her feel better, it didn't. Victoria only sent Verbena from her room and stared out the window, watching the screeching blue jay as it visited the tree.

She begged off from attending a dinner party that night; instead, as soon as her mother left to trade gossip and jokes with the other *ton* ladies, Victoria slipped out of the house from the back door. She was dressed in her split-skirt gown, specially made for hunting vampires.

That night she tracked and staked five undead.

The next night, three more.

The third night she only found one. It felt bloody good when she drove that stake into the vampire's chest.

But it wasn't enough, so she wandered the streets near Covent Garden and allowed herself to be accosted by several mortal criminals. After showing them her pistol and the expertise, with which she could kick and punch, Victoria ran them off into the darkness and felt a bit more satisfied.

She didn't return to Grantworth House until after dawn. Then she fell into bed and slept restlessly.

When Aunt Eustacia sent a summons on the fourth day after Phillip burst into Victoria's bedchamber, she considered ignoring it. She didn't feel the need to meet with her aunt or Max, who would certainly be there. She was doing her job hunting and killing the undead; they'd retrieved the Book of Antwartha, which she had hidden at the chapel at St Heath's Row before she and Rockley broke things off.

What could her aunt want to meet about?

Her decision was made when Lady Melly poked her head in her bedroom. 'I'm attending tea at Winnie's; she and Petronilla were hoping you'd come too so we could discuss seating arrangements for the wedding. I haven't seen Rockley for a few days, Victoria. Is he ill?'

Apparently her mother didn't see the red rims of her own daughter's eyes, nor the black circles underscoring them. 'Not that I know of. He's been very busy. And, unfortunately, I promised Aunt Eustacia I would visit today. It's been nearly a week.'

She really did have to tell her mother.

Every day she didn't, she risked it appearing in the papers before Lady Melly knew. It wasn't fair to her mother that she might be blindsided. The Society ladies would have a field day at her expense if that happened.

'Mother, I have to tell you something. Rockley and I had an argument. We…' Her voice trailed off when she saw the stricken look on Lady Melly's face.

'Well, surely you can mend the fence, Victoria! You cannot ruin your future over one small argument!'

One small argument.

'I wanted you to know in the event that you heard any rumours,' she added lamely. *Blast.* She could single-handedly take down three vampires; why couldn't she tell her mother the truth?

'Well, I expect you to speak with him at the Mullingtons' ball next week and fix things! No excuses, Victoria. It's the duke's fiftieth birthday; everyone will be there. Including you.'

Victoria nodded. She had no choice, and Phillip possibly wouldn't attend anyway. He hated those affairs. And if there was even a hint of a rumour that he was eligible once again…well, he would be cornered before he took three steps into the room.

'Now, I will see you tonight. We leave at seven thirty. Be ready. And put something over those black circles under your eyes, Victoria. You look horridly exhausted.'

But in the end Victoria didn't go to Aunt Eustacia's. She sent a message back, after her mother left, that she was obligated to spend the day making calls.

And she spent the rest of the afternoon in her room.

That night she had no choice but to attend a musicale with Lady Melly. The only redeeming factor was that it was sure to be an early night, which would allow her to sneak out of the house and go what she had come to think of as patrolling for vampires.

The musicale was just as unexciting as the one she'd attended at the Straithwaites'; perhaps more so, since this time Rockley didn't make an appearance.

Neither, unfortunately, did any vampires.

It was after midnight when Grantworth House had settled to sleep, and Victoria slipped out the back door.

Barth, her trusty mode of transport, was waiting just around the corner, and as had become their habit, he merely nodded as she climbed into the hackney. He knew his duty by now and drove the carriage to a dangerous part of town. It varied each night; Victoria didn't care. She trusted Barth to know the best places to go and to take her there.

The cobbled streets were damp from a light summer rain, glistening like grey teeth in the moonlight. Victoria left the hackney and told Barth to come for her in two hours.

As the carriage trundled off, she walked to the centre of the empty street and stood there, looking around. Daring any danger to accost her.

Everything was silent. Grey and black and silent.

She favoured this section of the city – wherever it was; she didn't care and didn't need to know – because the street lamps had either burnt out or not been lit tonight. It was the perfect breeding ground for vampires…or other thieves who needed to be taught a lesson. She wasn't particular.

After the first night of patrolling by herself, dressed in men's clothing, Victoria had elected to wear her split skirt on subsequent trips. Garbed as a woman, she attracted more attention from those who wanted to prey on the weak.

But tonight it appeared that the streets were devoid of any dangers for men or women.

She walked down the centre of the road, bold and quick, watching for anything that might move in the shadows. Feeling for any faint chill over the back of her neck.

Nothing.

Nothing until she rounded the corner of her third block and saw the shift in an alley. And the back of her neck chilled.

Her lips stretching in a nasty smile, Victoria started toward the shadowy movement. She had her stake in her hand, hidden in the folds of her cloak, and she walked along nonchalantly. She passed the alley, her movements nearly shouting innocence and temptation.

She expected him or her to charge out and attack her, but when nothing had happened after half a block, she stopped and turned to look behind. No one was there; the coolness at the back of her neck had eased.

Just as she turned to walk back to the alley, a black carriage, high sprung and elegant, wheeled around the corner. Victoria turned to look; it was unusual to see such an expensive coach in this part of town.

The carriage eased to a stop in the street in front of her. Its two black horses rolled their eyes, the only pure white in the grey of night, and stamped their feet. The driver did not look at Victoria as he sat unmoving.

Then the door opened.

'Victoria.'

It was Sebastian, and he was beckoning to her; just his gloved hand was visible, but she recognised his voice, the way he said her name.

She stepped toward the carriage, walking up to the door, and looked in. Sebastian sat alone inside, leaning forward from his seat just enough to stretch his hand out. Offering his assistance to her in climbing in.

'Come. You won't find anyone to hunt tonight, my lovely Venator.'

'Why is that?' She stood directly in front of the door, hands on her hips, suddenly unaccountably angry.

'Come for a ride with me. We can enjoy the full moon and I will tell you all about it.'

'Unless there's a vampire in there that's ready to die, I'll walk. Thank you.' She turned and started away.

He moved so quickly she had no time to react; he was out of the carriage and had his arm wrapped around her waist, whirling her back toward the vehicle in what seemed like an instantaneous movement. She stumbled over a stone that marked the edge of the road, falling toward the carriage. Her hands slamming into the wall were the only things that kept her from landing in the mud.

'So you're in the mood for a fight, are you?' Sebastian said in her ear as his hands planted on either side of hers. 'That's the word on the streets. It's been the talk at the Chalice.'

She whipped her arms out, knocking his hands away, and turned. He was right there, so close she could count every eyelash and smell cloves on his breath. 'You're no match for me,' she hissed. She didn't understand where this anger was coming from; she just knew she needed an outlet.

'Try me.'

She moved, but he was fast, and he caught her wrists, one in each hand, and pulled them straight down so her arms were extended past her hips. Victoria struggled, but before she could break his grip he placed a foot next to hers and yanked her to the side. She lost her balance, and he picked her up and shoved her into the carriage.

Sebastian was up and inside before she could scramble to her feet, locking the door. He pounded a long walking stick on the ceiling for the driver to start just as Victoria sprang up from the floor.

'Have a seat, my dear,' he said, looking up at her standing over him as if she'd just called for tea. 'If you want to fight, I'll fight. You appear to be in need of some kind of…release. Or…you can take a seat safely over there.'

Victoria sat. She was breathing hard, and a little shaken at how easily he'd bested her. Well, not bested her exactly – he'd caught her off guard, but she was not subdued. Not by any stretch of the imagination.

'What do you want?'

'That, my dear, is a dangerous question to ask. Are you quite certain you want my answer?'

She considered him, the way his eyes gleamed and a half smile curved his lips. And decided she wasn't ready to have the answer. So she asked a different question: 'What did you mean, that I wouldn't find anyone to hunt tonight?'

'I mean that the undead have made themselves scarce on the streets the last few nights because of the rampage you've been on. They've all been biding their time at the Chalice, padding my pockets.' He smiled fully. 'So I thought that I might find you walking the streets, frustrated at your lack of success.'

'Rampage? Hunting and staking vampires is what Venators do. No different from what Max has been doing for years.'

'Maximilian is known for his cold and calculating kills, true, but apparently your particular technique of late has sent the undead scurrying. It may have something to do with the fact that you still have in your possession the Book of Antwartha and are one up on Lilith; I am not certain. I just know that the vampires have been more wont to drink kegged blood than fresh in the last few nights.'

'So you've come to take me to the Chalice, so I can hunt there?'

A look of horror washed the charm off his face. 'Absolutely not!' And then when he saw the faint smile she'd allowed, he laughed. 'Touché, my dear.'

'Why do you want to protect the vampires?' asked Victoria, feeling a bit less restive. A little more relaxed.

'I don't protect vampires.'

'By offering them a safe place to congregate, you certainly do.'

'Perhaps I find it beneficial to provide a place where they will come and take their ease. Perhaps having that public place where their tongues will loosen and information might flow is valuable to me, as well as others. And there is, of course, money to be made – both from the undead, and from the ones who merely wish to interact with them.'

She raised an eyebrow.

'Some people find it pleasurable to allow a vampire to drink their blood.'

'Pleasurable?'

'You've been bitten by a vampire, Victoria. You know what it felt like just before he sank his teeth into your neck. And how, after he did, you wanted to just let go and let him take you.'

He was looking at her in such a way that she felt hardly able to breathe. But she managed to reply, 'How do you know I was bitten by a vampire?'

Suddenly Sebastian was on the seat next to her, his walking stick clattering to the floor. His leg pushed into the side of her thigh as he turned to lean over her. Stripping off his glove, he reached for the collar of her cloak and pulled it away. The fresh air rushed over her skin. 'Because I saw this the first time we met.'

He traced his bare finger over her neck, following the tendon that led to the small pool at the base of her throat. He dipped his thumb there, filling the soft, elastic indentation as the rest of his hand moved to cup the side of her neck that was not scarred.

She couldn't move away. She could barely breathe as her pulse throbbed in the V of his hand, making his grip tighten and then loosen in rhythm with her heartbeat.

'Remember this?' he murmured, tipping her head so that she rested in his hand, opening the marked side of her neck to the whole of the carriage, open and vulnerable as he bent toward her.

She closed her eyes and felt it: lips, tongue, teeth; biting, licking, scraping gently over her sensitive skin, coaxing and convincing. She wanted to twist from him, to sigh, to press into him for more.

Her cloak loosened and fell away, her shoulders bare to the top of her low bodice. His weight pressed down on her more now, his warm hands – one bare, one gloved – moving over her shoulders. The leather of his covered hand moved like sticky flesh against her skin, the thick seams and buttons rough where they touched her.

Victoria's mouth was still free; she breathed a long sigh; perhaps she said his name, she wasn't sure. He raised her arms above her head, pushing her wrists into the corner of the carriage where she lay. This brought his face close to hers, his clove breath warm on her chin, his fingers tangling in the hair at the top of her head.

Victoria closed her eyes. She could pull away; she could break his grip and sit up and shove him back to the other side of the carriage for the liberties he was taking…but it felt so delicious, so reckless, so *right* for the way she was feeling.

Phillip – dear Phillip – had made her feel warm and liquid and malleable when he kissed her…but he was gone now, and Sebastian's mouth on her neck evoked a different sort of response…sharper…deeper and improper, and made her hungry for more of whatever he was offering. Or taking.

'So easy,' he was whispering into her ear. 'You are yearning for passion, Victoria. Is your marquess nothing but a cold fish?'

She was too lulled to experience the annoyance his comment should have sparked. 'My marquess is no longer my marquess,' she replied in a voice that was not her own.

'Indeed?' Sebastian pulled away so quickly that she opened her eyes. 'Well, if that is the case, then I will feel not the least bit of guilt for this incident.'

Despite the fact that her lungs seemed too full to draw in another breath, Victoria replied, 'I doubt that guilt is an emotion that ever crosses your mind, regardless of the circumstance.'

He laughed, dropped a brief kiss onto her lips

for the first time, and said, 'Well, one must at least appear to make the effort.' And then, as if realising how good her mouth tasted, he kissed her again. Hard and rough were his kisses, and Victoria, as though released from some sort of restriction, kissed him back.

This was nothing like Phillip. In the back of her mind it saddened her, because their passion had been true, without the underlying brutality of the one she shared with Sebastian.

When he moved, releasing her wrists and allowing her hands to delve into his loose curls, she shifted her hips to keep from sliding off the seat, and her foot landed, unbalanced, on the round walking stick. Sebastian pressed his weight into her, as if to implant her into the bench, and matched his hips to hers. A kind of burning tingling between her legs surprised her, and she pushed up closer, wanting more, feeling the hard ridge of him through their clothing.

Sebastian moved again, and suddenly Victoria felt cool fresh air splay over her breasts. She gasped in surprise and her first instinct was to struggle away, but when he laughed over her skin and closed his lips over one of her nipples, she fell back against the seat.

Good heavens...she'd had no idea!

He tugged and sucked, and she pulled him closer, and even when his hands whisked impatiently at her split skirt, inching each half up to the top of her hips, she didn't push him away. There was freedom in knowing she could at any moment.

And for the moment, she was going to indulge in whatever this was. She needed it.

Sebastian had known she needed it.

When his hands slid to the tops of her thighs she pressed them together as much as she could, but one of his legs was trapped between them. He chuckled against the underside of her breast and looked up with gleaming golden eyes half hidden by the jut of his brow and the tips of curls falling over his forehead with the rhythm of the carriage movement. 'Are you still an innocent, my dear?'

'In some ways,' she replied with more honesty than she should have been able to at that moment.

He withdrew his hands from her skirt and moved to her waist, pulling the waistband down and baring her cotton shift to the bare flashes of street lamps and moonlight. He gave a soft, low sigh when he found what he wanted.

Both hands cupped around the slight swell of her belly and slid together until his fingers touched her *vis bulla*. 'Ahh,' he said in a molten voice. And he lowered his face to the warm silver.

The faint brush of lips over her skin made her want to jerk and twist away – and press up into his mouth for more.

But then suddenly, like a dousing of cold water, she realised that the back of her neck was cool.

Victoria stilled, listening. Yes, it was.

Sebastian stopped as though he too had noticed a change in the air, just as the carriage lurched to a halt.

'Vampires,' Victoria said, pushing him away and her skirts down. She pulled her bodice back up over her breasts and felt the iciness at the back of her neck with an unusual portent. Checking to make sure her stakes hadn't become dislodged during this last interval with Sebastian, she stood, shook out her skirts, and reached for the handle of the door.

The night was uncomfortably silent.

Sebastian reached out just as she would have turned the handle. His fingers closed over her wrist. 'Be careful, Victoria.'

She looked down at him. 'I am a Venator.' And she opened the door.

Standing in the grey street stood an Imperial and three Guardian vampires. They ringed the door side of the carriage. She understood: This was not a random attack; they were waiting for her.

An ugly yet unsurprising thought snapped into her mind. She turned back to Sebastian, closed the door and barred it. 'Did you bring me to them?'

His expression was unreadable. 'Why would I have saved your life by telling you about the Book of Antwartha, then do such a thing?'

A loud thud against the carriage door caused the vehicle to lurch to one side, then rock back into place.

Victoria reached for the walking stick at the bottom of the carriage and, resting its metal tip at the edge of the seat, slammed her foot down on it. The end broke off, leaving a lethally jagged end and turning it into a stake that could be used to combat a sword like the ones the Imperials carried.

Her hands were damp, her heart racing faster than usual. She'd never fought an Imperial. Nor taken on three Guardians alone.

'Venator! Show yourself!'

She was no coward, but she knew the odds were completely against her.

One of the windows shattered, spraying glass over Sebastian's black wool coat draped over the seat. He hissed angrily and gathered it up, sending the glass tinkling to the floor. Yet he said nothing to Victoria.

A leering vampire face showed in the broken window, reaching in to scrabble his hand around to find the door latch. Victoria reacted, shoving the stake through and miraculously catching him in the chest. *Poof!* One Guardian was gone.

But she couldn't stay in here forever. They weren't going anywhere, and Sebastian didn't appear to be promising any help.

Victoria leant out of the jagged window and said, 'Who calls "Venator"?'

'I do.' The Imperial vampire stepped toward the carriage. It was a greasy-haired woman, and her eyes were the red-violet hue of her status. She carried a sword, as had the ones Max had battled, and she wore trousers – slim, leg-hugging trousers that afforded greater movement than the ones Victoria wore.

'What do you want?'

'I have come to bring you to my mistress. She wishes to meet the newest Venator.'

Victoria dodged back in as one of the Guardians lunged toward the carriage in a vain attempt to catch her and pull her out. 'Please give Lilith my regrets, but I receive callers only on Tuesdays and Wednesdays between the afternoon hours of two and half past three. Unfortunately, we do not serve her favourite beverage.'

She reached out and grabbed at the vampire who'd just missed closing his hand around her. Her fingers gripped his jacket, trying to pull him into the coach. If she could just…get…them…one by one…

He slipped free of her grasp and thudded to the ground, and suddenly what had appeared to be a stalemate took a turn for the worse. The remaining three vampires moved toward the carriage as though flying, and slammed into it with the entire force of their power.

The carriage rose up high on one side, held for a moment in midair, then slammed onto its other side.

Victoria and Sebastian landed in a heap on the far windows, and in the furore, a slim pale arm reached in from what was now the top and had been merely a broken window, fumbling around for the door catch.

Victoria scrambled to her feet, climbing on the vertical seats. She ignored the pain in her head and stepped over Sebastian, who lay in a heap on the floor.

The door opened before Victoria could prevent it, but she was ready with her stake and stabbed out at the torso that came through the entrance. With a grunt of triumph she drove it into the body, and blood spurted out.

And then she realised, as it was flung away, that one of the vampires had used what had been Sebastian's driver as a human shield.

But that was her last thought, for suddenly everything went dark and close as something heavy was thrown over her. Victoria struggled, but whatever was holding the stifling cloth down over her person was strong and unmoving.

She couldn't breathe, couldn't take in any more lungfuls of oxygen that weren't laden with lint or dusty or stale or tight…too tight. She struggled against that tightness and tried to pull in more air…and finally lost the battle.

The blackness became reality.

Chapter Nineteen

The Marquee Cuts In

Something pulled at her, nudging her into semi-consciousness. It was too difficult…she couldn't drag her eyes open.

'Victoria!'

There it was again – that hissing voice, bothering her.

Then suddenly she came awake, remembered the Guardians and the Imperial, Sebastian and his coach.

But even with her eyes open, she saw nothing. Blackness. The voice was closer, but she didn't know whose it was…it was too low. She made her mouth move. 'Here.'

Something was covering her, wrapped around her so that she couldn't move and could barely breathe. No wonder she hadn't wanted to wake up…it was much too difficult to try to draw in air under this heavy cloth. But she had to.

Stealthy movement told her someone was coming toward her. Then hands were moving, pulling at the knots, stripping the ties away, and finally plucking the stifling woollen cloth from her face.

Victoria had never felt anything so wonderful as those deep, clean breaths of air…despite the fact that they were laced with the stench of rotting fish. She was not complaining.

'Max. How did you get here?' she asked, even as she pulled herself to her feet, checking for stakes. They appeared to be in a warehouse, and based on quiet lapping sounds below, not to mention the odours, it was near the wharves.

'They're coming back for you anytime; let's go,' he said, grabbing her arm. 'The sun will rise in less than an hour, so they will hurry.'

He led the way out of the room and she followed, shaking off his grip and trying to figure out how he'd found her. She must not have been unconscious for long if the sun hadn't risen yet.

Once outside, Victoria took in greater breaths tinged with the scent of seaweed and salt. Much better.

A hackney was waiting around the corner from the warehouse, and Victoria recognised it as Barth's. She looked at Max, but he was already answering her. 'When you didn't show up at your meeting place,

Barth came and found me. I learnt the rest from Sebastian. Climb in.'

He stepped in after her, and the hackney took off with an enthusiastic lurch. Barth was just as ready to call it a night as Victoria.

'They were taking me to see Lilith,' Victoria told him. 'Why did they leave me there? Why didn't they just take me right to her?'

'I can only guess, Victoria, since I wasn't there and am not, unfortunately, privy to their plans…but I would assume it was because they weren't certain of her location or whether she was quite available to… eh…receive you.'

She settled back in her seat, thankful that for whatever reason, she hadn't been brought face-to-face with the queen of the vampires whilst unconscious and wrapped up in a heavy black cloth. She would meet Lilith someday, but Victoria truly hoped it would be more on her terms than on Lilith's.

The last thing Victoria wanted to do was attend the party celebrating the Duke of Mullington's fiftieth birthday. But she had no choice.

Her mother was in a fine fettle, for she'd realised that it had indeed been over a sennight since the Marquess of Rockley had called on his betrothed. Victoria had been avoiding the subject and hiding in her room, trying to figure out just what to tell her, but that had only added fuel to the fire of her mother's concern. There was no way on earth Melly was going to allow the engagement to be broken. Rockley was too fine a match to let go. He'd asked for Victoria, and her mother was going to see to it that he would take her.

Thus, on a sticky summer evening, Lady Melly herded her daughter to the Grantworth carriage and watched with a tapping foot as the groom helped her climb aboard. She clambered in after her and settled on the seat across the way.

'Your maid did a fine job dressing your hair this evening, Victoria,' she commented. 'Though she seems rather obsessed with those sticks in your coiffure. Why does she not use feathers or beads instead of those Chinese objects?' The ones tonight were painted with pink-and-green swirling designs, Verbena's own creation, of which the maid was quite proud.

'She likes to try different styles,' Victoria replied, hoping to stave off a long lecture. 'I think it looks rather unique.'

Fortunately Melly seemed to accept the comment, and turned her attention to fussing with her own gown and fan and indispensable, digging the thick white invitation from its depths and reviewing it once again, and murmuring to herself that it was quite a feat for Duke Mullington to have actually attained the age of fifty, with all of his sins and vices.

Her daughter forbore to mention that his sins,

great as they might be, were nothing compared to those of others socialising about London.

Victoria's gown was spring-green silk, a bit heavy for such a warm night, but fashion was fashion. Silk looked and felt expensive, and, according to Lady Melly, Rockley's betrothed must be dressed appropriately. For she was still the fiancée of the marquess, and Melly would ensure she looked every inch of it. Small pink and white rosebuds, trimmed with dark green leaves, blossomed in the lace along her bodice, at the cap sleeves on her arms, and along the furrows of trim near the bottom of the skirt. Now, in the coach, Victoria held a crocheted pink wrap bundled in her lap, and a matching pink indispensable. Her gloves were dark green.

Victoria knew she looked well; if only she *felt* it. It was all she could do to listen to her mother prattle on about how she must act if she saw Phillip – no, she must think of him as Rockley again – at the ball; how she must be demure and polite and a hint mysterious so as to recapture his attention – *if* it were indeed waning.

Of course, Lady Melly didn't understand what Victoria had been trying to tell her – his interest hadn't waned so much as evaporated. *Poof!*

The ride to the Mullingtons' seemed both interminable and much too brief. Victoria was weary from a week of forays into the night, and the events of early this morning in Sebastian's coach and at the hands of the Imperials and Guardians had left her feeling a bit off.

In fact, although she dreaded what would happen when she came face-to-face with Rockley, she was rather relieved to be thrust into what promised to be an evening of normalcy, when she could eat and drink, dance and flirt, gossip and jest with people who didn't have red eyes and long fangs.

Or angelic golden features and very naughty kisses.

Verbena had outfitted her with her stakes, of course, and there was the chance that a stray vampire might show him- or herself at the ball…but it was unlikely, for Mullington House had formerly been an abbey and bore religious relics and symbols throughout, including at the entrance gate. Along with what Sebastian had told her about the vampires holing up in the Chalice due to Victoria's aggressive hunting, she felt certain that it would be an uneventful night. But she was prepared nevertheless.

Sebastian. Victoria felt alternately ill, confused, and uncomfortably warm when she thought about him and what had transpired. He'd kissed her *bosom!* And she'd let him…enjoyed it, in fact. Quite enjoyed it. Quite, *quite* enjoyed it.

Even now, at the memory, a gush of warmth reminded her how dangerous and warm and titillating it had been to have those moist lips brushing over her private skin. How, even as it had been happening, she'd struggled with the right and wrong of it. And that it had been no hardship at all to kiss him back.

Had he really delivered her to those vampires?

She couldn't believe he would do that…yet it had happened so smoothly. And…the thing that bothered her most – the things, actually – were, first, that he did not deny it; and second, that he seemed to know they'd arrived just before the carriage had stopped. Just about the time Victoria felt the telltale chill at the back of her neck and sensed that they were in trouble.

'Victoria, stop your wool-gathering. We've arrived, and you haven't arranged your shawl!'

Oh, yes, the shawl. She must arrange her shawl.

Victoria stood as straight as she could in the carriage, tilting her head so her hair nearly brushed its roof. She drew the wrap around her shoulders, then let it slip just so to her elbows. The coach staggered as it moved ahead in the line of vehicles waiting to unload the guests, causing her to lurch to one side. She readjusted her wrap and waited, feet spread in an unladylike manner to give her stability.

'Sit down, Victoria,' her mother said impatiently.

'I'll stand. We are almost to the head of the line.' She was suddenly too jumpy to sit and wait passively. Her stomach twisted and leapt. She knew Rockley would be here tonight. He might have avoided his other societal obligations in the last two weeks, but he would be here. The Mullingtons were distant cousins.

At last she alighted from the warm carriage and into the humid air. The sun had nearly set, sending a pink glow radiating from the horizon, but night's blue-grey tint had already coloured the rooftops and stone walls in the distance. Sconces and lamps sent a warm yellow glow over the brick walkway to the grand entrance of the home, open to guests.

When they were announced, Victoria swept her eyes over the crush of guests below the sweeping foyer staircase. She did not see Phillip, thank heaven. Perhaps he hadn't arrived yet. Or perhaps he wasn't going to come at all.

Gwendolyn Starcasset was there, and she greeted Victoria as though she were a long-lost friend. Perhaps she was; Victoria hadn't thought about it recently, but she and Gwendolyn had shared some enjoyable conversation at past events. 'How good it is to see you, Victoria!' said the diminutive blond. 'I have missed standing on the sidelines with you and discussing the best way to make our picks from the eligibles. But you, of course, have made the match of the Season, so you mustn't worry about that any longer!'

'Indeed.' Those two syllables were difficult to bring forth, but Victoria did manage. Why hadn't Phillip posted the announcement in the *Times*? Why cause her this agony of waiting for that shoe to fall? As soon as it did, she would be ostracised. And then she could stop making these appearances at balls and musicales, and concentrate on hunting vampires.

After all, that was her destiny. That was why she'd given up Phillip.

'My brother George was greatly disappointed to hear that Rockley had claimed your hand. He was quite taken with you at the Steerings' ball.'

'And what of your prospects?' asked Victoria, trying to keep from glancing toward the main entrance. She really didn't want to see Rockley anyway. Surely he would cut her, and she would be mortified. Not to mention Lady Melly.

Oh, lud, why hadn't she made sure her mother understood what had happened?

Gwendolyn chattered away about the three eligible men who'd shown interest, until one of them claimed her for a dance. Victoria would have tried to slip off to the room being used as the ladies' lounge, but she did not have a chance. Sir Everett Campington approached and, bowing most elegantly, requested her to join him for the quadrille.

Glad to have something to do other than try not to stare at the main entrance, Victoria agreed and actually found herself beginning to enjoy the lively movement of the quadrille. She and Sir Everett stepped together, then apart, then promenaded down between a row of other couples. Victoria twirled and swirled, curtsied and spun, and realised after a while that she was smiling.

There was only one moment during the dance when she forgot herself, and that was when she and

Sir Everett did one particularly enthusiastic spin, linked elbow to elbow. Victoria forgot that she was much stronger than he, and sent her dance partner stumbling across the floor with the force of her movement.

It was when he returned and they linked arms again, this time side by side, that she looked up and laughed in pure pleasure, then executed a turn that sent her facing the cluster of people standing on the edge of the floor. And whirled right past Phillip.

Victoria didn't even stumble. She wasn't sure how she managed that, but she was thankful beyond belief. When the dance ended, Sir Everett looked down at her and asked, 'Shall we find Rockley? I'm certain he will want to claim the next dance.'

'Oh, I had rather hoped for something to drink,' Victoria replied airily, firmly facing in the direction away from where she'd seen Phillip. 'I'm not certain whether Rockley has even arrived tonight.'

Sir Everett bowed in acquiescence, and if he knew she was lying, he was too gentlemanly to correct her. 'Of course, Miss Grantworth. Let us find some punch.'

Victoria managed to keep herself very busy for the next thirty minutes. She danced with three other gentlemen, including Gwendolyn's brother, who was just as blond and pretty as his sister. She drank at least six glasses of punch, thankfully, for with all the exertion of dancing on such a hot evening, she was thirsty. And because of those six glasses of punch, she was obligated to visit the necessary twice.

But at last she could avoid the confrontation no longer.

Just as she was turning to walk onto the dance floor with Lord Waverley, a calm voice stopped her in her tracks.

'Waverley, I believe this dance is mine.'

She turned, her throat suddenly dry when she tried to swallow. 'Rockley.' She tried to sound delighted but failed miserably.

Lud, but he looked…handsome, defeated, irritated, tired…familiar. Comfortable. His eyes might be a bit heavier-lidded, the blue in them might be a little colder, his mouth might be thinner. But he was still Phillip. And he was holding out a bent arm for her to take.

She took it, sliding her green-gloved hand around it in a gentle grip. They walked away from Waverley without another word to him or to each other.

It was a waltz. Of course.

He spun her perhaps a bit too quickly, too abruptly, into the waltz position, square in the centre of the room, as if to be sure everyone saw them. And they began to dance.

Victoria kept her attention focused over his shoulder; she was afraid to meet his eyes. The irony of the situation didn't fail to amuse her, somewhere deep inside where she couldn't laugh: she had no qualms

about facing two, three, even eight deadly vampires…
but to look in the eyes of the man she loved took
more courage than she had at that time.

After two full turns about the dance floor, he said,
'It might be nice if you looked at me, Victoria. Perhaps
even smiled a bit. People will begin to talk.'

She obliged by looking up, but could not form
much of a smile.

'You look very beautiful tonight,' he told her,
holding her eyes for a moment even as he executed
a perfect manoeuvre around a couple who were out
of time with the music. 'It's no wonder you had no
shortage of dance partners.'

One…two – three; *one*…two – three…There was
nothing between them but the count of the music
and the sense of unfinished business.

'I expected you to cut me. Why did you ask me
to dance?'

His eyebrows rose and his eyelids lifted. 'In the
eyes of Society you are still my fiancée, Victoria. I was
not about to let you waltz with someone else.'

'Then why do we not put an end to what Society
thinks, Phillip? There is no sense in prolonging it. You
will be free to court whomever you like, and I'll be
free to do what I like.'

Her unanswered question hung between them
until the dance ended. Phillip released her hand and
shifted the arm that had been around her waist to
allow her to grip his elbow again, then led her off the

floor. 'Would you care for some fresh air? You look a bit flushed.'

She was flushed, and – heaven forbid! – perspiring from all of the activity. 'Yes, that would be lovely.' She dug out her fan, snapped it open, and began to wave it in hopes of drying the gentle moisture on her bosom.

They paused near the edge of the dance floor to obtain two small glasses of iced tea, or what had been iced tea until the heat turned it lukewarm. Sipping the sweet drink, Victoria allowed Phillip to escort her through the doorless entrances hung with vines of clematis to keep the flies out but let the fresh air in. He brushed aside the leafy, flowering strands and she stepped out into the welcome air.

Instead of stopping on the terrace where the potted gardenias and roses added scent and colour to the evening, Phillip drew her along with him past the end of the brick terrace and down one of the four paths that spiked from it.

As his healthy stride slowed to a stroll and he remained silent, Victoria could hold back no longer. 'Why have you not posted the announcement in the *Times*?'

'I have been wondering the same thing about you.'

'But…thank you. That's very kind of you to help me save face. But it's no matter to me.'

They had walked quite far from the party, and

Victoria was just about to speak again when they rounded a bend in the pea-gravel path and came upon a small arbour. A stone bench sat under the archway, and more clematis and climbing roses were tangled in it.

Victoria thought Phillip meant for her to sit when he slid his arm from her grip, but as she moved toward the bench, he pulled her back – and into his arms.

He kissed her…oh, he kissed her. She recognised there the same emotion she'd felt upon seeing him again: familiarity, comfort, and something new… need. It told her all she needed to know.

After a long interval, in which she found her fingers loosening the hair clubbed at the nape of his neck and her belly pulled up against his, Phillip pulled back and looked down at her. 'I have missed you. I meant to stay away and let you do what you would tonight, for I have no further claim to you, but in the end, I could not. And it wasn't because of what Society thinks. It was because of what I wanted.'

Victoria blinked rapidly. 'I've missed you too, Phillip. I checked the paper every day, sure that the announcement would appear. And it never did.'

'I thought you would be the one to cry off.'

'But I did not. Phillip, you said…' She stepped back and he let the hands clasped at the base of her back release. 'Nothing has changed. I cannot tell you what you wish to know.'

'I have been thinking – doing much thinking at

my club, riding through the park at dawn, in my study.' His smile was crooked. 'In all of the places that I would be certain not to run into you.'

She smiled back. She'd been doing the same…in all the places she was certain not to run into him, like the streets of St Giles after midnight. The bowels of London.

'You mentioned destiny. Your destiny. You said it was indelible, unchangeable. But Victoria, I do not believe destiny is a fixed thing. There is some choice that comes with it.

'For example. I was destined to love you – I know that is true, for I never forgot you from that summer. I did not even think to seek a wife until this Season… and you were in mourning for two years after you should have come out. As if you were waiting for me, and for the right time. Or as if I were waiting for you…to be ready.

'My destiny is to love you. But I have a choice as to how I can fulfil this certain thing, this destiny. I can love you and be with you, or I can love you from afar. After tonight it became clear to me that I cannot love you from afar. That I must love you *with* me.' He took her hands and raised them, gloves and all, to kiss the backs of them, looking at her over them as he did so.

'Phillip—'

He moved her hands up to press against her mouth. 'Victoria. Whatever is your destiny, you do have some choice. You can decide how to handle it, whether to embrace it or fight it. Whether to share it or hide it.'

'Phillip, I swear to you...I swear that this thing between us is nothing that I can change and nothing that I can tell you about. But...' It was her turn to press gloved fingers to his mouth to keep him from responding. 'But if you will still have me, I can promise you that I will make the *choice* to balance that part of my life with the life we'll build together. That is the part of my legacy that I can control.'

Closing his fingers around her wrist, he tugged her hand away from his mouth. 'Then, since there is not and could never be anyone for me but you, Victoria, we will have to let our destinies live together.'

And he kissed her.

Chapter Twenty

Maximilian Is Pressed into Service

'I received this today.' Max flung a thick ivory envelope onto Eustacia's piecrust table. It slid to the edge of the highly polished oak, knocking her stake aside. 'I cannot believe she is going to go through with this madness.'

Eustacia knew what it was; she had received her invitation to Victoria's wedding a week earlier. She exchanged glances with Kritanu, who was working on fitting the wooden pieces of a new weapon he'd created. 'I didn't realise you were on the guest list.'

He snorted. 'She's asked me to attend in order to make certain…as she puts it, "nothing untoward happens". She wants me to patrol for vampires while she gets married!'

Eustacia camouflaged her chuckle with a cough. 'Well, she certainly can't be doing it herself, now, can she? And I am in no position to help out, with my arthritis. The rest of the family thinks I'm mad anyway. They would send me off to Bedlam if they saw me skulking about with a stake! Max, Max…I have my reservations about her choice, but I can't stand in her way. She deserves the chance to try it if she feels so strongly about it.'

Max stalked over to the sideboard and helped himself to a glass of whiskey. 'It's ridiculous. You could forbid her, Eustacia.'

'And face the wrath of my niece Melly? I'd rather come up against Lilith in person than that.' As a joke went, it was a feeble attempt, and she knew it. But Kritanu, bless him, gave a little laugh and went back to what he was doing. But not before she saw the sympathy in his jet-black eyes.

It had been so much simpler when it was just the two of them, fighting, studying, loving.

'Max, really. She's managed to help us locate and steal the Book of Antwartha; she's been hunting and executing vampires on a regular basis even while maintaining her societal duties. And it has been a great help to us for her to have access to some of these events, where she can move about freely and find and kill any vampires that have managed to penetrate that level of the *ton*. That is something not as easy for you or I to do, being from Italy, and something we have needed for a long time. As the Marchioness of Rockley, she'll have even more access to these kinds of venues. And perhaps even have the chance to do so at court.'

'Yes, and when she's the Marchioness of Rockley, she'll have a husband who will want to follow her when she comes out on patrol, as he did two weeks ago. Or who won't let her go at all, and because he's her husband he'll be able to keep her in on the nights we might need her. Or enforce her presence at more and more of those ridiculous balls, or evenings at Almack's, or weekends in Bath...We have a life-and-death business here, and my concern is that she'll be less available for help when we need it.' As always, when he became impassioned about something, his English grew thicker with their homeland accent.

'You've never been one to want to work with someone, Max, so why are you so concerned about it now?'

'Lilith grows stronger every month, and we need to work together. All of us. And what happens, Eustacia, when Victoria begets an heir for the Marquess of Rockley? She can't be hunting vampires in that condition.'

Porca l'oca! Max was right. Eustacia had her own worries, but she'd tried to push them away, tried to play devil's advocate with him because she didn't want the rift between him and Victoria to grow any wider. But she could not argue with his points, and indeed, had spent some sleepless nights worrying on them herself.

From all aspects, it could not work. She could not believe it would, had never known it to happen. Yet Eustacia had learnt not to live by absolutes. Just because it hadn't happened didn't mean that it could not.

Time to change the subject.

'And the marquess – I presume he has recovered from his experience at the Silver Chalice and is not rushing about London trying to hunt vampires?'

Max grimaced, presumably a reaction to the large gulp of whiskey he downed. 'He called on me the day following the incident. Did I not tell you that?'

'No…you did not.'

'He wanted to know why I put the *salvi* in his drink. He was quite…agitated. We nearly came to fisticuffs. He appeared to be under the impression that I had taken Victoria to the Silver Chalice, and that it was I who influenced her so. He was babbling on about destiny…and from what I was able to glean, he had just come from her home. He left me with the impression that they were calling off the wedding. Which is the reason I was quite surprised to receive *that.*'

Eustacia could think of nothing to say. She merely raised her eyebrows, hoping he would continue. When he did not, and instead sat glaring at the offending invitation, she prompted, 'Whatever did you tell him? About the *salvi*?'

'I told him the truth – that it was for his protection.

That he'd walked into a nest of vipers that he had no hopes of understanding, and that the only way I knew to get him out safely was to make him sick. Unfortunately, it did not work as planned.'

And that he'd been bested by a non-Venator was probably the largest reason it sat like a stone in his belly.

'If he follows her again, he could easily jeopardise our work.'

True. Too true. 'Victoria will have to find a way to manage that, Max. I trust that she will be able to.'

She prayed her niece would be able to.

'It would have to be raining today, of all days,' Melly muttered to Winnie as she watched her beautiful daughter exchange vows with the catch of the Season. 'A fortnight of sunshine, and today must be overcast!' Despite her annoyance, she cast a satisfied glance over her shoulder, gleeful at the expressions of some of the other mamas who hadn't been quite as successful in their matchmaking endeavours. Today was truly a coup!

Indeed, a soft, summer rain was falling on this, the day of the Marquess of Rockley's wedding. The sky was coloured with pearl-gray clouds, and the steady rain brought the smell of peat and summer flowers to the air. The overflow guests were huddled outside the chapel under hastily erected tents, and more than one pair of spectacles had fogged or misted up. Melly's lorgnette was damp, but that was from tears of joy… not the rain.

'The drizzle isn't bothering them,' Winnie whispered back. 'I've never seen Victoria look so beautiful, and so happy.' She dabbed at her eyes, then snorted, bull-like, into her lacy handkerchief.

Melly had helped her daughter dress at St Heath's Row in a slip of soft lemon silk, with a lacy white gauze skirt over it. The lace was embroidered with seed pearls, twists of satin ribbon, and ocean pearls, giving the whole of it a gentle glittering sort of glow. Madame LeClaire had outdone herself!

Victoria's maid had drawn up only the topmost of her curls onto the crown of her head, leaving the rest of the unruly mass to cascade down her back and over her shoulders. Melly had forbidden the use of those ridiculous sticks in the bridal coiffure, and so more pearls, and also ice-white diamonds, had been woven into the corkscrew tresses. Still more created a wrap around the top of her cluster of curls, holding them in a crown-like position.

Moments after the heaviest of the rain showers eased, Victoria had walked down the aisle at the small stone chapel on the grounds of St Heath's Row carrying a cluster of lilies of the valley and yellow roses. English ivy, wrapped around the stems, trailed to the ground at her feet.

The marquess was resplendent in a dove-grey coat and ink-black breeches. His boots shone like jet, and his waistcoat was rich claret patterned with black-and-grey paisley. His neckcloth, a solid colour matching the waistcoat, had been tied to within an inch of its life, and was as crisp as a bloodstain on his perfect white shirt. Such exquisite fashion sense!

Rockley's thick walnut hair was brushed back high off his forehead, and did not dare fall from its place even when he tipped his head to look down at his bride. The long sideburns that framed the very edges of his cheeks had been trimmed and lay flat and smooth against his skin. His eyes, half-lidded as they always were, were fixed with great emotion on the glowing bride next to him as he spoke his vows clearly and for all to hear.

As his mellow voice boomed his promise to love her daughter until death did they part, Melly couldn't resist looking over at Lady Seedham-Jones, whose three single daughters – all of whom had come out in the last four years – were sitting next to her. The lady in question had the look of a wrinkled prune about her face.

That was when Melly noticed the Italian gentleman who seemed to know her aunt Eustacia quite well. Maximilian someone-or-other – since he didn't have a title, Melly hadn't bothered to learn his last name. 'Whatever does that Maximilian person have in his hand?'

Winnie turned to look at the tall dark-haired man with the arrogant face. He sat in the back row of the chapel, looking rather bored, and as Melly watched he slipped something – a long, pointed stick – from the sleeve of his jacket. He hefted it in his hand, then slid it back into the starched white cuff. More than once.

'How very odd,' Winnie murmured, fingering the crucifix that dangled from her neck. 'It almost looks like a stake one would use to impale a—'

'Don't say it!' Melly hissed. 'Do not even breathe your foolish thoughts here at my daughter's wedding!'

'But, Melly, you know—'

'Hush! They are about to be presented as husband and wife!'

Winnie complied and closed her mouth, but her eyes darted back to the Italian gentleman sitting in the last row. Melly pretended not to notice, but she did keep a wary eye on the man for the rest of the wedding celebration.

However, he remained on the outskirts of the revelry and never once left the fete. So it was most certain that Winnie's imagination had run away with her yet again.

Silly woman.

Victoria had never seen the bare chest of an adult male, but she found it exceedingly captivating when, late on the day of her wedding, in the privacy of his bedchamber, her new husband whipped off his shirt.

The starched white broadcloth fell in a crumple on the floor and Phillip stepped over it, moving toward her outstretched hand. She wanted to feel the smooth skin that had been hidden under his shirt. Who would have known that such a proper gentleman had such firm, golden ridges dusted with dark hair, of all things! But the curls felt soft and interesting when she finally touched them, and if the gentle intake of his breath was any indication, he did not mind her questing fingers at all.

Not at all.

Victoria was still garbed in the night rail that Verbena had hustled her into, after all of the guests had left St Heath's Row. The faintest sounds of clattering dishes and servants ordering one another about during their effort to clean up did reach her ears, up there in the suite of rooms that belonged to her husband, but Victoria's attention was quite focused elsewhere. In particular, on the hands of her husband, which were industriously unbuttoning the tiny buttons that Verbena had done up a mere fifteen minutes earlier.

She held her breath when the flimsy cotton lawn, trimmed with an abundance of lace and satin that she was certain had gone wholly unappreciated by her new husband, fell away, baring her shoulders and a great deal of her bosom.

And whilst Phillip, the man she loved, carried her to the bed they would share, if she happened to think, ever so briefly, that he was not the first man to see her breasts bared…well, that thought was immediately driven from her mind when he replaced smoothing hands with his lips.

It felt quite delicious, and Victoria was gratified that the pleasant tingle between her legs grew stronger and moister under her husband's ministrations. And that she was feeling his warm skin under her hands and nails as they ruffled the scattering of hair that grew in so many unusual places – on his muscular arms, over the flat expanse of his chest, down a long, thin line that disappeared into his trousers.

He'd left off kissing her breasts to move back up to her mouth and then along the most sensitive area of her neck, where the vampire bite was all but gone. For the first time in her memory, his hair had moved out of place and fell forward on the sides, brushing his sideburns and the edge of his jaw.

Phillip moved back, away and off, and shucked off his breeches. With a covert glance, as if to check her reaction to the bulge thus revealed, he took a bit longer to slip out of his drawers and then stood looking down at her.

Victoria felt hot and trembly all over when she saw the part of him that most obviously wanted her.

He came back toward the bed, where she'd hiked herself up on one elbow to watch him undress. Sprawling next to her, his nakedness lining the length of her night rail, he trailed a hand along her body, from her throat down along between her breasts and into the deep V from the part of her gown he'd impatiently left buttoned. But not for long.

His fingers deftly slipped the remaining buttons from their loops as he bent forward to kiss her. And then, as his hands brushed over the newly exposed skin, he stopped.

'What…?' He sat up, away, and pulled the edges of her nightgown aside to expose the soft rounding of her stomach and the glint of silver that lay there. 'What is that?'

Of course. She'd realised he'd ask about it. He wouldn't recognise a *vis bulla*, as Verbena or Sebastian would. But she hadn't expected the expression on his face to be one of such…displeasure.

She'd already decided how to explain it. 'A Gardella family tradition,' she told him, reaching for the squared-off roundness of his shoulder to pull him back toward her.

He resisted, and though she was strong enough to keep him moving toward her, she released him.

'Why?'

'It's believed to offer a kind of protection. As I said, it is a family tradition that Aunt Eustacia requested I follow.'

'It is…unusual. Does it hurt?' He reached a finger to touch the silver cross.

'No. Not at all.' She flicked the cross and its small hoop to demonstrate.

'I'm not at all certain I like it, or that it's appropriate.'

Victoria stared at him for a moment, then told herself it was her wedding night and she did not want it to be spoilt. 'I can take it out for tonight, if it would make you feel better.'

'Feel better? I'm not certain I agree with your choice of words…but, yes, Victoria, I think I would rather look only at your beautiful body without any adornments.'

'I will be right back, then.' She had no intention of removing the *vis bulla* and leaving it in his bedchamber to be lost. Pulling on a robe she'd discarded almost as soon as she entered the room, she hurried to her adjoining chamber. In the low light she untwisted the silver ring and slipped it from its mooring at the lip of her navel. When she pulled it out and placed it on her dressing table, she had to sit for a moment. Its absence left her light-headed and clammy, and she found she needed to rest her head on the table for a moment.

She could put the *vis bulla* back in, in the morning. And perhaps Phillip would grow used to it.

She turned toward the door that joined their bedchambers, and started…for he was standing there, her husband, in all of his naked beauty. Dark hair, heavy blue eyes…lean limbs shadowed with the glow from the candle on her dressing table. Her breath caught for a moment and she felt muzzy-headed again…and this time it was not from the removal of her *vis bulla*.

'Come here, darling,' Phillip said, holding out his hands to her. His shoulders flexed easily in the flickering candlelight. 'I hope I did not spoil the mood.' He smiled in a manner that reminded her uncomfortably of Sebastian – a bit wicked, edged with promise…yet there was a tenderness there in his eyes, something she'd never seen in Sebastian's golden ones.

And why was she comparing him to Sebastian? Her husband, on their wedding night? Perhaps it was only normal for one to compare and contrast when confronted with something unfamiliar…and exciting.

She stepped into his arms, glad that he'd come to her and apologised. She felt the warmth of his body, long and textured against hers, and the prod of his erection was gentle against her hip. Her half-donned robe gusted around them, and she slipped it off her shoulders. It collapsed onto the floor, pooling at her ankles as her naked breasts pressed against his chest.

Phillip kissed her along the side of her neck, where her skin was the most sensitive, and where the bare brush of his lips made her toes curl and her breasts tighten. Somehow his mouth didn't stop its tasting of her as he brought them to the bed – her bed, not his – and tumbled her onto it.

'So beautiful, my darling,' he told her, propping

himself up on an elbow above her. His body cast a shadow over half of hers, and she watched in fascinated interest as he drew his finger gently down between her breasts, along the irregular line of dark and light. The tingling that had begun in her belly, then between her legs, tightened almost painfully as he bent to draw her nipple into his mouth.

As he sucked and tugged, the sensation grew and ebbed with the rhythm of his mouth and the slide of his tongue. His breathing became deeper, warm and moist over her skin, and when he slipped his fingers between her legs, Victoria didn't know whether to press her knees together…or let them fall away.

'Let me, Victoria, my wife,' he whispered against her neck, drawing his mouth along her jaw as he positioned himself over her. 'I will be very gentle… and after a moment, you will feel only pleasure.'

She did. She let him, and opened her legs in a wanton manner, one that would have horrified her if she'd thought about it…but she did not. She let him. Let his fingers stroke and slide, dip and delve, until she did not know what was happening…only that it was pleasure beyond anything she'd imagined.

And then…the pain. The sharp, quick pain as he moved his hips between hers, and then, as he had promised, only pleasure.

Only easy, rising, fulfilling pleasure.

Chapter Twenty-One

Wherein the Marchioness Proves Herself an Excellent Storyteller

Victoria felt better when she reinserted her *vis bulla* the next day. It took a little bit of jimmying and tugging to get the silver hoop back in place, but she managed it with a bit of help from Verbena, and once that was done she finished dressing.

She was pleasantly sore from the activities of the night before, and, so far, quite delighted with her new marital status. Over breakfast she and Phillip ate kippers and eggs, sausages and biscuits, preserves and clotted cream. And then they boarded his travelling coach, which had already been loaded with their trunks, and embarked on a two-week honeymoon.

When they returned, she was rosy-cheeked and no longer sore.

On the morning after their return, Phillip left St Heath's Row early to take care of some business in town with his solicitor and banker. Victoria worked diligently if reluctantly on her correspondence, but was saved from an entire afternoon of tedium by a missive from Aunt Eustacia inviting her for tea.

'You look lovely, my dear marchioness,' said her elderly aunt when Kritanu showed Victoria into the sitting room. 'Rested and quite happy.'

Victoria bent to kiss her aunt's uncommonly soft, unlined face. 'Indeed I am, Aunt. But I am also quite desirous of returning to the task at hand.'

'We are delighted to hear that,' drawled Max, who was standing across the room.

'Max. I never did thank you for agreeing to attend the wedding,' Victoria replied. She had expected him to be there, and as part of her new position, she'd decided she was no longer going to allow him to nettle her. Her happiness made it much easier for her to pity his dark moods and what could only be great loneliness.

He bowed. 'I was happy to be of assistance.'

Perhaps he too had decided to be less combative.

'And how was the wedding trip?' Max continued, standing until Victoria took her seat. 'I trust the marquess is well and has given no indication he plans to revisit the Silver Chalice.'

Perhaps not.

'We haven't spoken of that evening since it

occurred,' Victoria told him, keeping her voice mild.

'Victoria, I realise it is your first day back from your honeymoon, but I felt it necessary to contact you,' interjected Aunt Eustacia. 'We've learnt that a group of vampires has planned a raid of sorts on Vauxhall Gardens early in the morning. Despite Max's expertise, we felt there should be two Venators in order to keep them from succeeding.'

Victoria felt the thrill of the fight tic in her heartbeat, but then she recalled. 'I am bound to attend the theatre with Phillip tonight. But…what time would I need to be ready?'

'Midnight, of course,' Max said from the corner. 'I am certain that you could invent *some* reason for returning to your home earlier rather than later in the evening. Having just returned from your honeymoon.'

Victoria did not allow the flush to warm her cheeks; she stopped it cold. 'Indeed, you are right. It will be no hardship to entice my husband to return home early. Of course, I might be otherwise occupied for a time…'

Max nodded, his eyes dark and cool. 'Of course. Do you think you could perhaps adjust your schedule so that I could pick you up at midnight? So that too many people aren't killed before we arrive?'

'You don't have to pick me up,' Victoria reminded him, wondering where her resolve had gone. 'I can meet you there.'

'I will pick you up. You would never locate me in Vauxhall.'

'I will have to find a way to leave the house without Phillip knowing.'

'I should expect him to sleep quite well after such an evening,' Max said mildly. 'Or perhaps you could assist him…with this.' He reached in his pocket and pulled out a small vial. 'If you are concerned that he might awaken and find his wife missing.'

Victoria caught it when he tossed it lightly through the air. 'What is it?' But she already knew. It was a drug. Max was suggesting that she drug her husband.

'It is called *salvi*. Protection. Safety. It comes in quite handy.'

'As long as you aren't caught administering it and forced to drink it yourself.' Victoria looked at the small vial, then glanced at Eustacia, who'd been unusually silent during their exchange. It was almost as if she'd realised her intervention would be useless.

Could she actually drug Phillip?

Was it necessary?

If she didn't would he awaken to find her gone? If she wasn't beside him, where she'd become quite used to sleeping in the last two weeks, would he seek her out in her own bedchamber?

The liquid was nearly clear; just the faintest blue tinged the thin, watery fluid. She would have to. To protect him, she not only had to lie to him…but drug him as well.

For she could not chance his awakening and putting himself in danger again.

Never again.

'I am feeling quite exhausted,' Victoria murmured into Phillip's ear as they sat in the box he'd let at the theatre. 'I would much rather be in bed…wouldn't you?' She dipped the tip of her tongue into the innermost part of his ear – quickly, like a tease – then moved away and returned her attention to the stage. Prim and proper she was then, with her hands folded neatly in her lap.

Phillip shifted next to her in a manner that told her he, too, was thinking of things other than the play…which she was rather enjoying. 'We can slip out during the next intermission – ah! What perfect timing,' he amended, as the actors exited the stage.

Victoria clung to his arm as they pushed through the bustle of people leaving their boxes to mingle and be seen.

Phillip handed her into the carriage and climbed in after her. Instead of sitting on the seat across, he settled next to her and drew her near, kissing her with promise.

'My dear, your neck is so cold! Are you quite comfortable?' he asked, pulling away.

'I am not chilled, but oh, Phillip! I left my

indispensable in our box; I'm certain of it! And it has Aunt Eustacia's brooch in it… Could you hurry back in and retrieve it for me?'

'Of course, my darling. You wait here – I won't be above a minute!'

She hoped that wasn't true, and waited until she saw him hurry back into the theatre before she slipped the stake from a hidden pocket in her underskirt and climbed quietly out of the carriage – hoping the groom wouldn't hear her.

The walkway was crowded, more with carriage grooms and hackney drivers than theatregoers. Victoria wasn't certain where the vampire was, but she followed her instinct and hurried around the corner. The street was darker here, and not so busy – but when she approached the third hackney in the row, she knew she'd come to the right place.

A deep, muffled groan came from inside, and seeing that the driver was missing, Victoria flung open the door.

The vampire was a woman and, from the looks of it, had just finished feeding – or, at least, had already started. She was dressed in a dark cloak, and her brown hair was arranged quite prettily in an intricate coiffure, complete with gemstones and ribbons. In fact, if it weren't for the bright red blood trickling from the corner of her mouth, and the odd-coloured eyes, she would have looked like an innocent society miss.

'How nice of you to join us,' she greeted Victoria.

Quick as a flash she lunged forward and grabbed at her. It took little effort for her to draw Victoria into the hackney – mainly because Victoria did not resist.

But once Victoria was sprawled, half in, half out of the carriage, she took matters into her own hands and scrambled to a seat on the opposite side.

That was when the vampire saw the stake.

She drew back in fear, and her red eyes widened. 'Venator!'

'Pleased to meet you,' Victoria told her as she slammed the stake into her chest.

Poof! She was gone, and Victoria was alone with the man she presumed was the driver of the hackney, based on the less than elegant clothing he wore.

She shifted his body to examine the bite and determine whether he was still alive and able to be saved. The bite was deep and still running with bright red blood. She felt the other side of his neck, trying to find a pulse…but her hand came away wet. The vampire had already been there too.

If they had come out of the theatre a few moments earlier, she might have sensed the vampire sooner, in time to stop this.

But there was nothing she could do for the man. He was already dead.

When Victoria opened the hackney door, she froze, then quickly shut it. Phillip was standing on the street, calling for her.

Damn and blast!

She peered out the window, waiting for him to pass by so she could sneak out and hurry back to their carriage.

As soon as he went beyond the hackney, she did slip out and rush back…but just as she rounded the corner, she realised she was leaving Phillip alone – where another vampire could easily appear.

The back of her neck remained warm, but she still paused at the corner, peering around to watch for him.

To her relief he came back into view, striding along as if to hurry back and search in a different direction. She made her way to the carriage, where Tom, the groom, rushed up to her in relief.

'My lady! Where did you go?'

She did not answer, for at that moment Phillip came around the corner and caught sight of her.

'Victoria! Where did you go? And what is that on your gown? Is that blood?' He stared at her, appalled.

'Let us get in the carriage and I will tell you.' It was nearly eleven, and if she was going to be ready for Max, they needed to get started.

Phillip helped her into the carriage, and Victoria took her seat, thinking quickly. 'Did you find my indispensable?'

'No, there was nothing in the box. Victoria—'

'Oh, my dear, here it is! It was under the cushion all along!' she said, retrieving her little pouch. 'I am so sorry for sending you on such a goose chase.'

'Yes, just as you were last week when you thought you left your shawl at the inn where we dined.'

'I can't imagine how I've become so fiddle-minded!' Victoria said, and because she recognised that he was only so patient and able to be distracted for so long, she said, 'I did not mean to give you a fright, Phillip, but I saw an acquaintance of my mother's and hurried out to greet her. I walked with her and her husband to their carriage – just a few down from ours – and she bade me come in and greet her daughter, and as we climbed in, the door of the carriage slammed into her husband's nose, and it began to bleed quite dreadfully. He was so embarrassed that he bled on my skirt. I couldn't just rush off…so I stayed until I was certain he did not feel at fault. I am so sorry I did not tell Tom that I was leaving!'

'Well, I hope that you don't just hie off again without telling someone. First, it is not safe – there are many miscreants lurking about, waiting for an opportunity to rob an unsuspecting straggler…and second, you are a marchioness now and not only have a position to uphold, but you are very valuable and worth quite a bit of money to someone nefarious – and much more to me. I want you to be safe.'

'Of course, Phillip. I won't do such a thing again.' And she meant it. Next time she'd plan better.

They snuggled together, during the rest of the way home, as newly weds were wont to do. Victoria plotting how she would slip the *salvi* to Phillip, and Phillip thinking about how he was going to slip something into Victoria.

It was a quarter past midnight when Victoria rapped lightly on Max's coach.

The door swung open and she climbed in without help. To her surprise Max, who lounged in the corner of one seat, didn't say anything about her tardiness.

Instead, he knocked on the ceiling for Briyani to go, and the carriage started off.

Victoria sat silently across from him, trying riot to think about how she'd betrayed her husband.

She'd added the *salvi*, which Max had assured her was tasteless and odourless, to Phillip's glass of scotch, then brought it to him after they made love.

Curling up in the large feather bed next to him, Victoria pretended to fall asleep whilst waiting for the drug to take effect.

'Did you use the *salvi*?' Max's question snapped her back to the present...but not away from the guilt.

'Yes. I had no other choice to ensure his safety, did I?'

He looked at her. 'You did have a choice, Victoria... and you know that I believe you made the wrong one.'

Anger boiled inside her, topping off the simmering of guilt. 'And you know that your opinion means little to me.'

'A fact which wounds me deeply.'

'Do you know what I think?'

Max inclined his head, and in the low light she could see one eyebrow lift. 'I am certain you are about to tell me.'

She continued. 'I think you are jealous. Purely, simply jealous, and that is why you have nothing nice to say.'

'Jealous?'

'Yes, jealous of what I have with Phillip. What you don't have and never will because you are so cold and cruel.' The words tumbled out, almost as if she didn't know what she was saying – but she did know, and she knew she wanted to wound him, just as he'd wounded her by rubbing salt in her already tender heart. Her guilty, tender heart.

It frightened her, the way she felt – the strength of the emotions roiling inside her – because…she feared, deep inside, that perhaps Max was right after all.

Perhaps she'd made a mistake.

Max sat like stone for the remainder of the carriage ride to Vauxhall Gardens.

When they arrived he gave instructions to his driver, paid the four shillings for himself and Victoria to enter the gardens, and, with the barest of glances at her, started along the winding pathway.

Lamps of orange, blue, yellow, and red hung throughout the gardens, casting brightly coloured circles on the stone path and the booths that offered ham slices, biscuits, and punch. Although she'd never been in the gardens before, she knew there were hidden alcoves and mysterious grottoes throughout the park – the perfect places for an assignation, or for a vampire attack. People strolled about – couples, clusters of young people with their chaperones, and groups of young men looking for adventure. The fireworks display had finished thirty minutes earlier, and the patrons were beginning to head back to their carriages.

It wasn't far into the gardens before Victoria's neck iced over. Definitely at least ten vampires in the vicinity, she guessed. She had dressed in trousers and a man's shirt tonight, needing the freedom of movement.

Max led the way, and just about the time Victoria thought her neck must surely be white with frost, they came upon a group of four undead toying with a septet of young men.

Perhaps both Victoria and Max had an equal amount of temper to vent, for the battle was brief and fairly one-sided…all four vampires were staked barely before their intended victims could run for safety.

Since only a few fangs had been bared, and the seven young men were quite in their cups, Max did not feel they needed to be hypnotised out of their memories. Instead he urged Victoria to follow him down a darker path.

As they rounded the corner of a tall, thick bush,

three vampires leapt out at them. One of them was carrying a knife, and before she could react Victoria felt a hot, sharp pain down her left arm.

With a cry of fury she raised her right arm and plunged the stake into his chest. She heard two soft pops as Max dispatched the others, and she turned to continue along the path without another word.

Her arm burnt, and when she reached over to touch it, the jacket sleeve was damp. The only good thing about the wound was that the scent of blood would attract any other vampires, making it much easier for her and Max to finish their job and get back to the carriage.

And for Victoria to get back into bed with her husband, who slept peacefully and dreamlessly, thanks to his unscrupulous wife.

Anger with herself helped propel her striking arm during the other two short-lived incidents; she and Max were efficient and silent as they finished off the cluster of vampires that had dared to invade Vauxhall Gardens on a night that they patrolled.

On the way back to Max's carriage, Victoria held her wounded arm, which throbbed and stung, radiating pain up into her shoulder. She walked behind Max, who did not bother to shorten his long strides in deference to her shorter ones.

It wasn't until they got in the carriage, each in their own corners, that he saw her holding her arm. He rapped on the ceiling, and as the carriage jolted into motion he said, 'What's wrong with your arm?'

Before she could reply, he sniffed the air, then reached across and pulled her hand away. 'You're bloody bleeding through your coat!'

'It worked quite well to attract the vampires. We finished up rather more quickly than I'd thought we would.'

'Take off your coat. You're bleeding all over yourself, and probably on my seat as well.'

Victoria glared at him, but she did shrug out of her jacket. It hurt like blazes when she tugged the tight sleeve over her arm, and when she bent her elbow to pull the other side off. The white sleeve of her shirt was dark with blood from shoulder to past her elbow. Max took one look in the low light and swore. 'Bloody hell, Victoria, why didn't you say something? How did that happen?'

'One of those three who jumped from the trees had a knife, and he caught me by surprise.'

Max was cursing under his breath as he rummaged in a small drawer under his seat. He sat back up holding a mass of white cloth, a small jar, and a knife.

With brief, angry movements, he sliced the clean blade down her shirtsleeve, cutting the fabric from her shoulder to her wrist and pulling it away to bare her arm. 'Hold still.' He sopped at the blood with some of the cloth and, holding it tightly, told her, 'Keep this here for a minute. It's starting to slow.'

She held the cloth there while he opened the small

jar. The smell of rosemary and something else that she couldn't identify filled the carriage, and when Max pulled the cloth away, she allowed her free hand to fall into her lap. 'Hold this,' he said, slamming the jar into her open palm. He scooped roughly into the jar and slapped some of the cool, thick salve all along the cut, then wrapped white strips of cloth none too gently around her arm. Victoria felt her fingers begin to tingle as the blood was cut off, but she said nothing.

At last, when they were nearly back to St Heath's Row, Max stuffed the unused cloth and the jar back into the drawer and settled into his seat. 'You'd better start thinking of a good story, Victoria, because you're going to have a bloody time of it trying to explain that to your husband.'

Chapter Twenty-Two

Incident at Bridge and Stokes'

Phillip found his wife already sitting down to breakfast when he came downstairs the morning after their visit to the theatre. He felt muzzy-headed and sluggish, though he had slept later than usual after a satisfactory bout of love-making.

'Good morning, my dear,' he said, breathing in the scent of crisp bacon and coddled eggs. They were alone in the dining room, so he bent to press a kiss to her bare neck and said quietly, 'I was greatly disappointed to find my bed bereft of you. Why so early to rise?'

'I woke early and did not wish to disturb you,' she replied. But the dark circles under her eyes told a different story.

'I must have slept like a stone not to hear you get up,' he commented, filling his plate, wondering why her expression seemed so guarded. 'I cannot recall even moving after resting my head on the pillow; indeed, I believe I woke in the exact same position in which I lay down. That is quite unusual for me. It must be your fault.' He said it lightly, with a teasing smile, but Victoria did not seem to find it amusing.

She took a sip of tea and appeared to have difficulty swallowing a small bite of toast. Phillip shook his head; he still felt cloudy-minded. Perhaps his little joke hadn't been as funny as he'd thought.

'Are you cold?' he asked, trying another tack. 'I'm rather warm, but you are wearing a pelisse.'

'Yes, I am a bit chilled,' Victoria replied. But her cheeks were pink, and if he was not mistaken, there was the slightest sheen on her forehead.

'Are you not feeling well?' he asked.

'No, in fact, I am not feeling quite the thing.'

A thought struck him, a wonderful thought. But it was too early…it had been only two weeks. But he spoke anyway. 'Perhaps…is it possible you might be carrying my heir? I know it has been only a few weeks…'

Victoria looked up from her breakfast at him, her face pale and her dark green-flecked eyes wide, shocked. 'N-no…I think it is too soon, Phillip.'

He smiled. 'Then we shall have to work harder at it.'

'I am not feeling well,' Victoria said, standing abruptly. 'I believe I shall lie down for a bit. Are you off to your club today?'

'I have some business to attend to…but if you are not feeling well, Victoria, I will stay nearby.'

'No. No, Phillip, I will be fine. I just need some rest. I did not sleep as well as you did last night.'

He watched her hurry from the room, and noticed something very odd: when she brushed through the doorway, she bumped her left arm on the edge. The way she grabbed at it and gasped told him it was more than a minor pain due to clumsiness. Something else was wrong.

Dear heavens! A baby! Phillip wanted a baby!

Victoria collapsed on the bed in her private chamber, forgetting and falling on her left side and then rolling over when pain burnt down her arm.

She couldn't have a baby. She couldn't keep drugging her husband every night she had to sneak out and patrol… She couldn't keep 'forgetting' items and sending him back for them. She couldn't continue to make up ridiculous stories about bleeding noses to explain blood on her skirt. She couldn't keep taking out her *vis bulla* every time they made love.

How was she going to do this?

She could tell him the truth…but if she did that, he would simply follow her. Put himself in danger again.

Or worse…he would think she was mad.

The door opened and Victoria bolted upright, but it wasn't Phillip.

'Now, my lady, what ever is the matter?' It

was Verbena. Her orange hair tufting with every movement, she sailed over to the bed and sat next to her mistress. 'Is it your arm paining you again?'

'No, since you cleaned it up last night it has hardly hurt me at all, except when I bumped against the door. It's the marquess.'

Verbena nodded. 'Aye, yes, I see that. I see that you must take your *vis bulla* out at night. He don't understand, and ye can't tell him. What did ye do to him to make him sleep so well? Franks said as how he could barely stir him this mornin'.'

Victoria shook her head. It was her knowledge to bear and no one else's. 'It is better if I do not speak of it. But the marquess wants an heir.'

'Of course he does. But you cannot be fighting vampires if you are carrying a babe! You will have to make certain this does not happen.'

'I cannot deny him!'

'Why would you want to do that? There are other ways to prevent a baby from coming, my lady. Your aunt will know how Venators prevent babies.' Verbena nodded her head sagely. 'And I know some tricks myself, my lady. If your aunt cannot help you, I will.'

Victoria nodded, feeling a bit relieved, but at the same time as though she were sinking ever more deeply into a quagmire of lies and deceit.

Perhaps Aunt Eustacia would have some words of wisdom.

* * *

To Victoria's relief, the ever-present Max was not at Aunt Eustacia's home when she called later that morning. Kritanu served them a light nuncheon, then disappeared discreetly when it became obvious that Victoria was not there to practice her *kalaripayattu*.

'How is your arm?' Aunt Eustacia asked.

Apparently Max had been there.

'It is fine.'

'It will heal quickly; Max's salve is miraculous, and you carry the protection of the *vis bulla*.'

Victoria ate a bite of cheese, wondering how to tell her aunt she didn't think she could go on. That she needed to change something about being a Venator.

'Aunt Eustacia, I need your advice. I don't know what to do.'

'It is much more difficult than you believed it would be, isn't it, *cara*?'

'Phillip wants an heir, and I cannot give him *salvi* every night!'

Her aunt nodded, her black hair gleaming like the night. 'It is a very difficult situation you are in, Victoria. As for the baby...well, that is easily preventable. I am surprised you did not ask about that sooner.'

She did not reply. Her aunt was right that she should have been concerned with this before now.

'I will give you a tonic. If you drink it regularly, it will keep you from having a baby. Victoria...'

The way Eustacia said her name brought Victoria's face up to look at her.

'Lilith has not forgotten that you and Max retrieved the Book of Antwartha. I know it is safely hidden at St Heath's Row, but Lilith will not rest until she gets the book in her possession. It may seem that in the last two months undead activity has waned. It may appear that you are not needed, that Max and I can handle any threats that come along. But do not be fooled. You are a Venator and have been forever marked as one. Never forget you have dealt Lilith a great defeat – for she will not forget. She will not rest until she has exacted her revenge.'

Evening fashions were not conducive to hiding wounds on one's arm, so Victoria found herself in quite a quandary that night. Verbena helped her to pull on the longest pair of gloves she owned, melon-coloured ones that extended past the elbow, but there was a great expanse of bare skin exposed, due to the flimsy puffed sleeves that barely covered the edges of her shoulders.

'You will have to keep your wrap about your arms at all times,' Verbena clucked. The dressing had been removed, and true to Aunt Eustacia's word, the cut had already begun to heal and was hardly sore at all. But the long red gash was still quite noticeable, so Victoria wrapped her shawl around her upper arm twice, letting the rest of it swag gently across the base of her spine and over her right arm. 'Under no circumstances can you take that wrap from your arms.'

Phillip had sent word that he would be at his club for the evening, and would not be attending the dinner dance at which Victoria was expected to make an appearance. She considered crying off, but felt that it would be better to attend for a short while in order to appease her mother, and return home before midnight.

Thus she was greatly surprised when, as she was leaving the dance floor after a country dance, she saw Max striding across the room toward her.

Victoria excused herself from her dance partner, the younger son of an earl, and hurried to meet him. 'I know that you aren't here to partake of Society at its best,' she said by way of greeting.

'Lilith's minions are on the move. There's to be another group attack tonight,' he told her, casting his glance about the room. 'I do not wish to ruin your evening, but it would likely save some lives if you were to accompany me. Can you get away?'

'Yes, of course.' She was already walking toward the main entrance of the house.

'I don't see the marquess. Don't you need to tell him you are leaving?'

'He is not here this evening.'

Max easily kept in stride with her as she made her way up the sweeping flight of stairs. 'Where is he?'

'At his club.'

'Which one is that?'

'Bridge and Stokes, I believe, although why it matters to you I – what is it?'

He'd grabbed her arm, nearly jerking her off her feet near the top of the steps. The butler eyed them curiously, but she ignored him, for when Max spun her about to look at him the expression on his face sent a sick feeling worming into her stomach.

'The raid tonight is to be at a particular gentlemen's club.'

Their eyes met and he needed say nothing more; she was already pushing past the gawking butler and a cluster of people arriving at the dance.

He caught up with her outside, where she was trying to spot the Rockley carriage in the long line of vehicles around the circular drive. She had no time to wait for the valet to call for it. 'Are you certain you want to come? What if Rockley recognises you?'

'I'm going.'

'Then get in here.' He flung open the door of a black carriage, one she was more than familiar with, and lent her a hand to climb in.

Victoria scrambled to her seat, and had barely settled when the coach started off. Her long skirts were tangled among their four legs, and her wrap had slid to bare her cut arm.

'Here.' Max tossed her a large bundle of cloth, and when she sorted through it she found a shirt, trousers, a coat, and a long strip of cloth. 'Verbena gave them to me when I came to find you.'

Victoria looked down at the clothing and back at him.

'You can't fight in a ball gown, Victoria, and you needn't pretend modesty to me. I have no interest in watching you undress in a carriage, unlike your friend Sebastian, who would likely offer to assist you.' With that he tilted his head back against the top of his seat and closed his eyes. When she didn't move, he snapped, 'Be quick about it.'

Her gown was not easily removed, but Victoria struggled through and managed to unhook the flat copper hooks that held the bodice together in the back. When she pulled the gown up and over her head, the fabric wafted in a cloud of gauze over the interior of the carriage, brushing Max's stoic face – but he did not shift or give any indication that he felt it.

With her gown off, Victoria was dressed only in a light chemise and corset. It would be impossible to remove the stays without assistance, so she pulled the man's shirt over the fitted undergarment.

She could not pull it down over her generous bosom, cupped up and pushed together as it was. Victoria must have made a sound of frustration, for Max said, 'Do you need assistance? I'm so sorry I did not think to bring your maid.'

Her attention snapped from her bosom to him, but he was still relaxing, eyes closed as if nothing more urgent than a picnic were on the agenda.

'In a moment.' She would have to take the corset off and bind her breasts in order to get the shirt on. For a moment she considered remaining in her gown... but that was ridiculous. Not only would she not be able to fight, but she would stand out unacceptably in the club. If she even got in.

She turned around on her seat, presenting as much of her back to Max as possible. 'Can you...I can't unlace my...my corset.'

There was a pause; then she heard him stir behind her. The back hem of the shirt moved, and she resisted the urge to pull it down in front. If she did, he would not be able to reach up under it and unlace the corset.

His hands were quick and impersonal, and he managed to move them up and under the shirt and untie the laces, loosening them from top to bottom. She kept expecting to feel his fingers – would they be warm or cool? – brush over her skin, but they did not.

Victoria felt the garment give way as each row of laces loosened, and she held it to the front of her chest as it began to sag from behind. When he was finished, Max did not linger. She felt him move away, heard him settle back into his seat without a word.

Victoria wrapped herself with the strip of cloth Verbena had thoughtfully provided, awkward and rushed, allowing the shirt to slip almost completely from her shoulders as she did so. Her wounded arm ached faintly with the odd angle, but she was not about to ask Max for any more help.

'Are you nearly finished? I'm getting a crick in my neck.'

'Almost.' The collar buttons fumbled under her fingers because of her haste, but at last the shirt was done, the trousers were pulled on, and her coat was shrugged into.

'There are shoes on the floor,' Max said, still without moving.

At last she was ready. 'I'm finished. Thank you.'

Max opened his eyes. 'You have to do something about your hair.'

Victoria yanked the pins from the intricate curls and whorls Verbena had spent an hour on, knowing that her only option was to take it down and smooth it back.

'Do you have anything I can tie it with?' she asked, using her fingers to scrape it into a long, low tail at the nape of her neck.

Max, who seemed prepared for any eventuality, produced a thin leather cord from under the same seat the salve had been stored in, and, ordering her to turn, helped her bind and braid it. Their fingers clashed, and his cool ones brushed her neck as he helped her stuff the long tail down the back of her shirt.

By the time they were finished, the carriage was rolling to a stop.

'Here we are,' Max said, slamming a hat on top of her head. 'If Rockley sees you, the game is up. Otherwise…you can pass for a man.'

So much for Sebastian's opinion that she was unable to hide her gender while dressed in men's clothing.

Max tossed three stakes her way, and as she shoved them into her coat she saw him pocket a gun and slip a small dagger into his boot. Then she followed him out of the coach.

Victoria had barely had the chance to wonder how Max intended to gain admittance to the private gentlemen's club with the small, discreet BRIDGE & STOKES sign when he approached the doorman.

'Guests of the Marquess of Rockley,' he told him coolly. Victoria edged up the steps to stand next to him. Her neck was still warm.

The doorman allowed them to step into the foyer of the narrow building, effectively turning them over to the butler. 'May I help you?'

'We are here as guests of the Marquess of Rockley,' Max said again. 'Maximilian Pesaro and his companion.'

Victoria wanted to kick Max. What in the blazes was he doing? If Phillip saw her… But when the butler turned, ostensibly to call for Phillip, Max shoved her none too gently toward the curl of stairs that swept up from the entrance and into a balcony above. 'I'll get Rockley out of here; you go up there and see what you can find,' he said in an undertone.

She dashed up the steps and was just disappearing from sight when she heard the butler return. The voices below were a low rumble, but then she discerned Max's tones pitched loud enough for her to hear him say, 'He is above-stairs? I shall go up and find him myself then, thank you.'

Victoria had reached the top of the staircase and now she froze. She heard Max making his way up in her wake, continuing to assure the butler that he would locate the marquess on his own.

And just as Max reached the top of the stairs, facing her, two things happened: one of the doors along the hallway overlooking the balcony opened and Phillip walked out...and Victoria felt her neck ice over.

She looked at Max and they both moved at the same time – Victoria turned and hurried down the hall in the opposite direction as Max whirled to face Rockley, who stopped when he recognised him. He was with another man, who looked annoyed.

'Pesaro? I did not know you were a member here.' There was no warmth in his voice or his face; clearly he did not believe Max belonged there.

'I am not. I came at Victoria's behest. She asked me to call for you to return home.'

Victoria, who had moved several steps down the hall and ducked into an open doorway, held back a gasp at his audacity.

It was gratifying, in a matter of speaking, to hear

her husband's panic when he replied, 'Is she ill? Is she hurt?'

'I believe she will be fine, but she did wish to see you most urgently.'

It would have worked. It should have worked to get Phillip out of the club before the vampires struck, but they were just a little too late.

Victoria felt the chill at the back of her neck sharpen so suddenly that she stiffened in surprise. Still standing in a shadowed doorway, she pulled one of the stakes from her pocket just as her husband's companion opened his mouth.

She saw the flash of white fangs and the sudden glint of red in his eyes. Fortunately the sound she made drew Phillip's attention toward her and gave Max the opportunity to slam his own stake into the vampire behind him.

Phillip, who was peering at Victoria, took several steps toward her and did not appear to hear the *poof*. 'Do I know you?' he asked uncertainly.

Victoria, taking care to keep her head angled away and tucked under the hat she wore, felt the presence of another vampire.

'Rockley, get out of here,' Max said angrily. 'Get home to Victoria. She is waiting for you!'

She was thankful he drew Phillip's attention from her, and then a loud shout and altercation from below completed the distraction.

'What the bloody hell?' Phillip turned and began

to bound down the stairs, Max in his wake, barely touching the steps.

Victoria watched the two men go and knew that Max would see that Phillip was safe. That left her to handle the second floor.

She hurried down the hall, throwing doors open in search of the three vampires she sensed were up there. She found one just beginning to seduce his intended victim with a game of cards, and when she blasted into the room, he barely had the chance to throw down his hand before she staked him.

The sounds of fighting and shouts from below urged her on more quickly. Max was easily outnumbered, if the sensation on the back of her neck was accurate – and it always was. She had to find two more up here, and then she could go down to help.

As it turned out, they found her first, coming down the hallway shoulder-to-shoulder. They appeared to recognise her.

'There she is!' one of them growled, and suddenly he was next to her, grabbing at her arms. Victoria ducked and threw herself at his legs, sending him tumbling onto the floor just as the other one approached.

Using all the strength in her legs, Victoria shoved and slammed the second vampire onto the first one, then vaulted to her feet. One stake in each hand, she whirled and slammed them, one, two, into their chests.

She started toward the stairs and paused, looking

down at the fracas below. Max stood in the centre of the room using a fireplace poker to stave off what appeared to be two Guardians and an Imperial. Three other vampires stood waiting their turn, unable to get close enough to join the fray. Dark drops of blood flew with each of Max's movements; he was obviously hurt somewhere.

There were no other men in sight. Presumably the club members had taken themselves off…or were lying unconscious somewhere in the back. Phillip was nowhere to be seen.

Victoria flipped herself over the balcony rail, landing as planned on top of two vampires. They tussled on the floor before she had the opportunity to stake one of them; then with a somersault, she rolled away and leapt to her feet. The clatter of metal on the ground drew her attention, and she saw that the Imperial's sword had fallen when Max staked him.

She snatched it up and, whirling back up and around, sliced the head off a Guardian in one swoop. He poofed and she turned toward Max, who was easily holding the three other vampires at bay. When Victoria came toward them, one of them saw her and spun around to dash out the front door. She let him go in favour of checking the back rooms to make sure there weren't any other vampires – or victims. The back of her neck had become warmer, and she didn't expect to find any other undead.

She did find four gentlemen who'd obviously been

playing faro before they lost the battle with a vampire or two.

Victoria had not seen the results of many vampire attacks; in her limited experience she had most often prevented them from happening. Even the driver of the hackney two nights ago had been fed upon, but not destroyed and mutilated as these four men were.

Her stomach twisted as she walked into the card room. Blood was everywhere, clogging the room with its brutal stench. Shirts and jackets were in shreds, chests and necks torn open as though a mad dog had terrorised the men with teeth and claws. One man's gaping wound still showed the twisted blue-grey of his veins and muscles in his scored-open neck.

Vampires had fed on them, but they had also destroyed them.

"'Hell hath no fury…'"

Victoria turned. Max looked weary, and his swarthy face was as pale as its olive colour would allow. Three dark stains dampened his black coat. He held a stake in his hand.

'I presume the woman you speak of is Lilith?' she replied, proud that her voice was steady.

'Calling her a woman is a bit of a stretch, but yes, I would say this is her message to us.'

'We got all the vampires except one who bolted. Are there any victims who can be saved?'

Max shook his head.

'Phillip?'

'He's gone. Sent home in my carriage, which no vampire will dare attack. Briyani knows what to do. He'll drive him around for a few hours before taking him back to St Heath's Row. He was to give him some *salvi*; you'll be home before your husband, so you can tell him any story you like.' His voice was strained.

'Max, you look like you're going to fall over.'

'I've been worse. Let's get out of here before the Runners arrive. I don't want to have to clean their minds tonight too.'

They stepped out together into the starry, moonless night. It was peaceful and warm and the streets were nearly empty. There was nothing to indicate that a horror had just occurred in the narrow brick building behind them.

Chapter Twenty-Three

In Which the Truth Comes Out

Max would not let Victoria see to his wounds. He snarled at her when she tried to pull his jacket off to look at them, so she gave up and settled onto the threadbare seat of the hackney they'd been forced to hire to get them home.

The edge of the horizon had just begun to colour with the faintest grey-yellow of approaching dawn. Victoria couldn't help but breathe a sigh of relief. No more vampires to deal with until the night.

Now all she had to handle was her husband.

Despite the fact that he was growing grey and breathing more shallowly, Max insisted that the hackney drop Victoria off at St Heath's Row before taking him home. And he wouldn't even consider coming into her house to have his wounds – whatever they were – attended to. Thus, when she climbed down from the hackney, she told the driver where to take him – not to his house, but to Aunt Eustacia's – and gave him an extra shilling to make certain he got Max inside and into her aunt's care.

It wasn't until she walked up the steps to the entrance of St Heath's Row that Victoria realised she was still garbed in men's clothing, and that what was left of her gown was still in Max's carriage. It wouldn't seem so odd to Lettender, the butler, that she would arrive home at dawn in a hired hackney…but to arrive dressed as she was would certainly be cause for some comment and curious looks.

However, she was the marchioness, and though the austere butler might look at her askance, he surely would not dare to ask any questions.

The biggest concern Victoria had at that moment was whether Phillip was home. She rapped on the door, knowing that the household was already up, although perhaps Lettender was still snoring in his back room. One of the under-butlers opened the door, and from the bored look on his face Victoria knew that she had arrived home before Phillip.

Thank God.

She walked past the young man as if it were an everyday occurrence that she should leave in a ball gown and arrive home in men's clothing, and hurried up the stairs to her chamber. Verbena stumbled to her feet when she walked in, her springy hair smashed flat on the same side of her face that had sleep marks.

'My lady! You are home! How is your arm?'

'I am fine. Thank you for sending this clothing for me,' Victoria said. 'But quickly, now, I must get dressed in my nightclothes. The marquess should be arriving home shortly, and I do not want to him to see me dressed thus.'

They worked quickly, and none too soon, for just as the sun began to show its glowing edge against the rooftops of London, Max's carriage pulled up in front of the estate.

Victoria flung on a cloak and dashed back down the stairs, skirts and hems held high.

Kritanu's nephew Briyani, a short, narrow-faced man with large muscles and the same bronze skin colour of his uncle, was helping Phillip out of the carriage.

'Thank you for taking care of him,' Victoria murmured to Max's driver. 'Has he been awake?'

'Not so much, just as we were arriving home.' He handed Verbena a bundle of frothy material – her ball gown, now crumpled and soiled beyond repair, but at least it would not remain in the carriage.

'Max is at your uncle's home, and he is injured quite badly,' Victoria told him.

He nodded and climbed back into his perch, starting the carriage off. 'I will go and see how he is.'

'Victoria!'

Phillip was standing at the door of the house, looking bedraggled and exhausted. His eyes, always at half-mast, looked particularly weary.

'Darling! You are home at last.' Victoria said brightly, slipping her arm around his.

'Max came to my club; he said you called for me to come home. And then there was some great altercation there – I left in the midst of it.' He shook his head as if to clear it, and Victoria felt a renewed stab of guilt. 'I must have fallen asleep on the way home.'

Lies and more lies. Subterfuge and deceit. Phillip was an innocent bystander who just wanted to live a normal, happy life with the wife he loved…and he was caught up in a mess that he could not comprehend. And he didn't even know it.

How long could she continue to expend energy in making certain he didn't know? Making certain he was safe? Living a dual life?

Victoria drew him into her arms right there on the stoop of St Heath's Row, just beyond the stone walls that separated their estate from the streets of London.

'I am fine. I am afraid there was no urgency for you to return home; I merely told Max, when I saw him at the Guilderstons' dinner dance, that if he should see you to let you know that I would be home early and would like to speak with you.'

Perhaps another wife would have asked about his evening, about the altercation that apparently he faintly remembered at Bridge and Stokes, but Victoria could not take the charade that far.

'Come, you look exhausted. Why do you not take a rest?'

He slid his arm around her waist and propelled her with surprising strength into the house. 'I will if you will join me, my lovely wife.'

'That I will.' Could he sense the relief in her voice? Could he tell that the tension had slipped from her as he appeared to accept so easily what had happened?

Victoria wasn't certain whether she should be relieved or disappointed that Phillip was too tired to make love to her, as he'd certainly intended. She curled up next to him and tried to sleep, knowing that something had to change before she went mad.

Her dreams were filled with the images and smells of the scene at Bridge and Stokes, of shredded flesh and pools of blood, vacant eyes and mouths sagging open in shocked and ecstatic screams...of red eyes and gleaming fangs and the whir of a metal blade, slicing and slicing and slicing...

When she awoke it was from a restless movement, and she was looking into the clear blue eyes of her husband. He was not smiling.

'You were there last night. At the club. At my club.'

She was so taken by surprise, Victoria could do nothing but move her mouth, trying to speak, but her lips would not form words.

'You were with your cousin. Is he really your cousin?' He was propped on one elbow, half sitting.

The sheet had fallen from his bare chest and showed the curve of his arm and the dip of his elbow.

'No, I mean, yes, he is my cousin,' she stammered, pulling herself up to sit. Too late, she remembered the scar on her left arm…In their haste the night before, Verbena had dressed her in a gown that had no sleeves. The gash on her arm, though healing quickly, was long and red and impossible not to notice.

Phillip did notice it, and he reached for her arm, pulling her off balance. 'What is this? When did this happen?'

Victoria pulled away hard and broke his grip with little effort. She hadn't taken off her *vis bulla* the night before. 'A few days ago. It was an accident in the stables – I cut myself on one of the farrier's tools.'

'That is a very deep cut,' Phillip replied, his voice neutral. 'When did you say it happened?'

Victoria swallowed. The last time he had seen her nude and with bare arms was when they made love after returning from the theatre – just before she drugged him, only two nights ago. 'I believe it was yesterday morning, after you left to go to your club.'

He looked at her. 'Yesterday? It appears to have healed quite rapidly.'

Her heart was pounding rampantly. 'Yes, I am quite surprised. My aunt gave me some particularly effective salve.'

Phillip threw back the blankets so hard they whipped over her face, falling on her head then slipping down into her lap. He moved off the bed, naked and beautiful, and very, very angry.

He stalked over to look out of the window that spanned the height of the wall from ceiling to floor, crossing his arms in front of him. As he had done before, he spoke to the wall, not to her...though the words were for her.

'Victoria, I want to know why you were at my club last night dressed in men's clothing with that Italian man you claim is your cousin. And I want to know the truth of how you received such a dangerous injury that has healed so quickly.'

She drew in a deep breath. She had wanted something to change. This would be it.

'I was at the club because we – Max and I, and yes, he is my distant cousin – learnt that there was going to be an attack there. I wanted to be certain you were safe.'

'You wanted to be certain I was safe?' He spun from the window, and the yellow sunshine cast a beautiful golden shadow over his skin and hair. Unfortunately she was in no position to appreciate it. 'What kind of nonsense are you speaking, Victoria? What could you do besides put yourself in danger?' He gestured to her arm. 'It appears you already have!'

She was angry at the derision in his voice, and exhausted, and over the top with stress. She should have ended the conversation there, told him nothing else. Let him be angry.

But she didn't.

'I work with Max. It is part of our family legacy.'

'You *work* with Max? Marchionesses don't work.'

'I do.' She swallowed. 'I hunt vampires.'

He stared at her. And stared.

And stared.

And then he said in a terrible voice, 'You are mad.'

'I am not mad, Phillip. It's true.'

'You are mad.'

Her temper snapped. She vaulted off the bed and marched over to him, stopping so close that the hem of her night rail brushed against his bare legs. 'Give me your hands.'

When he reluctantly offered them, she grabbed his wrists and said, 'Try to break my grip.'

He tried, and he couldn't. She forced his arms down to his sides, watching the expression on his face turn from anger to shock to incomprehension.

She released him. 'I am a vampire hunter. It is my family legacy. I have no choice; it is what I must do.'

Phillip stepped away from her, bumping into the window behind him. 'I don't believe in vampires.'

'That is quite foolish of you, as one nearly bit you last night…just before you saw me. Max dispatched him whilst you were talking to me.'

He shook his head. 'Whether they exist or not, you cannot hunt vampires, Victoria. You are a marchioness. You are a pillar of Society. I forbid it. As your husband, I forbid it.'

'Phillip, it is not something you can forbid. It is in my…my blood. It is my destiny.'

'You may believe that. You may think you have no choice, but if you do not leave the house to hunt vampires, you are making the choice not to follow your destiny.'

'And I should just ignore it when I learn that there are to be vampire attacks…at places such as Bridge and Stokes? Let people die? You escaped, Phillip, because Max told you a lie to get you to leave. But you did not see the carnage that was left behind…of some of your friends. It was beyond horrible.'

'I forbid it, Victoria.'

'I'll not stand by and let people die that way.'

He pushed away from the window and stalked past her into his dressing room, bellowing for his valet. 'Franks!' Phillip paused at the door that adjoined the two rooms, holding the edge and looking down at the floor. 'You should have confessed this before we were married, Victoria. It is unforgivable that you did not.'

And he shut the door. Softly. But ever so loudly.

'They have been home from their wedding trip only two days, Nilly,' said Melly complaisantly, 'but I am sure I can prevail upon the *ton*'s newest fashionable couple to attend your niece's ball.'

'That would be divine!' gushed Petronilla, eyeing the platter of orange-cinnamon finger cakes. They smelt delicious, but it was that odd carroty hue that put her off. Perhaps she would have a talk with Freda about toning down the colour. At least the lime biscuits weren't the nasty green shade they had been the last time Freda had made them. Now they looked rather appetising, even with the thin veneer of white icing.

'Where is Winnie? I thought she wanted to hear all of the details of the wedding trip,' Melly complained. She had none of her friend's hesitation; she snatched up two of the cakes and began to nibble on a third.

'I am here!' As if on cue, the parlour door opened and in sailed the Duchess of Farnham. She jingled and clunked.

'What on earth is that?' asked Melly, staring in askance at the large crucifix that hung from her waist like a chatelaine's ring of keys would have done in medieval times. Only the crucifix was much larger than any ring of keys. 'And *that*?'

'It's her stake, of course,' Petronilla explained as if Melly had lost her mind…when, in fact, it appeared to Lady Grantworth that it was her two dearest friends who had done so. 'Winnie, I do hope you haven't any thought of using such a thing! That would be so cruel!'

Winifred plopped down in her favourite seat in Petronilla's parlour, somehow managing to slide four finger cakes and three lime biscuits onto a plate and pour herself a cup of tea in the process. 'I am not foolish enough to be prancing about without protection, and you two ladies would be wise to do the same!'

'No, no, no, *no!*…Winnie, do not tell me you are still afraid that a vampire is going to jump out of the shadows at you some night!' Melly stuffed the rest of the orange finger cake into her mouth and swallowed a gulp of tea, shaking her head and rolling her eyes.

'I should say so!' Winifred poured a generous amount of cream into her tea, disdaining the sugar, and stirred with gentle, elegant strokes to disperse it. 'You did hear about the incident at that gentleman's club last night, Bridge and Stokes, did you not? When I heard about that, I went right out to one of the footmen and demanded that he take one of the duke's old walking sticks and make it into a stake for me. I'm going nowhere without it!'

'Incident at Bridge and Stokes?' echoed Petronilla, her pale blue eyes wide with interest. 'Whatever are you talking about? Were there vampires there? Did anyone get bitten?' There was a breathy note to her voice at this last.

'Those were not vampires, Winnie!' Melly shook her head and smoothed her skirts. 'I know the incident you are talking about – and it was not vampires. How many times must I tell you that they simply don't exist? They are the product of Polidori's imagination, fuelled by legend and ghost tales.'

'What happened at Bridge and Stokes?' asked Petronilla again.

'How can you not have heard about it? It has been roaring through the servant gossip mill faster than a fire in a dry field!' Melly replied archly.

'I have been indisposed all morning,' Petronilla replied delicately.

Melly snorted, but Winnie deigned, at last, to explain. 'Five men were found dead after some passers-by reported to the Runners that there had been a loud altercation there early this morning. No gunshots were reported, and from what I have heard, the bodies were found quite destroyed, torn up, even. Very messy.' She reached for another biscuit, thought better of it, and set it back on her plate. Apparently there were some things that affected her appetite.

'Lord Jellington, my cousin, called on me first thing this morning,' Melly interceded. 'Because the marquess belongs to the club in question, and had, in fact, been there last night. But apparently he left before the incident occurred, and Jellington wished to assure me that he was not involved.'

'Knowing Jellington, I am quite sure that was not all he wished to accomplish by calling on his attractive third cousin,' Petronilla commented slyly.

'Oh, do go on! Jellington has never looked twice… well, perhaps twice, but definitely not thrice…at me in that fashion,' Melly replied, burying her face in a cup of tea.

'It was vampires that did it.' Winnie steered the

conversation back on track. 'That's why there were no gunshots! They don't need guns to get what they want.'

Melly was shaking her head. 'No, Jellington says it was likely one or two people with knives who attacked the members of the club. Perhaps in some sort of vigilante manner; for all of the ones found dead – except one, who may have been an accidental casualty – were quite in debt and owed much money to some of those nasty moneylenders they speak of from St Giles. The Runners believe it was an attempt to collect funds due them, or to make an example of those men for not paying back their debts.' She sniffed and set down her teacup.

It was Winnie's turn to snort. 'That is what the Runners are saying. But I don't believe them. They don't want there to be a mass panic from everyone in London believing that there are vampires running about.'

'If there are vampires causing all of this,' Melly returned, 'why has no one reported seeing one?'

'They are very careful…they sneak about in the dead of night,' Winnie replied. 'Make certain your bedroom windows are closed and bolted.'

'I shall ensure that mine are locked up tightly,' Petronilla replied a bit too earnestly. 'They do sneak around in the dead of night, don't they? But I heard they can change into mist or fog and slip through the crack of your window…and then turn themselves back into men. Right in your bedroom! Oh, dear, and Mr Fenworth sleeps in his own chamber across the hall! I will be quite alone and unprotected!' Her voice was pitched loud, as though to make certain any vampires lurking about might hear.

'If they sneak around in the dead of night, then that is most definitely an indication that vampires – if they do exist – weren't responsible for the attack at Bridge and Stokes.' Melly leant forward to drop a small lump of sugar in her tea.

'And what about that incident at Vauxhall Gardens the night before last?' Winnie commented. 'Did Jellington tell you anything about that?'

'No.'

'There was some sort of altercation there, but no one was hurt or injured.'

Melly raised her eyebrows. 'No one was hurt, injured, or – heaven forbid! – bitten…and you ascribe the incident – whatever it was – to nonexistent vampires? Winnie, my dear, you really are taking those gothic novels too seriously. Everything violent or unexpected that happens in this city cannot be attributed to creatures like vampires. There is enough evil perpetrated by man that we don't need to invent paranormal beings to blame it on.

'Now, let us dispense with this nonsense and talk about something much more interesting…such as how soon we might have a little marquess on our hands!'

* * *

His wife was mad. She had to be mad, for the alternative was terrifying.

For the first time he could remember, Phillip de Lacy, Marquess of Rockley, did not know what to do.

He left St Heath's Row and drove his curricle into town. He stopped at White's, another of the clubs he frequented, and sat at a table by himself. He had several glasses of whiskey, a large hunk of beef that tasted like sawdust, and a slab of bread that could have carried weevils for all he noticed.

After White's, he felt restless and left to visit another gentleman's club, although he did not wish to be sociable at all. At Bertrand's he avoided his friends and sat in an empty room, ignoring the buzz about the unfortunates who had perished at Bridge and Stokes last night.

Perhaps that was the reason he did not wish to talk with anyone.

He did not want to know whether Victoria was right or wrong. He did not want to have to think about what it meant if she was right…or if she was wrong.

When Phillip had not returned to St Heath's Row the next morning, Victoria could stand it no longer. She called for the carriage to come around and took herself off to Aunt Eustacia's home.

Her aunt took one look at her and understood. 'He knows.'

Victoria sank into a chair, angry that her hands were trembling and that tears threatened her eyes. She nodded. 'He's forbidden me to continue to hunt.'

Eustacia waited. She knew the power of silence. The sound of the clock ticking marked the minutes, paring away at the hope she'd placed in Victoria.

'I told him I could not stand by and let people die.'

Eustacia nodded. That was good.

'He became angry and left. He hasn't been home since we quarrelled yesterday morning.'

'He saw you at his club?' Max had told Eustacia about the attack at Bridge and Stokes while she was tending to his wounds. It had been his attempt to keep her from lecturing him about taking better care of his injuries; she saw through it, and let him think he'd had his way. Then after he was finished, she chastised him roundly. Even Venators had to care for their wounds, she reminded him.

'Yes, he recognised me. I told him the truth; I couldn't hide it any longer, Aunt. I couldn't live the lie, keep feeding him *salvi*.'

'Of course you couldn't, *cara*. It is not in your nature to be deceitful. I realised it was a possibility that you would have to tell him at some time. I did not expect it to be so soon, and in the midst of this very precarious time—'

'What do you mean?'

'You and Max have had to stop two raids in the

last three nights; perhaps there was even one last night that we weren't aware of. Lilith is gathering her forces. She is ready to make her move against you in retaliation for your besting her. She wants the book back, and she's put some plan in place to get it.' She rubbed the knuckles on her left hand, where the sharp sting of arthritis jolted her.

'Max is in no condition to be out, but he has been at the Silver Chalice since yesterday, trying to learn what is going on.' He'd suspected that Rockley would have recognised Victoria and that they would have had a confrontation, so he'd refused to let Eustacia get Victoria involved, insisting he'd handle it alone while she tended her home fires, as he put it so cynically.

'I knew he was badly injured, but he would not let me tend to them.'

'I know. He confessed it to me.' Eustacia sighed. She had other suspicions about Max's motivations, but now was not the time to air them. Instead she said, 'He doesn't like to be coddled.'

'Aunt Eustacia, did I do the wrong thing in telling Phillip?'

'I don't know how you could have done otherwise; but I do believe there will be consequences. They may be as simple as the marquess trying to prevent you from leaving when we need you; or they may be more severe. You must impress upon him that this is not something he can be involved in, as much as he might want to protect you. He cannot. You must make it clear to him; or send him to me, and I will do it.'

Victoria nodded. She would do that – if he ever came back to St Heath's Row.

'Now, *cara*, you must go home and get some rest. Your husband loves you; he will return in his own time, when he has come to terms with your confession. And we need you. Max cannot do this alone.'

Victoria nodded…but for the first time she truly regretted her decision to accept the Legacy. She wished she had turned it down and had her mind cleared.

She wished for ignorance. And a normal life.

Chapter Twenty-Four

In Which Three Gentlemen Meet Up

Late in the second day after Victoria had told him her fantastical story, Phillip realised what he needed to do.

Certainly, he'd already visited Bridge and Stokes, and found it closed, 'due to death'. And there definitely had been rumblings about the attacks that had happened there; but no one had mentioned vampires.

He'd even gone so far as to drive his curricle to Victoria's cousin Maximilian's home, planning to confront him as he had done before…but the man was not home, and the dark-skinned butler was unable to tell Phillip when his master would return within a day.

One thing he knew he could not do, yet, was to face Victoria. So he did not return to St Heath's Row.

Instead he hired a hackney to take him to St Giles. To the place he'd followed Victoria, to the establishment called the Silver Chalice.

There he would find the answer.

Oh, he wasn't foolish. Numb, perhaps, dull and mind-fractured with grief and pain...but not foolish. He prepared: he wore a crucifix under his coat. He stuffed full bulbs of garlic in his pockets. He even found something that could be used as a wooden stake – a broken walking stick in the cloakroom at White's.

Phillip didn't believe in vampires, and though he hadn't wasted his time reading that ridiculous novel by Polidori, he knew what lore said about protecting oneself from the undead.

But he also pocketed a gun.

When Max walked into the Silver Chalice for the third night in a row, he knew something bad was going to happen.

It was about time; he'd been waiting for it all to explode for three days. Ever since that first raid at Vauxhall, followed by the one at Bridge and Stokes, he'd known this was leading up to something.

Lilith's patience had worn thin.

What he didn't expect – couldn't have fathomed finding – was the Marquess of Rockley sitting companion-ably at a table with Sebastian Vioget.

Before he had a chance to wonder about it, Vioget

looked up and saw him standing at the entrance. The faintest flare of a smile tipped his mouth, and he nodded to Max.

Max started toward them. No matter how cunning Lilith was, this could not be part of her plan.

'Good evening, Rockley,' Max said as he approached the table.

'Pesaro. Why am I not surprised to see you here.' True to his words, there was no inflection in his voice.

'Perhaps, but it is I who am at a disadvantage. I would have believed that after your last visit, you would have actually learnt something. Namely that there are places where you are not welcome…and not safe.'

'Vioget here has assured me that that is not the case, that I have nothing to fear while I am in his establishment. Victoria has told me everything.'

'Indeed? But you did not believe her, so you came here to find out for yourself. Foolish man. If I had not arrived, you would be at the mercy of this man's whim.' So she had told him. Max's eyes slitted as they scored over the marquess: his sleepy eyes, perfect hair, tailored and pressed clothing. The man had walked into this den of the undead, disbelieving, and wholly unprepared to face the results of his actions.

He was as good as dead unless Max intervened. Again.

'If you had not arrived, we would have continued

our conversation most pleasantly,' Vioget returned coolly. 'Now, if you please, Maximilian—'

But before he could finish, a bad sound behind Max grabbed the attention of both of them. He whirled as Sebastian bolted to his feet.

Imperials. Five of them – more than Max had ever seen together at one time – standing at the bottom of the stairs, swords drawn, red-violet eyes glowing. Only one of them smiled, and his fangs gleamed.

Max heard Rockley's intake of breath. Too late, poor bastard.

The room had quieted, and the tension pulsed like a dying heartbeat.

'Good evening and welcome to the Silver Chalice.' Max had to give Vioget credit; his voice was as smooth and unruffled as if he'd been greeting a lady for tea. But Max knew that five Imperials were not here for tea, or for libation of any kind. Even the fresh sort.

Lilith had sent them.

The leader of the Imperials took three steps. The undead at the tables near him shrank away. Imperials, when angered, had been known to cannibalise their own.

'Sebastian Vioget, we have been sent to escort you to the presence of our mistress.'

'Please give her my apologies, but as you can see, I am otherwise engaged this evening.'

Max noticed that Vioget had shifted himself back toward the brick wall behind Rockley. Under the guise of adjusting his coat, Max moved to the left of Rockley, placing him between Sebastian and himself and only a few inches from the hidden doorway. Max wasn't about to let Vioget get through there without the two of them.

Not for the first time, he wondered how he had been saddled with babysitting a marquess…yet again.

'You are amusing, Vioget. Now, you can make this simple…or you can make it difficult.' The way the Imperial leader caressed his lower lip with his left fang indicated that he much preferred difficulties.

Max touched Rockley and felt the rigidity of his shoulder. 'Be ready,' he said softly, without moving his lips. 'Behind you.'

But they never had a chance.

Suddenly the room was a flurry of movement – a table went flying, swords flashed, chairs splintered; there were shouts, screams, and the thuds of flesh on flesh.

Max grabbed Rockley and threw him under the table, then followed. Forget the hidden door; they would try to slink out by edging along the walls.

Phillip, who had found himself unable to move, suddenly knew his only chance to escape was to follow Victoria's cousin on the floor under the tables. He let go of the gun in his pocket, realising, at last, what Pesaro and Victoria had been trying to tell him. Too late.

It hadn't been enough – the hypnotic tug and pull of the eyes of the customers in the inn, the way they seemed to bore into him and soften him…no, it wasn't until those five men, with burning eyes and lethal weapons, had exploded into the place that he realised that he was going to die.

He was going to die with accusations and anger toward his wife hanging between them.

Knowing instinctively that the crucifix in his pocket would be little protection against the five creatures, Phillip scrambled across the floor after Max, pinning his only hope of survival on the man who seemed to know what to do. Shards of glass and splinters of wood cut into his fine breeches, sliced into his hands. Something dark and sticky spilt onto his head and shoulders from the tables above. Rust's stench filled his nose. There was a loud crash behind them, and he smelt the spill of lantern oil and, closely thereafter, the clogging scent of raging fire.

He and Pesaro miraculously reached the curve of wall that ended at the bottom of the stairs to this place he would forever think of as hell. Shouts and the sounds of fighting followed them as they inched along the wall under the cover of a sudden thick smoke, and Phillip wanted to shout in triumph when they touched the bottom stair.

Stumbling up the steps, Phillip saw his guide look back, pausing on the stairs. He pushed past Max, onward, recognising that there was no hope of helping Vioget. Or anyone else in the way of those five monsters.

But when he reached the top – freedom – he found himself facing two more of the creatures. Their eyes were red, and they did not carry swords. One was a woman. But, as unfamiliar with these demons as he was, Phillip recognised that they were vampires by the way he slogged into futile motions when he was caught by her gaze.

'How lovely,' she said in a throaty voice. 'Just what I needed. And I thought I would miss all the fun, being stationed up here.'

He couldn't fight it; her eyes trapped him. He was picked up and carried effortlessly away…away somewhere. He struggled; he couldn't break free…she held him close, and he felt her heart beating in him, through him, as if wrapped in some kind of tendril that tightened with each struggle.

She shoved him somewhere; he fell onto something upholstered and struggled to get away. He was in a carriage; he could see out the door; they had Pesaro. They were dragging him toward the carriage, but she pulled him back, away from the opening.

'Now, my lovely,' she said, and he looked into her eyes. He couldn't help it. They compelled him like nothing ever had. He was vaguely aware of a heavy burden tossed in next to him, for it broke the connection for the barest of moments.

'My lovely,' she said again, and her strong fingers filtered through his hair like a lover's. Like Victoria's. Then she tightened them, pulled his head back hard, and he cried out at the shock. She bent to him; her lips were warm and cool at the same time. They touched the curve of his neck, the soft part now open and bare.

He struggled, but she pulled away and looked at him, settling him with her eyes. 'It won't hurt, my lovely...my lovely.' She licked his face, closed her mouth over his, and thrust her tongue into it. Choking him...yet pleasing him. When she pulled away, he tasted blood...and she was licking her lips. He wanted to lick them too.

Someone was struggling next to him in the carriage. It jolted him, and the female vampire hissed, 'Subdue the Venator. But control yourself. The mistress will have your heart if you feed on him.'

Then she returned to Phillip, smiling, calling him with her eyes. 'And what is your name, my lovely? You are too pretty to remain nameless. Perhaps I will keep you.'

He wanted to answer; he didn't want to answer... He had no choice. Her red eyes, circled with black, pinpointed with black too, compelled him to respond. 'Phillip...' he managed. 'Rockley...'

Her eyes widened in shock; her control slipped. Sharp nails dug into his scalp and into the upper arm she held. 'You are Rockley? Married to Victoria?'

Faintly, above the rushing in his ears, he heard a desperate '*No!*' but Pesaro's groan could not stop him from responding, 'Yes.'

The woman vampire smiled, looking at him. Her fangs were long and pretty. He wanted them on him, in him. His cock throbbed in anticipation. He drew in a deep breath when she bent to his flesh. She teased him for a moment, her lips, her tongue, her fangs nicking, nibbling. 'That changes things,' she murmured, and sank her fangs into his ear.

He groaned as pleasure and pain stormed through him...like nothing he'd felt before. Warm liquid dripped on his neck; he could smell it – smell it on her breath when she came back to his mouth. He wanted to breathe it too.

'I won't have to kill you now.' She drew in a long breath and exhaled, slowly, delicately...breathing warm into his flesh and blood as she sank her teeth into his shoulder.

Chapter Twenty-Five

The Marquess, the Venator, and the Innkeeper Go Missing

Victoria had just returned to St Heath's Row after a dinner party at Grantworth House when the message arrived.

She'd been hard-pressed to explain to her mother why her new husband hadn't attended with her; and it was even more difficult to extricate herself from the after-dinner socialising…but she had pleaded exhaustion. Apparently the blue-black circles under her eyes were enough to convince her mother that she was unfit for a late night. And if Lady Melly believed the reason was due to an impending happy event, well, Victoria was too heartsick to fight with her on it.

Thus, she had just begun to unpin her hair when the messenger arrived to deliver a note.

She didn't recognise the handwriting, but the seal

was gold and bore the imprint of a bold V surrounded by trellises and cups. It could be from only one person... she tore it open.

I am in possession of something of apparent value to you, although your actions in my coach led me to believe otherwise. He will be safe until you arrive. You have my word.

S.

His word?

She threw the note on her dresser and called for Verbena to help her change. A visit to the Silver Chalice required some preparation.

But when Victoria arrived at the Chalice, or what had been the Chalice, it became clear that no preparation could have readied her for the scene that faced her.

It was three o'clock in the morning, and where the bar should have been overflowing with customers coming and going on the steps, it was silent. The acrid smell of burnt wood, spilt blood, and fear assailed her as she hurried down the steps.

The place was in shambles. Tables, cups, chairs, bottles...even bodies, the piano...everything was strewn all over the floor. Half of it was burnt; the place stank of ash and oil.

Victoria walked into the room, hoping to find something...anything to tell her what had happened.

Max was supposed to be here, she remembered suddenly.

Had he been caught in this? Was he dead?

And Phillip? Sebastian had promised to keep him safe.

Cold settled over her, a deep, penetrating, final iciness.

Max. Phillip. Sebastian.

They had all been there.

Max opened his eyes.

The room was hot and shadowed, the only illumination from flames licking one long wall. At first he thought he was in hell…but then he realised he wasn't so lucky.

'Maximilian.' He tried to block her voice…but he was too weary. His strength sapped away, he had little resistance. Especially to her.

'Look at me, Maximilian,' she crooned, her words bumping over him like a gentle hand.

He closed his eyes.

'Why do you turn away? You know you cannot deny yourself.'

He pulled himself up from his sprawled position on the floor. His hands were not restrained, but she would have no need to do that. He was powerless in many ways in her presence.

'It has been so long since you have come to me, Maximilian.'

The way she said his name made him feel as though a thousand centipedes scuttled over his skin…yet…it lingered on the air, his name from her lips. A chain that bound them together.

'I did not come to you, Lilith.' It took all he had to make those words easy, smooth. To say her name to her face.

Her laugh, low like barely a breath, curled around him. 'You always did need a bit of persuasion. Come here, Maximilian. Come to me.'

He stood, then forced his limbs to do his bidding and not hers…and leant against the wall, settling one of his hands over his left nipple, touching his *vis bulla*. Thank God even she could not touch that.

A wave of strength flowed through him and he concentrated on it, pulled the force from the holy silver he wore.

And he turned, then, against the wall to look at her.

She lounged on a long white chaise. Her eyes – he could meet them for only a moment – were almond-shaped, beautifully lashed, deep-set…and blue ringed with red.

'Ah, you are more yourself now, aren't you, Maximilian? I much prefer you in your alpha state than that mass of weakness my servants dumped here last night.'

'Last night?'

She nodded once, regally.

'Is Rockley dead?'

'Rockley? Oh, no…no, my dear, I have other uses for him.'

Max closed his eyes. If the man had kept his mouth shut, and never told the vampire his name, he would be dead. And safe.

The connection to Victoria wouldn't have been made.

'Now, Max, my dear, it has been too long. You must come to me.' The liquid summons in her voice pulled at him. His hands and feet began to tremble with the effort of keeping them motionless, under his control.

Sweat gathered at his frozen nape, dripped down beneath his shirt. The scars on his neck burnt and throbbed, responding to her call.

Still he resisted. He rolled along the wall, away from her.

He felt her move; his eyes were closed in concentration, but he felt her come toward him. He steeled himself, felt the wall under his hands and cheek, and tried to grip it. It was too smooth.

Tall as a man, she breathed on him from behind. Her presence cloaked him, smothering and stifling… and she was not yet touching him. One of her hands reached up – he felt the air move – and she touched his hair, smoothed it, stroked it, while she drew in her breath in a long, languorous caress…and exhaled.

She tipped his head to the side gently. He let her.

She stepped closer and now he felt her breasts and the curve of her mound pressing into his spine and his rear. He moved his hand between himself and the wall, touching the *vis bulla*, and breathed.

His neck was open to her; she was tall, tall enough to press her lips, one cold, one hot, to the skin there. He shuddered when she touched him. Closed his eyes. Waited.

She toyed with him. Laughed against his skin, breathed on its moisture, scraped him with one sharp incisor. Her heartbeat became one with his. She melted into him from behind. His shirt was wet everywhere; he could hear nothing but her pulse.

When she ran her long, sharp nails from his shoulder to the base of his back, he felt his shirt give under them. It fell away under her hands, and when she pressed up behind him again, touching his bare back, he wanted to let go. Stop fighting.

The smell of his blood from her scoring nails filled his nostrils…she closed her lips over the edge of his shoulder, where the cuts had begun, and where they were the deepest, and he felt her tongue slip through the wetness.

She sighed, and her lips curved with pleasure against him. 'Maximilian…you taste like no one else.'

He marshalled his strength. 'I do not consider that a compliment.'

Laughing in delight, she sucked hard at his shoulder. 'Taste.' She pulled his head back at an impossible angle, and covered his mouth with her blooded lips.

He tasted it, the heavy iron flavour, her cold, slick tongue. He took her kiss and wanted more. Damn it. He wanted *more*.

Her hands slipped around under his arms, over his belly. They curled up over the centre of his chest, raising the hair that grew there. He arched back, lifting his chest, tipping his head back at the command of her hands. They slipped apart, to the sides and over his nipples, and she jerked, startled, and removed them. Laughing.

'That is another thing about you, Maximilian… you are the only one to give me pleasure and pain, rolled into one.' And then she pulled away, stepped back; he felt the coolness of her absence on his bare skin.

He breathed deeply, resting his forehead against the wall. When she brushed his *vis bulla*, her pain had given him a needed jolt of strength. It had been like that every time before…she craved that combination of pleasure and the unexpected zaps of pain when she came near the holy silver cross. She liked the power it gave him, too, the added strength that allowed him to fight her when he touched it.

Because she knew she would always win.

Max became aware that she was speaking to someone, and he turned, focusing, in time to see Lilith's gleaming white smile. 'I'm afraid you will have to wait a bit longer, dear Maximilian. My guest has arrived, and they are showing her in.'

Max turned from the wall, the fog and rapture sliding away. Things had gone from worse to unimaginable. The guest could only be Victoria.

Chapter Twenty-Six

The Marchioness Is Received

Victoria shifted the heavy satchel over one shoulder, holding its heavy bulk against her hip as she followed the two Imperials into a large room. She had to blink to allow her eyes to adjust to the dark room after being in the morning sunshine.

The Imperials, swathed in black from head to toe, had led her from the meeting place Lilith had specified into the cavernous room of a ruined estate ten miles outside of London. Kritanu and Briyani, who had accompanied her, had been ordered to remain with the carriage — an order, Victoria knew, they would ignore as soon as the vampires had taken her within.

The windows were painted black and covered with boards to keep the dangerous sun from filtering in. Inside, the cool, damp air and low light made her skin feel clammy, but when they rounded the corner into what appeared to be a receiving room, there were blazing fires in large fireplaces at every corner.

Sunlight burnt the undead; fire did not. A vampire could walk through a blaze and be unscathed.

At one end of the chamber was a low dais that made her think of a throne room, or a great hall in a medieval castle. In fact, this room, with tall windows boarded over and a ceiling that stretched into a large black-painted dome likely was the hall at one time. Vampires of all types were in the room, perhaps two dozen of them all told: regular undead, Guardians, and several Imperials. To the side of the dais was a large shallow dish that held a tall, roaring blaze, giving heat and illumination to the woman who sat on a massive chair in the centre of the dais.

Lilith, of course.

Victoria looked at the vampire queen, meeting her blue-red eyes for only a brief moment, as Aunt Eustacia had warned, and then letting her attention skitter over the rest of her figure, which was slender, almost emaciated. Her skin was the blue-white hue Victoria had expected...but her hair, long and rippling down either side of her shoulders and over her breasts, was brilliant copper. It burnt the eye, it was so bright.

She must have been older than Victoria when she was turned undead; her immortal age was near thirty. She was not beautiful, but horribly elegant. The lids of her eyes were so thin and cold they were purple; her cheekbones jutted out, forming the same coloured hollows below.

Her lips curved in a welcome smile, the grey-blue of them plump and sensual. Her hands, gathered in her lap, boasted long, pointed nails. And she had five dark marks that, even from her distance, Victoria could see formed the span of a half-moon from the top of her cheekbone to the side of her chin.

Lilith the Dark was not so much dark as she was burning and frigid at the same time – ethereal, with her fair skin and narrow wrists, sinewy neck, and long, elegantly crossed legs.

'Victoria Gardella. How pleased I am that you have joined us.'

'Where is my husband?' Her voice came out strong and bold.

'Where are your manners, Marchioness?'

'I am here to make an exchange, not to have tea.'

'Well, then let us get on with it. You have interrupted my pleasure.'

Victoria followed Lilith's gesture and stopped breathing. Max. That was Max.

He stood to one side of the dais, having been in the shadows until Lilith's gesture caused someone from behind to jab him forward. His shirt hung in shreds about his waist; his arms hung at his sides. Blood streaked his shoulders, and his bare torso was covered with dark hair, slashing scars, and sweat. Her attention focused on the glint of silver that pierced one flat nipple. As she gaped, he raised his face and looked at her. His eyes were flat and chill.

Rattled and suddenly terrified, Victoria turned her attention away and back onto Lilith, who had been watching with interest. 'Two Venators as guests at one time. I have never been so fortunate.'

'Now, where is my husband?'

Then she heard him. 'Victoria!'

She spun and saw that he was being brought in the room, chained – as if poor Phillip could do any damage to the creatures in this room! – but alive. And walking on his own.

Victoria turned back to Lilith. 'He does not need to be chained. Let him loose and we will discuss our exchange.'

'Discuss? There is nothing to discuss. If you wish to have your husband back, you will provide me with the Book of Antwartha.'

Victoria smiled at her. Wayren had been at Aunt Eustacia's when the message came from Lilith. 'I will provide you with the book when you have met my requirements. The protection has changed, and the book must be given to you freely, or it will do you no good. You cannot take it from me or it will crumple into ash.'

Lilith returned the smile, and Victoria did not like the expression in her eyes that accompanied it. 'Ah, a formidable negotiator, and one who plans well. I would have expected nothing less from Eustacia's blood.' She whipped her hand and the Guardian holding Phillip dropped the chains from his wrists. 'Of course, that assumes that you really have changed the protection and aren't merely bluffing.'

'Is Sebastian Vioget here as well?'

Lilith raised her copper-orange brows. 'He is not. I sent for him, but he did not see fit to accept my invitation.' Her eyes narrowed. 'I suspected he was the reason you were able to come by the Book of Antwartha so easily.'

Victoria didn't think the events of that evening could be called easy, but she said nothing.

'He told you how to get the book, did he not?'

'Do you think I would be foolish enough to believe a man like Sebastian Vioget?'

Lilith leant back in her chair, laughing in delight. It was like smoke – delicate, penetrating, and stifling. 'Ah, I have missed matching wits with a woman. Your aunt was a formidable opponent during her time as well. As for him' – she glanced at Max – 'he is a man, and has certain weaknesses that are a pleasure to exploit.'

Her attention returned to Victoria contemplatively.

Victoria's hair rose along her arms, and she knew she must keep control of the conversation. Now she would have to get both Max and Phillip to safety. 'I have the book here, Lilith, but my terms are different from the ones you offered in your message.'

'Indeed. Why does that not surprise me.' Lilith made a slight movement, and Max moved forward as if he had lost his will. She closed her fingers around his wrist, barely fitting them there, and manipulated him so that he knelt in front of her, on the far side of the fire. 'Let me guess. You want to guarantee the Venator's safety as well.'

Victoria nodded.

Then Lilith's eyes changed. Not colour…no, they stayed sapphire blue, encircled with a thick red ring… but something else in their depths moved. Victoria could not look away. She was trapped, felt soft and foggy. The floor slogged beneath her. The air billowed, pushing in on her.

'What is it that you really want, Victoria Gardella?' Lilith's voice came from far away, yet it was in her ear, for her alone. Her mouth didn't move. Her eyes did not blink. 'Your husband?'

Phillip moved next to her, a puppet responding to her cue, and Victoria touched his arm. He was cold, chilled; she wanted to pull him to her and keep him safe. They bumped against each other, and through the fog Lilith had wisped around her, Victoria felt a heavy weight in his pocket.

Victoria raised her hand and pressed her eyelids closed, breaking the connection with Lilith. A tremor passed through her as Lilith struggled, then surrendered. Momentarily. Victoria must not look at her again…but it was impossible when those eyes seemed to be able to catch her gaze at will.

'Why do you want the book so badly?' Victoria asked, slipping her hand into Phillip's pocket and closing her fingers around the pistol. Foolish of the vampires not to have relieved him of it, even if it was harmless to them.

'There are many secrets within,' Lilith told her conversationally. She stroked Max's dark hair, clutching a handful and pulling so that he rose to his knees. 'I am particularly interested in the spell that will enable me to raise an army of demons on the night of any full moon. And then there is the decoction that I can drink and give to my servants so that a Venator cannot detect our presence. That would be most helpful, I am sure you realise.'

Without warning, she yanked Max's head aside and sank her teeth into his skin.

Victoria watched in horror as she drank from the distended veins, her needle teeth sliding in like a knife through butter. Max closed his eyes; she could see him struggle to breathe, watched his chest rise and fall, the silver *vis bulla* trembling with his efforts. His hands closed in on each other; his throat convulsed.

Next to her Phillip stirred, his breathing deepening, becoming ragged as his eyes fixed on the scene. Victoria tore away to look at him, saw the feral gleam in his gaze and the unconscious gaping of his jaw…and she knew. Horror sank into her even before she saw the gleam of his fangs…the glint of red in his eyes.

'No!' she screamed.

Lilith released Max and he sagged to the floor. She smiled, her white teeth gleaming. She'd fed elegantly; not a drop of red anywhere.

Phillip had fallen to his knees, panting, next to Victoria.

His eyes were wild, tinted red, for he was still newly undead, and need burnt off him. Victoria could smell it, and it sickened her. Her stomach heaved; her head spun.

She clutched the satchel and forced her fingers to still from their trembling.

'You do not like my little surprise? I am sorry that I did not allow him to finish feeding before you arrived. I only allowed him to sample me in order to take the edge off his appetite. He will still enjoy you when I give him the word.' She gestured at Phillip. 'Rise! You will have what you need when the time is right.'

Phillip obeyed and stood next to Victoria, and she realised what Lilith intended when he smoothed a hand possessively down her arm. Her stomach pitched.

'Now we will negotiate, my dear. Although I don't know that there is much room for that; as you can see, I hold all of the cards.'

'I still have the book.' Although what good it did her, Victoria did not know. *Phillip*. What had she done to him? By marrying him, by giving in to her selfish needs…she'd brought him here.

Grief numbed her. He was gone, and she could not get him back. He was damned. Evil. Immortal.

'Yes, but the book is worth more to you if you give it to me than if you keep it.'

Victoria struggled to turn her attention from the shock and horror of her husband's condition and focused on Lilith. 'What do you mean?'

'With the book I can give you what you want, Victoria.' Lilith's eyelids sank lower, and she pierced Victoria with her intent. Red glowed, beaming from her blue irises. 'I can give you back your husband. Whole. Pure. Mortal, for he has not yet fed on a mortal being.'

'How?'

Lilith rose for the first time, and stepped down one step. Her slender hands clasped in earnest at her middle, the long, fitted gown she wore trailed down the steps after her. 'It is in the book.'

'Why should I believe you?' Victoria's mind worked frantically. She could save Phillip! It was worth it to save a life, to give Lilith the book.

'Because you have no choice. And why would I lie? I have the advantage. I don't need to do anything for you.'

'Why would you?'

That was when Lilith stepped right up to her. Victoria kept her eyes focused over the vampire queen's shoulder, but the woman's proximity sent her pulse speeding, snagged her breath and made it her own. She could feel Phillip next to her, struggling to control himself. 'Because, my dear, I can give you something else that will also benefit me.'

She smelt like roses. Fresh, dewy, beautiful roses. This icon of evil, of rapaciousness, smelt like a summer flower. The epitome of feminity. She smelt like Victoria's mother.

Victoria wanted to gag. She replied instead, 'I beg you, don't keep me in suspense.'

'I can release you from your vow. I can make you a person, not a Venator. I can set you free. You and your husband.'

Her heart hammered. Her hands slickened. Victoria closed her eyes; Lilith continued to speak. 'Your aunt didn't tell you there was a way out, did she?'

Victoria shook her head.

'There is always a way out…well, nearly always.' Lilith laughed. The sound filled Victoria's ears, echoed inside her brain. 'Some of us are bound forever…but not you, Victoria. Not your marquess. You can be free, have a normal life. Is that not what you wish?'

'Ah, yes, I'll give up my powers so you can kill me. That's quite a deal.' It was a struggle to form the words, but they sounded cool – at least to Victoria's ears.

She waited to be convinced…she waited to hear Lilith's line of reasoning, praying that it would give her the freedom to make the choice.

'Oh, no, didn't I mention? Along with the release from your vow, there is also an incantation that provides you and your lover with infinite protection from the undead. You will be free to live as you wish…have a child, even…and be protected from all vampires. If you give me the book.'

Victoria drew in a deep breath. Everything she wanted. For the price of an old book.

A book that had spells in it that could help Lilith gain power. She would be able to raise demons. She would be able to mask herself from Venators.

Victoria swallowed. The book hung heavy in the bag at her side, along with her conscience. Her heart was numb.

Phillip stood, panting, next to her. Victoria looked at him, and he faced her as if drawn by some invisible thread. The red had faded from his eyes, and his fangs retracted. He looked like the man she loved. The one she'd stood up at the altar with, promised her love and fidelity to.

The one she'd pledged to be bound to for the rest of their lives.

You should have confessed this before we were married, Victoria. It is unforgivable that you did not.

His last words to her hung in her memory, harsh and brutally true.

She had wronged him beyond anything he could have imagined, damning him to hell once his immortal life was ended by someone like her…or to hell on earth as an evil creature living off the blood of helpless victims.

She loved him, and she'd brought him to this.

She could save him…and she could also get what she wanted: freedom from this life. A clear conscience. A mind ignorant of these evils. The same blissful ignorance her mother now had.

And protection from them.

Isolation from the knowledge and reality of the undead.

Victoria's heart beat faster. Her hands moved, digging into the satchel. The leather cover of the book felt rough, the binding split. The pages crackled when she moved them.

'Give me the book.' Lilith stood close, but she didn't dare touch it until Victoria gave it to her. Freely.

Victoria could feel her anxiety, her lust for the set of bound pages.

What was she trading? Her life, Phillip's life…for a book.

A book that contained…perhaps…great powers. And perhaps not.

'Stand back,' Victoria said to Lilith. Her decision was made. 'I will make the trade.'

Chapter Twenty-Seven

A Most Fortuitous Length of Rope

When Lilith stepped away from him, focusing all of her power and attention on Victoria, Max was finally able to set the rhythm of his own breath. His neck throbbed and burnt, but he knew from experience that it could have been worse.

Much worse.

Warm blood trickled over his skin. He pushed himself upright with trembling arms, forced himself to his feet, and shot a hard look at the Guardian who dared to move toward him. No one would risk touching the property of Lilith, which branded him safe – in a manner of speaking.

Rockley had been turned undead. Max had suspected, but wasn't certain until now, when he saw the way Rockley gazed with unleashed lust on his wife. At Lilith's word, he'd feed on Victoria until she died – or worse. But not until he was given leave by his mistress. Not only had she allowed him to feed from herself, but Lilith was holding him off to ensure his complete devotion.

Touching his *vis bulla*, Max closed his eyes, inhaled the power, and let Lilith's evil seep from his pores. They had to find a way to get out of this place with the book. There was no hope for Rockley.

Then he heard Victoria. 'Stand back. I will make the trade.'

What?

Give Lilith the book? Undo all they had worked for?

No!

He moved, started down the steps of the dais… and was blocked by the swords of two Imperials.

Victoria had seen; she looked at him. Hard. Then her eyes swept away to his left, quickly up and then down. Back to the satchel, which hung across the front of her body. She was feeling through the bag with one hand; the other fell alongside the loose white trousers she wore.

She'd dressed for battle, so to speak. Her hair was pulled back, severe and black, twisted into a knot at the base of her neck, leaving her eyes wide and dark in a face the colour of health…not death. Despite Lilith's vibrant hair, Victoria was the one who glowed, standing next to her.

Max took a deep breath. Focused. To his left was

the large, shallow dish of fire, sitting in its cradle of metal arms. Next to it was a pile of wood…much too thick to be used as stakes. But the fire itself…

'Stand away,' Victoria said to Lilith, and suddenly Max saw why. She had a pistol in her hand. That was helpful.

Lilith stepped back, but did not appear surprised. 'You took that from your husband. There is no bullet in there that can harm me. You are the only one in danger from such a weapon.' Then she turned to look at Max, still held captive behind two crossed swords. 'Or he.' Her brows lifted and she sent him a scorching smile. 'Perhaps you wish to eliminate any witnesses to your…change of heart.'

Victoria raised the pistol and pointed it at Max. It had been a while since he'd been on the wrong side of a barrel, and he hadn't missed the predicament one whit. The Imperials even shifted their swords, as if to give her a better shot. 'I would not wish my aunt to know that I had forsaken my vow; instead, Max and Phillip and I will simply disappear.'

'I am not finished with him yet,' Lilith replied.

'Nor am I.' Victoria looked at Max again and, giving a spare nod, pointed the pistol straight above her head and pulled the trigger. The black-painted dome burst, and shards of glass rained down on the centre of the floor…and noon sunlight blasted through the opening in the ceiling.

Lilith screamed and fell away, rolling out of the

generous ring of light in the centre of the floor. Phillip, who was standing on the edge of the sunlight-infused area, dodged from the danger zone.

Max had moved just as Victoria nodded, shoving the vessel of fire onto the Imperials. One of them caught flames at the edge of his trousers, and when he dropped his sword Max leapt for it.

Max vaulted to his feet, slicing the head from the burning Imperial. He whipped around and took two more heads from the unprepared vampires who stood gawking along the walls, and spun toward Victoria.

Victoria hesitated, looking at her husband, but then Max was storming toward her. He leapt, landing next to her in the middle of the room. Sunlight bathed them both standing in the circle of safety. The fire he'd tipped over caught at the upholstery on Lilith's chair, and began to tear through the carpet. Smoke clouded the fringes of the room, rising to the open air above.

Most of the vampires had advanced, collecting around them, blocking them into the round yellow area that spanned perhaps eight feet. Lilith stood a short distance away, screaming orders and rubbing her hands over her body as if to brush away the burns from the sunlight. One of her Guardians was wiping a fine layer of burnt skin from her face and bosom, leaving raw pink underskin in its wake.

Max looked down. He noticed the warm yellow had dulled at their feet. A cloud was moving over the sky and soon would block the sun. Their sanctuary would disappear.

'I don't suppose you thought this through any further,' he said, brandishing the sword at a younger undead who dared take a step toward them.

'I was rather hoping that, since I got us this far, you'd have an idea.'

The smoke was getting thicker, and some of the furnishings were starting to kindle. It would be a very short time until the entire room erupted in flames; the dry, rotting curtains that hung at the black windows were already suffused with angry orange and red tongues.

Something quick and dark snaked from the circle of vampires, whipping in, and Max turned in time to see Victoria struggling in Phillip's arms. The light and dark divided them: She was in the sunbeams, he in the safety of shadows, trying to pull her into the shade. Part of his arm was in the sun, and his face twisted from the pain of sunshine blasting down on him, but he did not release her. Victoria's feet were planted far apart, her arms pulled behind her, and as Max watched, Phillip looped an arm around her waist and swept her out of the light.

She reared up, struggling to break free. Her face was wet with tears, and she seemed to be saying something over and over...and finally she bowed her head and slammed it back into Phillip's nose. He released her, and, seizing the opportunity, Max hefted his sword and brought it back in a strong swing.

But before he could finish it and cleave the Marquess of Rockley's head from his body, Victoria staggered back into the yellow light and grabbed his sword arm, sending the powerful blow slicing through the sun and shadow, down Phillip's body and to the floor. 'No, Max!' she cried. 'No!'

'You can't save him, Victoria,' he shouted back, furious and suddenly frightened. She couldn't save him. Didn't she understand that?

'No!' Victoria cried.

'You cannot leave me, Victoria,' Phillip said, inching closer, his voice a hollow echo of what it had been. 'You belong here with me.' Compelling. So compelling, so sweet and alluring. And unavoidable.

Max grabbed her arm when she would have moved toward him. The pull… He understood that. What he didn't understand was the strength of Phillip's call to Victoria, as such a young undead. She was a Venator.

'Phillip,' she sobbed, but she had a stake in her hand.

'Come to me, Victoria,' her husband said. 'Your friend can go…but you must come to me. I need you. She promised me I would have you.'

Then Max heard her, moving toward them in their circle of warm light. Lilith. She had recovered. He felt the pull, the demand already. She was calling him… and it was with fury this time. He would die. The games were over.

They had no way out.

Then, as the light tipped even paler, he caught a movement from above. They looked up and saw a rope hurtling down from the broken dome above. More glass tumbled below as the rope brushed against the fragile edge, and as the shadows kicked at the remains.

'Kritanu!' Victoria breathed.

Max saw the dark face of her trainer, and then Briyani's as the two bent over the hole in the ceiling. The timing could have been no better...they truly were doing holy work.

One of the vampires leapt, trying to grab the rope as it swung near the edge of the light. He caught it but lost his balance and fell at their feet in the pool of sun. Screaming in agony, he tried to roll away, still holding the rope. Max brought his sword down and the screaming stopped. The rope hung free again.

'Go!' Victoria shouted, shoving a handful of rope toward Max.

'I'll not leave you—'

'I have the book,' she said fiercely. 'And you've been bitten. Go *now!*'

The vampires were closing in, their fangs gleaming as the sun began to fade under a swath of clouds. Lilith stood at the very edge of the line of light and dark, but she did not step farther. The smoke filtered up through the hole, hanging at the very upper edge of the room, and the flames were close enough that

Max could feel their searing heat. Even if the sun weren't fading, the curling edges of fire would drive them from their safe area before long.

When Lilith would have reached for him, Victoria lifted her satchel and held it in front of her. 'One move, Lilith, and I will throw the book into the fire.'

Just then another rope dropped. Max caught it and wrapped it around Victoria's waist, tying it tightly. 'Pull!' he shouted above, and immediately he found himself rising through the air. He swung back and forth like a pendulum, and, looking down, he could see his shadow cut through the circle of sun in a rhythmic pattern, the moving blemish in the yellow sphere growing smaller as he rose higher.

Victoria held on to her satchel, so she could not climb as well, but Max had tied the knot tightly and she was lifted slightly off the ground. As she rose, Phillip leapt into the light and grabbed at her foot, pulling her back.

'No!' he shouted.

Max was halfway to the top when he looked down and saw Phillip pulling on her. Victoria didn't seem to be struggling; she seemed frozen, hung suspended in the air, the heavy satchel pressed to her chest. Phillip had her foot and had angled her out of the light. He was nearly climbing up her legs to pull her back down, adding his weight and strength to the burden Kritanu struggled to raise.

'Victoria!' Max shouted. He couldn't go back; they were pulling him up, and he couldn't climb down.

She wasn't fighting; she wasn't struggling.

Phillip reached the rope around her waist, tugging on it, and Max watched in disbelief as the rope he'd just tied loosened and Victoria fell to the floor, half in the light and half in the dark.

The rope dangled uselessly from the dome.

'Phillip,' Max heard Victoria say. She was not moving, just looking up at him. Her husband looked down at her, then at Lilith, as if asking for permission.

'Put me back. Now!' Max shouted up to Kritanu, but the rope continued to rise inexorably. Kritanu's face was no longer looking down from the dome; he had moved away in order to pull up the heavy weight. 'Kritanu!' He struggled to loosen the knot, his fingers digging into the rough hemp around his waist.

Phillip pulled Victoria to her feet, and she was no longer in the sun. The rope hung behind her, still swaying.

'You can't save him!' Max shouted, trying to untie the rope around his waist so he could drop back down and help her. But his weight and the pull of gravity had tightened the knot so that he couldn't pull it apart. He was nearly to the top of the dome and was just beginning to notice the smoke.

The room was so large that the smoke, which should have been clogging and choking them, dissipated and hung near the tall ceiling; the fire was a greater danger than the smoke.

He saw movement as Lilith swept her arm in permission. Phillip fell on Victoria, and her head tipped back as though he'd commanded it. Max could almost hear the groan of need from him as he bent toward her open neck.

'The book, Lilith! He will destroy it!' Max shouted, swinging more wildly with his agitation. He could see the wall of flame moving toward the circle of vampires; but they were unconcerned. Fire would not harm them. Only Victoria.

'Stop!' shouted Lilith, extending her arm and reaching for Phillip through the air.

Phillip stiffened as though she had grabbed his neck, whimpering, but he did not move. Max could hear his laboured breathing, and, thank God, Lilith's power released her and Victoria came to herself. She pulled away.

She fell back into the sunlight, and Phillip did not stop her. She lay back, sprawling in a much smaller circle of light than had been there moments before.

'If you want the book,' she said, her voice steadier than Max would have expected it, 'you let me go. I will give it to you.'

Max looked down, tried to see what was happening below. And then, as his rope spun him in a gentle circle, he saw the line next to him move, tighten. 'Pull!' he shouted above. 'She's ready! Go!'

As Victoria rose through the smoke, he could hear her. 'The Book of Antwartha. Lilith, the book is yours! You will search for it no longer!'

'No! Victoria, no!' Max shouted, and then heard the dull thud as the book hit the ground far below. And then, through the faint haze of smoke, he saw the manuscript, sitting in its circle of glowing yellow, waiting to be snatched up by the vampires.

Then he could see no more.

From below a woman screamed, shrieking in pain and rage, and suddenly Max was being dragged out of the smoky air into the fresh, beautiful sunlight.

He scrambled aside and set to helping Kritanu and Briyani raise Victoria.

When she finally reached the top, her face smudged with black, he helped pull her over the glass edges, careful not to cut her. But that didn't stop him from lighting into her in another way.

'You gave her the book?' he shouted. 'Victoria!'

'What is left of it,' she replied calmly, as if she'd just stopped by for tea. 'I dropped it, and the book turned to dust. It is gone forever.'

Max stepped back, planting his foot firmly on the sloping roof. 'I presume...' He paused, because if he didn't measure his words carefully, he might kill her. 'I presume you did that knowing it would be the effect.'

'Of course. As soon as the sunlight touched it, it crumbled, just as Wayren planned.' She turned to follow Kritanu and Briyani off the roof of the burning building, leaving Max to follow behind.

He had several other things to say to her, but they would have to wait. Though she'd tried to hide them, he had seen the tears.

Chapter Twenty-Eight

In Which Eustacia Makes a Confession

'We saw the black dome break,' Kritanu explained when they had returned to Aunt Eustacia's home. 'And recognised that something was happening in that portion of the mansion. And then the smoke came out.' He shrugged. 'We knew.'

'You could not have appeared any more fortuitously,' Max replied.

Victoria looked at the ugly red welts at his neck. The bleeding had stopped, and she'd had the pleasure of pouring salted holy water on his bite during their drive back into London. She had said very little since they left Lilith's hideout, leaving Max to explain what he could.

'Venators do holy work,' Eustacia said from her chair. 'The most miraculous things happen when we are fighting evil.'

Miraculous? Victoria closed her eyes. She could not dismiss Phillip's face from her memory, the deep hunger…the pleading…the curve of his lips and the line of his nose. The beloved face, turned desperate and vacant.

You cannot save him.

Max's angry words reverberated in her mind. She could not save him; indeed, she had condemned him.

'The book was destroyed?' Eustacia's question brought Victoria back, and she looked up to see all eyes focused on her.

'I never intended to give it to her.' She looked at Max.

He bowed his head in acknowledgment, but said nothing. He'd been uncharacteristically kind to her since they'd climbed down off the roof of the mansion and sat in the carriage, watching the house burn. Lilith's stronghold was destroyed, but there was no reason to believe that she was. Or Phillip.

There would be more battles in the future. Lilith would rise to power again, and they would face her.

And as Aunt Eustacia told her, the vampire queen would never forget Victoria's role in her downfall.

'Do you know what happened to Sebastian?' she asked suddenly, looking at Max.

'No. I presume he either perished in the fire or was killed by the Imperials. He would have preferred it, rather than face Lilith.'

She did not miss the disdain in his voice, and she did not begrudge him that. She'd seen firsthand the power Lilith had, and had felt the inexorable allure of a vampire's complete hold. Perhaps death was better than being unable to control one's own actions and desires.

But not for her.

'Aunt Eustacia, may I speak with you?'

'I have been waiting for you to ask.'

When they were alone, her aunt spoke before she did. 'I have no words for how sorry I am about Phillip, Victoria.' Her jet eyes held grief and remorse, and her soft, knobby hands reached for those of her niece. 'If I had known—'

'But you didn't. You couldn't. And you – and Max – tried to stop me.' Victoria gripped her aunt's fingers and blinked back the tears. 'Is there nothing that could be done to save him?'

Eustacia shook her head. 'If a vampire has fed on a mortal, he is damned for all eternity. Perhaps prayer or great sacrifice might save his soul, but there is no guarantee.'

Victoria closed her eyes. 'It was my selfishness that caused it. I should never have married him. I loved him, and I should have loved him enough to release him.' She raised her face, wiping away the tears. 'He told me that his destiny was to love me – whether we were together or not. Now he cannot do even that.'

'It is hard, Victoria. I know. It is beyond anything

you ever imagined. You have given your life for this cause, and never forget that it is the right and true thing. You help to rid the world of evil, to keep it at bay. If you and Max and I and the others were not here, giving up our lives, this earth would have been overrun by evil long ago. In return for our extraordinary powers and protections, we sacrifice.' She hesitated, then said, 'Lilith offered to release you, did she not?'

Victoria nodded, her wet face hot and sticky. 'I *wanted* it, Aunt Eustacia. I wanted it. She would have given me Phillip...or she said she would have. Could she have?'

'Perhaps. I do not know.' Eustacia drew in a long, long breath. Exhaled. 'Victoria, I have not been fully honest with you. About the choices and vocations of a Venator.

'Some Venators are born, as you were. Some choose, as you know, through great danger and sacrifice, to take on the role. Once the decision is made to accept the responsibility, there is only one way a Venator can cease being—'

'No.' Victoria stopped her, shaking her head, certain. 'No. Do not say it.'

Her aunt paused, looking at her. 'I know it is too late for you and Phillip, but, if you wish it, I will. Your sacrifice has been great.'

Victoria stood, walking over to the cabinet where the Gardella Bible was locked in safety like a host in a sacristy. 'No. It is no longer an option for me, if it ever was. When I first accepted the Legacy, I did so innocently – but I did not *understand*.

'I thought it was fun – to be strong, to be able to walk the streets alone at night, and know that I could defend myself better than any man could. It gave me freedom that I had never imagined a woman could have!

'With the freedom, with the strength and power, comes pain and sacrifice. The impossibility of having a normal life. Responsibility.

'I can never go back, Aunt Eustacia, even if you gave me that chance. I cannot, because it's no longer a game for me. It's no longer merely a task – to hunt evil and send it to hell. Lilith has made it most personal.'

Epilogue

A Farewell

He moved through the silent house like smoke – quick, dark, noiseless. His house. His home he could enter uninvited.

If one of the servants saw him, they would think nothing of it. Nothing but that the master had returned home at last.

But no one saw him as he moved silently up the stairs. Need pulsed through him, and as he thought of the taste of her, of being sated at last, he felt her heartbeat moving with his. Even from that distance.

He smelt her, and his hands trembled at the relief that would soon be his. The awful need would dissolve, and he could think again. Breathe on his own. Rest. Feel something beyond hunger.

He would take her with him, be with her…forever. Make her like him, immortal. She was his destiny… had been, always would be.

He stood in the doorway of her chamber. Not hesitating…savouring. Experiencing the pull, her draw…and the stronger bond that he controlled. He knew it was strong enough. Their love was deep enough. He could do it… Powerful as she was, he could turn her.

She lay on her side, covered by nothing but a filmy white gown that left her arms and bosom bare, and the blue filter of moonlight through the open window. Her dark hair curled over the pillow. Her eyes were closed, deep in shadows.

He stepped in, his heart – no, her heart – pounding in his chest, his temples, his belly, his cock. His breathing deepened, slowed, as he thought of the relief he would have, sinking into her. His eternal love.

Victoria was waiting. She'd known he would come, had been expecting him since she returned home, refusing Max or Eustacia to accompany her. She sent Verbena away, gave the servants the night off.

She wanted to be alone when he came.

As he brushed against the side of the bed, she felt her breathing change. It was no longer hers. They drew in together, exhaled together. She opened her eyes and looked at him.

He was Phillip…beloved Phillip. She reached for him, and he fell onto the bed.

He kissed her, touched her, pulled the gown from her shoulders, and she let him. She allowed herself the desire, the comfort.

She felt it when he changed: the edge to his breath, the harshness of his pulse storming through her. The slip of his control. His eyes glinted rosy, and when he raised his face, his fangs glinted dull white and lethal.

But his voice was Phillip's. Unchanged. Familiar. Loving. 'Let me, Victoria, my wife,' he murmured… as he had done before. 'I will be very gentle…and soon you will feel only pleasure. We will be together forever. My destiny.'

When his incisors scraped over her flesh, at the tender joint of neck and shoulder, readying to sink in, she stiffened…sighed. Closed her eyes. Tears leaked from them.

She groped in the sheets, closed her fingers around the smooth wood. 'I will always love you, Phillip.' And she stabbed him.

When she opened her wet eyes, she saw someone standing in the door of her chamber.

Max. His stake was outlined by the moonlight.

'I followed him.'

'I knew he would come.'

He bowed his head, then looked up at her. 'You saved him. You stopped him in time.'

'I hope.' She drew in her breath. 'You were right about it all, Max.'

'For that, and for this, I am sorry.'

'You were right about me – I am a foolish woman.'

'No. You are a Venator.'

A year later, Victoria is back on the streets of London, determined to keep them safe from bloodthirsty vampires. Don't miss her next adventure in The Gardella Vampire Chronicles...

Rises The Night

Excerpt from Rises the Night

Victoria tightened her fingers around the ash stake, more out of habit than necessity, and peered around the rough brick corner. It was dark, and damp, as London was wont to be shortly after midnight, and the streets just past the safety of Drury Lane were strewn with refuse and scattered with the occasional thief, prostitute, and other such dodgy persons.

Unfortunately, none of said dodgy persons were wreaking any havoc, picking any pockets, or biting any necks.

Now a year had passed since Lilith had left London, and Victoria was back on the streets hunting for vampires for the first time since the night she'd removed her *vis bulla*. She'd spent the last twelve months practicing her fighting skills, learning to control the rage and grief that had driven her to nearly kill the man in St Giles. She wanted to be sure she was ready, and able to temper those emotions before reinserting her strength amulet. The silver cross shivered in the hollow of her navel when she walked, and Victoria felt complete again. She was ready.

Which was why she'd been taking to the streets late at night, stake in one hand, pistol in her other. Looking for something to do. Someone to save.

She would never stop looking for someone to save.

Victoria shook her head abruptly to dislodge the memory and chase away the guilt that still crawled along her nerves. Her temple scraped against the brick, sending crumbles of mortar dusting to the ground and a dull pain over her skin. And she returned her thoughts to the matter at hand.

Barth would be along shortly in his hackney to pick her up and take her back to the echoingly empty Rockley estate known as St Heath's Row.

No sooner had she had the thought than the hackney in question rumbled around the corner and came to a rather slower stop than usual. It wasn't that Barth's driving had improved – it was that he'd been combing the streets, looking for Victoria.

As she climbed into the carriage, she made the decision she'd been putting off for a week. 'Barth, I'm not ready to go home yet…Take me to St Giles. To the Chalice.'

And before he could protest, she closed the door.

There was a bit of a wait, as though he was considering arguing, but then she heard Barth cluck to the horses and she lurched as they started off at a smart pace. Victoria settled back in her seat and tried not to think about the last time she'd been to the Silver Chalice. More than a year ago.

It was well past midnight, and the streets of St Giles were deserted. Only very foolish or very brave people ventured into this area of London during the relative protection of daylight; at night, even fewer would dare to trespass. As they rumbled along St. Martin's Lane, and crossed the intersection of the seven roads known as the Dials, Victoria cast her glance down one of them. She had not forgotten Great St. Andrew's Street, nor even the block, where she'd nearly killed the man. She could find it again in her sleep, for though she did not recall the actual event in all of its terrible detail, the location had imprinted itself on her brain.

Perhaps someday she would return.

Several streets later, the hackney jerked to a stop, drawing her from her uncomfortable reverie. Anticipating the jolt, Victoria had already put out a hand to brace herself. Lifting the small lantern from the interior wall, she ducked out of the vehicle and slipped away before Barth could speak or follow her.

Her feet were soundless on the cobbled street as they skirted piles of trash and stepped over small puddles left from an early-evening rain. The stench no longer bothered her, nor did the weight of eyes peering from the shadows.

Let them come. She was ready for a fight.

Across the street and down she walked, head held high, hand on her pistol, the legs of her men's breeches swishing faintly against each other, the lantern light slicing through her shadow. A welcome summer breeze lifted the smell of rotting carcasses and animal waste back to her consciousness, then brushed on away. The back of her neck cooled slightly under the beaver topper she wore, but it was from the wind, rather than a sign of approaching danger.

Victoria stood in front of what had been the doorway to the Silver Chalice. She had not visited the place since the night she came looking for Phillip, and found instead the smouldering ruins of what had been an establishment that served vampires and mortals alike.

Did she imagine it, or was the oaky smell of ash still on the air? It couldn't be, all these months later…

The chill had returned to the back of her neck.

She froze, stopping her breath to listen. To feel.

Yes, it was there. It was real, raising the hair on her nape in a warning she hadn't felt for a twelvemonth: A vampire was near. Below.

Now, the rush of anticipation fuelling her actions, Victoria climbed over the rickety remains of the doorframe and started down the steps into the cavernous chamber. She felt along the stones with her left hand whilst her right carried the lantern, shining onto the wood and stone rubble that littered the steps. If she could have approached without the illumination, she would have done so; but seeing in the dark was not one of the gifts bestowed upon Venators. Some of the element of surprise would be diminished, but that was better than trying to make her way through the mess silently, and in the dark.

Miraculously, the ceiling had not completely caved in over the stairs, and she soon found herself at the bottom. Victoria paused, thrusting the lantern behind her to block some of its light, and peered around the corner into the dark, misshapen cellar.

What was left of Sebastian's place.

Although the tingle at the back of her neck still played there, confirming her instinct, she did not feel or hear any sign of movement. She stilled, but for the fingers slipping into the deep pocket of her coat.

The stake felt comfortable in her hand, but she did not withdraw it yet. She let her grip close around the wood, warm from her body, and waited, listening and feeling.

The chill on her neck edged colder, and she breathed the proximity of the vampire and the impending exhilaration of battle. Her heart rate picked up speed, and her nostrils flared, as if to smell the presence of an undead.

At last, satisfied that she was alone in the chamber, Victoria drew the lamp forth. Shining it around, she saw the same scene of destruction that had greeted her months ago; but now, her mind was not numbed by fear and apprehension. Now she saw the blackened ceiling beams, the splintered tables and broken glasses...Perhaps she even smelt the faint tinge of blood in the air.

The lantern bobbed as she climbed over a fractured chair, and glass crunched like gravel beneath her feet. She was making her way toward the innermost, darkest part of the wall, hidden under a lowering ceiling. The growing sensation at the back of her neck told her she was moving in the right direction.

Sebastian Vioget had disappeared the night the Silver Chalice burnt. Max had been there too that night, and he told Victoria he didn't know whether Sebastian had escaped from the fire; and she knew that he didn't give a whit what had happened either way.

Victoria knew she shouldn't care either...but she had not been able to forget the bronze-haired man who welcomed vampires into his establishment. He'd once told Victoria that it was better to know them and to offer them a place where they might find ease, where their tongues might loosen and information might be gained...

She found the secret door Sebastian had taken her through the very first night she'd met him. Tucked away under a low stone ceiling and set in among the stone walls, it remained fairly unscathed. Marked with black streaks, it was ajar.

And the cold at her nape tingled more sharply.

Victoria pushed through the door, leaving the

lantern at the entrance of the passageway. She felt the weight of the pistol in her pocket as it bumped against the edge of stone – the pistol, useless against a vampire, of course, but helpful for other purposes. In the dark, narrow passageway, Victoria couldn't help but remember facing Sebastian, with the damp brick behind her, and him much too close for propriety's sake as he reached to sweep off the hat of her gentleman's disguise.

He hadn't kissed her that time.

Moving down the faintly lit hallway, quickly, as though to leave the thoughts behind her, Victoria made her way to the small room on the left, the one Sebastian had used as an office and sitting room.

He, she, it, or they…were in this room.

Her lips curled in a feral smile and adrenaline kicked up her pulse. She had been ready for this for months.

The door was ajar, giving her the opportunity to peer around into the room. It was lit from within; only a large lantern could illuminate the chamber well enough for her to see the intricate brocade design on the sofa from where she stood. Interesting that a vampire or two would use a lantern.

From what she could see through the open door, the room had been untouched by the fire, with the exception of a lingering smoke smell that had likely been trapped in the couch and chair upholstery. There was no sign of any disturbance…The books were still lining shelves, the pillows perfectly arranged on the furniture... Even the silver tray with the brandy and sherry bottles was in place across the room.

The only things out of place were the two figures bent over Sebastian's desk. At least one vampire.

Slipping the stake from her pocket, Victoria let it hang behind the folds of her jacket and stepped into the room.

'Good evening, gentlemen,' she said as they turned. 'Are you looking for something?'

Her year of grief had made her a bit slow.

One of them was at her before she expected it, his eyes blood-red and his incisors flashing. Victoria stepped back, felt the wall behind her, and twisted away. He followed, and she tripped over the leg of a chair, nearly stumbling to the floor. The error made her more determined, and the skills Kritanu had taught her came flooding back to her muscles like the fit of a well-worn glove.

When Victoria gained her balance, the vampire was reaching for her, inadvertently opening his chest to her driving stake. She slammed it in, felt the familiar pop and stepped back as he disintegrated into dust.

Barely breathing hard, she looked up at the other man, who'd not moved. He watched her with a twitch of a smile, but he'd not changed. Instead, he adjusted his jacket and looked at her with glinting black eyes.

'Came prepared, did you?' he asked, walking easily

from around the other side of the desk. Coming closer, but easy. Unthreatening, and unthreatened.

'What are you doing here?' Victoria wanted some answers before she staked him too. It could be no coincidence that they'd both chosen this night to visit Sebastian's rooms; and by the amount of dust here, and the neatness of the room, she gathered this was the first visit anyone had made.

'Merely curiosity.' He stood so that the sofa was between them. 'This is what remains of the infamous Silver Chalice. I was interested in seeing the place owned by Sebastian Vioget.' His fangs had not protruded; his eyes remained an unexceptional grey.

'Do you know him?' she asked.

The vampire, who was no taller than most other men in London, had nondescript brown hair brushed back from his face. His nose, a bit too large to make his face attractive, rounded on the end like a garlic bulb. And his brows were straight, narrow strips over his eyes. He shook his head in response to her question. 'I'm afraid I haven't the pleasure of meeting Monsieur Vioget. From what I have heard, I'm not altogether certain it is any longer possible to do so.'

'I haven't seen a vampire here in London for months,' Victoria said, watching him. 'Since Lilith took herself and her followers off. Did she send you back to ascertain whether it was safe for her to return?'

He looked at her for a moment; then recognition

shifted into his dark eyes. Not red, not yet. They were normal. He looked like nothing more than an average English gentleman, except for his ill-fitting clothing. 'You are the woman Venator.'

Victoria bowed her head in acknowledgment.

His eyes narrowed thoughtfully. 'What a coup it would be for me to bring you to Nedas. He would reward me greatly.'

A spike of anticipation jolted through her. 'You could certainly attempt it. I'm certain that whoever Nedas is, he would appreciate your martyrdom.'

'I'm not quite as capricious as my dearly departed companion,' he replied. 'But I am much stronger and faster.'

Then he was there, across the room, next to her, reaching for her throat. Victoria spun away, but he grabbed at her arm, and he was indeed strong.

She tried to wrench away, caught in his suddenly glowing red eyes, and felt the sofa against her legs. She pretended to stumble, dodged, and knocked him off balance. He came after her again, close behind, without giving her a chance to catch her breath, and the next thing she knew, she was whirling back to face him.

Raising her stake at shoulder level, she lifted her face to look at him, ready to slam it home, and faltered. *Phillip*.

It was Phillip.

It was as if her body had turned to ice, and then

raging fire. The stake fell from her limp fingers and the scream was knocked out of her as he shoved her aside, sending her to the floor.

On the rug, dragging dust and lint into her panicked breath, Victoria looked up at the figure looming over her. How?

But it wasn't Phillip who bent over her. It was the same nondescript man, now with glowing eyes and a determined line for a mouth.

She scrabbled for her stake…Surely it hadn't rolled far on the rug. He lunged for her and she twisted away, suddenly trapped against the edge of the sofa. She felt something under her hip, round and hard and long, and rolled sharply away, toward his feet, grabbing the stake.

The force of her motion upset him, and Victoria propelled herself to her feet, stick in hand. She turned, using the momentum of her leg to whip around, then shifted her centre of balance as she plunged the stake into the centre of his chest. She pulled it away, stepping back to watch him dust to the floor.

Nothing happened.

And he came at her again, his mouth drawn in a frightening, feral smile.

Victoria recoiled in shock, stumbling backward, and tripped over the flipped-up corner of the thick Persian rug. She tumbled to the floor, slamming her head against the wall as she fell, and stared up at the red-eyed man who advanced toward her.

Calm and steady he moved and Victoria could barely get her mind around the fact that she'd stabbed him, sunk a stake into his chest, and *nothing had happened*. Neither blood nor dust…he'd just come after her again.

**Other titles available in
The Gardella Chronicles
from Allison & Busby**

Rises the Night
978-0-7490-7966-6 • £6.99 • Paperback

All Allison & Busby titles can be ordered
from our website,
www.allisonandbusby.com,
or from your local bookshop and are also
available by post from:

Bookpost, PO Box 29, Douglas, Isle of Man, IM99 1BQ
Credit cards accepted. For details:
Telephone: +44(0)1624 677237
Fax: +44(0)1624 670923
Email: bookshop@enterprise.net
www.bookpost.co.uk

Free postage and packing in the United Kingdom

Prices shown above were correct at the time of going to press.
Allison & Busby reserve the right to show new retail prices on
covers which
may differ from those previously advertised in the text or
elsewhere.